blood toys

tech | dark | powerful | troubling

Floyd Wray

Start Here

1. Confirm that the camera is enabled to read QR-code.

2. In the SETTINGS application, also confirm that you're connected to the Internet. Return to home screen.

3. Tap the CAMERA icon to open the camera on your phone/tablet.

4. Aim the camera at the square QR-code box (above).

5. Click the permission screen that appears on the device screen. (Best practice: use widescreen orientation)

6. Set audio levels, pause, play, reverse, forward using the media-controller on your phone-tablet.

https://vimeo.com/762072780

blood toys

Floyd Wray

Motionbooks.com, LLC
Springfield, Missouri
65804

ISBN: 979-8-218-02885-5   978-1-607-02384-5

Floyd Wray
Blood Toys
Published by: Motionbooks.com, LLC

Cover Design-Trail Boss & AI Wrangler: Chipp Walters

Additional Graphics: Nancy Wray

Audio Effects licensed by The Hollywood Edge Sound Effects Library, The Premiere Edition

All music licensed from musicloops.com.

AI Voice Generation licensed by Blaster Suite/Speechelo. Additional vocal work created by the author

A CIP record for this book is available from the Library of Congress Cataloging-in-Publication Data

Distributed by Motionbooks.com, LLC
2733 East Battlefield Road, #217
Springfield, Missouri, 65804

... for my amazing Nancy

blood toys

1 Firefly

The engineers in Austin were astonished. They'd done this in simulation a thousand times. Still, to see the real Firefly burning a real trail across the radar was nothing short of astounding. One of the techs leaned over to the woman at the next console and half-whispered, *UFOs away*. It was really not a very smart thing to say.

00:25

Myles Koepler glanced to the little blondie at the back of the control room, then strolled over to the tech who, by now, suspected the depth of his sin. Standing behind the man's chair, Koepler thumped him. A seriously sharp flick to the man's right ear. And the little blondie had heard. When Koepler stepped away from the chair, Claire Whitlock also noticed the crimson ear. Myles Koepler ran the lab like a football coach teaching science.

The radar-technician flipped out to a wider scan. This cued the data-capture tech to take the transceiver off standby. Claire had compassion for everyone on this project, except Koepler maybe, because it had been a tough contract. More than they'd bargained for. And the work was so sensitive, one infinitesimally small problem could result in the yanking of a seventy-five million dollar deal. Everyone in the control room knew this. And everyone in the control room was so *flexed* at this prospect, most of them were sitting a quarter-of-an-inch higher than usual.

01:42

The incoming signal from Firefly hit Z-O like a hurricane.

Massive waves of data blew into the servers, gobbling up space at speeds unheard-of. The video monitors flashed with the first images. Fishing boats off-shore. Inland villages. Firefly was now fifteen minutes from the skies over São Paulo.

02:05

Firefly's exterior skin captured audio/video data in a most peculiar manner. Simply described, it was an omnidirectional camera and microphone. It could see and hear everything in the flight path. Left. Right. Ahead. Above. Behind. Below. When Firefly's strange technology had been described initially, the engineers at Z-O were not only astonished at the flight characteristics, they saw what appeared to be an unsolvable problem. Almost immediately. You can't display a spherical frame on a traditional monitor. Even if you could, the view would be disorienting. Humans see the universe through windows. So, in addition to inventing an assortment of non-traditional navigation controls, the engineers created software that opened an interactive portal on the spherical video stream. Whether live or recorded, a temporary observation stage could be placed anywhere along the image surface.

03:10

Claire knew something else. The portal had been written twice. First, when Firefly was at Lockheed. Then, at Grumman in the 1980s, where it had been codenamed *Superman.* But it was the speed. Over the two-year life of the contract, that was the thing the engineers at Z-O couldn't quite get their heads around. According to extended specification, the unit would eventually zip past Mach 6, and do it in an acceleration burst of mere seconds. The other part of the profile that defied convention were the sudden stops. Firefly could instantly decelerate, then hover for hours.

03:51

The sober-minded guess was that the hardware had come from another defense contractor. Like Lockheed-Martin. Privately, though, most of the engineers at Z-O suspected, the machine had really black roots. As in *UFO-technology-black.*

Technicians who'd taken much of their livelihood from the darker side of defense contracting, quietly entertained the thought that the original contractor had almond-eyes and enjoyed playing with cows when no one was looking. Still, you wouldn't talk about that sort of thing. UFOs and little green men, or gray men, or whatever they were, they were a definite *no-no*, conversationally.

04:38

As the numbers spilled across the screens, as the tension let up, Koepler turned to Claire and smiled. Such a pretty little doctoral student in jeans and cowboy boots. Of course, Koepler had no illusions about who she was, really, and he was starting to worry, a bit, about how she might report the evening.

05:01

Firefly came to a dead-bang stop over São Paulo. This was the promise. You could place Firefly anywhere, focusing on target-data without anyone knowing. It was zoomable, fully-directional, and there were other things. Once Firefly achieved target, the NSA controllers at Fort Meade could not only listen in and knock out electrical service on the ground, they would eventually *fry from on high*. On the poor, unsuspecting victim, there'd be no visible signs. No burn marks or blown out eye sockets. Just a surprised body, dead for no good reason other than a focused micro-blast of high-frequency energy. That was the ultimate promise here, though *promise* might not be quite the right word.

05:56

Tonight, Z-O's flight plan called for nailing exact coordinates. Then zooming in on *sub-targets* per-request. Within a minute of arriving on-station, the first directive appeared on the controller's screen.

Zoom fifty-percent.

Down in São Paulo the party was just starting. There were cars and people everywhere. Plenty of targets. So the folks in Texas … cruised, driving the portal from one end of the street to the other.

Woman with a purse.

The tech scanned the street, chasing the field from his window on high until he located her.

Head shot.

He locked her in. Then zoomed down until it seemed, Firefly was tagging along just above her right shoulder. This had been a major specification, to isolate and track. But in Fort Meade another bit of technology was about to be flipped on, another layer of technology riding piggyback, but unknown to the folks in Texas.

07:01

NSA's Jerry Terance told the NSA-team in Fort Meade to *read* her.

The players in Texas thought they knew what Firefly was up to, but they were downstream on that score. Quite a ways downstream. The wizards at NSA had concocted something not even Superman could do. They looked inside skulls.

07:24

Terance and a handful of NSA personnel studied the monitor. They weren't observing the woman from the outside. They tracked the blood-pooling and electromagnetic fields in her brain. For the watchers in Texas she merely passed from light to shadow, from one flashing bar sign to another. At Fort Meade, though, she passed from *premeditation* to *target-acquisition*, as these zones of her brain lit the truth of her working life. It wasn't mind-reading. You didn't know what she was thinking, but in a way you did. Given the context, early-morning on a street filled with crawling drunks, the woman was on the prowl. Just as Firefly was on the prowl, overhead.

She finally locked onto someone. It was fascinating to observe, whether you were in Texas or Maryland. But at Fort Meade they saw so much more.

The woman's premeditation was eclipsed by a storm that flickered to light in the amygdaloidal nucleus of the anterior temporal lobe. A kaleidoscope bomb went off in her head. The colors flashed from one lobe to the other. Nailing every color in the rainbow. So much, so fast, they temporarily lost track of the read. Of course, none of this was visible on the scopes in Austin, at Z-O.

08:52

For the behavioral scientists at NSA, the scan suggested multiple transactions. The woman was *reading her client*.

They figured as much in Austin too. Most men in the room read the context, but the voyeurs at NSA knew it the instant the two on the street reached accommodation. The woman's head-storm subsided. Blood pooling returned to normal.

Focus the male.

The tech dialed in a new view. The woman's client was in his late twenties, wore a light colored shirt, white tennis shoes, had a mustache and matted hair. In Austin, that's what they saw, and all they knew. In Fort Meade, the scan suggested something else. A trail of light. Embers at the edge of a dark, murderous conscience, exploding forward like a gasoline-fire, driving hellish passion into flesh and muscle and hand and bone. As the couple shuffled into the shadows, then down the alley, Terance called it off. Told the boys in Texas to shut down. The folks at Z-O were a little put off, to say the least, but with so much hanging in the balance, they knew better than to leave the camera open. They closed the eye in the sky and prepared to launch back to the east.

10:18

In Austin, they thought they knew what would happen next. In Fort Meade, they knew, *absolutely*. Within minutes, the woman would be seriously injured, probably. Maybe dead. Because that's what the scan prophesied.

10:34

Firefly stood to become the Swiss Army knife-of-choice for American intelligence. The spooks would soon preside over humanity with unlimited vision, and a weapon without equal.

2 Jazz

Claire pulled out of Z-O a little before 6:00 a.m. Traffic was light. Within the hour, Austin would grind to a halt as it did every day, pretty much gridlocked.

In Austin, traffic-management hadn't been a priority. In the goofball logic that was *keep-it-weird-Austin-think*, t raffic had been initially seen as a barrier to outsiders. Except it hadn't worked. The population had exploded in the last decade; the steel-clotted streets were now competitive with anything Houston or Dallas could offer. Austin was a city that really wanted to be a town.

00:40

The Four Seasons in downtown Austin was not *standard* government issue. Claire made up the difference from her own pocket, but it was worth it. The quiet little hotel on the banks of the Colorado River, known to locals as *Town Lake*, was a sanctuary. There was a hike and bike trail down by the river. A bridge with a million bats. Great places to eat. All in walking distance. If you had to go to Texas, if you had to be in Austin, the Four Seasons was the way to go native.

On the drive in, Claire had a spur-of-the-moment Austin-idea. Migas. There was a little Mexican café a few blocks from the hotel. It would be the perfect way to end, and begin the day. She would call Terance as she walked over. Finish off with breakfast. Then go back to the room and crash.

01:34

In Fort Meade, of course, he expected her call. When the phone rang, the first thing he said was, "Nice job."

She asked if he was serious, or merely trying to boost her confidence. This had been her first shot at running a field operation. She was a little needy. But Terance didn't have much else to say, no suggestion to improve anything, or follow-up. Evidently, he meant what he said. She'd done her job well. Period. As the conversation trailed off, he asked what she was doing now, and she said. "Going for migas. After that, heading back to the room."

"Going for what?"

"Migas, Jerry. Tex-Mex."

02:18

Downtown Austin was in high form in 1996. Some of the most promising software startups in the world were there. As Claire entered Avenue Café/Las Manitas, she was surprised, but also delighted to see the place empty. Too early for programmers. She could eat in peace, and proceed to break the code on the migas.

She scooted into a booth, opened her briefcase and pulled out the yellow pad. Automatically, the waitress brought coffee; then five minutes later, the migas arrived. She scribbled out the identifiable ingredients. *Eggs*, of course, *tortilla chips* and *chilies*. She had that much already figured out, but there was something else. Some kind of piercing, sweet taste. And that was the secret. Claire was lost in analysis, having just realized the obvious: the sweet taste wasn't from the eggs, of course, but the salsa, which made sense. It was *cilantro*. As she scribbled away, someone came in and plopped down at the table next to her.

03:22

"Why are we here so early?" said the stranger.

The young man told her his name was Garrison. He was a programmer with Human Code, working in Director at the moment. Whatever that meant. But he planned to go on to C+ when the project wrapped in a couple of months. He'd gone all the way through high school, flunking math, and stuff like that, and no one back in San Antonio believed he had what it took to be a programmer. He was shameless. He was clueless. He was, in Claire's way of thinking, also mildly delusional. A programmer. He droned and droned. Finally, she looked up and told him plainly to go away, adding that she had a gun. He studied her for a few seconds. Maybe he had mistaken her for younger. Claire was a tricky guess. The pale-perfect skin and dimples and soft blue eyes conjured visions of a cheerleader on-the-loose. Ultimately, he must have decided she didn't look all that dangerous because he cranked it up again, asking what she did, and was she just teasing about the gun?

"No, I actually have one." Claire turned her attention back to the yellow pad. "I have a Glock-26 if you're really interested."

He snorted a half-laugh. Nervous, but not enough to shut up. At some point on the other side of unveiling his master plan, how he was going to get into movies and do special effects, she realized she was going to have to get serious with this guy.

"Wha-what do you do?" he wanted to know. Getting back to his original question.

"You say your name is Garrison?" she said. She cocked her head to the side as if now, she really cared. Anyone who knew her would have noticed the slight squint, and recognized that Claire had reached the limit.

05:18

He said he'd been *Gary*, originally, through about fifth grade, but *Garrison* was where the name came from, and it sounded better to be *Garrison*, or even *Graham*, than just *Gary*, don't you think?

"What do you do?" she asked.

Well, he'd already answered that one in excruciating detail, except now, maybe she was listening. Head-a-quiver, he wondered why she wanted to know.

"Computers are so interesting," she told him. Dishing him a saccharine smile, with dimples. "I just don't know how you guys figure them out. So complicated."

That's all it took. Gary cranked it up again. Saying what he'd said before, adding that he had another job, in addition to Human Code.

There were so many startups in Austin, Bicycle Cowboy paid him to do Director, after-hours. Plus, they paid cash, for obvious reasons.

06:16

Claire perked up. "Keeping a secret from your boss? Or …"

He told her that was also true, but then he made a face.

"Maybe I shouldn't say it, but mostly, it's Uncle Sam."

She almost giggled out loud. It was a gift from God. Tucked inside the briefcase, Claire carried a stash of business cards made just for her. Little *back-stories* for use if the need arose, and Gary had just traipsed into one of them. The one that identified her as a *field agent* with the IRS.

"Well, maybe you shouldn't have told me," said Claire, shaking her head. She couldn't have engineered it any better, if she'd had a week to set it up.

"So you're breaking the law, based on a higher morality?" she said. "How does that help the poor?"

It was a simple question, but Garrison was at a loss. He grabbed the first thing that floated into his brain. He told her … he told her … he told her *he tithed.*

"What?"

07:21

Gave money to a mission. And he figured he gave about sixty-percent of his income from Bicycle Cowboy, to Austin's street people. Directly. No guns. No bombs. And he didn't care if he didn't get tax credit. He put cash in an envelope and slid it anonymously under the door at the soup kitchen over on-um … *over on Seventh Street.* Worn out from invention, Garrison began to slow up with the backstory. Then stopped talking, altogether. And stared at Claire. He asked again, *what she did.*

Without saying a word, she opened her briefcase, felt for the slot in the liner, and produced a business card. Perhaps, better described as a *paper grenade,* given the way it seemed to blow up in Garrison's hand. He read it twice. Blanched, then shuddered, actually shuddered. Then read it a third time, before finally looking up. Blinking.

"The IRS?" he said.

"I'm a field investigator. What about you? Do you have a business card, Gary?"

He was reeling. "You're kidding, right?"

"No, actually I'm not. One of my colleagues will definitely have a few questions for you."

08:44

Garrison definitely had very white lips at the moment. And was unable to form even the shortest sentence. She was weary with the whole little melodrama and told him they would be able to look him up. Anyway, the government would be mostly interested in talking to the guys at Bicycle Cowboy, who were the *bigger fish* here.

"Are you okay?"

He didn't say. He looked like he might be about to throw up. Of course, he might also just sit there in a funk for the rest of the morning.

"Well, got to go to the office," she told him. "You ought to work for IRS. Liars. Cheats. Crooks. The line never ends, does it?"

She scooped up her papers, the briefcase and the check, and headed for the door. But as she walked past Garrison's table, she bent over and whispered that whatever happened, she wished him the best. She paid. Walked out. As much as she loved migas, she wouldn't be back. Avenue Café lost two customers that morning. Permanently. One of them was seriously thinking of moving to Guadalajara.

09:52

Claire tossed the briefcase to the table, then plopped on the edge of the bed where she began taking off the boots. They were genuine Texas boots bought right here in Austin, but she'd been wearing them for the last twenty hours, straight. She and her feet needed a break from Texas.

Her first impulse had been to crawl into bed. But sparkles on the water lured her to the balcony. And the breeze there. And the beauty of a morning that had – until now – gone unnoticed. She leaned over the rail and closed her eyes.

Except for the occasional *male-pestilence*, she felt pretty good about the way things were working out. It had taken sacrifice and hard work to get to this balcony in Texas. But it was worth it. All she had to do now was survive a bit of arcane corporate culture, and her destiny was set.

It fascinated her how people like Gary believed they could free-form it. They could opt out of preparation. They could make it in life because there was *more to them than the folks back in San Antonio* could've guessed. And this delusional man-child believed, this was the secret. The future would find you, because life was like jazz. And you don't compose jazz.

11:11

Claire had come to another conclusion. *Self-importance* was mostly a male-thing. Sure, women could be guilty too, but the real players, the real delusionoids were men. The engineers at Z-O weren't far behind Gary in terms of conceit. They believed they were the keepers of a great secret.

Naively, they thought, Firefly was about navigating the heavens with a basketball. But the real secret was at Fort Meade. A civilian contractor (Z-O) was providing developmental cover for a high-tech, robotic assassin. And while their position on the food-chain was higher, the engineers at Fort Meade were no less absorbed in their own secret worth. Logically, there was probably another control room somewhere, higher up, where an even greater secret was being hatched. One that included both NSA and Z-O within its borders. Though probably not Gary. Or whatever his name really was. During her time at NSA, Claire discovered, there were always secrets. Always something hidden.

12:22

Her fading attention drifted to the banks of Town Lake

where a woman jogged the trail. After that, she noticed a
couple. The little female couldn't have been more than sixteen,
and her boyfriend, not much older. The two were walking.
Pausing to embrace. Given her current state-of-mind, Claire
wanted to yell, they were *too young*. They should've *gone home
last night*. Jazz. Even at a distance she saw the clues. The cud-
dles and whispers. The caress of a finger. The little stranger was
completely disoriented. Upended by her emotions. It made
Claire want to cry. She slid to a sitting position behind the rail.
She watched with morbid fascination. The couple stopped and
looked out at the river. Arms interlocked. Good grief, she'd
seen this before. Seen it exactly.

13:20

Z-O was northeast of downtown, next to, and a little under
the landfill on Highway 290. Work at the facility, and the brain-
trust there, were a source of Austin-civic pride. But for Claire,
a military-contractor surrounded by garbage, was more than a
metaphor. Z-O, undoubtedly, had nasty secrets, and probably
an equally nasty habit of illegal dumping. Just a guess.

13:49

As she pulled into the parking garage, she wondered why the
city council hadn't taken action. Some of these DOD companies buried toxic by-products that infected the planet for thousands of years. She knew the answer about the city council,
though, or suspected it. Koepler had probably bought them off.

It had been a fleeting thought, but it kept coming back.
When she left Austin, when the work at Z-O was finished, perhaps she would pass an anonymous message to the Save Barton
Springs people, one of the environmental organizations in
town. Give them a few names of employees inside the company, with a list of probable by-products.

It wouldn't take much effort to conjure a major stink for the
lab. Z-O didn't need that kind of publicity. But of course, for
Claire this was just an urge of righteous indignation, an urge
to be resisted. You didn't let convictions interfere with your
profession. Break that rule and you would end up in the dou-

ble-wide next to Gary.

14:50

Claire parked. Took the underground tram to the north side of the facility, and the control room.

One of the younger techs, hands punched into his pockets, strolled over to Claire's desk. He was extremely shy, but somehow worked up enough courage to observe that *she'd come back for more.* Claire told him, she found it all *so very interesting.*

"By the way," she said, offering her hand, "congratulations on last night."

The tech was overcome, momentarily. He blushed, looked down at his feet.

"You should be very proud of yourself," she told him.

He agreed, it had been miraculous. He wasn't sure, anyone but Z-O could have pulled it off. "They tell you about tonight?" he asked.

"No," said Claire. A lie.

"Africa," said the engineer. "Opposite direction." He leaned over and whispered: "Victoria Falls, which is in Zimbabwe, towards the bottom of the continent."

"Really?"

"We're doing spherical aberration tests. You probably don't know what I'm talking about, but ... "

Claire interrupted him. She knew what a spherical aberration test was.

15:59

It turned out, the tech wasn't as resilient as Gary. He swallowed so hard, she heard it. With red cheeks, hands fisted deep into his pockets, he rushed back to the console, and Claire was immediately sorry she'd reacted the way she had, and would've followed him back to his desk. And reassured him. But Myles Koepler walked up.

"You're back," he said, rubbing his palms together. Obviously, he also had something to say, but didn't know quite how to start. He'd seen Claire's reaction to the tech. Not only was his timing bad, but his comment came totally out of left field.

"You're working on your doctorate, then? That's funny. You don't look like a doctoral student. But I'm sure you've heard that before."

"No-first time. What should I look like?"

16:48

At least he hadn't referred to her as *his little blondie* this time. Unlike the poor tech before him, Koepler did have enough conversational sense to hold his own, however. He asked when she would be defending her dissertation. Obviously, he didn't believe anything, he'd been told.

"Who are you working for?"

"I don't know what that means," she said. "I'm a grad student. My dissertation is on ultraviolet lensing. What do you want, Dr. Koepler?"

He stared at her, partly because, while he didn't believe her, he couldn't afford to say much more. He didn't want to make her mad. He may have been socially inept, but Koepler knew where the edges were. So he smiled. Nodded his head. That was it. Not another word. He wheeled around and walked back to his chair.

17:35

The stick light came up at exactly 12:06 a.m. As Firefly screamed toward the African coast.

Tonight, Claire sensed that while the engineers were noticeably tense, they were also confident. Every control, every tracking device, every single box they'd built had performed according to spec. When Firefly reached height and speed, Koepler took off his headset and strolled around. Studying the room. Double-checking everything. Admonishing everyone. Finally, he called for their attention. With Firefly on the way, Koepler wanted to launch a quick speech about the corporate mission, and how solutions were in the DNA at Z-0.

18:20

"I'm proud," he told them. "When I started this place fifteen years ago, we had to rent a warehouse in south Austin, which I know, some of you have heard me refer to, from time-to-time.

"In those days we had no idea, Z-O was going to be ... this, what you see, today. We've come to a ..."

Koepler hadn't gotten past his *page-one* yet, when an alarm went off. A split-second later, it was joined by others. In short order, the control room pulsed with warnings from every workstation. Koepler immediately switched gears. From motivational speaker, he transformed instantly into a football coach. More specifically, a coach in the process of losing a state championship. Almost screaming. Almost cursing. No more affirmation. No more DNA. He demanded to know what was going on, but no one could tell him. There was no tracking data, whatsoever. It was as if Firefly had fallen from the sky.

19:25

He ordered the engineer to *recheck the coordinates*, then told the video tech to *replay the last minute*. The engineer rewound the data, opening a window on the horizon. The unspoken fear was, the small globe had collided with an aircraft. The prospect of losing Firefly was horrifying enough, but the additional disaster of smashing into a commercial passenger jet was definitely the worst-case scenario. They studied the footage, flipping the window up, down, back, above ... nothing. Someone said, maybe it was the *transmitter*, or maybe it just *wasn't sending a signal*. Which might have been a possibility, except for one thing, Firefly had also *disappeared from radar*.

20:14

The phone rang in the control room. Claire knew it would be Fort Meade. She watched Koepler's face as he lifted the receiver. It would have been the civilized thing to do, to have shown a little compassion, but she couldn't find any. If you wanted to be a player in this business, you had to assume a tough game.

Claire slipped the legal pad into the briefcase and headed for the door. She would have wished Koepler good luck, but he didn't turn around. She reached for the handle, but as she did, telemetry chatter exploded from the speakers. Firefly was back.

20:50

What she knew, and they didn't: this exact thing had happened at both Grumman and Lockheed. No one in Fort Meade would be all that surprised, that it had happened again. Sure, there would be a few stiff memos, purely for corporate consumption, but in the end, no one would blame Z-O. Or question the engineering. Firefly simply had some kind of ongoing, internal problem. Claire returned to her desk as the flight controller announced: heaven's little basketball had made its way to an *un-programmed stop over Havana, at sixty-thousand feet*. Needless to say, there were serious issues here. Firefly had evidently made a U-turn, and gone in the opposite direction. And something else. The math was wrong. To reach Havana in thirty-five minutes was technically impossible. It was too far, too fast. Koepler ordered the unit back over international waters. This time, Firefly behaved, accelerating in a southeasterly direction at a little over Mach 3.

21:56

A second call came in over the secure line. Claire knew this would be from the Atlantic. The NSA controllers would be crawling back into the driver's seat. She slipped out. Climbed into the car. And headed back to the Four Seasons. She knew, with a little bit of luck, she would be going back in Maryland, perhaps within the next couple of weeks.

3 Halloween

Koepler's office was pretty much what you would expect. Except for the slab of granite that served as his desk. Practically every surface in the room was chrome, black leather or glass. It actually crossed her mind, he'd bought out a furniture expo somewhere. Only the desk. She had no idea where you found something like that. You could've buried five or six normal-sized people under it. The panorama behind the desk was even more outrageous. A fish tank, five meters by ten. Maybe more.

00:35

As Koepler pointed to a chair, meaning she could sit, he said he had intended to invite her over for a couple of months. And hoped she was enjoying Texas.

"My schedule is crazy, he told her, "getting crazier every single day. Feels like I've spent six months here without going home." He paused. "You're looking at my fish."

She said she was trying to figure out *how much something like that would cost.*

He motioned for her to come around to his side for a closer look, then explained, four years ago, when he had first heard about the contract, he thought it was all about submersible-RCVs.

01:14

"We'd done a couple of 'em for the Navy. Diving on wrecks. That sort of thing. So before we saw the actual specs on Firefly, I had the guys put this in. We would've used it as one of our testing tanks. Do you notice anything unusual?"

Well, something was odd about Koepler's monster aquarium. But not obvious.

"You're looking through three water zones. Three dimensions. The barracuda are in the saltwater. The salmon and lobsters, colder saltwater. And the pretty little yellow fish in the middle, they're my fresh-water babies. Tropical."

Claire asked how they had gotten all three, side-by-side. "Glass?"

"Nice observation. Actually, we've got a product called *Invisible Steel*. That's the codename. Here, take a look." He handed over a piece of finely woven screen. Practically translucent. And so light, Claire barely felt it in her hand.

"Tough as Kevlar," he told her, "non-permeable, with a thermal-transference less than two-percent. Put it in water, it disappears completely. Watch."

02:29

With a remote, he dialed down the lights, spotlighting the fish in the mid-dimension. They darted back and forth, oblivious, or unimpressed, by the predatory shadows circling around. What was most intriguing, there was no optical distortion. It was perfectly invisible. A steel wall. If Koepler wasn't overstating it.

"Once it's in place, you can't break it. Blast it. Cut it with a torch. Or drive a sub through. We're hoping to fence off all open water access to our nukes."

She said it was impressive, and thanked him for showing it to her.

"One other thing, actually," he told her. He paused to organize his thoughts. "Okay, here's the deal. I've been wanting to say this. We were lucky to get the contract. And we know it. Goes for both Z-O and Austin. So please, tell everyone what a good job we've done, because we have. Last night was just one of those things. I've got the guys on it twenty-four/seven. Won't happen again. My word."

03:37

Claire stared at the fish. She'd heard what he said, but pretended to be more interested in what was going on behind him, in the tank. When he realized this, he handed over the controller.

"Play with it," he said. "See what happens."

"Must make them crazy," she told him, meaning the barracuda. "Being able to just see lunch, but not be able to get at it."

"That's why we keep them hungry. That way, they do product testing for us, in a manner of speaking."

As if on cue, the largest predator in the tank lunged for the salmon. Or maybe the brightly lit, yellow water babies in the middle. But it was like hitting a wall. He bounced off, then swam away in a daze. She smiled. It was impressive technology.

"Soooo … getting back. Why don't you tell your people all the good things about us. We've got first-rate research in this town," he told her.

04:35

Claire handed back the controller and made her way back to the other side of the slab.

"You know something Miss Whitlock, I'm not convinced about you, not convinced you're a student. But I've got a pretty good idea who you work for."

Claire stood behind the chair. She told him, she didn't understand the point he was trying to make.

"I don't want to come off like a broken record, but when you don't work for the federal government, employment is pretty much day-to-day, what you can get. Maybe that's the point. We need contract work in this town. Tell your people, with the university, the other military contractors, and all this first-rate engineering we've got, Austin's like … we've got it all. Plus, we are the live music capitol of the world."

"*My people?* What's that supposed to mean?" she said. "I'm working my dissertation. What is it about that, you don't get?"

"Oh-right," he said, "but of course, my guess is, you probably already have a doctorate. You're here, basically tracking the project. And that's okay. We expect as much. But if there's anything you can do, help us get the word out about Austin."

One more time, she told him, she was *a student*, and had *a research grant*. That was all. And this was what the grant involved: looking in on related projects.

"Is that all Dr. Koepler?"

"No. One more thing. Since we're just having a sociable conversation here, let me say this. I read you better than you think. You've got nothing but contempt for military contracting. Which is a bit weird given who you work for."

06:20

Claire didn't blink.

"It doesn't matter if you respect me or not, or what we do," he told her, "or if you think this is a prostitution of science."

"What?"

"Please," said Koepler. "Just give NSA the good news. Z-O and Austin can take them anywhere they need to go. Technically."

Claire was thinking the word: *Havana*. But she didn't say it out loud.

He went on. "And you're probably ... maybe you're thinking, this guy isn't going to know, one way or the other, how I write it up. And that's true. But one thing, Dr. Whitlock. I know who you work for. Think about that. Me knowing who you are means, maybe NSA needs someone with a little more opacity. It's not a threat. But I hope you give us an *A* when you give us a grade."

No, actually, it *was a threat*, and a respectable one at that.

07:24

Halloween. Claire sat at the back of the control room. Watching the preflight. As usual, everyone was tense. There wasn't an explanation for the little side trip to Havana. And of course, Claire knew it would *probably* happen again. There was no predicting, when it came to Firefly.

The launch light went green. Somewhere out there, halfway around the world, Firefly ascended into the skies. Heading for Victoria Falls. Lift-off plus one, plus two, plus three. Everything looked good for almost ten minutes. But Firefly was about to enter a reality, never seen before. Not at Z-O. Not at Lockheed. Not at Grumman.

08:10

Twenty-minutes in, Firefly disappeared from the scopes. Koepler went ballistic. Stomping back and forth. A tech pointed at a monitor. What had been a blank screen, now strobed dark-to-light. And on the dark cycle, something was fading in. More visible with each flash. At first, the scene appeared to be underwater, suggesting, Firefly *had gone down.*

"I think it's kelp," said the tech, pointing to the stalks. The strobing continued a few seconds, then stopped. Firefly seemed to be floating.

08:50

Claire had been an observer, to this point, so when she took command of the room, everyone except Koepler, sat there. Mouths agape. Not just because of what was going on with Firefly, but because the *little blondie* wasn't just a little blondie.

She walked to the video monitor. The charade was over, and she wasn't unhappy to see it go. She wasn't upset with Koepler, either. It wasn't his fault. To be honest, she was thrilled at the bizarre turn-of-events, taking place on her watch.

Her mind raced, sorting the short list of explanations, when a human voice entered the control room via the speakers. Wherever it was, Firefly seemed to be listening in on a conversation. In perfect German, the voice said, "Are you finished?" Then, "Don't be afraid."

Claire translated for the others. The words were repeated a second time, before the cell phone rumbled.

"Jerry," she said. "What's going on?"

09:54

She listened to her boss for a few seconds, then started relaying instructions from Fort Meade, to the engineers at Z-O. First thing, they needed to see if there were any controls. The flight engineer grabbed the stick. To everyone's surprise, the unit *executed* to his touch.

"Jerry, we are still driving."

There was a quick instruction to *park Firefly,* while the team in Maryland tried to figure out what to do next. After a few seconds, Claire relayed the command to *maneuver Firefly up, above the kelp.* The dark stalks turned out to be incredibly long. Not unlike like ribbons streaming from a fan. Firefly chased them upward until unexpectedly breaking into free space. And not quite as dark. Claire told the flight-controller to do *a 360.* When he did, a landform came into view on the horizon. Claire pointed and instructed the tech to *go there.*

Thirty-minutes earlier, she had been at the back of the room watching. Playing the role of an outsider. Now she was running the show at Z-O.

11:05

The engineer pushed the stick. Firefly moved forward, as it was supposed to. But it wasn't floating in a waterscape. The kelp seemed to be *free-standing.*

The unit made it across, then hovered at the shoreline. A shoreline with ridges and mounds, and nondescript landforms. Like the surface of the moon.

"Do you hear that?" she said into the cell phone. From the speakers came the boom and crack of thunder. Followed by a flash. Onscreen.

11:37

Claire instructed the tech to *guide Firefly up the bank, to the top of the ridge.* The explosions were coming from the other side. When it got to the top, Firefly gazed down into a world, nothing short of astonishing. It made sense in a remote way, but it was also unlike anything any of them had ever seen. She ordered the tech to *turn off the monitor.* When no one moved, she reached up and turned it off, herself. She told them to wait for her in the conference room. She had to say it a second time. Only then did the techs shuffle to their feet, in a complete daze, and make their way out. Koepler remained in his chair.

"Do you mind?" she said, nodding to the door. Koepler got up, quietly. And walked out.

Claire was alone. She powered the monitor back up. But by now, the image was gone. Firefly had stopped transmitting. At least they *had* the footage. It was a major, and wonderful malfunction, as far as she was concerned. Where Firefly had just gone would be the most interesting problem with the platform so far. And she would be *first in line* to be project manager. Hopefully.

By cell, Terance ordered her to remove the ClearRAM™ drives, and *get them to the airport*. A company jet would pick her up within an hour. Claire was going home to pursue what she imagined would be a great adventure.

4 Overlay

Overlaying a black project with a white one proved an extraordinary tactic, and something NSA had gotten pretty good at by the 1990s. Neither the public, nor many in government knew *just how good*. Thanks to Firefly's recent excursions, however, the veil was about to lift. Slightly. And a few political functionaries would gain a rare entrée into one of the agency's most secret operations. They would debate costs. Revel in the vanity that comes with oversight. And walk away with a sense that things were under control. NSA was accountable. And that was the ultimate genius of it. Investigating the topside of an overlay satisfied political vanities without compromising the important stuff, beneath. *Brain-peeking*, for instance.

00:53

Hosted at NSA's Bohnert Theater, the symposium included bureaucrats from the Pentagon, General Accounting Office, a couple of oversight committees, the CIA, NSA, and significantly, the President's science advisor. Claire's boss, Jerry Terance, hosted the event. Terance was a pleasant man. With a smile that appeared genuine. And whose voice resonated assurance. He welcomed the visitors to Bonhert. Then paused, giving everyone a chance to settle into their seats. When the audience was focused and ready, he began the presentation.

"We have a surveillance platform that's been around for fifty-years or so. It originated at the Foreign Technology Desk back in the 1950s. That's not very descriptive, but most of this is classified. Firefly is what the Luftwaffe were doing out at the Fiat plant near Lake Garda, in 1944. In those days, we knew the

German *Firefly* by another name. *Feu-fighter. Feu-ball.*"

Onscreen, a black and white slide clicked in showing an old man. Beneath the picture was a bulleted overview of Terance's forthcoming presentation.

02:11

"What we learned about Garda came from a man by the name of W. O. Schumann. He came in with Paperclip. He led us to a couple of working Feus. Most of the others were destroyed by the SS, the last weeks of the war."

The President's science advisor, an outspoken African-American in her mid-fifties, interrupted. Of all the people in the room, Terance feared her questions the most. The Administration didn't have to know about these things. In fact, it was better if they didn't. He would have to exercise great caution when answering her.

"So the Feus weren't UFOs?" she said.

This was tricky. The question hinted, she knew more about the answer than she was allowing. So he was *tricky* back. He didn't answer directly. He said, "Toward the end of the war, the Germans had been trying to knock our planes out of the skies. Using Feus. And while there was pretty advanced radio work going on, it didn't have anything to do with ETs."

Which was true, to an extent.

"They got to the point where they could guide a unit into our formations, then self-lock and chase. We don't think they ever succeeded, but it was far more advanced than anyone knew at the time."

03:34

Terance told them that NSA had been back-engineering the technology since the 1960s. He touched on the work at Lockheed, then Grumman in the 1980s, and now Z-O Tech.

"As a surveillance platform, Firefly is what I'd like to describe as the *ultimate look-down*. That's the good news. The bad news is, we've lost eight units over the course of the program. Firefly has all this amazing promise, if we can just keep it in the air without hitting something."

Terance's introduction was followed by three technical reports. Each about forty-five minutes. The session everyone was most interested in, though, was scheduled for early afternoon. And the only thing on the agenda for the rest of the day. The Firefly video.

04:21

After lunch, everyone returned to the auditorium to discover a stage, slightly rearranged. A video screen had been lowered from the ceiling. On the platform, encircled by strands of cabling, was the console from Austin. Complete with the original Clear RAM™ drives, the portal-generator, a keyboard, and an NSA technician. They settled in as the lights went down. Though Terance had seen it a hundred times, like everyone else, he was spellbound by the stream of images. It was a visual mystery, where the only knowable measurement was the 115-seconds across which it played.

05:01

When the voice from the video came up, Terance translated. "Are you finished?"

After that, everyone leaned forward, studying the kelp. The frames fore, starboard, and port, showed fronds being pushed aside. In the aft-window, they drifted back, as if on a wave.

Firefly moved higher, out of the kelp. There were flashes of light and a distant rumbling. If the kelp-field was like a river, if the landform resembled a river-bank, the flashes and booming sounded like a thunderstorm. Except, it wasn't *a river, river-bank or thunderstorm.* Not in the traditional sense. Fourteen seconds from the end, Firefly ascended for a peek over the ridge. Here, the field-of-view transformed into a bizarre world. A rugged place filled with shadows. *Not at all unlike the surface of the moon,* as Claire had suggested back in Austin. But the most astonishing feature was what appeared to be a light storm, swirling in the distance. A massive tempest. Churning bright and dark. Throwing off thunderbolts. And great belches of flame. Like the surface of the sun. During one particularly massive strike, the illumination flashed to the kelp-field, be-hind and below Firefly.

"And here it is," said Terance. "The image is only visible for two frames."

The tech clicked into slow-mo. As the footage stepped forward, one frame at a time, he rotated the portal, zooming in on a remote section of the kelp-field. At the flash, he hit *pause*. Partly obscured within the rippling fronds was a human face. Gaunt. Pale. Frightened. It produced a collective gasp from the audience.

"What're we seeing?"

Terance said, *he didn't know*. After two weeks, no one had an answer. *If Firefly was a look-down platform, what planet was it looking down on?*

07:15

A gentleman in a tweed sport coat – assumed to be CIA – commented on the audio. He exhaustively speculated that the words must somehow *link to the face in the shadows*. Terance agreed. That was the working assumption.

"I think it's also significant, the words are German. The country-of-origin for this technology."

The science advisor stood up. "You're telling us, all this … this is from the 1940s? The Nazis were working on this?"

When she said *Nazi*, Claire knew it was coming to her. She was the weapons-expert. Koepler had been wrong about her having a Ph.D. She had two. One in physics. One in the history of military technology.

"Wait a minute," said the President's advisor, "most of us know there's more here than we can talk about publicly, but don't paint over it Jerry. Don't tell us *the Germans were doing this a half-century ago*."

08:14

Operating from great discretion, Terance didn't reply. In-stead, he looked over to Claire and nodded. He would let the experts take it from here. Claire stood.

"The Nazis were doing incredible science," she said. For reasons, pretty understandable to anyone who's looked at history. After the Treaty of Versailles, they had to approach war-science from a completely different perspective. They couldn't just go out and have a traditional air force. Or navy. I mean, they couldn't go out and openly develop a new tank. They were under international prohibition. So they took up what we would – today – consider to be far-out projects, but outside the restrictions of Versailles. The explanation isn't as interesting as *ETs and UFOs*, but if you stand back and look at the context, it makes sense that the Feus showed up in Germany when they did."

09:10

Claire's performance was perfect. It was also a lie. A lie with roots. NSA's charter had been drafted in the Truman administration as a secret agency with an overlay. The topside involved signal intelligence. Through faxes, phone conversations and later, email, they monitored communication streams, serving the cause of national security. The bottom side of the overlay was opaque. Even to many of the employees at NSA. But here was the agency's true charter: signal intercepts from *beyond*. Evidence of civilizations on other planets. And the greatest secret of all: battlefields on both the moon and Mars. Stuff, whispered at the edges. Stuff that marked you as crazy, but also ... *made you crazy*. That was the ultimate reason for the secrecy.

10:09

Some of the reality, hidden in the little black NSA-bag, made people nuts. Even so, the dark end of the overlay was meant to be as shadowy to those in the Oval office, as the man-in-the-street. And when someone like Claire drew the curtain saying, there was *an alternative explanation*, that the exotic German technology was somehow logical, they had reached a line, not to be crossed. Even by the president. The bureaucrats at Bonhert let it drop. Then contented themselves in the idle-but-ignorant peace shared with most of their delusional countrymen. There couldn't be much to the subject of visitors, off-world. Just goofy delusions of them. And hyper-imagination, running wild.

10:55

At the back of the auditorium, a frizzy-haired old man raised his hand. Dr. Millard Nunnally. Long past an age when most people retired, Nunnally was still going strong. He'd been with NSA since the 1950s. Claire wasn't sure whether they *couldn't get rid of him*, or *couldn't afford* to get rid of him. The difference being significant.

"I think we're being a little too quick on this," he said. "It is true, what Claire said about Versailles. But something extraordinary was going on in Germany, and I think it's time we start giving the subject a little more respect."

"What's he saying?" said the science advisor.

"I'm saying, don't dismiss the German question out-of-hand, like everything is known," said Dr. Nunnally. "You want to do a little archeology, consider this. There's no fossil record for a lot of what the Nazis were doing. And if you're brave, ask yourself *why*?"

11:49

Attempting to head off what he believed was about to happen, Terance uncharacteristically *jumped the gun*. He said they shouldn't *veer off into UFOs or Nazi mysticism*, but stay on-target. It was clumsy rhetoric. Here was a room filled with ambitious functionaries, all of whom had just witnessed one of the most baffling video segments ever captured, only to have a distinguished scientist from NSA, and the team-leader on a classified project, traipse into a subject better suited to a comic-book convention. Terance was quick enough to realize he'd overplayed. He scrambled for redirection.

"Uh, Dr. Whitlock was at Z-O during the test," he said. "Claire, how would you respond to the point Dr. Nunnally is making?"

12:39

She agreed, there might be a few odd gaps in Nazi science, *in the fossil record*, so to speak. In some cases, where there should have been a traceable, evolutionary technology, the

Germans achieved breakthroughs, not predicated on anything that had gone before. Things just appeared out of nowhere. That's the way it seemed, at least.

"Dr. Nunnally knows, most of this is still a matter of national security," she said. "I can't fully speak to it, but what I can say …" her face brightened because she'd just come up with the punch line … "in that context, Nazi science *was an enigma.*"

Claire and Terance smiled at her witty reference. But they were the only ones in the room smiling.

13:24

As the session drew to a close, there were no hard-fast conclusions. Everyone agreed, the course for the technology was an appropriate course, and the expenditures, justified. Terance concluded, saying that they would do a postmortem later, then in a couple of years, *maybe re-let the contract.* Firefly would be operational at some future date. Guaranteed.

As everyone stood and stretched, and packed their briefcases, the only man still seated, called out again.

"What if this little remote-device of yours ended up in another dimension?"

The room went silent. Had the old man been a kook, they could've written him off. But Dr. Nunnally wasn't a kook. And what he said, here at the end, unsettled everyone. Especially his colleagues from NSA.

"Come on Millard. Time to go home," said Terance.

He and Claire exited quickly. Nunnally remained, alone in the auditorium. Still in his seat even when the lights went out.

14:31

Back in Terance's office, Terance and Claire were still in shock over the way it ended. Terance could see only one positive in the otherwise horrible conclusion. "I think it's enough to get him canned."

"Why's he still here? He's way past retirement," said Claire.

"Old school," replied Terance, staring off into space. "And he knows a lot."

Claire sensed, there was more to this than her boss was willing to explore.

"Seemed to me like he got pretty close to the edge," said Claire.

"Yeah, but it was a mistake. You can't say stuff like that without facing the consequences."

15:12

The conversation gradually trailed back into the good things. Anytime they gave Congress a scrap, it got them *off our backs for a while.*

"And I think overall, they were pretty impressed."

Claire agreed, then added, "Speaking of Austin and Z-O, you already know my opinion of Koepler, but as I was watching the footage again, I got to thinking, they did do a pretty good job. It's a shame they're going to take the hit on this. We should definitely try to use them again. If possible."

"Wh-what are you saying, Claire? You want to go back to Texas?"

"No ... n-not unless you need me to."

"Well good, because you're going to Chicago," he told her. "I know we don't usually do back-to-backs, but I think you're going to find this quite interesting."

Terance told her that *in late July, an abandoned sub-bunker had been discovered in northeastern Canada.*

"It may be Point 103," he told her. "That's what you are going to find out. Somehow, a TV-production crew did a documentary inside. Spent four days looking around."

"Are you serious? What did they find?"

"Well, they didn't find the Coler, but they did find a *strange little box.*"

What did he mean by that?

"The Blood Toys, Claire. Maybe."

15:39

It was totally unexpected, and she understood – immediately – the implications. And why someone from NSA would need to stay close to the project. She asked who was running the investigation.

"Well, we're not, at least not directly. We're trying to finesse the Canadians through the State Department. Right now, the miniature is under guard at the Chicago Museum of Military Technology. We're going in through JPL. And I assume, you would be interested in a quick trip to *Chi-town*."

"Absolutely," she said.

5 Baffin Island

Three months prior to the briefing at Bohnert, four months after Firefly's historic malfunction – mid-July 1996 – a production crew landed in Iqaluit, northern Canada, on Baffin Island. With some of the most spectacular granite walls on the planet, Baffin was a supremely rugged destination. From Iqaluit, the video crew traveled to Cape Dorset, where they hooked up with a fifty-foot trawler. The Dorset Blue. They sailed up Baffin's northwestern coast, eventually putting in at a fjord between Prince Charles and a small village. Igloolik.

00:38

During World War II, Baffin, along with other remote waypoints in the Canadian arctic, was highly valued by Nazi Germany. In this part of the world, storms blow northwest to southeast. And pretty much run the weather from North America to Europe. By setting up secret weather stations on places like Baffin, the Nazis could effectively forecast naval operations in the north Atlantic. But there was another secret. And the Allies found out about it half-way through the war. Not only were the Germans running clandestine weather stations, they were also running submarines. And the most notorious sub-bunker of all, Point 103, was never found after the war.

01:26

Like Nordhausen, Point 103 was described as a labyrinth of shafts and underground storage chambers cut deep into a mountain. Unlike Nordhausen, however, 103 had only one means of access. A small, naturally-formed ocean passage beneath ice and granite. The Point 103-complex, lost for half century, was about to be rediscovered at the end of a four-hundred foot climb.

01:56

The first four up the wall spent the night, dangling from nylon ropes, inside portaledge bags. Three were professional climbers from Canada. The fourth, Steven Kincaid, had chartered the expedition, and ran the production crew, still aboard the Dorset. Waiting for their turn at the wall. Though he had trained with a professional back in the States, after clinging to the granite at Baffin, Kincaid now hated climbing almost as much as he hated Canadians. And that was saying something. The only thing that kept him halfway sane was radio contact with the others on his production team, far below.

Kincaid radioed down that the Canadians were still running a half-hour behind schedule. Down on the boat, his co-producer, Dara Mishra, suggested, *maybe they should think about the batteries.* The video tech had been monitoring the wall through the Betacam's power-robbing view-finder.

"Hey boss, it's your call," said Bruce. Wilkes was the videographer.

"She's right, Bru. Save the camera. I have no idea how *perfunctory* it's going to be."

03:05

The list of his least-favorite things was quite long. And growing. Kincaid hated drizzle. Hated updrafts from the water. Hated Canadians. Hated the portaledge bag. And hated leg cramps. When he shifted left, pain rolled up the right calf. To the right, the left knotted up. He couldn't prove it, but he believed the Canadians knew how uncomfortable he was and were dragging things out, on purpose. Eventually, though, the last piton was driven in, followed by the careful positioning of the charge. Kincaid radioed down, they were *about to blow the port.* Finally. He gave a countdown. There was a sharp report, followed by a puff of smoke, and crumb-sized pieces of concrete raining into the ocean. The vent was open.

Kincaid was impatient. Immediately, he demanded to know if the two climbers, nearest the port, could see inside. They couldn't. Slowly, one of them drifted down until he could place a foot on the just-fractured lip of concrete.

"There's definitely a tube," he called out. "Goes way-back. Farther than I can see with the flashlight."

Given that the shaft was approximately a meter-and-a-half wide, it wasn't just a simple matter of stepping inside. The first man would have to drop past the opening, then crawl back up. Not impossible, but not the easiest maneuver either, encumbered as they were with gear.

04:45

It was afternoon before Kincaid eased out onto the wall. The final minutes would be the most dangerous. Kincaid swung over a few feet, then reattached to another spike. As his weight shifted, he imagined how it would feel if the piton pulled free. How it would feel, rocketing down to the water. Fortunately, the event only happened in his imagination. The Canadians had done their job well. They were careful with him. With one climber inside the vent pulling him in, and the other guiding him from below and beside, Kincaid hoisted himself into the port. Crawling in on his stomach.

It would be almost five hours before the professional climbers got back down to the Dorset. During that time, Kincaid would be alone. The first person inside the bunker since 1946. The official schedule called for him to rest until the others made it up, but it was Kincaid's charter. And his call, ultimately. No sooner were the Canadians back out, rappelling down the wall, but he shouldered his gear and struck off into the interior of the massive rock. Alone. Ready to make history.

06:05

The passage angled down at a grade of about five-degrees. Denying the impulse to rush ahead, he worked his way forward, methodically tracking the ceiling and floor with flashlights, as he went. One was a miner's light. The other, handheld. A hundred meters in, he saw something flickering in the illumination. A few steps later, he could just make out a ventilation fan, rusting in its mounts. Blocking the passage. When he reached it, he kicked it in. Past the fan, he noticed soot on the walls. Indication of a flash-fire. Odds were, the Nazis tried to destroy the bunker on their way out. Would there be any secrets left, to discover, he wondered?

The tube angled to the right. Kincaid clicked the stopwatch, logged the time, and sketched the rough location on his notepad.

What a job, boring through solid granite. That was one of the other things, often forgotten about the Nazis: their incredible skill at tunneling. Entombed here in their granite bunker, with only one underwater access, they could have held off the Allies indefinitely.

07:23

The last section of the vent ended at a grate. Kincaid attempted to peek through, hoping to see something on the other side. He logged the location and how much time it'd taken to get here. And then, like the fan, one kick and the thing crashed to the floor on the other side. With the obstruction cleared, what he discovered was a bit like a stairwell of a parking garage. There were steps up and down, a handrail, and a soot-covered light switch. He tore off a piece of paper, scribbled the words: *this way, follow me*, with an arrow. And placed it on the floor.

08:04

Next, he unhooked the nylon rope dangling from his pack. He secured it to one of the fasteners where the grate had been. Then tied his pack to the other and lowered it into the dark. With the rope fully extended, the pack dangled a couple of feet off the floor. He checked the rope, tugging it one last time. Testing it to see how secure it was. Then slid down. When he reached the landing, his heart was racing. He instinctively reached for the wall switch, not really expecting anything after half-a-century. But when he wound it, overhead there was a loud pop. Followed by glass and sparks. In an instant, his fear of not finding anything, melted away. There would be something. Like Claire Whitlock at NSA, Kincaid had an ecologist's heart for something the Nazi's had been working on at the end of the war. A device that generated free energy. If the mission to Baffin ended up with one of these generators, the world outside these granite walls would be changed forever.

He powered up the small handheld camera, held it with the lens aimed at his face, and delivered these lines, which would eventually be heard by millions around the world. That was the plan.

"I came down the rope," he said, still out of breath. "The stairway obviously goes somewhere, but what I want to show you is this."

09:34

He aimed the camera at the light switch and continued speaking. He wondered aloud, how there could *still be electricity*. And then hinted at the greater mystery. The thing that had brought him here in the first place.

"The Germans had a couple of technologies, like the Coler generator for example. A free-energy device that broke the *laws of electricity*. We may be on the trail of that notorious generator, uh-notorious technology that the Allies hid from us after the war."

After a rather ponderous, self-righteous soliloquy on greed and the American way, Kincaid shut off the camera. No one could stop him now. The plan was ticking like a clock, exactly as he had designed it. He re-shouldered the pack and headed down.

10:32

The stairs seemed to go on forever. He stopped a couple of times to record a few more observations. Toward the end of his second interview with himself, he despaired of ever reaching the bottom, but *what an incredible discovery. Point 103 would be the major archeological find of the decade.* He said that too, four or five times, actually. Eventually, he did reach the bottom, where he was overcome by a sense of ... maybe ... a presence in the darkness. Of course, he was alone. And his perceptions were only goofing with him. But the sense-of-someone else was so strong, a thought flashed through his mind. The darkness seemed to be almost ... breathing.

11:26

From the stairwell he made his way into a blackened hallway lined with doors, some of which were open. Kincaid scribbled another message. *This way*, with an arrow aimed down the hall. He placed it on the floor just to make sure they knew his direction. Then cautiously, he proceeded down the passage. Listening as he went.

6 End of the Line

The Canadian climbers, Taitenger, Rousseau and Fitzer, had worked Baffin for more than a decade. Masters of extreme climbing, they always went up, prepared to face anything the weather or the wall could throw at them. This particular charter was different, though. It involved something they'd never done before. They'd never explored the backside, the dark side of Baffin's granite walls. If Kincaid and the three members of his crew were troubled about the climb up, the Canadians worried about what happened after that. A full day after saying goodbye to the captain of the Dorset Blue, the professional climbers and the video crew made it to the port. Dara went in first, then Wilkes and Peterson, the sound engineer. To no one's surprise, Kincaid was gone.

00:51

Ben Fitzer, who went by the nickname, *Bang-Bang*, was the lead climber. He had earned his name in his wild youth, where – under the influence – he had put ten rounds into a water hose, masquerading as a timber rattler. Wild youth notwithstanding, Fitzer was now an even-tempered diplomat in his fifties. A conservative business professional. He solemnly observed that Kincaid had *taken a huge risk*.

"If he gets killed down here, we might never find him. I'm sorry to tell you this, but-uh we're going to have to catch up before he gets permanently lost. Or worse."

The original plan had them resting half-a-day, but now they would have to accelerate the schedule. They rested two hours. Hydrated. Reconfigured the packs and ate a couple of power bars, each. Climbing gear was stacked neatly. Boots and ice hammers, wiped down. When they'd finished, Fitzer took the point. The six of them, strung out in a line, headed deeper into the mountain, following Kincaid's paper trail.

02:00

By now, Kincaid had reached the end of the line. His trek conveyed him to the end of a platform overlooking what had been a cavernous harbor. It was impossible to gauge the full size of the chamber, darkness swallowed the frail beam from his light. But it was massive. He made his way across crumbling deck-boards. Looking for artifacts. He was also mystified by the presence of fresh air. Something was driving an air-exchange down here. A prospect almost as unlikely as an exploding light bulb. And there were other curious discoveries. Most significantly, a concrete pier, though there was no ocean. The evidence of soot suggested, the harbor had been blasted dry.

02:50

As Kincaid explored his just-discovered lost world, the descent for the others was slow, but uneventful. Everyone picked up smudge from the handrail. A grime that spread to jackets, shirts and boots. Like Kincaid before them, there was a point, they wondered if the stairs went on forever. But they did also reach the bottom, eventually, where they found Kincaid's final note. Fitzer pointed to the end of the hall. Barely visible, they could see a flickering illumination in the distance.

"I don't believe it," said the Canadian. "He built a fire."

Everyone arrived at the landing within seconds of each other, instantly silenced by the enormity of the space. At the end of the concrete pier, Kincaid had built a bonfire from scraps of deckboard. He stood. Waved them over. He called out, *not to worry. There was fresh air.* The others climbed across the debris and proceeded to the pier.

"Shine the light," said Kincaid. "This is where the sub-pen was. We found it guys! We made history!"

Almost immediately, the Canadians sauntered off to examine what remained of the loading dock. Hoping for a Canadian discovery, perhaps. While the Americans hung out around the fire.

"There are two other passages," Kincaid told them, pointing over to where the Canadians were walking. "And I hope you're ready for this, there's electricity down here."

They stared at him like he'd lost his mind. He proceeded to tell them about the exploding light bulb.

"You've got to think, there's a Coler, or something, and we're going to find it, kids. This is what it looks like, this is what history looks like, when you're making it."

The professional risk, Kincaid's crazy mission – this strange world they'd just discovered – it was all beyond what any of them expected. And if it came to an end in the next five minutes, the effort had already been worth it.

Dara could dump on Kincaid with the best of them, but in spite of herself, she found him, totally amazing. When it came to results, he was in a league by himself.

05:12

After a while, everyone gave up, trying to manage the grime. There was no way. Their faces were streaked, as were their hands and everything else. No one said it because who wanted to leave the chase, but each of them wondered if the soot might also be deadly. What you could see was bad enough. What were you inhaling?

There weren't many options for base camp. The Canadians were told to set it up on the pier. With military precision, they unrolled the bags and sorted provisions. The Americans, in the meantime, were ready to get it on. They unpacked, then headed off for a quick reconnaissance. Dara and Wilkes went down one of the corridors leading from the underground harbor. Kincaid and Peterson went down the other. Before leaving, Kincaid told the Canadians that they would be back in an hour, and would need a *nursing* dinner tonight. "One other thing, be careful with Bru's camera. It's rented."

06:13

Now this was said mostly for the benefit of Bruce Wilkes,

who'd had a hard time letting the Betacam out of his sight for even an hour. To the Canadians, though, Kincaid's admonition was unnecessary.

Just one more yank of the chain, going on since day-one. Kincaid hadn't concealed his contempt for all-things Canadian. And the Canadians hadn't concealed theirs, for him. The result of this mutual lack-of-respect would eventually bear consequences.

When the Americans disappeared, the conversation at the pier turned ugly. Taitenger, one of the climbers, wanted to give the Americans their money back and take over the charter. In the interest of the national sovereignty.

"This is a Canadian thing, I'm thinking."

"Don't start," said Fitzer. "What do we do? I'm being serious."

"Take 'em out."

"Meaning what?"said Fitzer, scratching his chin.

07:12

Well, Taitenger's plan was straightforward. They could *take them out*, as in lead them back to the boat. And if they refused, they could take them out as in *drag them out feet-first.*

"And toss them out the vent, I suppose. You think we'd ever climb Baffin again?" said Fitzer. He knew the proposal was only half-serious.

"This is a national treasure. They shouldn't be running it. The Yanks don't have to be in the middle of everyone else's business, Bang."

07:43

Rousseau piped up, a wiry, ex-sailor from Quebec. He was also in favor of *taking them out*, whatever that meant. Who cared if they never had another American client? That would suit him just fine. Maybe he would get regular again, he said.

"And what if we get a reward? Maybe they'll give us a million dollars and we won't have to climb for a living."

"Yeah, they'll give us a pat on the back," said Fitzer. "Now seriously, what do we do? Tie them up? It'll take a couple of days for someone to find us."

No one said anything for a few minutes, but Fitzer eventually had an idea.

"What if we could get someone down to the boat? Say we forgot something. We could call the MPs from the Dorset, and the Americans wouldn't suspect a thing. Meanwhile, we'll let them do all the work."

08:38

Within minutes of splitting off from the others, Dara and Wilkes hit paydirt. They opened the door on a workshop, almost completely itact. With the rest of the bunker basically monochromatic under a layer of soot, it was a shock to see color again. Along one wall were drums of dark red paint, long-since dried to the consistency of concrete. There were wooden worktables. Brushes, still in cleaning trays. A pile of rags. And stencils. One of which, caught Dara's eye immediately: a circle cut into a sheet of plastic. It was eerie business, exploring a room, abandoned for a half-century. As they worked their way down the hall, Kincaid and Peterson made an even greater discovery. The radio room. Receivers, transmitters, and assorted paraphernalia were still tuned to the last transmission. Peterson dropped the tool-bag and went for the dials like a five-year old. The controls clicked like new.

"Do you have any idea what these things are worth?"

"You mean if you could get them back to Chicago," said Kincaid, "but yeah, it's a complete exhibit all by itself."

On that point, Peterson asked how you would get stuff like this down a four-hundred foot wall. Particularly since everything in the bunker had been brought in originally, by sub.

"How do you get something like that …" Peterson pointed to a rack, " … through the shaft? And-uh what about the Canadians? What keeps them from claiming what we find?"

10:17

Kincaid was just starting to realize that he had made a huge miscalculation. Ultimately, this wasn't about getting vintage, short-wave radios back to the States. If they found the legendary Coler, the Canadians would make a jurisdictional claim.

Why hadn't he picked up on this little nuance before now? He was blown away by his own lack of foresight. And there was no one to blame. Standing in the radio room, he came to an unexpected realization. He had planned to seek, but not find. He had planned to do a ground-breaking documentary, write a book and retire, but hadn't counted on actual discovery. How incredibly stupid was that?

11:04

Peterson went back to playing with the radios. Guessing at the labels. Twiddling with the wiring harnesses. And then, behind the console, he discovered an electrical outlet.

Though preoccupied with his still-emerging, grim reality, Kincaid joined Peterson behind the unit. Together, they pushed it back. Peterson then opened the toolbag and retrieved the volt meter. Unrolled the leads.

"Moment of truth," he said as he tapped into the receptacle. Instantly, the needle jumped.

"We've got 25 cycles at 220-volts. Solid as a rock. Steven, you were right."

Peterson was now talking non-stop, fully convinced, all they needed were replacement tubes, and they could fire up the radios. Good as new. He was ready to pop the back on the main unit and fiddle with the insides, but the somber Kincaid took the screwdriver from his hand and pushed it back into the toolbag, along with the voltmeter.

"Hey!"

"Explore the rest of the hall first," Kincaid told him. "We don't have all day."

They had spent so much time with the radios, Kincaid suggested they split up. He sent Peterson to the offices down one side of the corridor. He checked the other.

12:22

The first door Kincaid opened was a storage closet. Inside were ancient brooms, mops, and a trashcan. Behind the next, a toilet. Incredibly clean after forty-years. Ready to use and flush, except it didn't, when he did. When he opened the next door, in the beam from the flashlight, he saw a desk and chair. The desk had carved legs and ivory inlay. He assumed, this was the administrative office. There was a filing cabinet. Drawers were open. Papers scattered everywhere. At one end of the room was an old-fashioned typewriter with a high faceplate and extra long carriage. It was wonderful. It was also depressing. He probably wouldn't be getting any of it back to Chicago.

Then the beam from the flashlight spilled to another door, leading into a warren of inner offices.

13:17

As Kincaid was exploring the administrative center, Peterson discovered the gymnasium. Like the paint shop, the room was huge. There were free weights. A jogging track. A yellowed towel, still draped across a bench. And lockers. Peterson opened them one by one. Inside were crumbling shoes, rotted workout clothes, with pictures of wives and girlfriends still taped to the doors.

Meanwhile, Kincaid eased deeper into the administrative center. The next office had oak paneling and a dark red carpet, now brown. Also, double-doors with an ornate set of tarnished handles. He opened them. And was instantly hit with a foul stench. But it was the jackpot. The Führer looked down at him from a painting on the wall. There were bookcases. A regal desk and over-sized chair. Behind the desk was a wall safe, opened and seemingly empty.

When he stepped around to check it out, though, the light fell to a grisly discovery. Human bones, wrapped in the decaying shreds of an officer's uniform. And close-by, a Lugar. That's when Kincaid saw the paper on the floor.

The mind blocks things it doesn't understand. So his first thought was one of coincidence. He picked it up. *This way* was written on the page, with an arrow next to the words. An exact duplicate of the note he had left on the stairwell. But most amazing, the writing appeared to be his own.

14:53

He steadied himself on the armrest and sat down, astraddle

the bones on the floor. The note would've been a nice joke if there'd been someone around to take credit. In fact, he did call out, hoping Dara or Wilkes would step forward and confess. But there was only silence. As hard as it was to believe, those were definitely *his* letters. His *t*. His *s*. His arrow. He realized something else. Based on the placement, where the paper had been when he entered the room, the arrow had been pointing to a door on the opposite wall. Not that he was frightened, necessarily, but definitely of two minds as to whether or not, to open it.

At last, he stood, bravely walked forward, turned the handle, and nothing jumped out, but on the floor he found a cherrywood box. And atop the box, another yellow sheet of paper. What he read this time set him reeling. In his own handwriting were these words: *What has been found will also be taken.*

15:56

By the time they all got back to the pier, all four Americans were covered. Skin and clothing verged on one color. Soot-black. Peterson, the only African-American on the charter, said the new skin tones were starting to be an improvement, but there were still anatomical problems to be considered. When he said this, there was a lot of laughing and finger pointing. Under her breath, Dara said, *men are stupid.*

All-in-all, though, everyone was on their best behavior. Even Kincaid. He went over-the-top, talking about the freeze-dried stew. Saying it was like *homemade.* And what had they done to make it so good?

Fitzer, for his part, was equally magnanimous. He complimented the Americans. Telling them they were first-rate explorers.

16:43

It was weird that no one got suspicious. There was simply too much good will. The Canadians, of course, were actually looking for an excuse to get back to the Dorset. Which explained their *conversational sunshine.* And Kincaid was trying to come up with something to outwit anyone who might try to take possession of what he now considered his own. One other thing. He had a secret. He had made a breathtaking discovery. A discovery that had come with a warning. *What has been found will also be taken.* As he listened to the others, Kincaid had another blast of intuition. A thought that would've been totally alien, a couple of hours earlier. It crossed his mind, he would have to forget the Coler. It was an odd, powerful impulse. It wasn't as if he was hearing voices, but a clear message seemed to be transmitting from a place beyond conscience. As if someone, somewhere, was trying to tell him to concentrate on getting the cherrywood box back, instead. This would be major a departure from his original intention.

17:56

Around the campfire, Peterson told about the volt meter. Finding a hot electrical outlet was totally mind-blowing. As he recalled the triumph, Dara got more and more excited, and finally, couldn't hold back. From a sitting position, she rose to her knees and waddled over to Kincaid. Threw her arms around him. Gave him a long hug. And he pretended to be repulsed. He told her to stop, she was nasty. By this point, everyone was covered. But it only egged her on. She grabbed him again, kissed him, rubbing grime from her cheeks to his, to much applause.

18:32

When he broke free, Kincaid said, *slow down.* It wasn't time to party. Not yet. There were problems and they couldn't *relent.* Not yet.

"Guys, we can't test the current," he told them. "We left the step-down transformer on the boat."

"We did?"

"Yeah, the thing weighed a ton," said Taitenger.

"And that's why we didn't bring it up," Kincaid said, "but, now don't say *no* until you hear me out. We're going to have to figure out a way to get a few radios down to the Dorsett. And then, someone's going to have to go back down for the transformer. We need it, if we're going to do the video."

Of course, there was no way the Canadians were going to turn down the invitation. After all, this was the very thing they wanted to do. Get back to the boat.

And ultimately, it was agreed. After a good night's sleep, the Americans would continue to explore, and as they did, Fitzer and Rousseau would set a line of Mini-Traxions down the wall, and Taitenger would hustle to the boat for the transformer. Oh, and a quick radio transmission.

19:37

Time for bed. Fitzer and his team harvested a stack of wooden planks to keep the fire burning. Everyone dragged their sleeping bags together, except for Dara and Kincaid. They paired off into the shadows, beyond the pier. There were assumptions about this.

Long after the others were asleep, the two of them were still whispering about the day. Kincaid went into more detail about the administrative office, but avoided saying anything about the bizarre note or cherrywood box. Still, Dara had a feeling he was trying to tell her something, because he kept saying how it would be better to *hit a single* than be *put out at second.*

Another thing he kept repeating. *Sometimes you cut your losses.*

20:26

Her lips practically touching his ear, she finally asked him point blank, what was he saying? He told her, they wouldn't be taking the Coler back.

"I think it's here, that or something, but we won't be the ones to discover it."

She was dumbfounded.

"How do you know we won't?"

"Because the Canadians will *abrogate* what we find, and put it into another closet somewhere."

"I think you mean *confiscate*," she said. "Isn't this a little too late to be thinking about this?"

He told her, that was why they had to get a first-rate video, showing the transformer in action. Maybe they could run a camera light, or charge a battery. Offer proof, unimpeachable evidence of a cover-up. The inevitable documentary of the mission to Baffin could thus be used to force the Canadians to go public with whatever they eventually found down here.

"Video footage is all we're going to have at the end of the day. That's the reality. Don't look at me like that."

"Steven, it's crazy. Look what's gone into this. And the Coler. It's got to be here. You know it. I know it."

He told her, it had never happened before, but something like an *admonition*, something very strong had come over him that afternoon. He knew, beyond a shadow of a doubt, what would happen next. They would be denied their rightful discoveries by the Canadians.

"*Premonition*," she said, correcting him.

22:01

The conversation lasted another half-hour, until Dara drifted off. She told him they would have to *take it up again in the morning.*

As she and the others slept, Kincaid quietly crawled out of the bag and made his way through the main cavern. Back into the passageways. Retracing his steps. Exploring the gym, again. And the paint shop. Hoping for a missed alcove, or door they had failed to notice.

22:28

He placed his palm on the wall, checking for structural quiver. The kind of vibration a generator might transfer to floors or ceilings. And then, turned off the flashlight to focus his hearing. Expecting a creek. Or a groan of geology against concrete. Leaning against the wall, listening hard, that's when the absolute quiet of Point 103 entered his soul. Quiet, but also noisy in a way. He began to have a definite sense of something else, something stronger than premonition lurking in the silence. A sense of breathing, again ... whispering. And the longer he stood in the passage, the light off, the louder it became. Even if it was only his imagination, though, it was too much. He switched on the flashlight, then hurried back to Dara's side. As he lay there sorting it out, that's when it fully hit him that someone or *some thing* had spoken to him, again. Clearly, though without words. It thoroughly rattled him.

23:38

Everything had made sense in the beginning, back in Chicago. But as the mission rolled forward, he was sinking into an unexpected sense of the paranormal. And with that realization, he did hear something. Hard to pinpoint the direction, but it seemed to be coming from the passage where he'd been, ten minutes earlier. Something distant. The scuff of a shoe against concrete, perhaps.

Try as he might to dismiss primal sensibilities, there was something tangible, out there in the dark. A spirituality that wouldn't have surprised his father.

He barely slept, after that.

7 Blood Toys Bunker

They shot video inside the paint shop, then the gym, where they ate lunch. After that, Kincaid led to the office-complex. Here, they rolled a lot of footage on the wall-map, and a line of push pins, tracking a sub-pack. Presumably. After that, they set up a couple of low angle shots on a typewriter. Then a staged shot of documents on the floor.

There was an argument over the human remains. Wilkes didn't have any problem, shooting a close-up. But Dara was adamant. Photographing the remains demonstrated no regard for the next-of-kin, but she didn't have the final say. Kincaid said it would be better to have an honest shot of the scene than a dishonest one, based on some simple-minded etiquette. So they set the camera and proceeded to capture several fearsome close-ups.

00:51

There was one other thing. The wall-safe. Hard to miss, though that's exactly what Kincaid seemed to be doing. Miss it. Finally, Dara asked when he going to *look inside*. He seemed a little surprised. *What safe?*

"That one," said Dara, pointing. "In the middle of the wall."

She didn't understand his behavior, nor what seemed like a sudden attack of blindness. When he did get around to no-ticing, he got excited all-of-a-sudden. And animated. Throw-ing grand, sweeping gestures, and head bobs, protesting, *I didn't even see it*. For Dara, it seemed a tad staged. With great flourish, careful not to cast shadows, Kincaid reached for the handle and opened the door. *What could this be?*

02:43

Inside, was a cherrywood box. The one he had found the day before. He told Wilkes to *keep shooting*. Gently, Kincaid lifted it to the desk and opened the lid. Inside, was another box. Smaller, but exquisite. It looked like an exotic jewelry box. Brass. Covered with ornamental molding and strange markings.

Mouth open, intending to convey surprise, perhaps, Kincaid looked into the camera and said he wasn't sure, but they may have just solved one of World War II's most *alluring* mysteries.

02:23

With Peterson watching for the Canadians, everyone else focused on the box. On the inside-lid were pockets of velvet, five across, four rows down. With his index finger, Kincaid fished inside each one, withdrawing what appeared to be small tuning forks. From another pocket, he withdrew something even smaller. Which he placed on the table. Through the macro on the Betacam they saw a near-microscopic Panzer with a broken barrel. The detail was astonishing.

"Kids, I don't know for a fact, but we may be looking at the famous Blood Toys bunker. Keep shooting, Bru. Ou-out to me."

03:07

Aware that his words were being recorded for posterity, and a network special – hopefully – Kincaid took a breath. He'd had all night to rehearse what he was going to say now, off-the-cuff.

"It would've been what, April 1944? On or about Hitler's birthday. The Führer was given a miniature bunker, supposedly containing a small replica of every weapon in the *Reich armada*. The pieces, some of them not much larger than a fingernail, were said to have had *uh-inscrutable* detail. I want my executive assistant to come in for a second. Dara, you've studied this, haven't you?"

She stepped into the frame. He hadn't said anything about an interview.

"There have been a lot of theories about what might've been inside, did anyone ever find out what happened to the bunker after the war?"

She told him, most of the information on Blood Toys miniature *originated with the Chancellery staff in Berlin.* Everyone seemed to agree, the piece disappeared before Hitler's final days in the bunker.

"What're the chances we just solved the mystery?"asked Kincaid.

She said, the box certainly *fit the rumors.*

"Didn't Hitler also tell someone it contained a prophecy of some sort, for the German people?" he asked.

Dara said, "Actually yes, and that story had even come up before the end of the war."

04:31

Their attention turned back to the miniature bunker. Kincaid had difficulty lifting it out, but he was finally able to get his fingers between the padding and the brass-colored artifact.

Slowly, he lifted. Wilkes grabbed a couple of different angles. Even in the harsh illumination, the piece was amazing. From some angles, the box seemed to be pure gold. But the most intriguing feature: the strange letters, etched into the outer surface. Dara thought they were *Runes.*

"Occult symbols."

05:08

On the backside of the bunker was an opening, roughly the size of a quarter. Kincaid rotated the box toward the light. Wilkes cranked the Sony even closer, until the lens was practically touching the outer surface. The lens conveyed them past the threshold into micro-reality. Where the depth-of-field was so shallow, it was like peeking through a keyhole. But inside, at least to the degree they could see inside, the interior space was photographically-perfect. There seemed to be more vehicles in the shadows, but what they saw most clearly was a tiny motorcycle. Wheels parked in a perfectly cast puddle of oil.

Peterson wondered how the box opened. There weren't visible latches or hinges. Didn't make sense to have all this stuff inside if you couldn't get a better look. And of course, legend had it, the Führer had seen inside. He'd seen several levels, inside. With weapons parked on each.

06:04

It had to remain a mystery for the time-being because no one wanted to accidentally shatter the piece, trying to peel back one of the corners. The first priority would be getting it back to Chicago. And this is where Kincaid's little plot began. Carefully, he steered the revelation down a predetermined path. He told the crew what he'd already told Dara. His premonition. How the Canadian government would – his word – *obfuscate* their discovery. He insisted, getting the Coler was still a priority, as it had always been, "But they'll *abduct* anything we find, particularly something as *notorious* as the Coler."

It was a little hard for the others to follow his logic. They were giving up because someone might be *abducted*?

"And for the record, I believe the Coler is here," he continued, "but for our purposes, it doesn't matter. We've got one option. We focus on making a video to show the wattage going on down here. Eh-we make the best production we can, then get the documentary to the networks. If we do the job right, the Canadians will have to admit what they find, publicly. So we wouldn't be the ones to haul it out, okay, but we'll still play a role. We have to be completely ... what's the word?"

"*Altruistic*," said Dara.

"Altruistic," he repeated. "The point is, we won't be leaving empty-handed. This thing right here is also pretty notorious. But since we can't get the Coler, we'll do a deal on the Blood Toys. See what I'm saying? How it ties together?"

07:45

Wilkes wondered how they would get the cherrywood box back to Chicago. "If the Canadians would take the Coler, they would certainly take the box."

Out of the clear blue, or maybe not, Kincaid suddenly realized that they were bringing up a transformer. Right? And it came packed in a small crate.

When he said that, Dara realized what had been going on during the freeze-dried love-fest the night before. Kincaid had

61

manipulated the conversation. He needed the crate. And that implied: he'd known, he was going to need it. The little surprise-discovery in the administrative center had been completely staged. He'd been hiding information from her. What she could not have guessed, though, was that the Canadians had been working their own angle, as well. Within hours, the Canadian authorities would be on their way to Baffin.

Peterson wanted to know about the radios. Dara picked up the story-thread, saying that they would take a few, for appearances, but the Canadians would definitely confiscate them, if Steven's intuition was right. To make sure the other two were on the same page, Dara spelled it out carefully. "So we're going to hide the bunker and the miniatures in the transformer crate, and use the radios as bait."

She looked over to Kincaid, who seemed a little surprised that she had been able to figure out his secret plan.

"That is your thinking, right?"

He didn't answer, but nodded. It was.

09:17

Peterson and Wilkes went back to the dock to intercept the transformer, first thing. Dara and Kincaid repacked the Blood Toys miniature. As they worked, a little under her breath, she said that he wasn't much of an actor.

"Totally rehearsed, Steven. You put the bunker inside the safe didn't you? Why didn't you tell me?"

"Well, you went to sleep on me. Besides, I thought it would be nice, *enigmatically*-speaking, to discover the bunker on-camera. As it happened."

"You mean *cinematically*-speaking?"

"No. Both," he said, "cinematically and enigmap … *enigmatically*. It is a word isn't it?"

"Oh yeah, they're both words. Sure."

"Well, that's what I mean."

10:06

Inside the radio room, camera rolling, the tests with the step-down transformer turned out to be interesting. Peterson considered them little more than redundant. The volt meter said all that needed to be said. He didn't need a quartz light plugged into a fifty-year old circuit to make the point any more clearly. Before they shut the light off, Kincaid set up one last monologue.

10:30

"We may be looking at the best kept secret of the war," he said. "If it turns out, the Allies hid this *generational* technology, like what we seem to be seeing here, some of us will demand a Nuremberg II for crimes against the planet. Imagine what the world would've been like today if we'd turned off fossil fuels after the war. Cut."

This time, during his little speech, the Canadians were watching from the sidelines. When the eye-light went off, they applauded, and Kincaid told them, *none of it could've been done without Canada.* Which was true, technically.

With the video-production behind them, the next task involved selecting, then breaking down the radios which were to be taken out. Meanwhile, Dara and Kincaid slipped back to the pier where they placed the cherrywood box inside the crate, padding it with underwear and t-shirts.

11:29

It was grueling. For the climb down, the Canadians rigged self-locking pulleys to secure the equipment. Fifteen-hours after leaving the dark realm of Point 103, the Canadians and Americans staggered onto the deck of the Dorset Blue.

The little scene played out exactly as predicted. Thirty-minutes north of Dorset Bay, the HMCS Algonquian lumbered across the Dorset's course. Through a bullhorn, the Algonquian's captain instructed the Dorset to standby for boarding. Six Royal Marines in wet suits, all carrying machine pistols, rafted over. The Dorset's crew were grilled, along with the climbers, but the Americans took the brunt of it.

Where had they been? Where were the production permits? What were they trying to take out of the country? It was against the law to smuggle historical artifacts.

Kincaid was totally fed up with the Canadians. If they thought they could violate a private charter, or bully an American citizen, they had no idea who they were dealing with.

"Well we probably don't," said one of the Marines. "And don't actually care, either."

12:36

The officer warned Kincaid that there were laws protecting the nation's artifacts, and if he didn't shut up, he might find himself in a Canadian jail on smuggling charges. The Marines forced the captain to take them down to the radios. Then they brought them all back up to the deck, one by one. Kincaid plead with them. He had to have the radios for the museum. He would bring them back if that's what the Canadian government wanted. He also had a documentary to finish. He needed the radios. *Please.*

The officer listened impassively. Told him to go through channels. And if he wanted to see the radios again, he could bring his camera back to Canada, anytime.

13:25

Finally, the Dorset's captain gave the boarding party, coordinates to Point 103, a few miles up the coast. As well as the approximate elevation of the port. As the Marines motored back over to the Algonquian, Fitzer whispered to his thick-headed American friend, he was sorry it had to end like this.

With as much sincerity as he could muster, Kincaid told the thick-headed Canadian *not to worry*. "I don't blame you Bang. It happens, sometimes."

What he could've also said: *sacrificing a few vintage radios for the Blood Toys Bunker wasn't a bad trade-off.* The radios had been the perfect cover.

8 Chicago

The Museum of Military Technology (MMT) on Lake Shore Drive in Chicago, is one of the largest of its kind in the country. When it opened in 1968, the Tribune called it a *frou-frou barn*, claiming, it looked like a huge, overwrought warehouse.

In 1995, the year before the Baffin expedition, the Air Force loaned the MMT-Foundation an SR-71 Blackbird. The monstrosity filled the center aisle of the main hall, with space left over for tanks, troop carriers and a collection of biplanes. And there was even more space available. Smaller, permanent displays were housed in a series of connecting halls that formed the perimeter around the main room.

00:49

Claire Whitlock landed late Tuesday. She checked into the Marriott, then drove out to the museum, where examination of the Blood Toys bunker was going on around-the-clock. There were armed guards at the back entrance. She gave her name. Then asked if someone could take her card to Terry Pember, the administrator at MMT.

Pember showed up 10-minutes later. Like Koepler in Texas, he knew the signs. And knew she wasn't a student. If she was, she was certainly the best-looking Ph.D. candidate he had ever seen. In any event, her VIP pass came from on-high at JPL. And that was all he needed to know. He escorted her to the workshop and didn't ask questions.

01:35

The most amazing part of it all, to this point was, Kincaid had pulled it off. The Canadians didn't have a clue about what had happened until a month after the Americans were back in Chicago. Then, when he decided the timing was right, Kincaid held a news conference, making the claim: *they had discovered a secret device that generated electricity. After the war, the Allies had kept the generator under wraps. It was nothing less than a conspiracy. Big oil. The public utility sector. The government.* The accusations created a fire-storm in the media. Kincaid's face flashed from newspaper-to-screen. A textbook example of how make the media monster promote, what would eventually be, a TV-special.

02:26

He didn't say a word about the Blood Toys, though. He kept that little tidbit up his sleeve. His goal was to hoist the back-story, the context for the discovery, first. Then, when the Baffin-angle started losing its edge, the other shoe dropped. The media began picking up rumors of another discovery on Baffin: the Blood Toys bunker – the legendary artifact from World War II.

With that, the media heat went full-blast, again. For more than forty-days straight, there was something about Kincaid, or the Blood Toys, or the Coler-generator, on the first or second page of every major newspaper in the country. Eventually, the intelligence community got into the act, for reasons that weren't obvious at the time. And the Canadians, of course, went ballistic. Kincaid was especially heartened by this. He hated the backstabbing Canadians with their prissy conceit and thievery. They'd gotten what they deserved. Radios. He'd gotten the Blood Toys. He had been vindicated by fate.

03:37

There was another rationale in play, one that kept the U.S. government just outside the investigation. Had an intelligence agency, or the Smithsonian, or some other governmental entity taken over, the project would have essentially put the U.S. in the position of having run a secret operation in northern Canada. Not unlike what the Germans had done, half-a-century earlier. By officially leaving the artifacts at the MMT, a private foundation, the research remained semi-private, and the State Department was left to bail the water. It explained the furious pace inside the museum's workshop. Engineers and scientists unloaded crates as quickly as they arrived. Then they turned their frantic attentions to the assembly and tuning of exotic machines.

As if to emphasize the sense of spectacle, a makeshift stage had been erected at the far end of the workshop. Above it, theater lights. When Claire walked in, she thought it was a bit over-the-top, but she also knew, this was how it worked. Scientific endeavors were subject to free-market forces. Just like everything else. It was a variation on the theme of *eat-or-be-eaten*. But in this case, it was more like *promote-or-die*. So, while she wasn't much impressed by the staged drama at MMT, what she found infinitely more dramatic was the rumored appearance of the Microbotic-Impeller, the Micro-I, from Shervol Industries. It was something she had only read about it. Claire loved technology, and the Micro-I was exactly the sort of thing that got her off.

05:23

There were more than a dozen people crowding in, watching the assembly of the Micro-I, most of which was being performed by a dark-skinned man of Indian descent. Next to him, a young woman, also dark-skinned.

Roughly the size of an industrial freezer, the Micro-I was secured atop a wheeled-riser. The stand on which the unit would be placed was already onstage, where lesser mortals were busy, ratcheting the pieces together.

Out of nowhere, a stocky man in a blue blazer stepped to Claire's side. He was huge, towering over her by more than a half-meter.

"Excuse me," he said. He motioned for her badge.

Claire unsnapped it and handed it over.

"Cal-Tech?"

Claire told him *yes*. But he seemed to be a little suspicious. "Technically, I'm an observer for JPL," she told him.

No sooner had she said the words, than a smaller, well-dressed man carrying a legal pad, appeared at the guard's side. The lead-engineer from Shervol. Whatever it was he whispered to the security guard, Claire's interrogation came to an end. The big man handed back the ID. Thanked her. And quickly faded into the background again.

"Sorry about that," said the engineer. "Please, you're more than welcome to watch."

Before he walked off, she asked about the little man up front, doing the work on the Micro-I.

"Ah, that's-that's Dr. Madu Jha," he told her. "Our superstar."

"That's what I thought," said Claire, "thank you."

07:02

By the time the techs were cranking the assembled unit to the stage, Claire had worked her way to Jha's side, where she introduced herself. Jha turned and nodded politely. He was in his sixties. But looked quite a bit younger. That was one of the things said about him. He was *boyish*.

"The pleasure is mine, Ms. Claire," he said.

He was courteous. He was attentive. He was warmly sincere. He even asked permission to return to his work.

"They might drop something," he told her.

The Micro-I inched its way higher and higher until its base was level to the stand. Jha bounded onstage. Quietly, he directed the techs. They cranked the unit in place. Two minutes later, the device was perfectly secure.

Jha applauded with everyone else and seemed greatly relieved. Getting the Micro-I to Chicago, getting it up and running, then back to Shervol, were his primary concerns. With the heavy lifting done, Jha asked if there was a good strong cup of coffee, close-by. The young woman Claire noticed earlier said there was. She would get one for him.

She wheeled around and made her way back out to the hall. And Claire followed.

08:23

They were the only two people in the corridor. Hearing

footsteps, the woman turned to see, she was suddenly trailing a blonde.

"You're going for coffee?" said Claire. She introduced herself. The woman gave her a chance to catch up.

"And you are …?"

"Dara," said the woman.

"That's a beautiful name. Indian?"

"Yes, it is, actually."

Dara was all-business as they walked. Didn't say much else.

"I guess this is what we do," said Claire. "I guess … we're women. We *step and fetch.*"

Dara said she didn't really mind. Dr. Jha was a great man. Claire asked how long she'd worked for him.

"I don't, actually, I work for the museum," replied Dara.

"Oh."

09:12

In the break room, Dara threw away the old filter, installed a new one, and loaded it with coffee. She was equally curious about Claire. How had she been able to get into the museum? Claire explained, JPL had taken care of the *red tape.* She considered herself very lucky.

Dara thought, she was either lucky, or had heavy-duty connections.

"Did you know Dr. Jha before?" asked Claire.

"No. I just met him."

Claire asked what she did at the museum.

"I'm an assistant ah-video director, and about three-thousand other things, I think."

"Video? Do you happen to know anyone who worked on the V2 documentary, the one you guys did last year?"

"I did."

"Are you serious?"

"I was also on the crew at Baffin."

"Seriously?"

"Yeah, I'm still scraping it off." Dara held up her left pinky-finger. There was what appeared to be a dark strip of grunge deep inside the nail.

Claire couldn't believe her luck. She said she'd love to hear about Baffin, if that was okay.

"What do you want to know?"

"Everything," said Claire.

10:26

Steven Kincaid wore a coat and tie. He always dressed that way for his visit to the old woman on West Chalmers. He brought flowers and chocolates; and tonight, wrapped carefully inside that box, was a surprise.

Miss Suzanne, not *Suzy*, pranced to the door in white gloves, black leather slacks, and a vest, over a red jersey. Her hair was brilliant white. And puffed as high as ever. She was in her 80s.

"You shouldn't have done this," she said, commandeering the flowers, heading straight to the kitchen with them.

"Oh, don't forget this," he said, holding up the candy.

She pinched his cheek. He was spoiling her.

"And I've got something for you, love," she said.

Near the phone on the kitchen counter was an envelope. She picked it up and handed it over.

"I didn't come for a check," he said.

"I know that, silly boy, but this saves me a stamp. Besides, the foundation needs to see a face on my contribution. If they see you, Steven, they see the rich old bitty on West Chalmers. Right?"

11:38

Miss Suzanne's house was located in a row of houses on a closed street in north Chicago. Constructed next to the old McCormick Seminary in the 1800s, the quaint community had its own private park, and a grand place in Chicago history. Many houses in the neighborhood survived the Great Fire of 1871. And in the more-than-a-hundred years since, had been renewed and refurbished on a regular basis. By the mid-1990s they were again stately, without pretense, expensive, but still very historical.

Upon stepping through Miss Suzanne's front door, though,

any elegance or simplicity outside, evaporated. Kincaid entered a cluttered world unlike any he had ever seen. The décor could've been the insane result of crossing a third-rate museum with a fourth rate, used-furniture store. Honestly, he'd never fully comprehended all the things parked inside: the sofas, daybeds, ceramic cats, doodads, figurines, beer steins, decorator plastic grapes, wooden bowls, lamps, end tables … the place was dense. And he had a mild fear that it might all be coming to him when the old girl passed.

12:59

Here was the routine. There was always a bit of small talk at first, mostly, her telling all that had happened during the week. He listened, seated at the dining table> Hemmed in on all sides by plastic trees. As she rattled, she toddled back and forth to the kitchen, carrying the various dishes. Tonight, the motif was *Hungarian.*

"You've never tasted anything like this," she told him. "Sour cherry soup. So what do you say? You like it?"

Well-uh-unlike some of her theme-night concoctions, it turned out to be pretty good. Next came the Öntött saláta. Nor was it all that exotic. There were bits of bacon mixed in, and a hint of lemon.

13:44

After the saláta, however, it got dicey. The main course was something called *Venison with Forest-Berry Relish.* A dish as wild as road-kill, in his humble opinion. He kept his composure, mostly, but shivered with an unmistakable twitch when the first fork-load went in.

"Steven!"

"No, it's all good, just a bit of a surprise ... when it hit the tongue."

"What is your face telling me?"

He assured her, the bright flavor of her culinary masterwork had merely caught him off guard. That was all.

"Appetite is instinct, Steven, taste … acquired."

Kincaid had to eat a second helping of the venison to assure her that indeed, his naughty-but-naive taste buds had come around. He'd learned to relish the new dish, especially the actual relish, which took the edge off. A couple of tablespoons and you almost didn't taste the skid-marks.

14:47

Desert was something he couldn't pronounce. Sponge cake, basically, with whipping cream and rum-soaked raisins. But something he could honestly praise; and the old girl loved praise. After two servings, she removed her gloves. They took coffee in the living room.

"So talk to me about Canada," she said, in the afterglow of a grand dinner-presentation. "I'm sure you found out for yourself, Canadians tend to be a bit more refined, don't you agree?"

He nodded. Smiled. Stirred the coffee. He loved those Canadians, that's a fact. Sipping from rose-decorated, antique china cups, Kincaid described the Dorset Blue, the granite wall, and how the vent port had been *exactly where she'd said.*

"What was it like, inside?" She said, she imagined there were great presences.

He told her, most definitely. At some point, they would have to talk about that. He described the soot, and how they'd found the radio room, and the workshop, and the gym.

"It looked like the Germans just walked away," he told her. "There was even a towel on one of the benches in the gym."

"But that's not the most important thing, is it?" she said.

"No," he told her, "it's not. The Blood Toys were definitely the most important thing."

"I think I'm more interested in hearing about that," she told him.

"Well, we were able to see inside, a little bit, through a peephole. I'm sure we'll see more. We just haven't figured out how to open the thing yet."

16:28

Miss Suzanne said she was proud of him.

"And I believe it pleases them too," she told him. "Though they really haven't said, one way or the other."

Kincaid never knew how to respond to such statements. Her words made him extremely uncomfortable, though. Reminded him of just how crazy the old girl was.

She continued. "They even assisted you at one point, am I right?"

Her *friends*, whoever they were, unnerved him too. He was going to ask about them again, but the phone rang. It was Dara.

She spoke briefly with Miss Suzanne, who told her how good it was to have *you kids back*. There was no place like sweet-home Chicago.

Dara wanted to know if Steven was still there.

"She wants to talk to you," said Miss Suzanne, handing over the phone.

17:19

Dara told him there had been *a change* in the schedule. JPL would be conducting the first radar pass sometime after midnight.

He looked at his watch. "Uh-on my way in thirty-minutes. Maybe forty-five," he told her.

By such subtle effect he was putting Miss Suzanne on notice that he had something else to do tonight. Breaking off with her was never easy. When the call ended, he put the receiver down, and returned to where he'd been sitting. Neither spoke, at first. She finally got around to the main event of the evening.

"So … what else did you bring?" she asked.

"Huh. What do you mean?"

She liked being teased. But the intuition *unnerved* him. He told her, there wasn't anything else. But when she pretended to pout, he walked back to the kitchen table for the box of chocolates.

"Open it," he said, handing over the box, "but be careful."

"Are we to assume there's a secret here?"

18:25

She removed the ribbon. Her long fingers slid between the paper and the box, snapping the tape that anchored it. Carefully, she lifted the lid. Surrounded by chocolates, was a small plastic box. Inside, was one of the Blood Toys: a tiny artillery unit attached to a half-track. He told her, he had carefully, secretly removed it from the liner of the cherrywood box. And he had kept a tank for himself.

"My advice is, don't show it to anyone," he told her. "No one else knows."

Miss Suzanne was deeply moved by the gift. She didn't speak for the longest. When she did, her voice was trembling.

"It's our secret, Steven," she said.

9 Doodle-cams

When Kincaid walked in, two men from the Science and Industry Museum in Ottawa were waiting.

"Mr. Kincaid?"

"Huh?"

"We-uh need to talk."

"Okay."

"Some of what you've been saying about the Blood Toys, in public, you really ought to tone it down."

"Ah-let me guess: Canadians, right?"

There was a pause in the cadence, and maybe a twitchy-smile from the stranger, before continuing. "If you believe, a good defense is a good offense, it's not. You're way out of line."

Kincaid didn't respond.

"Let me give you the big picture. We're working up charges, just so you'll know. You took something that belongs to the people of Canada. It's part of our history. I guarantee, we're going to extradite you at some point, so keep it up, what you're doing. Just know this. You're digging a hole."

Kincaid shrugged and walked off. "By the way, boys," he said, as an after-thought, "I can have you *rejected*."

"You're a thief, Mr. Kincaid, and that's a fact."

"Here's a fact for you," said Kincaid, bestowing a special gesture, one even a Canadian would understand.

01:19

Onstage, the bunker sparkled in the overhead light. Somehow, its small presence filled the large room. So many people were crowding-in, Bruce Wilkes had to set the Betacam atop a scaffold. The resulting close-up was patched through, and displayed on the giant screen.

In the initial tests, the bunker had proven not so much impenetrable, as *invisible*. Failing the X-ray, the next option had been radar. Again, nothing. The tech changed the gain, dialed in the table-surface and a fountain pen, placed there for reference. It was as if the structure didn't exist. Radar saw nothing. After the second series of tests, museum director Pember announced a six-hour break so they could complete the setup of the Micro-I. During that time, pool-photographers would be taking close-ups of the Blood Toys bunker.

"The photos should be available at the press table, first thing in the morning. Also, we hope to have a translation of the glyphs. So, feel free to hang around if you want, but it might be a good opportunity to grab a little shut-eye."

02:30

Dara invited Claire to spend what was left of the night, at her place. She lived in an apartment on Patterson, not far from the museum.

On the way over, Claire asked about the Canadians. Asked if Kincaid had any reason to worry about being hauled off to prison. Dara told her, they'd *gotten what they deserved.*

"Steven had a premonition, what they were going to do, that they would try to confiscate everything, and they followed the script. That's precisely what they did."

"But will they prosecute?"

"I doubt it. Too much publicity. He's going to be okay. He always lands on his feet."

"What about the generator?"

03:13

"The Coler?"

Dara told about Hans Coler and the vintage, World War II tale of free energy. A story with which Claire was also well-acquainted. According to the post-war legend, Coler had perfected a way to crank out energy that sustained itself in the cranking out of more energy. Most everyone who'd pursued the device after the war had come to a conclusion. If such a generator existed, the utilities industry would be a thing of the past. A pretty devastating economic outcome, actually. Logically, if the Coler existed, but disappeared from public record, the list of reasons for its disappearance was a short one.

Did Dara and Kincaid suspect that the Coler was still somewhere inside Point 103?

"I don't know if it was the Coler, but something was, and I think we're going to find out, eventually. Steven's going to keep the story on the front page. They won't be able to sweep it under the rug. He's going to hammer away until the Canadian government comes clean with what they find. Steven can be an ass, but he can also be a perfectly brilliant ass."

As Dara opened the front door to the apartment, Claire told her, there was one thing she didn't understand. "How'd you find Point 103?"

"Someone Steven knows."

"Who?"

"Won't tell us."

04:42

Claire borrowed pajamas and a robe. They ended up at the dining table, knees up, talking about practically anything that popped into their heads. Claire said it was nice to live so close to work. Dara told her it was also expensive.

"If I stay, I'm going to have to find something cheaper. I don't look forward to it."

"You're moving?"

If the Baffin production received even half as much exposure as the documentary on the V2, and there was every evidence it would, she said *she might be tempted* to head back out to LA and try her luck at breaking into films. Again.

"Or ... there's Plan B, I can always go home."

"Where's that?"

"Jaipur. My father's a doctor. Ever heard of Jaipur?"

Claire said she hadn't. "In India, right?"

"Yes, it's known as the *Pink City* because of all the sandstone," said Dara. "I miss it."

05:40

Claire dug a little deeper. "Anyone waiting for you back there?" she asked. "Are you escaping a boyfriend?"

"No," said Dara.

"So why'd you come over?"

"Movies. I love 'em. I wanted to meet Warren Beatty and Michael Douglas. I think father let me come, maybe just to get it out of my system. And he was right. I never told him, of course, but he was. Working in L.A. didn't live up to my fantasies, but that's all I've wanted to do, since I was five. Make movies. Tell stories."

"How long were you out there?"

"Six months in L.A. A total mistake. I knew people in Chicago, so after going south, so to speak, in L.A., I went north, to school here in Chicago. Been here ever since."

Claire asked if she thought she'd stay in the U.S., permanently.

"Father made a deal. I'll go back to Jaipur if he sets me up in my own production company. Only one condition. I have to show him contracts first, before he spends even one rupee. Of course, without the equipment, how do I get contracts? My father is tricky."

06:58

According to the script, empathy cuts two ways. Claire waited, expecting Dara to show an interest in her past at some point, and she did. It was Claire's turn to *show-and-tell*. She trotted out her well-worn fiction, based lightly on the truth. Tonight though, something happened that had never happened. Claire was telling how she'd worked at McDonald's for a whole year after graduation. Waiting for her boyfriend to get his act together. And that's when the tears started. She was talking about the waiting, and the hoping, and the slow-dawning terror when you realize, your intentions aren't shared. But it played perfectly. Claire couldn't believe, she was having such a marvelous breakdown in front of a total stranger. Ultimately, she was able to get a grip when she stumbled into the part of the story where she got fed up with boyfriends completely, and went to Cal-Tech.

"If it taught me a lesson," she said, in voice slightly more composed, "then it was the best thing that could've ever happened, and it taught me a lesson. Did it ever."

Over tea that night, Dara and Claire became each other's new, best friend.

08:15

A little past 2 a.m., they were still talking when the phone rang. The first thing Dara said to the person on the other end was to apologize, Claire's cue to head for the living room.

Dara told the caller, she'd been working night and day for six months.

"Steven, I need my life back, a piece of it, at least."

Steven was her boss. When Dara proceeded to say, "You've obviously gotten what you want," then slam the receiver, Claire had the full picture, instantly.

"Are we okay?" Claire called out.

At first there was no response. Dara ran water in the sink. Washed the tea cups. Sniffled. Eventually a small, delicate voice whispered, *I'm fine.*

"They want me back at the museum," she said. "I've got to set up an interview."

"Right this minute?"

"State Department is shutting us down in the morning."

"Really?" said Claire. This was a huge surprise.

"Can you go back?"

"Absolutely," said Claire, her mind was still spinning with the news.

09:24

Thirty-minutes later, when they got back, Dara rushed inside while Claire called Fort Meade from the car. She didn't reach Terance, but did connect with the desk-supervisor, who confirmed that the politics had heated up.

"So they take possession in the morning?"

The supervisor told her, *not necessarily*. The Canadians wouldn't be getting the bunker back until the work in Chicago was finished.

"And you're sure about that?"

"Positive."

Claire asked the supervisor to pass on a message: "… tell Jerry, I connected with someone who was at Baffin. If there's anything he wants me to find out, get back A-S-A-P."

The supervisor said she would pass the message.

"Oh, Dr. Whitlock, don't know if you're interested, but-uh, want to know what the runes say? Rough translation is: *follow me*, or *follow this way*. Thought you'd be interested."

It didn't hit her at first, but a couple of minutes later, as she made her way inside, the words bounced back into her conscience, somehow familiar, somehow troubling, though she didn't place them, immediately.

10:35

Claire stepped inside the workshop in time to see Kincaid ordering Dara to the stage. Dressed-down in torn jeans, a flannel shirt and hiking boots, Kincaid struck Claire as totally full of himself, along with a few other things, probably. In the extreme. Most everyone else was in khakis or slacks, with the odd sociopath or two in a white shirt and tie. Not Kincaid. His clothes, his tangled blond hair and fuzzy chin, suggested someone deeply committed to the conceit of *artist-in-residence*.

Claire chased Dara to the stage; where Jha was feverishly entering data.

"Dr. Jha?" Dara was tentative. "Excuse me. I know there's a lot going on, but is there any way you can give us a quick interview?"

"About what?"

"The Micro-I. Just a general explanation, for the museum."

Jha reminded her that the technology was both proprietary and classified.

Dara understood, but he was the only one who could give an accurate overview the technology. Dara spoke to him in Hindi. Claire couldn't tell what she was saying, beyond the obvious. She was turning on the charm. And it worked, evidentially. Jha nodded. And then, he noticed Claire.

"Hello Ms. Claire. Nice to see you."

Claire smiled.

12:06

Kincaid jumped onstage, walked over to Jha and introduced himself.

"If you're wondering, I *charted* the *exposition*," he said, "plus I'm the boss of her."

Jha congratulated him on having such a pretty employee.

Kincaid explained what to expect. "The way it works, she asks questions." He held up a sheet of paper and handed them over.

"This one," said Jha, after scanning the page, "how the Doodle-cams were constructed, we can't go into that."

Kincaid wheeled around. "Don't ask it," he said. That's when he noticed Claire for the first time.

"Who's she?"

Dara told him, she was a doctoral student, and her name was Claire.

"No one else onstage," he said. "Into the cheap seats lady, like the rest of us."

"Steven, she's helping us, actually."

"Not up here she's not. Sorry."

As he was speaking, an older man with a neatly-groomed beard showed up at the edge of the stage, interrupting what was well on the way to becoming an argument.

"Are you Mister Kincaid?" he asked.

Kincaid turned from Claire, to the stranger.

"Congratulations," said the man. "Do you know just how lucky you were at Baffin?"

13:22

Kincaid went into his spiel, talking about the challenges

he'd had to overcome. As he talked, the stranger glanced over to Claire, holding the gaze a little too long. Not scary, but strangely aware. Or so it seemed. Then the man said something that really got her attention.

"A lot about the Reich never made it into the history books, Mr. Kincaid. Step lightly."

Claire couldn't put her finger on it, but the man came off as being … *too-aware, overly-aware … risk-aware*. When he turned and got lost in the crowd, something else crossed her mind. Koepler.

What if he'd made good on his threat and tagged her? The stranger definitely came across as NSA. An in-house investigator, maybe. But she didn't have the luxury, or time, for fretting. Kincaid wheeled around picked up with his demands, right where he'd left off, insisting that the stage be cleared. Just as he seemed to be reaching maximum inflexibility, Dr. Jha spoke up. Claire was his friend, too. He wanted her on the platform. Period.

With that, Kincaid threw up his hands and descended into the crowd. Out to the cheap seats.

14:44

When the camera finally rolled, when the interview started, Dr. Jha turned white, all of a sudden. His voice went thin. His sentences were punctuated with gulps. It got so out-of-control, they had to stop, so Dara could calm him down.

"If it helps, just forget the camera, talk to me," she told him. "Like we're having a conversation."

"I can't. This is not the first time."

"You can. Come on. Let's try. Dr. Jha, what can you tell us about this new technology?"

He took a breath. Wiped his forehead. Licked his lips. And looked directly into Dara's dark-brown eyes.

"Well, it's made by Shervol. It's called a *Microbotic Impeller*. And it's based on *swarm* technology."

She asked him what that meant. Jha explained, the microbots were based on ants, and ant-behavior.

"Except, they're designed for close-in photography ... instead of picnics. Each little bot has an imaging element. That's how they got the name."

"Which is …?"

"Doodle-cams."

"How do they work?"

Jha said, each unit captured, then transmitted a piece of a larger picture.

"From what they send back, we create a photometric map."

"How many little Doodle-ants are going in?"

"Five-hundred," he told her. "Each, takes a snap, then moves to the next level, and the next, until they've mapped everything inside. And that's pretty much … it."

He took another breath.

"Okay?"

"Perfect."

16:34

After the interview, when the camera and lights clicked off, Dr. Jha slumped back into his chair. He said, he preferred working in a lab, where, if you made a mistake, you didn't have a thousand people looking over your shoulder. Or watching on a big screen.

"I don't like people standing around. Sometimes, it's okay, like you and Miss Whitlock, but beautiful women are the exception to my rule. In fact, very beautiful women can stand on my stage, anytime. Hmm."

Dara and Jha spoke briefly in Hindi. More charm. More wishing him the best in their own private language.

10 Microbotic Swarm

Massed like a Roman phalanx, the small machines were motionless, at first, but eventually they started moving forward. A few stalled, then one started going in circles, jamming up the others.

"Dara, could you get my tweezers?" said Jha.

She opened the toolkit, pulled out a pair of tweezers and placed them in his hand. With the closed end, he thumped the hyper-active Doodle. The microbot stopped, but charged straight ahead, now, double-timing it.

"A-D-D," said Jha. "He knows better than that."

00:33

Jha was as gentle and unassuming as anyone Claire had ever met. It was sweet to see such a distinguished man talking to his little made-things as if they were children. With more than half the units inside the miniature, Jha seemed to relax a little. He estimated, they were a good thirty-minutes from the first pictures.

"Look." He pointed to the green circles moving across the computer display. He was obviously proud. "That's where they are, inside ... you can see ..."

01:06

The little cameras seemed to be fanning out across the first level, taking up positions on the bunker's inner ceilings and walls. A few appeared to be crawling atop objects inside the small space, which made it look like, they were suspended, mid-air.

Dara tapped her on the shoulder, motioned her to the side.

"Did you happen to see Steven went, by any chance?"

"Over there somewhere." Claire pointed. "Why?"

Dara said she didn't know how he wanted to handle the screenshots, whether she should just take them off the monitors, or what.

"No. We can do better than that. Let me print hard copy," said Jha. "Much better than shooting the screen."

Dara thanked him, but mumbled something to the effect that her boss was unpredictable. She couldn't afford *to assume.*

"I don't have a choice," she told him, "so ... hold my seat."

With a bit of a twinkle, Jha said he would do that. Happily.

02:02

There were only two on stage, Claire and Dr. Jha, who seemed to be having more technical trouble.

"Some of them are horsing around," he said. "I like to horse around, but not when I'm working. Come on guys. Grow up. Spank those hormones."

He looked over at Claire and smiled. Then turned back to the console. She loved the way he talked to them and about them as living things. That was precisely how he saw his Doodle-cams. As the swarm continued, he asked about her dissertation. What was it about?

Claire told him: *high-rez photometrics.*

"This is right up your alley, then."

"That's why they let me come to Chicago," she told him.

"Maybe you'll have a job for my Doodles someday," said Jha.

Conveniently, Claire's research suddenly called for *swarm technology*, as a matter of fact.

"But we call them CARBS. C-A-R-B-S." Claire told him it stood for *Compact Area Reconnaissance Bio-sensor.*

"Micro or nano?" he asked.

03:09

Claire hoped he wouldn't drill much deeper. Three or four more questions and he would punch through the other end of her cover story.

"Micro," she said. "Pre-op for cancer, and of course, nano

eventually, that's the big dream."

"Ah-that's the ticket," he replied. He was about to say something else, but the dots onscreen caught his attention. "Ay-yi-yi."

Claire looked to the monitor. One dot was running in circles, probably the one from before.

"Mr. A-D-D is still horsing around. The way the algorithm works, if we don't stop him pretty soon, another Doodle will copy him and start transmitting. Then another, and another. Then, the whole swarm gets infected with A-D-D."

Then, out of left field, he said something completely unexpected. He told Claire, again, he *liked horsing around as much as the next guy, but not when you're working*. He winked, then just above a whisper said, "You-uh horse around when you're working?"

Whoa Nellie! There was no escaping the subtext, here.

"Maybe Miss Claire doesn't horse around at all. *To … horse, or not to horse*, I guess that is the question."

His words, his obvious intention, made her almost physically ill. It caught her so off-guard, she said the first thing, and the only thing that came to mind, "I … I don't like horses," she said.

04:42

Dr. Jha still had the look. He whispered, she just hadn't met the right horse yet, then he *neighed*.

Claire was crushed. No, worse than that. Nauseated. Had one of her post-grad projects covered the art of vomiting-on-command, she might've blown an ill-wind in his direction, or thumped him, maybe, if she'd had a polo mallet. One thing she had learned, though, was the art-of-the-subtle. Unless they'd been paying attention, no one in the workshop would've noticed the offhanded way Claire stepped away from Jha, onstage. She moved to the side and examined her flip-phone, as if something was going on, call-wise. Jha, of course, realized he'd overstepped. He focused on the keyboard and worked in silence, until Dara came back.

It was curious to see so many notables-of-science, sprawled out on the floor like preschoolers. Some read. A few played cards. The younger ones goofed around with their computers.

Of course, a small part of the first level had been seen previously, the area immediately surrounding the motorcycle, now there would be a panorama of everything else. After post-processing, up-sampling, and photometric calculation, everyone expected to see a stunning world, perhaps an open window on a secret time.

06:10

"Dara, could you-um do something?" asked Jha. He wanted her to speak to the audience in his behalf, to tell them, *the Doodle-Cams were now on their way to the next station.*

She looked over to Claire. The prospect terrified Dara.

"Please ...," said Jha, in Hindi, this time.

Dara walked to the middle of the stage. In a faltering voice she repeated what she'd been asked to say, that the Doodles had made their first transmission and were now in the process of *moving to the second station.*

Someone called out, wondering how long it would be before a fly-through?

Jha whispered: "Tell them, thirty minutes."

06:52

The Doodle-cams were programmed to find the first level, unassisted. When one discovered the way down, the others swarmed into a line behind. Simple, in the real-world; complicated, as an act of programming.

Still, some Doodles weren't performing according to specification. Jha attempted to get them back on target via a reset, but you could see it in his face, he was increasingly concerned about the behavior. Within ten-minutes, thirty-percent of his small machines weren't moving at all.

11 Inside

Photometry is the study of brightness. Originally
a tool of astronomy, photometrics enabled researchers to measure the shapes and distances of stars. By the mid-1990s it was
also being used to create virtual space. The process involved
taking pictures of an object from different perspectives. With
those perspectives, then, the object's size and shape could be
interpolated as three-dimensional data, as in terrain maps, for
example. The Air Force used photometrics to simulate mission-flyovers, with elevations, landmarks, all the things the
pilot would ultimately see from the air.

00:40

Based on that principle, once the Doodle-cams captured
their small snapshots inside the Blood Toys bunker, Jha would
use the resulting photometric map to navigate each level in a
fly-through. 'A virtual walkabout inside an otherwise inaccessible space. A virtual world revealing a hidden world.

Jha had the path-controller between his knees. He called
over to Dara, "I need to avoid distraction. If anyone wants to
see anything in particular, tell them, they can tell you, and you
tell me. That way I won't have to be listening for a lot of voices.
Just you. I'm not good with cameras or audiences."

Turning to Claire, Dara whispered, "Neither am I."

01:29

"Uh-never mind," said Jha. There was no reason they had
include anyone else, "but if either of you ladies want to see
something, just say the word." Then he winked. "I'll show you

anything you want. Really."

Claire was still rather sad about her limitation, with respect to projectile-vomiting, but she was also, just plain mad. How amazing, at this point in history, that someone would be injecting sex and innuendo into a work-situation.

02:02

Jha directed the virtual camera deeper into the data-map. On-screen, the emerging images were astonishing. Three vehicles rezzed in. Initially, they appeared to be motorcycles with a small distinction. Instead of a rear wheel, each was fitted with a half-track.

"Anyone know what we're seeing here?" Jha asked, as he steered the virtual-camera forward.

Claire knew, but didn't say. They were Kleines 2s, designed for a driver, two passengers, and powerful enough to tow a field-artillery piece. Further down the aisle were more motorcycles. Claire identified them as BMW R-75s, Germany's courier platform.

What struck Claire, almost immediately, was the apparent newness of the machines: the realistic gloss in the paint. The boot-black shine of the leather. It was as if they'd just rolled off an assembly line, somewhere.

03:01

Jha steered to a point just above the handlebars, where something caught his attention. In the shadow between two BMWs were tools. Crescent wrenches. Screw drivers. Jha went down to within a virtual meter before the image started to artifact.

"Mister … ah-doctor, could you do something for me?" It was Kincaid.

Onstage, in a couple of hops, he asked for a close-up of the wall behind the motorcycles.

"Follow the electrical *conductor*. I want to see where it goes."

"The *conduit* … you mean?"

"Yeah. Conducts electricity to the room."

Jha did as he'd been asked. He tracked the conduit to the floor, where it disappeared into the faux-concrete.

"Uh-go back toward the box, I'm looking for a switch, some-where."

Jha chased the pipe, coming eventually to a wall-switch. Only three people in the room would've recognized it. The fixture inside the miniature was an exact duplicate of the one at Baffin.

04:11

Field-howitzers and small tanks lined the next row. Claire recognized the artillery pieces as Leichte 28s. The tanks were Pumas. Parked nearby were Schützenpanzerwagen 251s. Troop transports. In the last row were two massive vehicles, wheels ringed with iron plates. Claire guessed they were mine-rollers, of some sort.

Eventually, the virtual camera drifted to an inner door, op-posite the entry, where Dara noticed something, dead center of the doorway.

"And what's that?" asked Kincaid. He'd seen it too.

It looked like a piece of paper. Dara and Kincaid glanced at each other. Dara was about to say something, but before she did, Kincaid wheeled around, slipped back down into the crowd and disappeared. Dara followed him out.

05:06

Something about the reaction, the way they suddenly walked away, tweaked Claire's curiosity. It was fairly strange, they'd seen something onscreen, even though Claire wasn't sure what.

She waited for them to clear the room, then followed, out into the hall. Claire was definitely taking a chance here. If they saw her following them, there wouldn't be an easy explanation. She tracked them to the production office where she put her ear to the closed-door.

"Stephen, I'm not blind," Dara could be heard to say. "We saw what we saw, and maybe it doesn't mean anything."

"And what, exactly, is that supposed to mean?"

"It was just like Baffin," she told him, "the piece of paper, just like the ones you left for us. Don't pretend you don't know."

He said it was all weird enough without trying to make it weirder.

Claire strained to distinguish the words. She heard movement. Perhaps ... motion, indicating an embrace, but that might've also been her imagination. There was more shuffling, more of what sounded like hands caressing fabric. After several moments of what sounded like intimacy, Dara announced, she was going back. It was Claire's cue to slip into the shadows of the next doorway.

Dara left first. Kincaid followed.

06:35

For Claire, it was an opportunity. When the other two disappeared into the workshop, she ducked into the office. Made her way around the room. Opening drawers. Thumbing through the filing cabinet.

Except for video magazines and a thermos, Dara's desk was unremarkable. Claire found a Bible in the top drawer of Kincaid's desk. Beneath it were receipts and a pizza menu. But the Bible, that was fairly unexpected. Tucked inside was a Sunday bulletin from a church in Naperville. A strange set-piece in an increasingly strange puzzle.

07:14

"Where did you go?" asked Dara when Claire got back on stage.

"Daily check-in, faculty advisor wants me to let him in on everything. So what's happening here?"

"Not much," said Dara. She looked around to check out who might be listening, but only she, Claire, and Jha were onstage at the moment.

"This place is making me crazy."

"You've got a pretty good job girl," said Claire, "a lot of people would love to take your place."

"Maybe I can sell it to you."

"Come on Dara. A museum is a great place to work."

"Um-not only the museum," said Dara. "Sometimes it just flies into my head. How did I get here, in my life? I mean I know, but it's almost like I didn't have anything to do with any of it, I just drifted into … this circumstance."

"You're in Chicago," said Jha, smiling. Winking. A gift of bile, for Claire who rolled her eyes, then turned to Dara and said, "Jazz."

Dara didn't understand.

"Sometimes you play the note," said Claire, "it just happens."

"Well, it just happened, then, but it doesn't feel like music."

"Well-sometimes it doesn't," said Claire. "Sometimes you have to compose a few notes, I guess."

"Let me say something. You beautiful ladies are stimulating company," said Jha. "Very stimulating … on many levels, I might add. *Princesses of philosophy*, if you don't mind my saying."

08:46

Claire's interior monologue flashed to the vomiting scene again. He was really yanking her gag-reflex, and he wasn't finished. He sighted-in on Dara

"How would you like to come work for me?" asked Jha. "I spend half-the-year at home, and half in the States, I could always use a beautiful lady-helper."

Dara's expression was blank. She wasn't sure she'd heard him right. "You mean ... work for you?"

Jha said, *absolutely.*

"I-I don't know what to say. Really?"

"Let's do this," he told her. "We'll take a break, go out for lunch or something, where we can talk in private." He shot Claire a quick glance, and lost the smile, momentarily.

"Is this on the level?" asked Dara.

Jha winked. Reflexively, Claire grabbed her arm, but she didn't notice, because she smiled a broad smile and said: "Sure," like a silly little female.

09:45

A few minutes later, Claire was alone, feeling conspicuous. Maybe now it would be best to go to the cheap seats until someone got back, or maybe even do a little lunch. But she noticed Kincaid and the stranger, the one with the prescient observations from earlier in the day. They were walking toward the stage. As they passed, she reached out and lightly touched Kincaid's arm. She hadn't thought this through. Not yet.

"By the way, thanks," she said.

"Huh?" He turned.

"Thanks for letting me stay."

"Uh-yeah. Welcome," he said.

"Why don't you let me take you to lunch?" she said, her words coming as a shock. Who was running her mouth at the moment?

10:34

At this, the old man smiled, and nodded, and walked off.

"You're asking me?" He seemed quite surprised, and then she was quite surprised when he declined.

"Maybe some other time," he told her. "Thanks anyway."

He didn't mean it, of course. He was merely taking perverse pleasure in seeing the refusal land; how the gorgeous face flushed; how blondie stammered. It got pretty awkward, pretty fast.

"Chill, girl. I'm only teasing," he told her. "Sure. Let's do it."

The opening moves had thrown her completely off-balance. She hadn't planned to ask him, on a conscious level, at least, and the little social-riff seemed to blow up in her face. After expressing a distaste for jazz to Dara, she'd proceeded to march off into some kind of atonal free-fall. When he asked where she wanted to go, the only thing that came to her nearly-blank, still trembling mind was *White Castle*. She said she'd never been. Then, she tried to erase the shock-lines that had to be all over her face.

11:42

Over lunch, she reestablished a small degree of composure. It felt like she'd been physically whacked by his initial rejection. She was still tasting the blood. It was definitely new ground for Claire, not on any script she'd ever practiced. Or even consid-ered. But she climbed back up onto the backstory again, and made chit-chat about Chicago. Her love-hate relationship with O'Hare. As she gained a little conversational traction, though, he started doing it again, going out of his way to be only half-interested in what she was saying. And it was totally freaking her out. Karmic payback, truly, for all the Garys of the world.

12:25

The conversation drifted to silence, finally. Claire had reached the end of her ad-hoc strategy. So for a second, they just stared at each other. Like animals taking measure of a threat.

He did eventually say something. "Dara told me you were at her place last night."

Claire nodded

"She's-um an *indigis … an indigenous … um … Indian*," he said, "if you didn't know."

"Yes," said Claire, "I-I knew."

"I think she's starting to miss home, though. You really can't get any real good curry in Chicago these days."

As he rambled, Claire began to right herself, strategically. Maybe because, in his way with words she'd seen a target, and the slightest display of arrogance as he spoke of Dara.

13:18

When it was her turn, she took a bead on his vanity and told him how much she really enjoyed *his* documentary on the V-2.

"You saw that?"

"Wouldn't have missed it," she told him. Flashing the dimples. "You're getting to be well known, Stephen."

"Well, if you liked *Secrets of the V-2*, you're going to love *Baffling Baffin*," he told her. "That's the working-title."

"So, what was it like, inside?" she asked.

He pushed back the half-eaten cheeseburger and told her she would have to wait and see, just like everyone else.

"You mean, wait in the cheap seats?"

He giggled at the reference.

"I was just bustin' your ... making trouble," he said. "Nothing personal."

14:06

She smiled. She tried so hard not to show it, but Steven Kincaid had a gift for thoroughly demolishing her confidence, both on a personal and a professional level. She was too addled to see it, and she might have on any other occasion, just not today. She didn't perceive that this was a strategy: one, long-practiced. He used it with all women. He liked to make them squirm. Let them know they weren't half as desirable as they imagined. He had discovered this *law of sexual-aggression* back in India, that the average, beautiful female was used to being chased. And wasn't programmed for anything less.

14:49

It was *a law-of-attraction* that was even more true in the States, where the most common result would be the woman switching from passive, to active.

For Steven Kincaid, whether it was India, Canada, France or the U.S., it was *glory hallelujah when the fox hunts you.* That was his strategy, pure and simple.

Claire, of course, didn't know this. In fact, she was in a deep funk by the time they got back. There was only one other bit of bad news as a result of their lunch together. She found Steven Kincaid totally irresistible.

12 The Reich Armory

With so many Doodles stalled out on the first level, the terrain map from the second, left something to be desired. Claire was still able to identify most of the miniatures. There were Panzers, light howitzers and troop transports, and parked in the back was a goliath piece of iron, the Marder-1 anti-tank gun, but visually-speaking, the resolution was starting to fade.

After the initial pass, Kincaid asked to see the electrical *conductor* again. As Jha worked the camera, Claire worked a conclusion. The machines on the second level were slightly more lethal, in an evolutionary sense, than those on the first. This was intriguing, and caused her to wonder what might be waiting for them, the next level down.

Dara asked to see the small doorway again. The threshold. Jha guided the camera forward, and they all saw it at the same time. Another piece of yellow paper. Just like before.

"Would you like to try and see if anything's written on it?" asked Jha.

01:07

He drove the camera deeper into the doorway, until the scene began to artifact. The lackluster resolution was really starting to take its toll, now. He said he could get in closer, but it might take time. "I'll have to retask the Doodles. Anyone have a problem with that?"

He punched in the commands. Immediately, most of the micro-bots in queue for the next level, turned and headed back the way they'd come.

Everyone in the cheap seats was feeling second-class by this point. A matronly woman in Birkenstocks, hair pulled hard across a large, jowly head, asked: "Could you speak up?"

Someone seconded the suggestion. Then a man on the opposite side of the platform complained, "I teach fine arts, and I'm wondering why you don't have other professionals up there to help you analyze some of this?"

02:00

The comment kicked off a lively discussion. Most of the onlookers were academics, so a bit of ego-scholarship followed. But it was informative. Particularly when someone suggested that it was getting harder to conceive of the miniatures as merely a piece of sculpture. A squirrelly little man, strapped to an antique Argus, said he was beginning to think, the scene might actually be a peculiar kind of a photograph. "A-uh dimensional-capture of a real place."

That was the spark. Someone disagreed, good-naturedly, intoning the theme from *The Twilight Zone*. Then someone rebuked the use of the theme as unprofessional. A cheap shot. Like a barroom brawl at Oxford, the Birkenstocks were soon attacking each other with pedantic sensibilities and last tags. *This was an issue of science, not art. Not literature.*

03:01

From the stage, it got pretty funny. Claire noticed how the history professors gravitated to each other, not unlike the cavalry at Little Bighorn. Hard sciences regrouped. In under two minutes, everyone was in an argument with everyone else. What Claire found particularly heart-warming: the fine arts people were being pushed outward, toward the walls, where their forlorn opinions were being expressed in the pale glow of the *Exit* sign. That was good. That was very, very good. And funny.

It seemed, the bunker had ignited a sense of the mystical, as the onlookers attempted to reconcile what they were seeing, with what they knew about the universe. But over-and-above all the spit-and-citation, one question in particular, kept turning up. *How had the Germans accomplished such an incredible feat more than half-century earlier?* It got rowdy. There was a lot of pent-up hostility, evidentially. Pember stepped in from the hall to see what was going on. It might have even escalated from there, but when the screen started rezzing-in, everyone turned to watch, and a hard-earned silence overwhelmed the room.

04:15

Jha took the virtual camera to a position just above the floor.

"Here we go," he said, as he drove into the shadows. The paper on the threshold looked real enough, like it had just been ripped from a tablet. And when it filled the screen, what could be seen, was written in English.

Two words: *this way*. And there was also a hand-drawn arrow.

Claire spun around to see Kincaid's reaction, but she only caught a glimpse of him as he stepped through the exit.

04:48

Kincaid raced off for a visit to the old woman on West Chalmers. He banged on the front door.

From inside, Miss Suzanne's small voice called out, "Who's there?"

"It's Steven."

"You didn't call, did you?" she said, through the door.

"I know, but we have to talk."

"You know the rules, Steven. You have to give me a little lead time."

"Please let me in."

05:15

Miss Suzanne told him *absolutely not. Not until she'd put on her face. He could sit on the bench in the park and wait.*

"But I don't have that long, I've got to get back," he told her, hoping she'd take a little pity.

"It isn't fair, it isn't fair to me," she told him. "Don't I have any rights?"

"Miss Suzanne please, this is the most important question,

and you're the only one who can answer. I want to know about your friends."

"You know the rules, Steven. They contact me. I contact you."

"There's something strange going on here," he told her.

"Are you talking about the paper inside the bunker?"

"How did you know that?" he asked.

"And now you're worried, aren't you? These aren't the real Blood Toys. That you've been tricked. Be confident Steven, the bunker is the very piece given to Mr. Hitler."

"But how's that possible? The note is in my handwriting."

06:14

Miss Suzanne couldn't understand why he was so upset.

"If the bunker was fabricated in the 1940s, what's my handwriting doing there, inside?"

"Why is this such a big deal?" she wanted to know.

He was now standing, nose against the door.

"Are we talking about someone in the government?"

"To a degree," she said.

"To a degree? And that's how they knew about Point 103?"

"To a degree," she said. "How would I get the directions any other way?"

"But Miss Suzanne ... *who*, specifically?"

She said she wasn't free to discuss the details.

"Can we call them?"

"Steven, we shouldn't be talking about this in public. Let me get dressed. You can come in."

She was still talking through the closed door as he made his way back to the car.

07:10

Early Saturday afternoon, the third level was ready to be explored. More people had wrangled their way in. The place was packed. Some were obviously from the government. You could tell by the suits and ties. But some were academics, branded and obvious by beard and Birkenstock, and that included more than a few of the women.

As the morning wore on, the audience started getting impatient. There were too many people crammed into too-small a space. The big blow-up came after Jha asked Dara to tell the audience, they were now *having trouble getting a signal from inside the bunker.* It wasn't true and Claire knew it. The signal was diminished, but due to the fact that seventy-five percent of the Doodle-Cams had stalled out on the upper levels. Jha was in a full sweat.

Dara gave a panicked look, then walked to the front of the stage.

08:05

Her voice was uneven. More tentative than before. "Dr. Jha says the images might not be as good, so if you'll bear with us."

"Why?" someone yelled out.

"I don't know. Just … uh-the signals, just don't seem to be getting through, I guess."

A hundred hands shot up.

"Please," said Dara, "that's all I can tell you. Dr. Jha, a little help, please."

Someone else yelled out, "Then how did you get a signal before? Why did it work then, and not now?"

It was a terrible spot to be in, but when she turned to Jha for guidance, he just shrugged.

There were still shapes, onscreen, but also, huge gaps. Even Claire couldn't discern all they were seeing. As the virtual camera traveled deeper, she was able to identify the wings and canopies of Nazi-era aircraft. What was most obvious, however, was the drastic change in scale, now twice as small as before, making the scene even more astonishing.

09:13

The more she studied the drifting images, the more she realized, these were not the Stukas and the Junkers. These were the *exotics.* The experimental machines. Claire left the stage and ran out to the car, where she called Fort Meade.

"Which exotics?" Terance wanted to know.

"Well the good news: nothing's very clear. The bad news: I see an ME-163X, maybe a Triebflugal, and an Ho-229B, and a huge delta-shaped craft of some sort. Kind of like the HO-18C."

09:53

Terance wanted to know how big it was, compared to the others.

"Twice the size. And it's got something that looks like a leading-edge stripe across the wing."

"All the way across?"

"Well, as far as I can tell. It's getting hard to see the details. And Jerry, in the clutter there are other things, obviously."

"Just as long as they all have wings," was his reply.

"That's the point. I can't be sure. Jha has a work-around. He can send the swarm to focus on one specific area, if he wants. Might be too late."

Terance rung off without saying *goodbye*.

13 Big Ears

Ten minutes after Claire got off the phone, Pember stepped to the stage and made a surprise-announcement.

"Everyone. Could I have your attention please? As we all know, there's a bit of a disagreement about some of what we're doing, about the discovery and the research, so … this is to inform everyone, we're suspending the investigation, in good faith, in the hope that all parties can come to an accommodation."

The announcement elicited a collective-gasp. Followed by silence.

00:32

He said he hoped it wouldn't be a *permanent* shutdown, but he was fairly confident, they could find a solution. And maybe they would be back up in a day or two.

A history professor wanted to know, on what legal grounds the shutdown was taking place.

"We're honoring a request from the State Department. That's all I can tell you."

A woman from the audience reminded him that this was a public institution. The government had *no rights* in this matter.

00:58

"Yeah, and what if we refuse to leave?"

Pember stared at the belligerent man. Baffled. Not really sure how to respond. Then the door opened, ten security guards filed in, and their presence provided the very thing needed, and the only response required. Raw threat. One glance to the back of the room where the big boys lined the wall, and almost immediately, packs and briefcases were being loaded, in silence. One by one, the *Birkenstocks* filed out. Pember, Jha and Dara were the only ones left inside the workshop.

01:33

Kincaid was upset. He pushed through the acquiescent mob, out to the parking lot. Not only was Dara quitting, he'd just been kicked out of his own investigation.

He jumped into the car and headed back to Miss Suzanne's. This time, though, he had the presence of mind to call, first. When he arrived, she was ready for him, regaled in her leathers, sweater, and gloves. Plus, the silly woman had had enough time to whip up a batch of her slightly ethereal brownies.

"I have to say, you hurt me a little, Steven." She led him to the parlor. She pointed where he was supposed to sit. "There's never an excuse for that kind of behavior, love."

Kincaid wanted to punch her, but instead, told her he was forever sorry and asked forgiveness.

"I-I know you're under pressure," she told him, "but we can do better than that, can't we? Yes, you've got questions, but I don't have all the answers. We've gone over this."

Kincaid told her what had just happened at the museum. How he had been *rejected*. "To top it off, Dara *duped* me. Doesn't want to work with me any more."

"Good for her," said Miss Suzanne. "Someone just got a piece of her sweet little heart back."

02:46

Kincaid didn't want to talk about that. There were more serious issues. In his dealings with Miss Suzanne, though, he had a strategy. He looked at her, blinked, then said: "I think you know how I feel about you. I haven't tried to hide it."

She turned from him, fixing her gaze on the plastic trees across from the sofa.

"I've often thought, it's a shame we weren't born closer in time. I think I would've made you a wonderful husband, Miss Suzanne."

It was a wicked way to manage her, but he had confidence,

it would work. She wouldn't read his true motives. She was too old, too invested in her melancholy, in her dreams, and fantasies. He had nothing to lose. And it turned out to be the right tactic, in much the way his dealings with Claire had been *right*. The old woman teared-up, and that gave him a wicked sense of pleasure. She thanked him, removed her gloves, dabbed her eyes with them, then asked what he wanted to know.

"But you do feel the same about me?" he said, driving it home before proceeding.

03:59

"Steven, what do you want to know?"

"How do they contact you?" he asked.

"Why is that so important?"

"Because, when they call next time, maybe we can trace the call."

She smiled, shook her head and turned back to the plastic trees.

"Miss Suzanne, here's the deal. I found other notes at Baffin. Notes I hadn't written, but in my handwriting. And now, we're finding them inside a fifty-year old artifact."

"Yes. I know. They told me," she said.

"They *told* you? Did they tell you about the … I don't know what to call it, the *admonition*? I didn't hear voices, but you asked if there were powerful presences in the bunker. Oh yeah. And that's what I'm trying to find out about. What are we dealing with here?"

Eventually she turned back and looked him straight in the eyes.

04:58

"Why should I tell you anything?" she asked.

"You don't have to, I guess, but if you care for me ..."

There was another long pause in the conversation, as if she was measuring the words before speaking them. Finally, she told him: "Some of us are born with big ears, Steven. And big eyes. Not that we sought them. They were given. Gifts, I suppose."

He caught himself staring at her ears, with those huge ball-earrings hanging hanging down, nearly to her shoulders. Minus the hardware, they really weren't actually all that big.

"It's not the size," she said, as if she'd heard his thoughts. "I've tried to tell people about this and it always comes out the same. Everyone looks at me like I'm crazy. If you ever looked at me that way, Steven …"

"Miss Suzanne, there's nothing you could say that would change my … my feelings for you."

05:59

Tears glistened, again, in her eyes.

"When I say *big*, that's how I explain it to myself," she told him. "Big in the sense, I hear things other people don't. Just like what you were saying about your *premonition*. Did that make you crazy?"

"I hope not," he told her. "Actually, I've been thinking about that. Dogs hear things we don't. It's just the equipment, maybe, and maybe that's what's going on with you."

"They talk to me," she said. "But they're not visible. They speak inside my heart, I guess you could say. The words aren't mine."

Kincaid's suspicions, his terrible suspicions, were confirmed. The old girl was barking mad.

"When I was six, they first began calling me," she said. "They told me secrets, sometimes. Things I didn't want to know, but how do you shut them out? And when I was a teen-ager they told me who they were."

06:58

She rested her head on the chair-back, eyes-closed, falling silent again.

"Miss Suzanne?"

"To whom much is given, much is required," she continued. "What you're about to do, Steven, it's dangerous, but you need to know. You have the power to accomplish your dreams."

Barking mad. It was just a head-flash, of course, words flying through his consciousness at the speed-of-thought, and Miss

Suzanne caught the broadcast, evidentially. She told him *no, as a matter of fact, she wasn't barking mad.*

Her words utterly terrified him. Could she read thoughts? It wasn't the first time this sort of thing had happened.

She went on. "There's another bunker in Chile. If you go, they will lead the way. If you succeed, the earth will be healed."

"I'm not sure what you're saying," he told her.

"They gave many gifts to Germany, Steven, but the Nazis used their gifts to make war. Now they offer them again. In the drawer beneath the phone is a tablet," she told him. "Bring it to me, and bring a pen."

08:12

Kincaid rushed to the kitchen, bringing back the things she requested. She started drawing. The first image looked a bit like an upright roulette wheel. When she finished, she preceded to draw a schematic, adding symbols to the various junctions. He thought he saw the word amps, but wouldn't confirm that until later. On a third sheet of paper she drew a map labeled: *Chile.* She noted the southern Andes and a small village on the coast there. *Puerto Montt.* She also wrote the name *Quiroga.* On the fourth sheet of paper she drew a series of parallel lines with a circle near the bottom of the page.

"There it is, love. That's your destination, what you're looking for," she told him, tapping the paper. "A gift and a miracle that will return us to the first-age."

08:59

She shuffled the pages then handed them over.

"One other thing, Steven. You'll never see me again."

"Not true," he said. "When I get back. First thing."

"I'm about to be only a memory for you, nothing more. Now, go to your new love."

"My what?"

"Are you dense? This is your problem. You don't trust what you see and hear. Follow your heart. That's why you were chosen. For your heart."

"I don't know what you're trying *to purport here,* but I

swear, I will come back. God is my witness."

He had a last question, the one he'd wanted to ask since the beginning. "Do you know who they are, the people who give all the gifts?"

Her eyes blinked, then she flashed him a quick-but-mischievous smile.

"The Pleiades, Steven, they're star people."

09:55

She opened the front door, stood on her toes and kissed him full, on the mouth.

"And by the way, you're not alone. I love you too. I would've made you a good wife." It was the last thing she said.

As he ran to the car, Kincaid was not quite sure what'd just happened. Over the months there'd been some pretty strange stuff going on with Miss Suzanne, but this was off-the-charts. And now that he'd had a couple of minutes to think about it, no, he probably wouldn't be coming back to see her, after Chile.

14 Resignation

The Blood Toys had slipped into the murky waters of international politics. Claire didn't know for sure that NSA was behind the shutdown, but it looked that way. She sat cross-legged in the hall, outside the workshop. All around were scientists, professors, and technicians. Many were upset with the Canadians. Most, though, blamed the U.S. Politically speaking, they were neurotic-to-delusional, but in this, they weren't all that far off the mark. She would've loved to discuss it with them, just to get a fix on just how close their paranoia ran to the truth.

00:37

Dara showed up an hour later. She had been booted as well. The workshop was pretty much empty except for Jha, who was still hard at work.

"Hey Claire ... office."

They pushed through the crowd, made their way down the administrative hall to the production office, and ducked inside.

"Get this," said Dara, shutting the door behind them.

"Steven says *he needs me*. Do you believe that?"

"Well?"

"Well, Madu wants me to go to India next week. First-class."

"Madu?"

01:16

"He's a great man, Claire. I mean. You know that. At lunch, he cried when he was telling me about how lonely he was. And you want to hear something really sweet? Sometimes he goes to the map shop at the mall and looks at the street maps of Bombay and Calcutta. Isn't that adorable?"

"And let me guess, his wife just died," said Claire. "Right?"

"He's just like us, Claire, he's alone."

"But of course, *Maaa-doooo* is old enough …"

"I know, old enough to be my father. Right. But it's not like that. He sees something in me," said Dara.

"Like … ?"

"Well, I don't know, a little of himself, maybe."

Claire was too polite to say it, but what he saw in her was most definitely not something he saw in himself. In the truest sense of the word, he did see something; or the prospect, at least, and he wanted it. Dara had flipped headlong into mushy-logic.

"How did you know about his wife?" asked Dara.

"Her … *dying*? Intuition." Claire told her. "Feminine intuition."

02:25

Kincaid stumbled in looking absolutely terrible. He said he'd had enough. He grabbed the phone on his desk and punched in Pember's extension. During the brief conversation, the museum director had even worse news. There was a chance the investigation would be suspended permanently. Kincaid demanded to know how they could do something like that.

"Have you forgotten how we're funded? They can make things pretty hard, Steven, we don't have a choice here."

"But close us down?"

"If that's what they want."

Kincaid slammed the receiver.

"What?" he said.

"Hmm … nothing." Then Dara told him, he was a *brat*.

03:09

He was also furious, fingering all his little hatreds again, raging at everyone.

"Grow up Steven. You don't always get your way."

"What's this *always*? I never get my way. Hey, I've got a ques-

109

tion, what about us, you and me?"

"There is no *us*," said Dara. "Only *you*."

He turned to Claire and blurted out that he wanted to talk to Dara alone. Would she leave? Dara reacted with a little heat: Claire was her friend and whatever he had to say, he could say it in front of her. Claire appreciated the allegiance, but knew it would be a good idea to let them work it out, whatever it was they had to work out.

"I'll wait outside," she said, and left.

When the door closed, or almost closed, Kincaid told Dara his secret. There was another bunker.

"And it's the big one."

04:05

He begged her to stay with the museum for a couple more months. "This time, no production crew, just us. We'll do the cameras. We'll pretend we're on vacation."

"Where are we going?"

"You have to agree first, before I tell you."

"Sorry, Steven, no more expeditions," she said.

"But this is more important than Baffin," he told her. This time they would hit it out of the park. There was, and he was completely certain of it -- beyond a shadow of a doubt -- there was a free-energy device waiting to be uncovered.

"Dara, if I've done something to hurt you, I'm sorry."

"It never ends does it? We're going to change the world, you and me. It's a great picture, but when I look closer, I never see myself in it," said Dara. "Not really. I see you."

"We'll control the whole thing this time, start to finish, and you know what the finish looks like this time? We're this close to a revolution."

"Sorry Steven, I'm giving Dr. Pember my notice. I'm not interested in making you famous. Don't you get it? You only need someone to carry the equipment. If I'd wanted to be a mule, I didn't have to leave India for that. You're an idiot."

05:21

Dara met with Dr. Pember. It was a cordial couple of minutes. She told him about the job-offer, and how she could jet between the U.S. and her home. It might lead to all sorts of things. Opportunities. Maybe even movies.

"But I want you to know how much I've enjoyed working at MMT," she said. "I learned a lot."

05:43

He told her he hated to see her go, but he did understand. He extended a hand and wished her the best. She gave him a hug.

That evening, Claire and Dara decided to celebrate. Claire had gotten caught up in Dara's new vision of herself. How could you be anything but happy for her? True, she would have to deal with the Dr. Jha's little *horsey-problem* at some point, but Dara was a big girl. Claire knew that you could ride the horse, but you could also *break* the horse. Women had been doing that since the beginning of time.

06:18

In the parking lot, the two were laughing, giggling, totally absorbed in the question of where they would spend the evening. But as she opened the car door to get in, Claire caught sight of a group of men climbing out of an SUV near the entrance to the loading dock. As the trail of men passed into the light, she saw Jerry Terance. Her boss. That was the first surprise. And the man behind him, none other than Dr. Millard Nunnally. That was the second. Seeing them together, after what had happened at Bonhert, was beyond any explanation she could imagine.

15 Gods of the Overlay

Jha was still inside the workshop, along with Terance, Nunnally, and Pember. They watched as he programmed the ever-decreasing swarm. Sector-by-sector, the objects faded into view. A small plane strapped to a jetpack, dialed-in. And in the shadows of the HO-18, something unexpected. Jha blurted it out. "Is that a UFO?"

They bent down for a closer look. Terance said, *he didn't think so*, wasn't sure what it was, the lack of resolution made it difficult.

Jha pointed at the screen, as if he was looking in the wrong place.

"Could be anything," said Terance. Jha glanced to Nunnally, then back to Terance, then he *got it*. He turned to the keyboard without further comment.

00:50

Barely sixty Doodle-cams were headed down to the last level, where there were no geometric shapes. Only twisted lines. Jha was told to *grid it off and examine it, section by section*. But the doodles seemed to be dying. There was no assurance, they would be able to fully map the last level.

01:11

Nunnally's cell phone rang. The old man turned away, answering, as he walked.

"Dr. Nunnally, this is Claire Whitlock. But please don't say my name."

"Where are you?" he wanted to know.

"Outside the building. Can you come out?"

"This minute?"

"I'm on the east side," said Claire, "but it's dark out here. Be careful."

"Okay," said Nunnally, "I guess so."

Snapping the phone closed, he stretched, practiced a few theatrical yawns, then decided to *go out for a little air.*

01:47

Past the guards, he cautiously made his way into the shadows. It was good that she'd warned him about how dark it was. Nunnally's heart wasn't up to a good scare, so as he went, he tried to anticipate her sudden appearance.

"Dr. Nunnally. Over here!" He turned to a figure, stepping from the shadows.

"It's me," she said, reaching for his arm, to assure him.

"Jerry didn't tell me you were in town."

This was a little odd, but not unexpected. Jerry hadn't told her that he and Nunnally had any professional association, whatsoever.

"How can I help you?"

02:26

She told him, she wasn't sure about this. She had questions. Would he be willing to listen to them? Just listen, if it wasn't too much to ask, and if he wanted, he could answer, or not.

With the bravery of someone jumping into an ice-flow, Claire started asking her questions, without order, or convenient narrative. She just blurted them out. She knew she was inviting risk, but again she said, she trusted him, and he could trust her. When she finally stopped to catch a breath, he asked why she wasn't taking this to Jerry.

"Puts me in a bit of an awkward spot," said Nunnally.

"I know."

His words awakened her fears. Maybe she had miscalculated. Maybe she'd just shot her career in the foot. Or worse. The head.

"Have I messed up?" she asked.

He did speak, eventually, but his voice had gone tender.

113

Grandfatherly.

"Let me guess," he told her, "your hunch is that I'm fed up with our *processes*, shall we call them."

"You give that impression. Yes."

"Well, you're in luck. Ask your questions again, but let's take them in some kind of order."

03:43

"Dr. Nunnally, you've got know about the *Special Projects Lab* and the *Nazi working groups*. I'll take whatever you're comfortable telling me … anything on the subjects."

"I should know," he told her. "I was at the Pentagon in '53, six weeks after they opened for business, almost before I owned a razor." He chuckled at the images spilling into his memory.

"The other day at the briefing, you said something about-uh … *another dimension*," said Claire.

"Ah-you want me to breech my security agreement, is that it?"

"No, but I would like to understand more than I do," she told him. "I've got a decision. I need perspective, if you've got any to spare."

It was too dark to see her face, but he looked over as if he might be gauging her intent.

"Well-let me do this," he said, at last. "I'll give you the-um fifty-cent tour."

"Okay," she told him. "Uh-I don't have any money on me …

"You can pay me later."

04:51

As they made their way across the grass, he handed her one of the two peppermints he'd just liberated from his pocket. He told her, peppermint was a comfort food. And she was about to need a little comfort.

A comment that struck her as odd, partly because she had a fairly good grasp of the subject, and by extension, what he might say. But she was wrong on both counts.

"In spite of what you've been led to believe, we aren't being visited by extraterrestrials, Miss Whitlock, but we are being visited. The ET-angle is actually a bit misleading."

"I-I don't I understand," she told him.

"They're *inter-dimensional*, Miss Whitlock, not *extraterrestrial*. Not from another planet. Not even another galaxy. They're from … we don't know, actually. A *parallel universe*, maybe. But wherever it is, they're also here. Also with us. From what crosses your desk, you probably assume, this is mostly about star people. That's more or less the line."

"That's more or less how I understand my job," she told him.

"Well-let's just say, imagine beings from another dimension, where there is no time and subsequently, no speed-of-light. How are we supposed to relate to that?"

06:14

Claire took his arm. Steadying him as they made their way deeper into the shadows, or perhaps, she was steadying herself.

"UFOs are a cover story. And the surprise: it's their cover, not ours. They've been what … *gods, ghosts, trolls, leprechauns* … at the heart of all religion and myth. And now, they're friendly little space folk who sometimes aren't all that friendly."

Claire couldn't think of what to say next. Her line-of-questioning had been heading somewhere else.

"That's the fifty-cent tour," he told her. "Should be enough to keep your wheels spinning."

"But we're still … basically … let me get this right, we're still talking about influences *off-planet*. Except you call them *inter-dimensionals*. I'm not sure the distinction matters."

"Oh, it matters," said Nunnally, "makes all the difference."

She asked *why*?

"Because they're hiding behind stagecraft, behind assumed identities. We have no idea, their intention."

07:27

Someone, who'd already made peace with the prospect of life on other worlds, had just come face-to-face with a possibility, far outside the bounds of corporate curriculum. Claire couldn't process it. Ignoring the outrageous suggestion, she cycled back. She had a decision to make. There was another bunker and she

115

suspected that Jerry would want to go for it. She asked him what he thought about that?

"Another bunker?"

She told him, *not a miniature this time, but something real,* and she might have to travel outside the States.

"If you're asking my advice," said Nunnally, "don't get involved."

"But the guy's going to go with us, or without us, it's the same guy who went to Baffin."

"Claire, a lot of people on that hunt don't come back."

08:15

"I want the technology," she said. "I don't care if it's from out there, or in here, or wherever, and if this guy finds something, we don't want to be on the outside."

"But it's not just about the technology," he told her. "It's about the forces that insinuate themselves into every gift they bring."

He suggested, there were three reasons the subject had been hidden, even from employees at NSA.

"First of all because it's terrifying, and far worse than *little green men*. Most of us can eventually deal with the concept of an ET, but not this. Second, inter-dimensional reality is crazy. Compares to nothing. The creatures appear and disappear, change form, migrate from the visible to invisible spectrum, at will. But the worst part is, there's nothing we can do about it. They have the options, Claire. They respect us, almost as much as we respect a herd of cattle."

"But if they were going to do something, they would've done it by now," she said.

"Well-that's a myth. You can't trust them," he told her. "They've stalked us since before the age of the Pharaohs, and the evidence over all that time is: they can't be trusted."

09:40

Claire asked why this inter-dimensional explanation hadn't leaked to the public.

"But it has, it's been finessed out to the fringe, out where the crazies are. Here's one for you. If you haven't seen it, read Lee

Van Atta's dispatch in the Chilean newspaper, El Mercurio. March 5, 1947. All the clues are there, poking up through the myth."

"Actually, I have read it," said Claire. "You're talking about Operation Highjump. The legend of the Antarctic and the Nazis, after the war."

"I wish it was a legend, but there's evidence. In 1957, with the advise and consent of the Soviet Union, the U.S. exploded three thermonuclear airbursts over Antarctica. The Argus-Project. You know why? We said we were trying to melt a hole in the polar cap. What we achieved, was punching a bigger hole in the ozone, and destabilizing the gravitational field."

"Melting the pole doesn't make any sense."

"No, not unless you know what was actually going on. We were trying to take out an installation beneath the ice, knock it out with an EMP. It was not a legend, Miss Whitlock, nor was it Nazi, strictly speaking, if you catch my drift."

11 :00

They came to the shadow's edge on Michigan Avenue. Another step would take them into the light.

"Dr. Nunnally, point me, then, which way should I go? Why shouldn't I see this as an opportunity?"

The old man stepped from the shadows into the light, fully aware of what he was doing. He stood there, almost in defiance, almost willing himself to be seen by everyone up and down Michigan Avenue.

"They're like scuba divers," he told her, "they splash into our reality to study us, or confound us, or kill us. They were ground zero in the Third Reich, behind the phobias, the racism and occult science."

"Ground zero?"

"Yeah, the first-force in National Socialism.

"I don't understand that at all," said Claire. "Why would Germany lose the war?"

"Now, we're speculating. Rivals, I think. Nothing else explains why they haven't run us out of the house yet."

"Some inter-dimensionals are on our side?" asked Claire.

"We've chased them around the skies for more than fifty years. In that time they could've destroyed us a million times over. The only possible explanation is that they're held in check. And it's not us doing the holding. If that doesn't send a shiver through your soul, you're not paying attention."

"Are we safe?" she asked.

"World War II was some kind of dry run for what happens next. There's some kind of huge operation, staged across thousands of years, and in a lifetime, you only see a small bit. I can't explain it beyond that."

For Claire, the words had a deep effect, less a shiver, and more, a depressive wave.

"Claire, it is confusing, but never forget the horse they bet on. The Nazis. These forces aided a cause that killed maybe as many as fifty-sixty million people, worldwide. They inspire us, invade our dreams, sort of become a background noise to reality, conjuring doctrines we think of as our own."

13:16

She took his arm, and led him back into the shadows. Wordlessly.

He now understood, she'd never been exposed to the riddles, within riddles, and he felt guilty for having bludgeoned her with too much.

"Are you going to be okay?" he asked.

"I think so."

13:36

Before they went their separate ways, he told her he believed the Blood Toys were a sign of … *something*, though he couldn't say what. He also left the door open. She could contact him again, if she needed. She still had a dime left on the fifty-cent tour. As an afterthought, he suggested: "If you haven't, look up Madam Blavatsky. Her contact with these forces, what she called *ascended masters*, was where World War II began, fifty-years before the first shot was fired."

In a flat, still-dazed-out voice, Claire said she knew about

Helena Blavatsky and her influence in pre-war Europe.

"Then you're not surprised by some of what we're saying."

Claire told him, *not completely.*

"People say, UFOs mean us no harm, otherwise they would've done something by now," he said, "but they have. And you call it *World War II.*"

"But, why the Blood Toys, Dr. Nunnally?"

"I don't know. Maybe our overlords are going to leverage *signs and wonders* to become our gods again."

He said he believed that someday, there would be a strong, competitive religion based on inter-dimensionals.

"They will try to be our messiahs, and that tyranny, Miss Whitlock, will be the last. The human family won't survive."

She thanked him. She said she would hold everything in confidence and consider his advice.

"There's one other thing," he told her. Maybe he was just offering a softer exit, conversationally, but it was also, a brilliant opportunity.

"Claire, at the company, they're trying to get me to retire, and someone is going to need to carry my voice into policy. I want you to think about it, because there's a lot more to be said, if you're interested."

15:36

Sunday morning, instead of heading back to the museum, Claire showered, dressed, and drove out to Naperville, where Sunday service was already, full-blast. True, it was a stab in the dark, but perhaps Kincaid attended, this *church from the bulletin.* Maybe they would run into each other. Maybe his guard would be down. But she didn't know her own mind. Was she stalking him out of personal or professional curiosity? Or both? Or was she just coming unhinged?

16:08

Inside the sanctuary, everyone was standing, hands raised. The music was as loud as any club or bar. It was actually a bit shocking for someone who hadn't been to church in a few years. She almost lost her nerve, but an usher grabbed her by the arm and led her to the middle of the auditorium, and an open seat near the aisle. There, she stood. With everyone else. Words to the songs were onscreen, the singing of which was far more spirited than she, a lapsed Lutheran, remembered. A couple of people in the next row were actually hopping up and down, which freaked her out completely. Would there also be snakes? Maybe that's why they were jumping.

Between songs, to cover the key change, the band invited the congregation to *praise the Lord*. And the shouts grew even more boisterous. What was Kincaid doing in a place like this?

17:04

It didn't seem to be a tightly scripted liturgy, though, and if it was, the scripter had been treated to a catechism of commas, only, no periods. This ecclesiastical conniption went on and on and on and on. After ten minutes, she despaired of ever sitting again. The songs circled back, in an endless loop, and if one did incidentally grind to a halt, they cranked it back up and started over. The same ones. Over and over. What happened to *A Mighty Fortress*, or *It Is Well With My Soul*? Church had definitely changed, and not necessarily for the better. Eventually, the minister, or priest, or whatever he was, invited everyone to sit. It was time for the offering, followed by a time to preach. As with the singing, the pulpiteering was far more energetic than she remembered. The day's homily was about the Apostle Paul and his encounter with a blinding light, a datapoint she'd once correlated with the UFO-event at Fatima, Portugal, in 1917.

18:09

The homily … also … went on forever. She'd been brought up with the fifteen-minute kind, and perhaps that was the difference between a Lutheran homily and a Baptist sermon – forty-five minutes, maybe an hour.

Claire was now *liturgically-sleepy*, almost to the point of being comatose. Then without warning, the preacher asked everyone to stand, again. It seemed to be, just about over. The speaker announced that the *Lord was dealing* with someone, who had a storm in their life. He invited them to the altar.

"We aren't here to judge," he told them. "Every believer in this sanctuary has done the very thing you're deliberating."

A woman, up front, made her way forward. The music was cranking again.

Claire had just started toying with the idea of making a run for it, when she heard movement in the aisle behind. To her astonishment, it was Kincaid, slouching toward the altar. Upon his arrival there, he was immediately surrounded by ten men, all of whom began praying, hands raised.

19:19

She temporarily forgot how ready she was to get out of there, and now she was feeling no small amount of sympathy for Kincaid, who was at the center of all the ruckus. Then came the miracle. As the prayer up front raged on, the congregation started to file out. The service was over, but Kincaid was still surrounded. She reached for her purse, glanced back to the altar one last time, but as she was about to head out, she noticed one of the men, praying. It was the strange little man, the one who'd seemed to know so much, from the museum. The one who'd looked her in the eye.

At the instant she was remembering him, he turned, then gazed across the congregation to where she was standing, just like before. Their eyes locked.

16 Shattered

By the time she got back to the museum, there were news vans everywhere. On the curb. Doubled up in the street. And the lobby was in chaos. She found out why from a reporter. Forty-five minutes earlier, the Bunker had shattered, accidentally.

"Word is, they were shipping it back to Canada," he told her.

"Shipping it ... *what*?"

Terance and Nunnally were against the far wall in the lobby, watching her from across a surging tide of reporters and academics. They nodded when she looked over, but seemed otherwise detached and unconcerned. Which struck her as suspicious. She crashed into the chaos, over to where they seemed to be nonchalantly biding their time.

"Jerry, what is this?"

"Some kind of accident. I guess."

"They were sending it back?"

00:50

There was no direct answer, but by the way Nunnally rolled his eyes, she suspected there was more to it.

"Jerry, are we going to opt-in, or what?"

He said, he hadn't decided. He was still trying to *get a handle* on everything.

"Look at this! It's getting ahead of us."

01:11

As she was speaking, Kincaid rushed into the lobby, pushing through to the opposite wall. Where Dr. Pember was standing. Technically, he was the boss, but anyone looking on would have assumed the opposite. Within seconds, Kincaid's nose was inches from his, and there was a lot of yelling. Unfortunately, with so much going on, you couldn't hear, but Claire could guess.

"That's the guy, right there," she said, "the one, *spitting*."

"He looks crazy," said Terance.

She grabbed her boss' arm: "It doesn't matter, he has another bunker, Jerry. And we're either in or out."

Terance scratched his ear. Seemed to be thinking.

"But how would we set up?"

"If he follows his routine, he'll be getting an expedition together in the next forty-eight hours. I might not even be able to get on."

02:03

Terance asked about field-support. How would that work?

"I was thinking maybe, a transceiver, at first. Then, put something together on the fly."

"I see. *Jazz*. But you're right about one thing. We don't have an option."

He authorized her to go ahead. *Provisionally*. It wasn't a *yes* or *no*. It was classic *C-Y-A*, but a good sign. It meant, he'd probably leave it up to Claire. She could live with that.

"I'll get you a transceiver," he told her. "Just stay flexible with me. Okay?"

"Deal."

02:40

Claire tracked Kincaid to the production office. His head was down on the desk. When she came in, he didn't even acknowledge her.

"I know about the bunker," she told him.

"Yeah. No kidding." He didn't look up.

"The real one. The new one."

That brought him round. "Who told you? No, second thought, let me guess." His head dropped back to the desk. "Tell Dara I've been *sidetracked*, thanks to her."

"What does that mean?"

"They pulled the rails out from under me. Especially Dara."

"You've got to be happy for her," said Claire. "Think about what this means."

"What about me?" said Kincaid. "Completely screws up what I'm doing." He looked up. "By the way, you were at church."

Claire trotted out the story. Her favorite aunt lived in Naperville. A couple of summers, she'd come to Chicago, and this was auntie's church. She said all this, but wasn't sure that he believed it.

"Are you religious?" he wanted to know.

"Absolutely," she told him. "But Steven, I also believe in free-energy. You may be the only person on the planet with a shot at recovering the technology."

"You're volunteering, I take it?"

"Ah-I don't know about that," said Claire, strategically, "but you should definitely go through with it."

"Yeah well, it's a little hard when your production team has just been *deduced to zero*."

04:10

Out on the loading dock, Dara and Jha were pondering the new reality. He sat on a crate, trying to muster courage. She stood at his side, her finger lightly running across his lapel.

At last he spoke. The situation had changed, drastically changed. He wouldn't be able to hire anyone.

04:31

Dara suspected as much, but to hear the words was a punch in the stomach. She'd just resigned. More significantly, she had invested every ounce of her emotion into a new identity, away from Chicago. Away from Steven Kincaid.

"What if we were back home?" she said. "Would that help?"

"The project's in trouble, Dara. The doodles were completely inactive. I was down to thirty-five."

She asked if he had any idea why they'd gone on a rampage. That was the assumption. *Jha's doodles had come to life.* And basically destroyed the small structure, inside-out.

"I don't know," he told her. "First time I ever saw the disorder was last night. So the board is reviewing the project. I'll probably lose my funding." He snapped his fingers. "Nothing ... is the same. Get back to you old boss. Talk to him. Tell him what happened. Maybe it's not too late."

05:29

Dara rushed to the production office, crying. Claire grabbed and held her.

"What do I do?" she said. "The job's off."

"Nice career move," said Kincaid, his feet up on the desk.

"Thanks." Dara's tone was bitter, but also, furious. Her pent up anger suddenly had focus. She went off on him. It was pretty standard stuff. *He'd used her.* That was repeated several times. Then she said he was *moody* She was the only one who'd invested in the relationship. She'd *given* and *forgiven* while he'd *gotten* and *forgotten.* Classic accusations, though probably true enough.

06:10

Claire found herself caught up in Dara's fury. She might have just finessed her way onto Kincaid's expedition, but seeing her best friend in such pain, excited the warrior-sister, inside.

Kincaid announced that Dara's rejection had forced him to *enfranchise* someone else. And with that news, Dara wilted.

"Wait," said Claire, "if she doesn't go, I don't either."

But that was fine, as far as Kincaid was concerned. Now he was screaming. He would go alone, if he had to.

It snapped Claire back to reality. She had just conspired against her own best interest.

"Does Dr. Pember know about this?" Dara asked.

"I don't owe anyone an explanation," he told her.

"No, after today Steven, the museum doesn't need your kind of publicity."

07:04

He countered. The museum would be happy for anything that put them on the map.

"Like *Canada*?"

125

Claire was actually dazzled at how Dara was managing the transaction. She was threatening him, now. But she also realized, with Dara back in, would she now be the expendable-one? Even if Kincaid was willing to take them both, how would Dara's presence complicate what she had to do?

Having consoled her friend, Claire just as suddenly needed her *un-consoled*.

07:37

Late Sunday, Terry Pember watched the engineer vacuuming up the last shards. Except for him, Claire and Pember were the only ones in the workshop. The party was over.

"Hard day," said Claire.

Pember nodded. Some things were self-evident.

"I don't mean to pry," she said, "but any idea what happened?"

Pember said, it sounded like a small explosion. "We'd gone for coffee. When we got back, it was gone."

Claire wondered what they were going to do with the pieces.

"We're sending what's in the bag, back to JPL," he told her.

"One more time," said Claire. "You went for coffee? You and Jha?"

"Right."

"So you weren't in the room when it happened. Could anyone else have seen?"

"Those guys from JPL, probably."

"They were here?"

"I think so."

"But you weren't here?"

"Look, don't think I'm being rude, but I've reached my limit on this. Somewhere, it's written down, at least twenty times. I didn't see it happen, but I definitely heard it. Okay? Okay."

With that, he headed for the exit. Only Claire and the engineer remained.

08:59

"Excuse me. Could I look inside the bag?" asked Claire.

The engineer said, he'd been told to *seal* the contents.

"If it makes any difference, I'm from JPL," she told him, producing her ID. "And that's where you're sending it. You heard what he said."

The man thought about it, then stepped aside. She had *one minute.*

"Thanks," she said, touching him lightly as she went by.

09:27

Kneeling at the vacuum, she positioned herself between the engineer and the collection table, so he couldn't see precisely what she was doing. It was disgusting, but necessary. Watching her from behind would occupy him with thoughts of flowers and candy – probably – and a lifetime commitment, and home, and family, and *to have* and *to hold* … and all that stuff.

As the engineer's heart presumably pounded, she picked her way through the bag, looking for large pieces. She twisted one way, then another, and by such method was able to extract not one, but two minutes from the man. Had she wanted, Claire was fairly confident she could've run the number up to a half-an-hour.

10:12

She hated it, of course.

"Thanks," she told him finally, walking out. Clutched in her hand were the largest shards from the bag.

This much she knew. They weren't pieces of the bunker. Terance had pulled a fast one. In all probability, the Blood Toys had not been destroyed, as advertised, but shanghaied into the dark planetary system at NSA.

17 Getting Suspicious

Monday, when Dara went for pizza, Claire hauled out the shards she'd taken from the vacuum bag. Spread them on the desk. And told Kincaid to take a look. He said it looked like *broken glass* to him.

"Exactly what I'm thinking," she told him.

"I don't get it. What we saw on screen looked real. But this."

She shook her head no, it didn't look the same. "By the way Steven, are you okay?"

"I'm totally exhausted," he told her, "but what's new?"

00:31

She stepped behind his chair. "I'll tell you what you need to do. You need to slow down."

Her soft hands slid into position across the back of his neck.

"Those little motorcycles we saw had color and lots of detail. I don't see any of that here."

She agreed. "If you hammered a soft drink bottle, my guess is, it'd look pretty much the same."

"What do you mean by that?"

"Maybe the bunker wasn't destroyed."

He looked back down to the shards.

"Then what is this?"

01:02

Her hands drifted from his neck. Out to his shoulders. Rubbing and releasing. Stroking and embracing the flesh beneath the shirt.

"What it is," she said, "someone must've seen something."

"That would be the Coler," he told her.

He slumped into the chair, thoroughly bewitched by Claire's fingers.

"Relax," she told him as she dug deeper. "Relax."

Exactly seventeen minutes after heading out, Dara burst back in with the pizza. Kincaid's eyes were closed. And Claire was behind his chair. Massaging the back of his head.

"Don't let me interrupt," said Dara. She shoved the box onto her desk, then started pulling packets of parmesan and red pepper from her pocket. Tossing them too.

"I think she figured it out," said Kincaid, "that's what's left of the bunker. She took it from the workshop. But we think it might be ordinary glass. Right?"

"Right," said Claire.

02:03

As they ate, there wasn't a lot of conversation. Kincaid continued looking at the shards, pizza in one hand, a magnifying glass in the other.

"Maybe we ought to get a bottle and a hammer and see if we can *reciprocate* the effect.

"Tell me something," said Claire. "How do you do it? Dara and I've talked about how you keep making these … uh-amazing discoveries. It's more than just luck."

"It's not," he said, "it's who you know, who you know, and who you know."

"So who do you know?"

02:38

He turned and smiled, then said: "It's like basketball. Like rebounding. Getting into position means you have to be a couple steps ahead of the play. I just think that way, I guess. Maybe that's my advantage."

Claire's strategy was having an impact. But there was no joy for her in any of it. It was also having an impact on Dara. But it was something she had to do. That's how she justified it. Flattery for Kincaid. Small diminishments for Dara. A female transaction, men can't see, but Dara could. She and Claire were engaged in their own, not-so-invisible war.

129

By the time they'd finished eating, when Claire had fully front-loaded his conceit, she offered to take out the pizza box, along with the rest of the trash.

"But where's the dumpster?"

"Just let Dara do it," said Kincaid, "she knows."

"No, it's my turn," said Claire. "She's done all the work so far, it's not fair."

"Back of the workshop," said Dara, "usually near the main dock."

03:29

Kincaid reacted. And it came off even better than Claire could've plotted. "You take it out," he said. "Claire doesn't work here, she doesn't know where anything is."

Dara said, the dumpster wasn't all that hard to find.

"If it's no big deal, then why don't you do it?" he said.

Dara grabbed the box, along with the greasy napkins, and stormed out. There was far more going on here than an empty pizza box. With great skill, Claire was managing her way into his graces, and when Dara stormed out, she saw an unexpected opportunity. She lowered her voice. Told him she was slightly concerned about something. *The three of them traveling together might not be the best idea. There would be three passports. Two American and one Indian.* Claire wondered if that would draw *unnecessary attention.*

"I don't know, hadn't thought about it," he said.

"Steven, your muscles are still so tight. Lie down. Come on. Lie down. Face down."

"W-what are you going to do?"

"Lie down and I'll show you."

04:50

When Dara got back to the office, this time she found Kincaid on the floor. On his stomach. Claire had taken off her boots and was walking, bare-footed across his back. Mustering phony innocence, but phoniness only visible to another woman, Claire said, "His back just needed to be popped."

It went pretty much downhill after that. When she finished,

he sat up. Stretched. He said he wanted to discuss the *over-arking strategy*. If they traveled together, two American passports and one Indian, how would that look to the authorities in Chile, he wondered?

Chile?

"What are you saying? I'm not going, now?" asked Dara.

"Did I say that?"

05:43

She defended her passport. Three friends traveling together, there was nothing wrong with that. And Claire agreed, taking Dara's side, but ever-so-lightly.

"You would shadow us, making sure we're not followed, watching the big picture, but we'll still be together."

Dara had been thus reposted to the number three position, and she didn't like it. Occasionally, Claire interjected something that passed for sisterly defense, but when the conversation reached the point-of-tears, she slipped on her boots and headed for the door. One thing Claire didn't want to do was break up anything.

"You're not breaking up anything, trust me," said Kincaid.

06:16

Claire loved it, though darkly loved it. Playing such an edgy strategy. Setting emotional traps. Forcing him to small pronouncements. Forcing him to commit emotional momentum. She loved it, but she hated it too. Hated what the little game was doing to her friend.

Emotions were running pretty high by the time Claire walked out. Her bet was, Kincaid would be her best advocate, but that wasn't a given.

06:45

There were three things she hoped for, at this point. First, that Dara would have such confused loyalty, she wouldn't go to Pember immediately. Second, she would quit the field for the sake of drama. *In the way of women.* Third, by the time, she changed her mind, it would be too late. Kincaid and Claire would be in Chile. Or on their way.

She never knew how it actually went down, but Dara stormed out of the office, two minutes later. She shoved past Claire, and Kincaid saw the shove. He invited Claire back in, where she consoled, encouraged, and shot more warm air up his ego. And now they were on their way, Hust the two of them.

07:28

By the time Claire got back to the hotel that night, she was emotionally exhausted. But she had a win. She planned to fall into bed, her clothes on, and sleep the sleep-of-the-dead. But if Claire expected a *night-light* for her win, she was mistaken. Dr. Nunnally's delusion was about to wake her up to realities for which her mind, her dreams, and nightmares, had no space. There would be no victory-sleep, tonight. No sleep at all.

07:59

As she passed through the lobby, she looked up to see him. Reading a newspaper.

"Dr. Nunnally, is that you?"

"Oh-hi."

"What are you doing here?" She thought he'd gone back to Maryland.

"I brought you something," he told her. He held up an envelope. "I suspect you've guessed already, we still have the bunker."

08:22

She led him to the elevator, then her room, where he placed the envelope on a table. And then sat. He'd come for one reason: to talk her out of what she was about to do. He said, he doubted she would discover anything new. Going to Chile was an unnecessary risk.

"Technology is a trap," he told her, "a trap, not worth chasing."

She said, she didn't realize, he was such a *Luddite.*

"Maybe I am, now that you mention it, but I noticed something over the last fifty-years.

"Fifty?"

"Okay, fifty-five."

She giggled. "Whatever makes you happy," she told him.

"Fifty-five plus, then," he said. "The point is, are we better off for the last thousand years of technology? We've gone from a small population, to over-population, pollution, and enough science to destroy the galaxy."

Even if she found the Coler, *it wouldn't matter.* "We've got bigger problems than technology is going to solve."

09:26

She told him, "A non-polluting energy source would be a good place to start."

"And you believe that?" he said.

"What are the options, Dr. Nunnally?"

"Well, assume for a second, you and your friends find this bunker in Chile."

"Who told you *Chile?*"

"Educated guess," he told her. "So you go to Chile, take these risks, and bring home evidence, of some sort. What next? Go with the long shot here, let's say it leads to an energy-break-through. And you succeed. And everyone moves off the grid with their new-fangled black box. Think about it a second. Think about the impact, if we spread out, if we're truly independent of each other."

10:09

Claire said, her motto was *fix the problems, one at a time.*

"If you only could," he told her, "but ultimately, it's not technology, Miss Whitlock. It's about us. We're not just sucking the planet dry, resource-wise. We're polluting it socially, politically, and spiritually. Technical achievements won't fix that. Your Coler will only end up giving us more children-per-family. Surely you see this. Every solution like this only extends human influence and destroys the earth, bit by bit. It's positively Faustian."

"So what's your best idea?" she said. "Ignore the fact that by the 1930s, Germany had solved most of our energy problems?"

"That's right Claire. For the truly cynical, I guess you could say that. They did us a favor by culling the herd. One less Jew, one less toilet to flush."

"Now that's not funny," she told him, "I hope you don't mean that."

"Not at all," he said. "These miracle-devices are a trap. They were like a dream to the Nazis, too, but it was a nightmare. Take a long, hard look at how much science we dig out when we're making weapons. That's got to tell you something."

Her face was rigid. She was tired, bothered, and strangely discouraged by all this pessimism. This was not a subject where she had many doubts.

"Have you seen the report I did last year?"

Claire said she didn't remember. What report?

11:46

It's *SAS*, unfortunately. There's got to be a way you can find a copy. It's called, *An Unexpected Harmonic.*

"What's in it?"

"The truth. The crazy, crazy truth."

"But if it's SAS, it's probably not part of the fifty-cent tour," she said. "So tell me."

"We did a few drafts, maybe one of them is still lying around. Listen to me, you've got to read it," he said. "It's not easy information, but it's a summary of everything. Unified theory. Religion. The nature of human existence. Can you remember the title? *An Unexpected Harmonic.* If you get a copy, you won't need my fifty-cents."

"Don't leave me hanging," she told him, "what's the deal here?"

12:36

The old man got up and went over to the bureau, where He opened the top drawer.

"Excuse me?" she said.

He dug past the panties and slips, down to a Gideon Bible buried deep in the silk.

"Much of it isn't new, Miss Whitlock."

He turned on the lamp, opened the Bible and began mumbling, and marking with a pen as he flipped pages.

"Genesis 3:14. Two tribes compete for the earth. The human tribe fails its test. God tells the villain in charge of the second tribe, that his seed and the woman's will now be at war. Genesis 6. The sons of the serpent have sex with women of earth … producing halflings. Didn't teach you that in Sunday School, I bet."

13:25

Claire told him that she'd grown up Lutheran. And it was all completely Greek to her.

He continued. "Genesis chapter fourteen, verse twenty-four. God views Israel and the forces of Egypt from a column of fire, a glowing observation platform, if you will. What we would call a *UFO*. Any of it getting through?"

13:49

Lutherans didn't believe this. She was pretty sure about that. Baptists maybe, Pentecostals … but not Lutherans.

He pressed on. "To preserve the gene-pool, to reduce cosmic interbreeding, Israel kept a simple genealogy to enforce the DNA-purity. By doing this, they were able to keep the human genome optimized as they waited for Messiah, the perfect one, the one who would *bruise the head of the serpent*."

He flipped more pages.

"Ezekiel 1:15. Read it for yourself," he said, circling the passage. "The prophet saw a wheel within a wheel flying through the air. What does that sound like? The whole Bible, cover to cover, is one big UFO event, viewed a certain way. The miracles, the angels, the destruction of cities and what have you, there's a bizarre coherence to this stuff. I'm not a Christian, Dr. Whitlock, but I am increasingly suspicious, and about half of us at the company are thinking the same way."

14:58

Claire had absolutely no comeback for any of this, beyond the thought that he might be a little crazy.

"The Bible has a high-strangeness," he continued. "Here,

135

in the book of Job you have an extraordinary conversation between God and the serpent. The serpent admitted, he'd been patrolling the earth, and had seen one man, Job. *Patrolling the earth?* High-strangeness was going on a long time before Roswell."

"So, what you're saying, let me see if I'm getting this right. What you're saying, religion is actually the ET-story, is that it?"

"Or the ET-story is actually religious," he told her. "But it's right here. Black and white. *A messiah is born of a virgin.* Ongoing seed war. A procreative connection to an off-planetary father. And there's a moving star leading the wisemen to Messiah, for crying out loud. A moving star, Dr. Whitlock."

Maybe it was time to speak to him in a soothing voice, and tell him, she appreciated his concern and she would certainly think about what he had said. Maybe then he would de-escalate a little.

"So, you'll be coming back to Fort Meade, then?" he said. "Please do."

"No promises," she told him.

16:24

His eyes took a faraway look. "There's another ancient book, the book of Enoch. In it, God condemns the *Watchers* for giving weapons to humanity. Passing technology. The ancients are telling us the same story. It's a deception. A game of half-truths. And at its root is a seed-war between humans and inter-dimensional forces."

The twinkle returned to his eye.

"Okay, one more thing. What was Nazi Germany's greatest crime? Race purity. You want to understand history, look at the way the shots are grouped. It's always the same. Seed-war. Race purity. And who was the ultimate target in World War II? The Jews. God's *Messianic gene pool.* Another evidence of the Nazi influence you seek: a force has been deployed against the Jews since the beginning."

17:25

He knew she was overcome by this, but there was one last

thing. Flipping through the Bible he found this passage.

"Luke, chapter twenty-one, verse eleven. *And great earthquakes shall be in divers places, and famines, and pestilences; and fearful sights and great signs shall there be from heaven.* Are you hearing these words from 2,000 years ago, *fearful sights* and *great signs?*

"Verse twenty-five. *And there shall be signs in the sun, and in the moon, and in the stars; and upon the earth, distress of nations, with perplexity; the sea and the waves roaring; men's hearts failing them for fear, and for looking after those things which are coming on the earth: for the powers of heaven and earth shall be shaken. And then shall they see the Son of man coming in a cloud with power and great glory. And when these things begin to come to pass, then look up, and lift up your heads; for your redeemer draweth nigh.* What if it turns out to be real? What if Christ knew how the serpent would ignite a final global disaster. I'm telling you, don't go to Chile. Find a good man. Have a baby. Fix the planet with new life, because you won't fix your mortal soul, or mine with new technology."

With that, he placed the pen inside the Bible, closed it, and handed it over.

18:56

"Before you go," said Claire, "animal mutilations, crop circles, what's up with that?"

He didn't miss a beat. He thought they amounted to taunts. The first mocked the Jewish Passover. The sacrificial lamb. The genetically perfect lamb. Christ was the ultimate *perfect lamb.*

"And the second," he said, "is on the order of tagging, what street gangs do. Except this gang is making a territorial claim on the planet. By the way, in which medium do they work, these cosmic taggers?"

"Wheat fields," she told him.

"Close. Harvest fields," Miss Whitlock. "Jesus loved harvest fields because they represented those who loved God. Put in that context, crop circles are a harvest-taunt, across eternity. I'm telling you, put the pieces together and you've got is an *unexpected harmonic.* Read my report first, then if you're still up to it, go to Chile."

"Problem is, these things are all relative," she told him. "What's good can be bad, and what's bad can be good. Who's to know?"

He nodded, then said: *"Those who claim to see no darkness, in truth, see no light. Those who say there is no right or wrong, only opinion, are a danger to themselves and small children. Those who ignore an enemy through affectations of nobility or claims of intellect, are soon to be dead."*

He told her, it was a quote. He didn't tell her, it was his.

20:44

Claire had a hard time sleeping. How could the Blood Toys indicate anything other than a breakthrough in fabrication? But how much confidence did she have in anything at this point?

These were the thoughts running through her head, when she remembered the envelope. At 3:00 a.m. she flipped on the lamp and there it was, still on the table where he'd left it. The last images from inside the miniature.

21:09

Five peppermints and five black-and-white photographs spilled onto the table. What she saw terrified her even more than his words. But there was something else. Eight pages of a draft report. The one Nunnally had written: *An Unexpected Harmonic.* She was suddenly wide-awake. The pictures, the amazing report excited her, frightened her, and upended everything she thought to be true. By morning, Claire had changed her mind about going to Chile.

18 New Luggage

When Claire checked out the next morning, there was a Fed Ex at the front desk, containing a headset. The kind joggers wear. It picked up local stations, but if you knew the boot-sequence, it also pulled down databursts from the Echelon array, in low-Earth orbit.

00:16

To initialize, Claire dialed FM 105. Held the button for ten seconds. And the unit started receiving. Holding the button down for another thirty seconds, the beeping was replaced by Terance's voice. Now unscrambled.

There, in the parking garage at the Marriott, Claire heard the final decision: "We spent the night going over the options," said Terance. "Seems like you might be on the right track. Burst us once a day. Keep us posted on your movement. We've got an extraction team in Argentina, so we're pretty well covered if you run into anything. Which you won't, of course."

00:53

He signed off, reminding her that in Chile the Nazis had been allowed to set-up and govern their own mini-nation, within the nation, after the war. Even the Chileans came and went from these *estancias* (ranches), if they came at all, as guests.

"You'll probably end up in one of the extraterritorial provinces like Colonia Dignidad. We've never had anyone inside, so, we can't offer any you SIGINT or Echelon legacy. Tell you what we'd really be interested in finding out, though: how they've blocked our look-down would be a pretty big Easter

139

egg, if you pull it off. Remember though, wherever it is you end up, you will be the only tourist."

The message didn't do much to kick up her resolve. Thanks to Nunnally, she was now the one with reservations. After the pictures, and especially after reading Nunnally's report, her original understanding fell far short of what was actually going on, in reality. There were too many unknowns, and some of them were freaking her out.

In any event, she still had to, at least, verify the burst. She pressed the power switch five times, then replied, with a hint, that she was having second-thoughts.

"Jerry, heads-up. I'm on my way to the airport." She wasn't quite sure how to tell him the next bit. "I may have changed my mind. Like you said, maybe there's *too much jazz*. Maybe we ought to talk about this a little more."

She pressed and held the button. The message scrambled, then uplinked.

02:40

As she maneuvered through the traffic, she thought about the words Terance had used. *Seems like you might be on the right track.* But that wasn't the same as: *we agree, you're ON the right track.* To anyone who'd ever worked for the agency, it would've been obvious. He was positioning himself, in the event the operation went south. Initiative wasn't always the best course. Claire's dilemma now, even though she'd done, practically a U-turn on her own recommendation, would her newly-found uncertainty come off as weakness? There were risks, both ways.

03:19

She dropped off the car, then proceeded to the ticket counter. And he was already there, cross-legged on the floor, next to a massive backpack.

"That's all you're taking?" he asked. He pointed to the rolling suitcase and garment bag.

"I'm going home, Steven. Emergency."

"What?"

"I'm sorry," she said.

"Sorry?"

"Didn't know until this morning."

"You can't do this to me."

"What can I say?"

"Come on Claire. You're killing me here."

This certainly didn't sound like the Steven Kincaid from White Castle. He hoisted his backpack and motioned for her to follow him to a bench at the far end of the ticket counter.

"Give me five-minutes," he told her. "I want to show you something."

From the pack he pulled out several sheets of paper, selecting one in particular. Handing it over.

"And that's it. That's the Coler," he told her, pointing to a drawing.

04:21

Claire studied the schematic. It was intriguing, but that didn't mean it worked, necessarily. Only that it had been drawn by someone who knew what they were doing. There was indication of load, along with junctions and voltages.

"And this," he said, handing over another page, "this is the bunker. Fourth level down. That's where we find it."

He explained the plan. Someone would *interconnect* with them in Chile and take them in. It would be zero risk. It wasn't enough to change her mind. Given Nunnally's sermon, the night before, the last thing she wanted was to go to South America and find herself in a firefight with the loony lost-tribe-of-Deutschland.

05:09

To his credit, Kincaid didn't give up. In a last ditch effort, he started parroting back things she'd said, like: "It's not about money or fame, it's about *eviscerating* a secret." And, "Don't you want to know the truth?"

She held her ground at first, but it was his appeal to her curiosity and altruism that penetrated her resolve. She did want to know. More than anything, Claire wanted to know the truth.

Maybe it was over-reaching, or perhaps she was only guilty of melodrama. But in the depths of her soul lay the conviction that the survival of the planet, and humanity, hung on just such an opportunity. It was Jazz. If she blew the wrong note, it meant a career, but sometimes you *didn't compose notes. / Sometimes,* as much as she hated to admit it, *sometimes … the notes played you.*

In the end, she stared at him for a long time, and he was careful not to speak. It paid off. Finally, she nodded *yes.*

06:21

They found a nylon backpack, almost as big as his, at one of the concourse-stores. Claire repacked it in the ladies room, leaving her old luggage atop the toilet seat. When she walked out, Kincaid was as warm and appreciative as she'd ever seen him. He grabbed her. He hugged her.

"This is huge, Claire." And he wasn't just referring to the new luggage.

19 Paperclip

On the flight back to Maryland, Nunnally got to thinking about what he'd said to Claire. Maybe this muddy, airtight vocation of his had created a back-pressure. And she'd merely given him a relief-valve. The other possibility. Perhaps he'd needed to hear the narrative again. In his own voice. The connection between religion and inter-dimensional visitation had emerged from reluctant evidence. The ripple in a small conversation, grown large over coffee, at the water-cooler, or lunch at his favorite deli. It was a simple suggestion, but also extravagant. Religion and UFOs had *faith* in common. Both were invested in origins and destinies. Both dealt in mysteries and the promise of salvation. Transcendence. Phenomena that begged to be seen as two windows on the same landscape. A view, neither Nunnally nor his colleagues pursued in the beginning.

00:58

Novelty. Curiosity. Belief. Most converts travel the same trail. And that's what happened at NSA. An informal working group had grown up around the subject. An older researcher by the name of W.W. Cothran had been tasked with putting together a steering-document with as much coherence on the subject, as possible. The document, *An Unexpected Harmonic* had been the result. After that, a small, but growing team coalesced around an ever-maturing theory. It was an informal working group, but one where the results earned the darkest of all classifications: SAS/ TS. It came to be known as the Cothran Working Group (CWG), and Nunnally was a charter member.

When he got back to town, Nunnally was exhausted, but intrigued at the awakened memories. Instead of going straight home, he drove out to the Legacy Media Archive in Virginia. The suitcase still in the trunk.

Most documents had gone digital by the 1960s, but NSA, loathe to destroy the originals, opted to warehouse acres of primary reference in an underground vault. It was here in the stacks, Nunnally had, himself, buried an extraordinary document in 1959 or '60. He wasn't sure. And that would be the first challenge. Remembering.

02:23

Officially, NSA had 239 documents on UFOs. These were the *alien-and-cow* stories. Someone saw lights in the sky. Or heard much mooing. Goofy stuff, for the most part, but soberly investigated. The more sinister cases had been filed *variously*, as they called it. Nunnally tucked away more than a few, deep inside the empires of war. The Second World War, in particular, was such a sprawling data-zone, there were plenty of abstracted places for *filing variously*.

03:00

Operation Paperclip. He would start there. Three long shelves on the sixth-level contained the recruitment files for former Nazi scientists. The boxes didn't have everything, but there were first-statements. Nunnally was especially anxious to see the field-interview with Werner von Braun. He remembered enough to know, the trail began there.

According to the cover page, Von Braun's initial session was conducted *20-September-1945*. He was described as eager and cooperative. Additional comments included a reference to his shoulder cast.

03:42

> *Maj. Gen X*
> *So what happened?*
>
> *Werner von Braun (WVB)*
> *(English)*

An automobile accident. Inconvenient. I think.

MGX
Was it your brother we talked to yesterday?

WVB
Mangus, yes.

MGX
About these documents, will we need to talk with someone else?

WVB
No one else knows about them. I hid them, along with three of my associates. But to be clear, this is in your best interest. What we want is safe passage, maybe amnesty.

MGX
Of course, that's not our decision. If you are who you say you are, and the documents, sufficiently interesting, that's when we'll talk amnesty.

04:24

WVB
Our best scientists are running for their lives. It would be a mistake if they're captured by the Soviets. That's my concern.

MGX
Okay. Concern noted. Your brother said you were at Peenemunde?

WVB
Yes. I directed research there.

MGZ
Is that where you're from?

WVB
My family is from Selesia, originally.

MGX
And that's in Germany?

WVB
Yes. We have an estate. Hopefully, we still have it.

MGX
"Estate," or "home?"

WVB
Forgive my English, but I think the word is "estate." It's a very large property. Other families work for us. Has a church.

MGX
A church?

WVB
Yes. My father – how do you say – picked up the tab for the church.

MGX
He was religious?

WVB
Yes.

MGX
And you?

WVB
I-I don't understand ... oh yes. I-I am religious. Yes.

05:25

It was interesting for Nunnally to remember how things used to be. During this interview, blank spaces began to show up in the transcription, where there'd been expletives. Such would never happen today, where even the coarsest word found ink. In the old days, though, a form of propriety was always engaged.

At one point the general let fly with a string blue words, nailing von Braun on the question of how a religious person could've gotten involved with the *blanking* National Socialists. There were blankings all over the page. Von Braun's reply, on the other hand, had none.

06:03

WVB
Imagine the dilemma. We didn't have a choice in this mat-ter. We were either going to be SS, or they would've killed us. When we heard what was happening in London, specifically about the V-2, God being my helper, we were cut to the heart. It was the worst possible use for our science.

MGX
Well, how did you deal with it? Knowing, the rockets you were sending into the air, were coming down in London, killing thousands of innocent people? Children.

WVB
This is hard to answer sir, knowing what I know, now. We worked to get them into the air, we had no control where they came down.

MGX
Hmm. Were you a professor?

WVB
No, but I was recruited by one. Dr. Oberth.

MGX
Dr. Oberth?

WVB
Yes.

06:53

That was it. Seeing the name Oberth, Nunnally's fog lifted a little more. Somewhere in the Oberth papers he'd hidden a fil-ing clue. He stuffed the von Braun originals back into the box, then raced back down the aisle. Would he have underlined the keywords in pencil? Blue pencil? That had been his method in those days. As standard practice, researchers marked up documents, with pen and pencil. Initially, he counted on the fact that his scribblings wouldn't stand out, though he hoped they would now. And that he would be able to remember them.

00:00

The first twenty pages established Oberth's scientific credentials. The next fifty-three aimed at discovering how much a Nazi he'd been, or had he also been *a conscripted-man-of-science?* Toward the end of this section, the OSS officer started pumping him for technical details. Nunnally found this on page 62.

07:26

> OSS
> *… was that before the war, or as late as the 1930s?*

> OBERTH
> *I was not directly involved in it, but I was told, the 1930s.*

> OSS
> *It was outside the scope of what you were doing, right? And your position is that you hadn't heard about any of it until the mid-1940s?*

> OBERTH
> *We heard rumors.*

> OSS
> *What does the word "Vril" mean?*

In the narrative, the transcriber noted: *Oberth flushes, clears throat.*

> OBERTH
> *The Vril Society was a secret organization. I had no contact with them, to my knowledge.*

OSS
Well, we continue hearing words like, "alternative energy," or "alternative science." What do you know about this?

OBERTH
Rumors.

OSS
But it does actually mean something?

Oberth
Yes. The-the occult, maybe.

08:42

Toward the end of the interview, the OSS officer started threatening Oberth. There were plenty of blank spots, as in the previous document, but mostly, the man said things that would have been a breach-of-protocol these days. Pursuing the question of occult-science, he bluntly said he would *rather shoot Oberth than cart him back to the US.*

09:01

OSS
So it would be in your best interest to tell me what you know about alternative science.

OBERTH
I've told you everything I know, but I have, I have a name. You should talk to someone by the name of Karl Haushofer. He knows about this.

09:17

Nunnally was jolted to reality by a faint blue line underscoring Haushofer's name. That was it! He'd hidden a file, not in Hausehofer's, but his son's file: *Albrecht Hausehofer.* In the early 1950s, he'd tangled the trail to such a degree, he could scarcely make it out, after all these years. In moments, he was chasing back through the stacks. High atop one of the shelves was Albrecht's box, covered in dust.

Young Haushofer had been executed by the Nazis before the

end of the war, and not a proper subject for Paperclip, which was why Nunnally had hidden the crazy-file there.

09:57

Sure enough, sandwiched inside a formidable clutter was the long lost, long-hidden Paperclip interview with a man by the name of Eberhardt Zeiss. Karl Haushofer's aide-de-camp. He was the first person to ever suggest the connection between inter-dimensionals and religion.

More than three decades after having first seen it, almost fifty years after its transcription, Dr. Nunnally embarked on a narrative, utterly irrational to him, decades before. He pulled out his legal pad, got comfortable, and started reading.

The cover page indicated that this was a subsequent interview, taking place on *2-August-1947*. Zeiss had been a walk-in at JIOA. A handwritten note said that he had spent six months in a detention center, and had developed close friendships with some of the American guards.

10:55

> *Allied Officer (AO)*
> *I see you brought it with you today.*

The statement suggested that Zeiss had carried a book, or a document into the interview.

> *ZEISS*
> *The man yesterday said I could read it into the record, if that's okay.*

> *AO*
> *First, uh-let's pick up with what we were talking about yesterday. My C-O wants you to repeat what Haushofer told you about the flying machines. I also have a question. Was he a heavy drinker?*

> *ZEISS*
> *No. He didn't indulge in alcohol, so far as I know, at least, not regularly.*

AO

Well, start with Haushofer, at the beginning.

ZEISS

He was a professor in Munich, at the university. One of his students was Rudolf Hess, with whom he co-authored Mein Kampf, at Landesberg in 1923.

AO

And Hitler too, I believe. Right?

ZEISS

Yes, that's my understanding. He said, Germany and Japan had their first alliance in secret societies, which were the direct result of him going to Japan in – I believe it was 1908. I'm not sure.

12:01

AO

Explain, "secret societies." Is that what you were talking about? What's that other, unusual word you mentioned yesterday?

ZEISS
The Vril?

AO
What does it mean?

ZEISS

I'm not sure, but the members of the Vril Society treat it like a religious force. I've heard, they have rituals, but I'm not really sure about that.

AO

Okay. We'll take that up later. Getting back to Haushofer, you told me, he joined this uh, the Green Dragons – a secret soci-ety, when he was in Japan. Is that right?

12:34

ZEISS

Yes, he was proud of that. He based the Vril Society in Germa-

ny on what the-the Dragons taught him.

AO
Any idea what that might be?

ZEISS
Not really. I know they believed they could contact other ...
um ... people ...

AO
What do you mean by that ... other what?

ZEISS
He told me, wh-when he was in Tibet, he discovered a ritual
that put him in contact with the ... the spirits.

AO
Say that again.

ZEISS
I don't know how you say it in English, but they talked to ...
ghosts or ... I don't know what the right word is ...

13:14

AO
Were they were having séances?

ZEISS
I don't know this "séance."

AO
It's-uh ... like people sitting at a table, holding hands, while
this medium talks to dead people. It's a little crazy.

ZEISS
No, no it's not. That's what I'm talking about. Séance.

AO
Well, we'll have to save that for another time, too. Yesterday,
you said something, another funny word, "Hanabu." What

does that mean? "Hanabu?"

13:41

ZEISS
It's a space-ship. Haushoffer said the spirit-beings crashed one in the Black Forest, and it was being repaired by Dr. Kammler. When he first said it, I thought he meant fixing it, but he may have be trying to copy some of wreckage, trying to figure out how it worked.

AO
And the year?

ZEISS
I'm not sure, 1936, maybe. Dr. Kammler was working on it at the end of the war. Dr. Hans Kammler.

AO
Haushauffer told you this?

ZEISS
I got it mostly from conversations, like when you walk through a room, or someone's on the telephone. Kammler and Haushauffer did meet one time. I don't know what they talked about, though.

14:22

Haushofer said, the spirit-beings wanted to help Germany restore the purity of the race. Nordic gods, and that sort of thing.

The officer responded saying, he'd just read that Himmler thought he was in contact with the spirit of a dead German King, who'd died in the 1300s. Was this the sort of thing Zeiss was talking about?

AO
So it was like a shared mental illness?

ZEISS
Perhaps a "spiritual illness."

Zeiss evidentially sensed, he was being written off. There were things he wanted to say, and of course, he wanted to read from the book. And the officer eventually gave in.

> *ZEISS*
> *There were two writers, very important to Haushofer. I told you about Guido Von List, and the other was Helana Blatvotsky. She also went to Tibet in the 1800s. What is interesting about Blavotsky, she also claimed to have encountered hidden spirits. What I'm about to read was based on information they gave her.*

15:26

The transcriber noted that Zeiss began to read a passage from a book entitled: *The Secret Doctrine*. The book he'd evidentially brought to the interview.

> *ZEISS (reading)*
> *"One of the most hidden secrets involves the so-called fall of Angels. Satan and his rebellious host will thus prove to have become the direct Saviors and Creators of divine man. Thus Satan, once he ceases to be viewed in the superstitious spirit of the church, grows into the grandiose image. It is Satan who is the God of our planet and the only God. Satan (or Lucifer) represents the Centrifugal Energy of the Universe, this ever-living symbol of self-sacrifice for the intellectual independence of humanity."*
>
> *Blavatsky wrote this before Herr Hitler was born, but this was the hand inside the puppet of National Socialism.*

16:21

As Nunnally read, here it was in black and white. The strange nexus of genetics, cosmic breeding, war, and technology. Themes-in-common. Strikingly shared between religion and UFOs. But as the interview wound down, there was a final, chilling revelation.

Zeiss said that Hitler believed he had been visited by spirit-beings in his bedroom, late one night.

ZEISS
Most of the staff thought it was a drug reaction, but Haushofer believed, dark forces actually came to Herr Hitler's room.

It was outrageous, and Nunnally could imagine the American officers trying to remain non-responsive. Still, Zeiss had one last sermon.

ZEISS
When I was a prisoner, I was given a Bible by the Gideons. That's what I read while I was in prison.

17:15

He went on to say, the forces that deceived Haushofer had been trying to destroy the human family since the book of Genesis. That is what he'd gotten from his study, during his stay in prison.

ZEISS
Their goal was to break down the seed-line to Messiah. Read about Noah. They were having sexual relations with the women of earth, attempting to spoil the seed, even then. I know it sounds crazy, and that's how it remains hidden. It is crazy. But what this is about is "seed war," between God's people and the spirits. The voices that spoke to Haushofer, hated the Jews, and that's the clue. They also hate God, just like Blavatsky.

18:00

The rabid, evangelical forthrightness brought a smile to Dr. Nunnally. Here's another thing that would've closed down the interview, had it been conducted fifty years later.

ZEISS
Think about it. Why didn't we win, the Nazis? The spirit beings couldn't make good on their promises. They told Adam and Eve that they would be like gods, if you remember. And they didn't make good. They promised us we would be like supermen. They didn't make good. That is why you won. The God of the Jews had no choice, but choose sides.

Dr. Nunnally hadn't seen the document in decades, but in some back corner of his mind, the words had not only prospered, they'd taken up residence. All the experiences at NSA, all the secrets, all the intercepts – this doctrine of seed-war had become foundational to his understanding of the UFO – and this was where the CWG started.

He was so caught up in his thoughts, he didn't hear the footsteps. Didn't realize, someone was walking through the stacks until they were standing there, staring down at him.

"Hey," said Terance. "So this is where you go to hide out."

Nunnally closed the file and invited him to pull up a chair.

"Still come down to the world of paper?"

"Nostalgia," said Nunnally. "I like the feel of paper."

"We need to talk, Millard. If you don't know already, Claire's going in."

The news caught the old man a little off-guard, but it wasn't entirely unexpected.

"So what did you tell her?"

"I told her not to do it," said Nunnally. "We've been chasing this for a half-century, and we're no closer to understanding. She's young, Jerry. Let her have a life. Fire her, why don't you?"

Terance asked: "Did you characterize the Blood Toys in any way?"

"Didn't have to. She's not stupid," said Nunnally.

"Which is why we went with her proposal. This Kincaid has connections. Maybe our friends are engaging us. Would that be bad?"

20:07

Nunnally told him, "Not if you could trust them. Jerry, they blind our science. What they give us, backfires. There isn't one favor they've ever given us that hasn't cost more than we can afford. For heaven's sake, be objective. They lie. They abduct. I don't think we should be trading with these Indians."

"Millard, I have a lot of respect for you, but you're dangerously close to breaching your security agreement. Not just with Claire. What you said the other day at Bonhert, you amaze me."

20:40

The old man was suddenly tired. Maybe it was his heart. And maybe that was the intent, to stress him out. He told Terance to say what he'd come to say.

"I think you know," said Terance.

He told Nunnally, there would always be respect, of course, for all he'd accomplished, but that wouldn't be a *get-out-of-jail-free card* if he compromised national security.

"With me gone, who's going to stand up to you?" asked the old man.

"No one. With you old war horses out of the way, maybe we'll be able to step up to the next level … and *vibrate at a higher frequency*."

This had become a half-joke at NSA, particularly since the CWG report, *An Unexpected Harmonic*, had gone into distribution.

"But they're not from space."

"Millard, there are fifty-three species of extraterrestrials on the planet."

"There's one," said Nunnally, "and fifty-three manifestations. And you know what Taylor believes. The grays are biological robots, manufactured from stem cells, and expendable."

"Reg Taylor is crazy," said Terance. "And you know what I think about his theory; I'm not going to get into another argument about this."

21:59

"You can't explain why they have the capability to take any form, to be seen or unseen, and still, they leave around all these little stage props. Crash victims. Screen memories. And then we build on their fiction. I know it's easier to believe the extraterrestrial story, but they're deceiving us with it," said Nunnally. "And the deception doesn't have a happy ending."

"You and your little fundamentalist cabal have been blocking the proper course for a long time, and now, it's time to go."

"And if I don't?"

"Come on Millard. We'll do what we have to do," said Terance. "And just so you hear it from my lips, it's on the fast track. Not months. Not weeks. Not even days."

"Hours?" asked the old man.

"Maybe minutes," said Terance. "I don't want it that way, but really, it's your call."

22:58

"Say I resign in a couple of weeks, What happens next? Car accident? Cancer? We both know I won't be retiring in peace."

"Well, that's your problem. You don't trust anyone."

"And that's your problem," said Nunnally, "you do."

With that, Terance pushed back and stood to leave. His movement was slow, however, meant to be slightly ominous.

"By the way Millard, you have the photos from the bunker. You need to drop them by archives."

The old man lied to him at this point. Told him he would.

23:35

A little after noon, the green Buick LeSabre pulled into a convenience store in Odenton, Maryland. Dr. Nunnally filled up the tank, then headed home, a few blocks away. It was good to be back. He pulled into the garage. Closed the door. Removed the suitcase from the trunk, and went inside.

After a week, the house was musty. He opened windows, then the front door to create a draft. This was a ritual. One that had evolved over the decades. He changed to his seersucker leisure suit. Washed a load of whites. Then pulled out the Lysol from beneath the kitchen sink. He sprayed every reasonable surface. He was quite phobic about the kitchen. He sprayed. Waited five minutes. Wiped it down with paper towels. Then sprayed again.

24:23

There wasn't a real need to vacuum, but he did anyway. After that, he pulled out a dust cloth and gave the furniture a quick once-over. Nothing betrayed housekeeping like dust on a lamp.

A little after 2:30 p.m., he shut the windows again. Locked

the front door. Took the .38 from the dresser, along with an un-opened bag of peppermints, and headed out for the last drive he planned to take.

An hour later he was on Interstate 95 heading south. That night he would be in Creedmoor, North Carolina. Where he had been born. And where he planned to die.

25:01

Dr. Nunnally drove down Northside Road, past a small frame church, then left onto a dirt road. It was a familiar place, though only at the greatest distance of memory. Long before highways, shopping malls, and churches, this had been as re-mote a place as could be found in North Carolina.

A blank spot in the trees was all that remained of his child-hood home. There was not one board, not one rock. Just a depression in the earth.

25:32

He removed the pistol from the glove box and got out. How far he had come since leaving? He thought of his parents. Of their small, simple lives. How many steps had he taken from this place? Had to be a number, a precise number. One mil-lion? Two? A hundred? Were he to walk back in time, one step at a time, what step-number was it, the day he left for Chapel Hill? The old man marked off the phantom numbers of his life.

He did not despise the tears that came, as he counted back. It had been a grand life. A surprise, really. He abandoned these lonely roads to superintend the great secrets of the world. How much more could you ask?

26:19

He stood where his home had been. He looked around for a welcoming thought. And he remembered this. Christmas, the year of the big snow. Everyone had a present that year. And that was not always the case. Children pass through such mo-ments, unaware. The brief hours of this long, lost holiday had been the best he would ever live. Childhood and family. Mys-teries and securities. It was the final thought he would take. A boy carrying firewood and a snowy night.

In an act of great duality, of hallowed memories juxtaposed to the physical act of lifting a gun, he steadied himself for what came next. It was assumed that one only had to get past a certain point. Then the gravities pulled you under. He put the barrel in his mouth. Closed his eyes. Then slipped to another place. A place of sound and splendor. A place of welcome.

20 Chile

A young Chilean in a chauffeur's beret watched as Claire and Kincaid made their way through customs. When their passports were stamped, he walked up and handed them a note. *Take the train to Puerto Montt. I will meet you there.* It was signed, *Quiroga.*

"And I will take you to the train," said the young man, tipping his cap.

00:21

Late that afternoon, they caught the southbound *Ferrocarriles del Estado.* The train to Puerto Montt. Most trains in South America run according to approximate schedules. *Approximate* to the point, you can't be sure when you'll actually arrive at your destination. They assumed their arrival would be sometime the following day.

Claire anticipated, the ride would be a bit tedious. And it was. After boarding the flight in Chicago, there was a subtle change in Kincaid. The bratty attitude subsided a bit. It was no less than the unmistakable ritual of attentiveness. The predictable male-prelude to a hopeful liaison. But it was her turn. She was going to flip back to the role she played best. Disinterested party. By the time they boarded the train in Chile, Claire had reached a landscape she knew well: *the domain of the panting male.*

01:20

As the train rumbled out past the gasworks, then heaps of tires and a rebar factory, Kincaid offered up the brave story of his life. He said he'd been tracking the *German supposition* for years.

"I think the word's *suppository*," she told him. As she said it, she denied herself the most painful smile she'd ever swallowed.

"Maybe so," he said with a bit of suspicion. "A *suppository*, because there's a *supposed* history. When we worked on the V-2 documentary, you saw it, right?"

Claire nodded, staring into his eyes, but resolutely denying him acknowledgement or commendation. As a matter of fact, she was still fighting with the smile.

"Before the documentary, there hadn't a lot about Germans, flying rockets. A lot of people didn't know until we *manifested* the program."

02:17

After a few more malaprops, the *suppository-smile* died a gentle death. If such a thing is possible. But he continued, he had new ones to replace it.

At twilight, they were told the train was passing into Chile's famous wine country. Claire could just make out the well-tended rows passing in the shadows. Kincaid continued rattling, totally oblivious. Finally, she pushed back in her seat and closed her eyes on him. It took him thirty-minutes before he finally got the message.

02:54

Next morning, she couldn't believe the change in scenery. Santiago had been a quaint, old-world community ringed with urban sprawl and scrub-oak. A few hours south, though, the scene transformed from the old-world, into cataclysmic and majestic. Southern Chile looked like the Alps.

As the sun drifted higher, blinding everyone on the east side of the dining car, Claire saw quaint dairies. Lush green hillsides. Holsteins. And lines of fog. Also, a great landform in the southeast. The conductor explained, it was the mighty *Orsono*, the grandfather volcano of southern Chile.

Twenty-two hours after leaving Santiago, the train pulled into Puerto Montt. Planted along the north shore of the Relocanvi Inlet, and protected on the west by Tenglo Island, the community was colorful, friendly and robustly European. Passing through the train station, they heard almost as much German, as Spanish. It was an unusual cultural mix.

Out on the street, the smell of the ocean awakened their senses, otherwise dulled by the night on the train.

"What now?" said Claire.

"We wait," he told her. "We wait for them to find us."

04:16

They stood there for a few minutes, looking for a friendly face.

"This is not good," he said, finally. "Quiroga should've been here."

"An-and you're sure about this?"

He said he was positive. "This is the train station. He said he would meet us at the train station. Actually, the note said he would meet us here. In Puerto Montt."

He checked his pockets for the note because he was certain she was wrong. She told him, he'd given it back to the guy who'd driven them to the station.

"You sure you don't have it?" he asked.

"You're the only one who touched it," she told him. "And you gave it back."

04:52

She paced back and forth. What a bust. And if it turned out to be a complete wild goose chase ... Claire didn't want to even think about that possibility.

"I'm going over to the shade," she told him, finally, "I'm going to listen to the radio."

Kincaid ordered her to *stay put*. Quiroga would be looking for two people. Not one.

"He's looking for an American," she corrected. "And you do look *American*."

"I wish you would *persevere* with me."

"Persevere?"

"Don't go anywhere."

"I'm not. I'm ... *persevering* over there," she told him.

She walked over to a small tree next to the sidewalk. As she went, she fished the headset from the pack. Claire pretended to listen to local radio. What she was actually doing, of course, was downloading a databurst. There, in front of the train station, as scores of strangers milled about, no one knew, Radio-NSA was filling her head. Not music from Puerto Montt's only station. This was the message she pulled down.

"Claire, I found out few things," said her boss.

"Nunnally was a bit—um indiscreet, talking with you the other night. We're not taking disciplinary action, but anything he told you is classified. You're responsible."

This was interesting. How could Terance have found out about the conversation? Would the old man have ratted her out?

006:22

Eyes closed, looking for all the world like someone singing along with her favorite song, Claire uploaded a reply.

She sang that they *had arrived in Puerto Montt. No one had met them yet.* She sang, *not to worry about Dr. N. Most of the stuff he said was already known. Or suspected.* Then came the verse. *Nothing new to report, but she would try to update him, later in the day.*

When she opened her eyes, twenty-meters away, Kincaid was talking to someone. A pretty young woman had noticed him. But she was pitching a bed-and-breakfast.

07:02

Her English was almost as nonexistent as their Spanish, but eventually both Claire and Kincaid understood the offer. Five dollars per night. Per person. A price that included breakfast. The woman said her name was Elena. Then she produced a card with *Wallflower Bed 'N Breakfast* written in English.

"Four blocks," she said, pointing in a general direction. "Four blocks."

When she left, Claire said she'd pay that much, even if she only slept for five minutes.

"Stay," Kincaid ordered. "We've got to be obvious."

"Guess what Steven, you are obvious. Why can't I take a nap? I'm tired."

He told her no. Emphatically. Quiroga would be looking for two.

"But how long am I supposed to sit here?"

"I don't know," he said. "But I expect you to be *conducive.*"

"I expect you to back off," she told him. "You may push Dara around, but I'm not Dara."

"I should have come alone," said Kincaid.

Oh my, how she was enjoying this. Claire's countenance clouded up. Then she went into a full-pout.

"I'm really tired! Do you understand?"

"I do," he told her, "but we're both tired."

She said *no*, he didn't understand. She should be at home, working on her dissertation. But no. Here she was at the tip-end of the world.

Finally, he couldn't take it any more. He told her to *go, go take a nap* or whatever it was she wanted to do, *waste five bucks.*

"Thank you." And with that, she hoisted her pack and walked away.

08:47

Finding the Wallflower was easy. When Claire walked up, the reason for the name was immediately obvious. Eye-level to the street, a wide crack in the plaster sliced across one corner of the building. And growing inside the crack, an abundance of brightly-colored flowers. Purples. Reds. Yellows. The place didn't really need a sign.

Elena was thrilled to see a customer walk up. Claire pointed to the crack. "I like that."

"Yes," said Elena. "Earthquake."

"Oh," said Claire.

A scan of the houses either side of the street revealed more cracks, though none had flowers growing from them.

"Very original," said Claire.

Elena nodded, smiled and offered to with the pack.

165

"Oh, that's okay. I can carry it."

By the time Kincaid stumbled in, four hours later, the two women had become hard, fast friends. Even with the language barrier.

"I see you got a lot of sleep," said Kincaid.

"I wasn't tired any more."

"Oh, isn't that nice," he said. "Where's the room?"

Elena pointed up the stairs. Claire told him his room was the second on the right. As he trudged up, he said to let him sleep in. When the door slammed upstairs, Claire made a nasty face. Elena put her hands to her mouth and giggled.

"El stupido," said Claire.

10:16

Next morning, Claire and Elena took a walking tour of Feria Artesanal, the open-air crafts market. Elena kept saying the words *beautiful* and *best in Chile*, as she strangled the language, describing the obvious.

The merchants were setting up booths. Even at this hour, there were baskets to purchase. Sweaters and blankets. Claire was particularly fascinated by the jewelry. She tried on a necklace, then pointed to the rings behind the glass. Both women tried on a dozen rings. Sometimes shaking their heads *yes*, sometimes *no*. There was one in particular, both agreed on. An extraordinary piece in white gold, capped with a blue sapphire. Claire was smitten. And the bargaining began. She couldn't understand what was actually being said, but Claire got the distinct impression, Elena thought the price too high. She tried to wave off the disagreement.

"Guys, it's okay," said Claire. "I was just looking. See? I've taken it off."

11:20

There would be no quick peace. Elena's voice went shrill. The shopkeeper waved a fist. Elena raised one back. Claire had no idea, this was tradition. Where was the fun in a simple transaction when you could have a little catharsis thrown in for free? Then out of nowhere, someone else joined fracas. A young man walked up. He listened to Elena's argument for a moment, then he started yelling at the merchant. Claire backed off. This little public disaster no longer involved her. Unexpectedly, the merchant threw up his hands, accepting whatever offer the young man had just made. From beneath the table he produced a small velveteen box.

"Oh no, I didn't intend to buy," said Claire.

"You don't have to," said the young man in perfect English. "It's yours, with our compliments."

12:15

Claire judged her benefactor to be in his mid-twenties. His olive face was lit with a blazing set of brown eyes and a gentle smile. The quintessential Latin: shirt opened a couple of buttons down. Collar turned up. A neck-scarf knotted sideways around his throat. He would be the *essential* Latin to Steven, no doubt.

"You speak English," said Claire.

"I am Quiroga. Rob-Q," he said, offering his hand.

Claire accepted it and introduced herself.

"Rob-Q, I can't keep the ring.

"Then I'll buy another," he said.

"No, that's not what I mean."

"Of course. This is your tradition. But please accept, as a present," he told her. "This is ours."

13:05

Her new friend Elena, while she couldn't understand English, interrupted Quiroga in Spanish. With the dust barely settled, another argument kicked off. Claire suspected her new friend was protecting her from the predations of a Latin lothario. A Latin ... Steven probably didn't have a word for *lothario.* Before it got completely out-of-hand, Rob-Q said something that seemed to placate Elena. Then he turned to Claire.

"You do not understand. I'm the one who is meeting you," he told her. "Roberto Quiroga."

Now it registered. *Quiroga.*

"Where is Mr. Kincaid?"

Elena answered in Spanish. "El Stupido?" Then pointed.

13:52

Draped across the bed, one leg twisted in the sheet and hanging off the side, El Stupido was still sleeping when they arrived.

"Hey," said Claire. "Wake up!"

He groaned.

Claire grabbed the sheet and ripped it away. Kincaid lay there pale and white. Hair sticking sideways. The slightly embarrassed Chileans retreated to the hall.

"What?" he said.

She told him to get up. She'd found Quiroga.

"You … found him? Where?"

"Just get up, please."

14:29

With Quiroga serving as their translator, Claire found out about Elena. She'd inherited the Wallflower from her grandparents, Germans who'd come over after the war.

Quick to pounce on a marketing opportunity, Elena put in another plug. She invited Claire to tell all of her friends about Puerto Montt. And to be sure and mention the Wallflower.

By taxi, Quiroga took them on a quick tour of the lakes. They saw Alpine-styled chalets. Grand residences of wood and glas. Some straight out of Gstaad or St. Moritz.

"Now you see why we call it *little Switzerland*," said Quiroga.

Claire made the point that it didn't just look like Switzerland, this part of Chile seemed very European. They'd noticed it in the train station. Quiroga explained that Europeans, Germans in particular, had been coming to Puerto Montt since the 1850s. Until now, it hadn't registered with Claire that a German community had been here at the turn of the century. It explained the ease with which *Third Reichers* had eventually slipped into residency.

Quiroga ended the tour at Angelmo Tipico, where Claire was amazed at the fresh seafood. She ordered buttered sea-bass with cilantro. Kincaid had scallops. The only thing Quiroga insisted on was something called a *Pisco Sour*.

"Grape brandy and lemon juice. You come to Puerto Montt, you must indulge."

He was right. It had a tart, rich taste, but no discernible kick. At least, not immediately. As the waiter cleared the table, Kincaid asked Quiroga to tell a little about himself. "How did you learn to speak such good English? Did you live ever live in the States?"

"Yes," he said, "I did actually. I attended the University of Texas. Hook'em horns." He held up the two-fingered salute.

16:29

Maybe it was the Pisco Sour, but Claire almost blurted out that she'd been to Austin, and not all that long ago. The alcohol had definitely loosened her tongue.

Kincaid said, English was hard to pick up, right ? Especially if it was a second language.

"Hard enough, but when you live there, it's not quite so bad. The hardest part for me is thinking in English," said Quiroga. "I start thinking in English, I think I want to buy a Buick, or Chevrolet."

Claire asked him what he wanted to buy when he was thinking in Spanish, and he smiled.

"Anything but a Buick or Chevrolet, I think. A Bugatti, maybe."

Claire wanted to know his major at UT. And he told her, *fine arts*.

"Wouldn't that be a little expensive for an international student?"

"I had a scholarship," he told her.

17:23

Going back to the point about language, Kincaid said he'd had to learn English as a second language. It hadn't been easy. Claire caught what he was actually saying. Offhandedly,

Kincaid was letting her know, he realized he used the wrong words sometimes. Sometimes his choices weren't even in the ballpark, but they were artifacts of a second language, learned late.

"So English is *your* second language?"

"Yes, Claire, it is. How many do you speak?"

She glared at him, and probably shouldn't have been so open, but he had hooked her with his little dig.

"I speak four, Steven."

"Oh yeah? What?"

"French, German, Italian and Russian. I can write in Cyrillic. And how about you, Steven?"

18:14

He applauded.

Kincaid wrangled the conversation back to the mysterious patrons for whom Quiroga worked.

"Should we assume they are German patriots?" he asked.

Quiroga hesitated, then said, the Europeans had gone out of their way to help Chile. They set up free hospitals, put charities in place to help the Indian communities, ... *and scholarships.* He didn't spell it out, but the two Americans understood this to mean, he had also benefited from their generosity.

18:49

When they got back to the Wallflower that afternoon, there were boxes on the front porch. Quiroga had taken the liberty of out-fitting the expedition. He apologized for having to guess the sizes, but as it turned out, he'd been fairly accurate. There were chilotes (ponchos), boots and alpaca sweaters.

"And you'll happy to see, I found smaller backpacks," he said. "Good? Good. Elena, have them at the pier at 4:30 in the morning, if that's okay."

Kincaid nodded, *sure.*

21 Exotic World

El Remolino (the Cowlick) pulled away from the dock at 4:45 a.m. For the most part, the captain piloted a twisting course down the coastline, keeping the craft nearly a half-kilometer offshore. Occasionally, he steered closer, and it made Claire nervous. He would glance over to the electronic readouts as he executed his maneuvers. But mostly, he chatted with everyone in the wheelhouse. And was fairly nonchalant about it all.

Claire whispered, she wondered if the captain was paying enough attention.

"This is pretty dangerous," she said.

"Many times I travel with him," said Rob Q. "Don't worry. By the way, he wants to know if-uh you're married."

"What? Oh. Si," she replied.

"Really?"

She shook her head *no*. Quiroga told the man *si*, anyway.

00:56

With dawn came glimpses of the intercostal waterway. Fog settled in across much of shoreline, but when it started to lift a little, Kincaid noticed, the walls were looking more and more like Baffin.

"Except, there's a lot more green," said Kincaid. "What kind of trees are those?"

Quiroga told him they were the symbol of his country. The Araucaria pine.

"They're unusual aren't they?"

Rob Q told him, not in Chile. In Chile they were pretty

usual.

"Oh, right."

01:32

During a slight break in the weather, Claire and Rob Q went out on deck where the wind was brisk and pungent. But the rain started again. Hard enough for the captain to turn on the wipers. They scrambled back into the wheelhouse, dripping a water-trail back to where they'd been sitting.

01:49

One of the crew brought over a large white towel, offering it to Claire.

"This, for you," he said.

"Gracious," she told him. "You're so kind. Bless your heart."

Claire had just made the man's day.

El Remolino was passing within twenty-meters of a sheer rock wall. Claire was busy with the towel, but increasingly distracted by the prospect of shipwreck. The captain then wheeled hard-left, steering into a channel. Claire hadn't even seen it until the last second.

"Are we sure about this guy?"

Quiroga explained, the passage was a shortcut. In fifteen minutes, *expect him to turn back right, toward the ocean*. It would *cut off an hour*.

"If we don't sink," said Claire.

Rob Q smiled. Not to worry.

02:43

For three hours, the tug drifted through an increasingly fractured seascape. They passed small islands, sailed into an estuary and finally a canyon, incredibly steep on three sides. The good news, the rain had given way to mist again; the bad: the deckhands were breaking out the tender. The easy part was now behind them.

Under Quiroga's supervision, Claire and Kincaid donned sweaters, shouldered their packs and slipped into rubber ponchos. Meanwhile, the captain throttled down and shifted to neutral. The crew told Claire *good-bye*, the one who'd given her the towel even kissed her hand.

"Well, thank you again," she said, flashing the dimples.

"Keep towel?"

"Oh no. Thank you anyway."

Kincaid closed his eyes and told her she was having too much fun.

"Yes I am, El stupido. I am indeed."

03:48

Five minutes later, the rubber boat was banging through the waves. Heading for the rock wall. Then, about a hundred meters out, they saw a trail leading up into the rock.

Over the whine of the outboard, Quiroga shouted that this was where they got off, and to *hold on*. There wasn't enough room to beach, so the tender bounced onto a shallow ledge. Against a rolling, dangerous footing, the three climbed out. Moments later, the whine of the outboard dissolved into rain against plastic, and the groan of a crashing sea.

"Ready?" said Quiroga.

Kincaid nodded. Claire wasn't sure. Quiroga did his best to build her confidence. He told her again, he'd been on this trail many times. *No problem.*

04:39

Kincaid wasn't worried because he'd done this sort of thing before, back at Baffin.

"You should-of seen those rocks, you want to see scary. They were massive, probably twice as big."

Ah, the wonders of comparison and the predictability of male ego. Claire closed her eyes at him and shook her head.

"What?" said Kincaid.

"El Stupido."

"Would you stop that? It's not funny."

"Wanna bet?" said Claire.

Quiroga interrupted the little spat, saying he would go first, then Claire, then Steven.

"Oh and Steve, catch her if she falls."

"What?"

"Just teasing. You're not going to fall."

Under less extreme conditions, Claire would've been provoked by such condescension. But even now, they were high enough on the trail, she had no qualms about Kincaid breaking her fall. Absolutely none.

05:39

For the first few minutes, the passage was manageable enough, but pretty slick in spots. Claire understood, without being told, to hunker down. To keep her cute little center-of-gravity tucked in. Then, about the time she thought she'd gotten the hang of it, her foot slipped. She flatted out against the rock. Hugging the trail, but not screaming. That would come later.

"You okay?" Quiroga called down. She said she was, but *could he take it a little slower?*

"I would, but it's going to rain," he told her, pointing to the sky. She was too high to look up any higher. She waved him on.

Unfortunately, the trail didn't get easier. They were halfway up when the angle became impossibly steep. Quiroga kept pushing, but she demanded they stop *to think about it.*

"Does it get worse?"

Quiroga told her the next fifteen minutes would be difficult, but she could do it.

06:43

Looking down to the water, Claire realized, there weren't many choices. Going down would be even more terrifying than going up.

"Are you okay?" Quiroga called out.

"No. But let's get it over with."

They were fifteen minutes from the top, fifteen minutes from safety, when the rains came again. Water washed over her hands and face, flooding away the stones. She dug in. Held on for dear life. When she looked to see how far they had to go, she saw Quiroga fighting his way up an almost perpendicular wall of rock and mud.

He slipped. For a split second, it looked as if he would send all three of them into the sea. It was the end. That's what Claire thought. She closed her eyes, but when the panic cleared, she was still there. Still hanging on.

"Claire! Pay attention," said Kincaid, "grab his hand, I'll *levitate* you."

Somehow, Quiroga made it to the top, and was reaching for her. His fingers were inches away.

Kincaid reached up and *gave her a little levity.* She screamed when his hand grabbed her rear and gave a push. Her digging hand lost grip, such was the shock. Gravity took a couple of quick swipes at her stomach. Almost immediately, though, Quiroga's strong hand had her. He yanked her up, pushed her toward a small Araucaria. Kincaid followed, a few seconds later. All three sat there, their legs and arms locked around their respective trees.

"See, It was easy," said Quiroga.

Claire's eyes were still closed.

08:23

The terror of the climb wore off in about three hours. Three hours of trudging up and down and around. The rain was constant, and miserable. Beyond that, the only thing Claire knew, they were heading east. Maybe, east.

On that rare moment when the mist thinned, the view was more amazing, each time. There were waterfalls, volcanoes in the distance, rising from the clouds. Most exquisite of all were the massive trees. Quiroga said, some of them were ancient. If there was any compensation for the climb, it was the scenery. Southern Chile was stunning.

09:06

By the end of the day, the rain transitioned from drizzle to a torrential downpour, but Quiroga kept the pace. He seemed to know where he was going. They took a right at a small waterfall, and the way he bounced along made Claire think they might be nearing their destination.

Moments later they walked up on a rickety old cabin.

"Our hotel for the night," said Quiroga.

There were puddles inside. And steady streams from the holes in the tin, but it was otherwise, a glorious sanctuary. They were out of the elements. If only barely.

"Sorry about the leaks," said Quiroga looking around. "It might be a good idea to get out of our wet clothes. Is that a problem, Claire?"

She said it wasn't for her, *as long as you boys don't make it one*. She was pretty sure she could trust Rob Q's honor in such matters, and if Kincaid tried anything, Quiroga was old school. He'd probably challenge him to pistols at dawn. Her virtue was safe enough.

Stacked next to the fireplace was more than enough wood for the night and Quiroga quickly set about building a fire. As he worked, Claire and Kincaid stripped off their ponchos, boots, wet socks and sweaters.

Against the wall was a stack of blankets covered with plastic. Thick wool. Itchy, but warm. When the fire crackled to life, it filled the air with the sweet perfume of burning pine. Great therapy for what had passed that day.

10:40

Claire awakened once during the night, thinking about the ladies' room. Remembering where she was, though, and how miserable the plumbing would be outside, she snuggled deeper into the blanket and pulled up the plastic. She would hold-and-forget. As she lay there, she thought she heard something outside, moving around, but fatigue gave way to silence and then sleep. She awakened next morning to light streaming from the holes in the roof. Holes previously dedicated to running water. She had things to do. She slipped on her now-dry socks and boots, quietly lifted her pack and eased out the door.

11:22

Slogging out behind the cabin, the night's blanket still draped across her shoulders, Claire was unprepared for the discovery she was about to make. She walked around the corner, coming face to face with three horses. Their saddles and harnesses were off to the side, next to a cast-iron skillet. Inside the skillet was a burlap bundle with a dozen eggs and a slab of bacon. Someone had come up in the night, in the rain. Tied the animals to the trees and then disappeared. That's probably what she'd heard.

11:54

It was an extraordinary place. Almost like a lost world. After relieving herself, she headed off on a quick expedition. The trees were massive, with stunted tufts of green sprouting from the top. Giants, cast across fifty generations of humanity, or more. Growing stronger, she thought, as the world of men extinguished itself. She drifted tree to tree, caressing the bark with her fingers. Smelling the pine needles scooped up from the ground.

Then quite unexpectedly, when she walked around an especially large tree, she stepped into a clearing. The first thing that came to her mind was *fire*. All around were massive, charred stumps rising from the earth like stalagmites. She guessed it to be the handiwork of one of the nearby volcanoes.

12:48

She removed the headset from her pack. For some reason, though, the thing wouldn't tune in. There was AM/FM spectrum in the form of noise, but nothing else. When she switched to the transceiver, it let out some kind of death-squeal, but no beep. Had she banged it during the climb? The last five meters had been violent. If she'd damaged the unit, that would be bad. There was another possibility, though. It might have to do with geology. Who knew what kind of metal had been blown across these fields? Maybe it was natural interference.

13:26

Claire re-shouldered the pack and turned back for camp. But now she saw something else out of the corner of her eye. Not a stump. Not a boulder. Something roughly the size of a pickup. When she was a hundred feet away from it, she realized it wasn't a boulder, but a glob of steel from an eruption of iron, most likely. As she looked it over, in the twisted, pitted surface,

Claire made another bizarre discovery. A straight edge. This was not an artifact of geology. She walked around the thing. It looked like armor plating after a very bad day. And on the backside, in a recess near the top, she found a hinge. Instantly, she recognized it. She was looking at what had been the hatch of an M1-Abrams tank. This chunk had been a tank. The plating on the M1 turret was a hardened laminate called *BRL-1*, designed to take a direct hit. The vehicle had obviously been decimated by a force beyond comprehension. A force that demolished the most powerful armor on earth like clay in a fire.

14:41

She took out the camera and grabbed snapshots from every angle, and close-ups. Then rushed back to camp. Along the way she came across other pieces of iron-debris, though nothing as large as the turret. A discovery she would keep to herself for the time-being.

22 Going In

After breakfast, they headed east on horseback. Quiroga avoided the steep elevations, sticking to valley-trails, when possible. Maybe he was trying to make up for the day before.

Claire couldn't get a couple of things off her mind. First, of course, was the tank. That presented her with a huge question mark. The second was more in the form of a distraction than anything. The strange world in which she now found herself. Clear streams. Lonely stands of Araucaria. She was thoroughly transfixed by it all. Dr. Nunnally's words also intruded a little, especially his proposition that living green, living off the grid invited widened occupancy of the planet. It was so terribly cynical, but there was truth in it, because she would live here.

00:53

Assuming a non-polluting electrical generator, she would move to the Chilean wilderness and never leave. As would millions of others, probably. And the human family would thus leach its way across the planet until there was no wilderness left. In a couple of conversations, Nunnally had reminded her that *the devil cured your cold to give you cancer.* As she bounced forward on horseback, her mind bounced to a thousand questions. But very few answers. Many of her long-held assumptions were coming unstuck.

01:30

Eventually, they came to a stream. The horses stepped in. Sipped with casual indifference. Then just as casually, strolled back onto the path. A few minutes after that, the trail ended. Claire found herself sitting on a horse at the base of an incline, with the sinking knowledge, there would be no detour.

"Drop the reins," said Quiroga. "Give them the lead."

"You're not serious!"

"They know where they're going. Both hands on the saddle-horn. Lean forward."

02:04

Would it ever end? Claire was so tired of revisiting the same terror, over and over. The climb was incredibly steep, but the animals dug in, lifting themselves and their passengers higher. Until finally, they made it to the top. Where Claire opened her eyes again.

"That's it," she said. "No more. Got that?"

Quiroga told her, *the horses were used to the trail. Trust them.*

"Many times they've made this trip."

Under her breath, Claire muttered, this would be her last.

They proceeded in a line across the ridge, precarious in spots, but the horses stepped with caution. And this is how the morning passed. No clouds. Plenty of time for meditation. Plenty of time to revise what you thought you knew about the cosmos. Plenty of time to wonder what you'd gotten yourself into.

02:57

That extraterrestrial life forms had been zipping around since forever, that was a settled reality. For half-a-century, an incredible amount of money had been poured into ET-management by the U.S. government. And within this enterprise were two groups, evidentially, though she hadn't realized it before. One, ready to embrace higher consciousness. The other, filled with religious paranoia: *the Germans had been in league with the devil.* And that's why the second side, Dr. Nunnally's side, was readying itself for cosmic war.

It was amazing, how clearly she saw it now. Both Terance and Nunnally had shown up in Chicago, senators from opposing political cults. And from the bid for her allegiance, Claire inferred, the old man's side was dying out. That bit of insight went a long way to explaining some of the policies at NSA. Politics, too.

03:58

When they stopped for lunch, Kincaid hustled firewood. Quiroga unpacked the coffee pot and skillet. As the men worked, Claire headed off into the woods. She walked for five minutes before pulling out the headset. This time the receiver picked up a comforting stream of beeps, followed by Terance's voice.

"Claire, you need to check in. We lost you last night. A couple of things. We got a little background on Kincaid. Didn't have much of a normal childhood, looks like. Grew up in India.

00:00

"His parents were missionaries, so he spent a lot of time in boarding schools. First trip to the states was to go to a religious college in Chicago. That's about all we know, at the moment. Will advise if something else shows up. Oh! Remember the 64-million dollar question. *How to see the lower levels in the Blood Toys bunker?* Well, the guys in the lab figured it out. We don't know how it works, but each level seems to be *frequency-sensitive.* That explains the tuning forks. Each one, when it's vibrating, lights up a specific level.

"It's incredible. You touch the surface with the fork while it's still vibrating, and the walls go clear for about 90-seconds, before reverting back. Revolutionary stuff. Otherwise that's pretty much it, but contact us, okay? You're a special lady, Claire. You're in our thoughts and prayers."

05:30

Wow! Was that weird or what? It sounded like Terance, voice-wise, but he never volunteered anything he didn't have to. And he never admitted to either *thoughts* or *prayers.* What was going on here?

She looked around, making sure she hadn't been followed, then uplinked a reply. She explained, they were on horseback, *somewhere between Chile and Argentina.* The only unexpected discovery, so far, had been the tank.

"It was an M1. Or what was left of it," she said. "I tried to GPS-you from there, but must have been in a radiation halo. The site is east of Puerto Montt. Jerry, what happened out here? Somebody's got to know something."

She described the ride on horseback, and how she'd nearly fallen into the ocean, and how they'd spent the night in a leaky cabin. She signed off saying, *wish you were here*. Then up-linked the message.

06:32

Quiroga and Kincaid were in an argument when she got back. Kincaid had started it. Not much surprise there. His *convention* was that the Germans were natural racists. Ever the gentleman, Quiroga quietly countered that you didn't libel an entire population just because of a few.

"You accuse them of racism. I suppose, everyone who lives in Texas wears funny hats and drives pickups?"

"I think so," said Kincaid. "You're making my point."

Quiroga said he'd lived in Texas. "You can't make a blanket statement like that. They aren't all cowboys."

"Well-they're either cowboys, or gay. Or gay cowboys."

"Maybe you ought to move there," said Claire, who was furious. How had she ever been attracted to this guy?

"Listen, here's the point I was trying to make," he said. "Actually, more of a question. Are we going to find Germans or Nazis at the end of this trail?"

Quiroga's eyes flashed. "Rest assured. Whatever we find, they'll have open minds."

"Unlike some we could name," said Claire.

07:45

A fairly nasty silence, followed. They climbed back onto the horses and headed out. At first, they went as before, in a single line, but passing into a scrub-field, Claire pulled alongside Quiroga. In a voice loud enough to be heard, she apologized for Kincaid.

"I don't think he knows what he's saying half-the-time."

"It's okay," said Rob Q. "His mind is a little closed, maybe."

They rode side-by-side. Quiroga told her what he knew about this part of Chile, and Patagonia, to the south. It was an incredible bit of wilderness. Largely unpopulated. Claire said it was the most beautiful place she'd ever seen. He was lucky to have grown up here.

As they chatted, Kincaid followed, thirty-meters back. Sulking.

Rob Q turned in the saddle a couple of times, making sure, he was still there.

"Is he going to be okay?"

Claire said, she didn't know. "He's got issues."

"Please don't be offended," said Rob Q, "but I don't think he likes it very much when you call him *El Stupido*."

"Well, he is," said Claire, "it's his maiden name. But you're probably right. I need to go a little easier on him."

Quiroga thought this was a good idea.

09:09

An hour later, Quiroga reigned in the horses and made an abrupt announcement.

"We leave the horses here," he told them. Dismounting. Tying the reins to a branch.

Though not expressly invited to do so, Kincaid climbed down and proceeded to help him unsaddle the horses.

"Look Rob, if I offended you, I'm sorry," said a penitent Kincaid.

"Oh no, my friend, I'm not offended. This is probably very stressful for you."

Kincaid said he hadn't intended to insult anyone with his *Nazi-comment*. He did, after all, understand the difference between Germans and Nazis.

09:50

When he said it, Claire who'd been listening from a few feet away, applauded him in much the same manner as he'd applauded her, for her languages.

Quiroga smiled, then when the moment passed, he turned

extremely serious. He told them, "What I'm about to say, you must listen very carefully. From now on, step where I step. Exactly. Don't leave the trail for any reason."

"Landmines?" asked Kincaid.

"I'm saying, just step where I step."

"No landmines?" asked Kincaid.

"Come on Steven. Just do what the man says."

"I'm not trying to be rude, I just think Rob Q ought to tell us."

Claire assumed, Quiroga would give assurances at this point, that the warning didn't have anything to do with land-mines. But he didn't.

"*Step where you step,*" said Kincaid. "Got it."

"Thank you," replied Rob Q.

10:49

The undergrowth was dense. Pushing through the spidery limbs, Claire let one fly over her shoulder. And it was practically an accident. It hit Kincaid in the nose. He yelled. She *almost* apologized.

"You did it on purpose."

"You're crazy."

"Please," said Quiroga, "someone could be listening to us, right now."

"Just try to be more careful," said Kincaid.

They walked another half-hour. When Quiroga's pace began to slow, he also became more tentative. Correcting course every few steps.

"Okay. Wait," he finally told them. "Wait until I check something. I'll be back."

Claire asked how long, exactly, would he be gone, and he told her, fifteen minutes.

He then, disappeared into the undergrowth.

11:42

Later, Claire would wonder what she'd been thinking. She had the sudden, bright idea to pull out the transceiver and attempt to flash a GPS-waypoint. She figured Kincaid probably wouldn't notice. It would be an *alertness* test.

"Hey, I hate to bust your bubble, but there's not a radio station in a hundred miles," he told her as she snapped the headset into place.

"You don't know that," said Claire, hitting the send-sequence on the unit.

It was brassy, it was that; flashing Echelon right under his nose. But she made a connection and proceeded to take it a step further. She stated her status, giving her report in such a way that it also served as a sort of distracted conversation with Kincaid.

For example, she said: "We've come to be some kind of boundary. We think there might be landmines, right Steven? We're resting at the moment while the guide checks something out. What a day, right Steven?"

12:42

Proneness to misstatement notwithstanding, Kincaid wasn't blind or deaf, or even as dumb as she'd come to think. He sensed, the conversation was *way off-axis*. A pun he would've definitely missed.

"What are you listening to?" he asked.

Claire twiddled with the tuner.

"Nothing … really. What are we going to find at the end of the trail Steven, Nazis or Germans? That was interesting, by the way."

She anticipated, his answer would be enlightening for the folks back in Maryland.

He told her, he didn't care. "Oh-by the way, I don't appreciate it when you take sides. You didn't even know what we were talking about. You just assume, he's right and I'm wrong."

"What are you talking about now?"

"My point had been that Germans tend to have a … *redundancy* … that's what I was saying."

"I think the word is *tendency*, but all Germans are racists? "

"There is a tendency, I believe that."

00:00

"Please, do us both a favor and don't say it out loud. I have a lot of German friends. And so does Rob Q. That was a stupid thing to say. Oh, and quite a few gay friends, who aren't from Texas."

"So, what are you listening to?" Kincaid asked again, enforcing the question by reaching for the headset. She grabbed it, held it in place with both her hands. Her little enterprise was backfiring.

"It's just static. Let go!"

A little too professionally, she let fly an open palm, connecting with him on the lower jaw. Knocking him to the ground. And stunning them both.

Quiroga stormed into the clearing. "What are you two doing?"

Kincaid didn't say it with conviction, but rubbing his jaw, he said nothing.

Rob Q told them it was time to go, but then mid-sentence, noticed Claire placing the headset back into the pack.

"What's that?" he said. "We're not supposed to be turning on electronics out here, I thought I told you."

"I guess I forgot," said Claire. "Sorry."

14:55

Both men were suspicious now, but Claire didn't miss a beat. Casually, she placed the headset inside the pack. Burying it deep. As Quiroga continued chiding her, she pressed the *send* button. A beep erupted from inside the pack. She'd pulled it off, but it had been close.

"We go single file," said Quiroga. "And please remember ... *exactly where I step*. And don't turn on anything electronic."

"Did you hear the man?" asked Kincaid.

"I heard the man ... El Stupido."

15:32

Rob Q continued. "We'll come to a fence. The gate should be opened. On the other side is a guard-station. Where we've got to be careful. Don't look left or right, just straight ahead. And if you do see someone, don't say anything. Don't nod, don't smile, keep your eyes forward."

"Did you turn off the radio?" whispered Kincaid.

"Shut up."

23 Hijacked

A hundred meters from where they'd left the horses, they walked into a clearing. It was exactly as Rob Q had said. There was a fence, a guard station, and a lot of serious technology in the form of towers, motion sensors, and cameras.

They followed Quiroga onto the gravel roadway He reminded them again, to keep their eyes forward. Even though he was the one looking side-to-side, at the moment. He seemed extremely tense. As they approached the gate, Claire couldn't help but wonder about the community on the other side. What were their values? Histories? She wondered if they'd evolved their own style of dress, over the decades. Or adopted the fashions of the day. Part of her expected to see a quaint little Bavarian village, on the other side. But the Nazis had also architected Auschwitz and Dachau. That was really the issue. It could be either extreme.

00:55

The guard station was an odd structure, like something that had been prefabricated and brought in by helicopter. Disappointing, in the architectural sense. Minus one point for quaint little Bavarian village.

More forcefully than ever, it was dawning on Claire that she had no idea, what she'd gotten herself into. And what about the headset? With all the obvious technology at the gate, what if they could detect its true function? Even powered down, anything that transacted electrons could be seen, theoretically. But the question was too late. It was in her pack, and she would have to leave it there.

She walked through the gate. And though she'd been told specifically not to, she glanced inside the station where she saw display screens and a blinking console of some sort. As far as she could tell, the place was empty. Claire was starting to breathe a sigh of relief when an alarm siren went off. Quiroga wheeled around. He didn't say anything, just stared at Kincaid, then Claire, and then back.

"Don't look at me," Kincaid told him. He held up his hands as if confirming his innocence.

02:11

No jack-booted storm troopers goose-stepped out of the building. There were no voices over loudspeakers. Or German Shepherds, springing from nowhere. And eventually the alarm went silent. Quiroga turned and continued walking forward, same pace as before. Not a word was said.

When they rested a few minutes later, Claire expected some sort of inquisition, but there was nothing. She was certain, the sensors had detected the transceiver, but for reasons unknown, she had been allowed to enter.

02:48

"We're halfway," Quiroga told them. "The next camp is two hours in that direction. But I need to warn you about something. In a few minutes we're coming to a junkyard. You're going to see a lot of stuff stacked around, and probably … my suggestion would be, we shouldn't touch anything."

"Radiation?" asked Claire. She was thinking about the *fried turret* from earlier in the day.

"As a matter of fact, yes. Low levels, but *yes*."

"Wait a second!" said Kincaid. "We're walking into a radioactive site?"

"That's not what I said. They're big into recycling, okay? And when you recycle, I mean … you never know."

"I think the question is, *will their recycling give us cancer?*" said Kincaid.

"A few X-ray plates, old medical equipment, that sort of

thing. But it's mostly junk. Nothing we need to worry about."

Claire's and Kincaid's eyes met briefly. For all their differences, they were thinking the same thing. He had dodged the question. One more hole was punching through Claire's reality. A hole where the honorable and attractive Rob Q once stood.

04:05

They arrived at the ridge-mound by late afternoon. Quiroga started up. Claire and Kincaid followed. At the top, they were confronted with the sounds of explosion, and a plain thickly covered with what appeared to be boulders, the color of rust. Presiding over the wasteland was an idling volcano. A storm billowed from its upturned lips. This was the source of the booming.

Just as Claire already suspected, Kincaid wondered if what lay strewn across the wasteland might actually have been manmade. Or *man-destroyed*. The ever blunt Kincaid had no hesitation when it came to saying what he thought.

"This was a battlefield. A dead zone."

Quiroga's counter was quick and rehearsed: He said, Kincaid was free to think what he wanted, then announced, their camp was in that direction. He pointed. And they had to get there before dark. Without another word, Quiroga stumbled down the ridge. Into the *dead-zone*.

05:13

Kincaid stepped in beside Claire. There was an interesting exchange between them, at this point. As they made their way down, he looked over and said, "Interesting."

She nodded, and repeated, "Interesting."

The *dead zone*, as Kincaid had called it, was filled with wreckage and junk. Some machines had expired there. Others had been dragged from somewhere else. Disobeying Quiroga's warning about not touching anything, Kincaid ran a finger across one of the rusting surfaces.

"Look," he said, holding the finger up for her to see.

"You better hope it doesn't fall off," she told him.

He rubbed his thumb and index finger together. There were traces of red, but more significantly, an oily smudge.

"See this? Saw it at Baffin."

Claire took his hand, holding it to her face for a closer look. She thought it smelled a bit like a petroleum residue. When Quiroga realized they had stopped walking, he yelled back. *What were they doing?*

Kincaid was quick. "I think I broke a blood vessel on the reins."

"We've got a long way to go," said Quiroga, "please keep up, and don't touch."

06:26

For the Americans, walking through the rusting machines-of-war was like walking among expired gods. And the pieces weren't just massive chunks of iron. There were smaller scraps as well. Along with droplets of steel, spewed across the earth like molten rain. The implications were staggering. NSA had to have known about this place, but they hadn't said anything. What happened next marked the beginning of Claire's loss of confidence in what was going on back in Maryland.

The next break, Quiroga picked a large open spot, well away from any upright debris. Kincaid asked if this was about radiation, but Quiroga replied, it was more about earthquakes. They were a regular event in this part of Chile. You always wanted to be out in the open, away from anything that might fall down on you.

"Why didn't you tell us before?" asked Kincaid.

"It's common knowledge. I thought you knew."

07:25

Kincaid said the answer *wasn't good enough*. It was time for Quiroga to tell all he knew about this place and what was going to happen next. Kincaid was obviously spoiling for an argument. Claire saw it as an opportunity to excuse herself and put in a GPS-call to NSA. As she walked away, the voices behind her got louder. She was starting to appreciate Kincaid's in-your-face approach. It was time Quiroga told them everything.

As she walked, she rummaged through the pack, half-slung across her shoulder. Then she spotted the perfect cover. A large chunk of sheet-metal. She squatted a few meters behind it and flashed Echelon. Seconds later, the headset chirped to life. The data burst came as a total shock because this time, it was from Dr. Nunnally. Terance was her controller. Under no circumstance should the old man have been able to tap into the com-channel. It was completely off-protocol, and set off even more alarms in Claire's head. Nunnally addressed those alarms, first thing. He said, *rules were made to be broken*. And *sometimes you had to leave the page,* so to speak. And play *a little jazz.* That's what his breaking protocol was all about. But not to worry. There were precedents, even though she might know them.

08:49

"By now you've seen for yourself," he said. "What happened on that battlefield is probably the question you'd like to ask. NATO, the Warsaw Pact, the OAS, the Soviet Union, were all there, where you are now. Fifty-thousand men died on that secret battlefield. And the forces against which they fought are still inside the fence. Along with our unburied dead. The spirits of the Reich live, Claire. What I said before about pure stagecraft, have you ever wondered about the stuff we recover with Pounce? Or the artifacts we deconstruct at SPL? Ever wonder how you can have a UFO-device flying through space and time. A device with hyper-technology. But a device that crashes in a simple thunderstorm? Such things happen only on the far side of human logic. And that's the point. That's where they play. Where they reveal themselves, in a context that makes no sense."

09:49

His words were always so oppressive. He continued.

"Theatrics, Claire. This UFO-business is not the government's secret. It's theirs. The inter-dimensionals are the ones who enforce the secrecy. They police their own little mystery. Do you understand now, how confusing it could get? Their prowess is almost mystical. They can circumvent our best security. Access our most secret files. And even recast anyone they want. If they plant themselves in the chain-of-command as a general, or assume the role of military police, even the President, suddenly, we're dealing in mirrors. Not looking through a glass. We've got a de-facto agreement which amounts to: we know they're there. But for the most part, we are in the audience watching. Just like everyone else. From the cheap seats.

Claire leaned out to see if Kincaid and Quiroga were still arguing. Good that she did, because Kincaid, though still at a distance, was strolling her way. Calling to her. Still squatting, she leaned back out of sight, hoping to get to the end of the message.

11:01

Nunnally went on. "Why haven't they made a move? What do they get for all this stagecraft? Simply … they're waiting for us to call them out. We must request our own slavery, as full-payment for salvation. Follow the logic. Given how long they've watched the human family, by now they know how we perceive threat. Right? When someone hides intent, or lies, or refuses to identify them-self, it adds up to danger. But that's just what they do. They know these things, but they threaten us anyway. If they meant no harm, they would've stepped in front of the curtain by now. Instead, there's a bigger game. When they've promised technology, or begged for us to disarm and not militarize space, it's very shabby theater. They give to get, and they want us weak. That's the point. That's why I'm hijacking the channel. The evidence suggests, now that the Cold War is over and they can't play off two competitor-states, the game entered a new round. The Blood Toys are a game-piece. As for the promise of the Coler, even if you find it, Claire, don't bring it out. Accepting from their hand only strengthens their hand."

12:23

When the message ended, she fell backwards onto the ground. Literally, knocked off her feet. Dr. Nunnally had just addressed her stream-of-contemplation for the last couple of days. By the time Kincaid got there, she was back on her feet, dusting herself off.

"Are you okay?"

"Yes and no," she said.

12:49

An hour after leaving the second debris-field, they stepped onto a footpath, twisting through the trees. It disappeared at a small stream, then continued on the other bank.

A little after 5 p.m. they walked into their campsite. Already set up. Three tents and a roaring fire. Steaks sizzling in a huge black skillet.

"They want you rested and strong for tomorrow," said Quiroga. "It's much easier from here."

Neither Claire nor Kincaid had much to say. By the time they took their boots off, Quiroga was shoveling steak onto large plastic plates.

"Where's the *sauerkrap* and sausage? And *snaps*?" asked Kincaid.

Good-naturedly, Quiroga said, he'd *put in a request*.

13:40

Even now, after a day with three or four pretty good-sized arguments under his belt, Claire could tell that Kincaid was ready for another. This time, she might be tempted to join him. On his side, for once.

"Why don't they come out and meet us?" asked Kincaid.

"Am I that disappointing?"

"I just hoped to see a real live Nazi. Or even a German. Now that I know there's a difference."

Quiroga didn't take the bait. He laughed and replied that he would put in a request for that, as well. A real live German and sauerkraut.

Kincaid jabbed away, bringing up the subject of radiation, again, and pointing out, they'd just passed through – not a *dump*, but a *battlefield.*

"And did you see any bones?" asked Quiroga. "If you didn't see any bones, how do you know it was a battlefield?" He made it seem like the craziest suggestion in the whole world.

"Uh-given their track record, they could've made soap or lampshades by now," said Kincaid.

The statement visibly tagged Quiroga. He offered a grim smile, stood and scraped trimmings into the fire.

"If you will excuse me," he said, "Now I must take some personal time."

"Wait. Where are you going now?"

Quiroga told Claire he would be back in fifteen minutes or so. Probably.

"*Probably?*"

15:08

When he had disappeared, Kincaid put the plate down and stared at Claire.

"Where do you think they are? Our hosts?"

Claire didn't have an answer. What she'd been thinking about were Nunnally's words. *They know how we perceive threat.* She wondered if you could trust your own human instincts in such questions. But really, what was the option? Instinct was pretty much all you had. When Claire did finally respond to the question, it was something along the lines of … *did the fact that they hadn't shown up indicate threat?* That was the point.

"I don't know, but that's how it feels," said Kincaid. "But after all this, I hope they'll let us take something home."

Claire tossed the steak into the fire. Placed her plate atop Quiroga's. And laid back, hands clasped over her forehead. She asked Kincaid how he had found out about this place.

"First questions first. Who do you work for, Claire? Because you aren't a grad student."

"I don't know how to take that," she told him.

"Take it for what it is, a simple question. Who do you for?"

"I'm working on an advanced degree in physics." Who did he think she was working for?

"The government, maybe."

"Okay," she said, pretending to be a little embarrassed, "It's time you know. Technically, I'm with JPL. If there is such a thing as free energy, who better than JPL to transfer the technology to the public? That's why I'm here."

16;47

"I knew it! So it's your job to protect the oil companies, I guess. And if they don't want competition, whatever we find goes under wraps."

She told him that JPL provided a sort of public trust in such matters. But Kincaid put his hands over his ears. Shook his head. And said, he was *going crazy.*

"Okay," she said. "Your turn. How did you find the Blood Toys?"

She noticed, he quivered slightly, from excitement, as if he had something to tell, but couldn't quite make up his mind to say it.

17:20

"I was born in India," he told her. "My parents ran an orphanage in Bombay. I think it was that *boomer-generation* thing. They were like hippies. Out there doing something for humanity."

"And that's how you and Dara met."

"My parents knew her parents. Her job at the museum was basically my doing. She owes me."

"Except, she's also in love with you."

"I never loved her. I mean, she's a friend. We've know each other since we were kids."

"If your parents worked at an orphanage Steven, were they religious?"

"Well, we did go to church, but they were mostly just living an *alternating* lifestyle."

"They weren't religious?"

"Of course, you can't say that. India is a very religious place," he told her.

18:14

He didn't realize it, of course, but he was revealing more than he knew. Claire interpreted his skirting the question as an embarrassment over his upbringing.

"You speak Hindi?" she asked. "Like Dara?"

"*Thandé puravil oru pampirikkunnu,*" he said.

When she asked what it meant, he told her: "*There's a snake behind you.*"

Claire jumped and squeaked, and went into *frantic.*

"Not really. It's Malayalam. My first language."

"There's no snake?"

He shook his head. *No.* "Just Malayalam. I was showing you the language."

18:52

When she realized what'd just happened, Claire started laughing at her overreaction. And it got him started. It wasn't that funny, but that wasn't the point. Kincaid had just mis-spoken again, but in his first language this time, and it struck them both as incredibly funny. It marked the first time they'd laughed *with*, and not *at.* Claire told him, snake or no snake, it was still his turn. How did he know about the bunker?

"It's sounds crazy," he said, "but there's an old woman in Chi-cago. Big-time patron. She has connections."

"And that's how you knew about Baffin?"

"Yes."

"And where you also got the drawings?"

He nodded.

"Who does she know?"

Kincaid drew his knees to his chin.

"I thought it was someone in the government, used to think that."

19:49

What did he mean?

"Turned out, no one in government is leaking this stuff. The old woman got the information through … *channeling.* You know what that is?"

"Hearing voices," said Claire, "like a medium."

"Before I left town, she told me up front, the *ET's were talking to her.* The day she drew these …," he reached over, opened his backpack and fished out the folded envelope. "Look again," he said. "She was sitting as close as you are now, and they were talking to her."

"You heard this?"

"No. My family has strong opinions about *hearing voices*."

"You're more religious than you let on, aren't you? Let me guess. You were over at her place, and she got off into this wizard stuff, and you went to church the next day," said Claire, "to wash off your soul a little. Is that what happened?"

He nodded once. Claire had nailed him.

20:52

She couldn't sleep. She lay there in her zipped-up tent, staring at the plastic crosspiece above her head. If an old woman could hear voices, if there was war between two cosmic adversaries, had she been actually talking to the real Dr. Nunnally? And before that, Terance? Given the technical virtuosity that kept popping up, the riddles within riddles, who was to say that someone hadn't hijacked a voice, or both of them, for that matter? The enigma was spiraling out of control. Beyond her logic.

But how else could you explain Dr. Nunnally showing up on a frequency, run exclusively by her controller? There was something even more troubling. How had the disembodied voice known her thoughts? Was someone out there, rummaging through her mind?

24 The Debate

When they set out next morning, the woods started to thin. Against the ragged, untended frame of the Andes, Claire noticed that the few Araucarias they now saw were aligned in rows, like landscape-art for a grand estate. They had to be nearing the end of the trek. But no one was prepared for what happened next.

As they made their way through the open field, the earth shuddered, without warning. Then convulsed. A powerful turbulence knocked all three to the ground. The trees toward which they'd been hiking, tossed skyward, straining to shake their roots. And it happened so fast. The hikers fell. Crawled. Struggled against the open waves of earth. Quiroga made them lie flat. Ten seconds later, the world went still again,. But Quiroga said to *stay put*, just in case there was an aftershock.

00:57

He'd no sooner gotten the words out, than the earth pitched a second time. Though not as violently.

There was some discussion about when it would be safe to proceed. The Chilean explained, earthquakes were unpredictable. When to pick up the trail again would be a matter of instinct. So they took an extended break. Well away from the trees. Stretched out and waited.

Claire was impatient. There was a large Araucaria fifty-meters away. It would amply provide the cover needed for her next *call*.

"I hate to bring it up," she said, "but I need a little privacy. You think I could go over there behind the tree if I'm careful?"

Quiroga thought about it, then told her to go. But stay alert. At the first sign of movement she had to be prepared to get out.

"Even if it's embarrassing. Get away from the trees as fast as you can."

01:59

On the backside of the great trunk, Claire squatted. Pulled out the headset and hit the power switch. There was a message waiting. This time it was her boss.

"Claire," he said, "Millard has a terrible habit of only telling half the story. The half he wants.

"It's true what he said, both we and the Soviets knew there were, shall we say, *contributors* to the Nazi war effort. It's why we're still involved with Nazi science. The Germans did stealth in the 1940s. We just started. Our first rockets were their last. And there's the electromagnetics,. Stuff we don't even talk about now. They were a brilliant people. And their benefactors, even more so.

"Here's what gets lost on Millard. It was never intended that the Nazis should do what they did. Yeah, there was a thing about race purity, but it was about gene repair. Not a mission to exterminate. Millard always wants to know why our cosmic friends got involved with the Nazis in the first place. It's simple. You know as well as I. After the Treaty of Versailles, Germany had a lot of problems. Our visitors assumed that having been oppressed, Germany would not *oppress*. What no one counted on, of course, was Hitler.

03:25

"Today, we need to rebuild and purify. We must. Don't let the fundamentalists destroy the restoration. Like it or not, fate may have selected you to be ambassador for the rest of us. So focus on two things. First, take anything they give you. Second, for the sake of the universe, our planet cannot remain parked in a hateful orbit. Tell them that. The time has come. Earth needs no more swords.

"God bless you Claire. Help us. Help us make the peace."
With that, the message ended.
Claire posted a response. Quickly punching in the sequence,

she uplinked this:

"Jerry, what am I supposed to do? I'm in the middle, here. And I don't understand how Dr. Nunnally logged onto this channel. In all the protocols, where's the part that says anyone who wants, can hijack the link? Who am I actually talking to? Even you. You don't sound like you. *God bless?* Unless you're ready to explain some of this, maybe the best thing for me would be head back to Santiago. You and Dr. Nunnally need to make the peace, first. Maybe we go from there."

04:48

She had just flipped the headset into the pack when Quiroga's voice rang out from the other side of the tree. He was close.

"Claire? You okay?"

"Just a second," she told him. "Finishing up."

"I thought I heard talking."

"Oh, I was singing. Not very musical, huh?"

As she stepped around the tree and took his arm, she told him that she'd always believed, just because you couldn't carry a tune, it shouldn't keep you from having *a song in your heart.*

"It's so beautiful here, Rob-Q. Look at this place. I promise, though, no matter how it inspires me. No more singing. Just humming."

He seemed to accept the explanation. As they walked toward Kincaid, she started humming. To fully sell the line.

05:40

Early afternoon, they stumbled into an arroyo. Quiroga turned, motioned for them to follow, and proceeded down the gully, heading south.

The passage was challenging. The rocks were large, and in some cases, sharp. Then, every fifty meters or so, they had to negotiate a fissure. Or dodge a puddle of oily water. Usually, they could step over, but a few required a detour.

When they arrived at an especially large fissure cutting across the stream bed, Quiroga noticed wisps of dust catching in the breeze, rising from the high side of the fracture. It indicated a recent break. Maybe from earlier that day.

201

The Americans stepped across, but Quiroga peered into the gap. Without telling them what he was doing, he scrambled up the bank. Ripped a branch from a scrawny Jarilla bush. And slid back down. He fished the limb into the crevice and when he withdrew it, there was a dark, syrupy substance dripping from the leaves.

"Do you have oil around here?" asked Kincaid.

"No. We import most of it."

Quiroga tossed the branch aside and motioned for them to continue.

"That was oil wasn't it?" said Claire.

"Looked like it," said the Chilean. "I don't know."

07:04

Eventually, they came to a boulder blocking the passage. And when they crawled around, a few meters on the other side, was a bridge. And parked on the bridge was an antique black Mercedes.

"For us?" Claire asked. "Is this the surprise?"

The Chilean nodded. It was. According to Quiroga it was a Mercedes Benz 770k. 1939. *Good as new, and five miles to the gallon, hopefully.*

The ride felt like silk. Particularly after the last couple of days. Occasionally, the massive vehicle would hit a crack in the pavement. Some could be quite jarring. But it was an almost sinful reprieve from climbing, hiking, horses, and earthquakes.

The road curved through lush fields. Past an orchard. And eventually, a pasture with Holsteins, another world. Claire got to thinking how magnificent it would be to live in a place like this. But she wondered, as maladjusted as modern humans were – immune systems in overdrive – she wondered if people could even survive the *green world* of a thousand years ago. Where the only particulates were the ones thrown off by nature. Where the water was pure. And the earth, rich and un-wounded by asphalt? The ecology of a thousand years ago, that was the voice that called her to Chile. Not the politics, really. Not even the technology. Except as it advanced the cause. That was what mattered most: the healing of the planet. Her day-dreams were interrupted suddenly as the Mercedes braked to a screeching stop.

08:53

Quiroga jumped out. Kincaid followed. There was a particularly menacing fracture across the roadway. Not so much a curb, but a half-wall, similar to what they'd seen in the arroyo. Quiroga pointed inside the fracture. Kincaid saw the same syrupy ooze as before.

"Sometimes the pavement buckles," said Quiroga, "but I've never seen the oil. We definitely have to go around."

In a four-wheel drive vehicle it would've been simple, but not an auto built a half-century ago. With Kincaid leading the way, guiding him, Quiroga drove the Mercedes off the shoulder, well off the roadway, and into the field. Eventually they were able to drive over the upthrust, where the shifting topsoil had absorbed most of the break.

Back on pavement, Quiroga slowed down, and admonished the other two to keep their eyes peeled for the next crack.

09:52

Drops of rain hit the windshield. For Claire, it was nice to be watching from inside an automobile this time. Especially when the drops turned torrential. The wipers slapped spastically, missing beats. Making it almost impossible to see out. It got so bad, Quiroga had to slow down even more. Claire estimated their speed to be at about ten miles an hour.

They rumbled across an old suspension bridge. Passed through more fields. Then groves. Then fog-crossed valleys. The rain followed them.

"Are we still in Chile?" Kincaid wanted to know.

Quiroga replied that borders *didn't matter* out here.

"But where are we going?" asked Claire.

"New Wewelsberg. You'll see the steeple in a minute or so."

The rain let up. The clouds opened, allowing light to stream through. It was a spectacular scene. The skies were still boiling, dark over the Andes. But the Mercedes was driving down a seam. A bright seam of sunlight. And in the valley, ahead and below, was a steeple poking up through the trees, just as Quiroga had said.

11:10

At a one-lane suspension bridge, Quiroga slowed the big automobile to a crawl. Then stopped midway across. He shut off the engine. The river was the only sound. The only smell: the pines and the rain-cleansed atmosphere.

"I have to go ahead," Quiroga told them. "I should be back in fifteen-minutes."

"You're leaving again?"

"Yes, there's a formality we have to observe. So sit, relax. There are more surprises."

Kincaid asked about traffic. Wasn't it a bad idea to leave a car parked on a one-lane bridge? Quiroga told him not to worry. There wasn't much of a rush hour in these parts. Then he walked away.

Kincaid opened the door. Stood, and stretched. And leaned over the rail. Claire did the same.

"I wonder what's going on?" he said.

Claire knew the question would sound weird. He was even more committed than she, but she asked anyway.

"Could there be a downside to renewable energy that we're not thinking about?"

12:23

He cocked his head as if he hadn't heard right.

"Now don't get me wrong, but our only real problem is too many people. Pollution is merely a sign that we've had babies.

"Where did that come from?"

She set up a small fiction. She said that one of her professors believed, when technology was too liberating, or too cheap, the human population tended to expand.

Kincaid said it would definitely be *a long time before that happened.*

She put it another way. Would he be tempted to move to the wilderness with the right technology? Green? Non-polluting?

He said he would.

"That's the problem," she told him. "So would I."

"Claire, that kind of thinking keeps us on our knees."

"But you have to admit, Steven, energy holds us together. Human community is based on centralized power grids. What happens when that goes away? It might also be, the human family might not survive if our enterprise goes green."

Kincaid told her *she thought too much*. It was a silly question. Claire backed off a little. Something had to be done. But what if was more true, that a really green planet was – by definition – an *empty* planet?

"You don't believe that," said Kincaid.

"I don't know. Maybe I do, maybe I don't," she said.

13:55

After 45-minutes waiting for Quiroga, the Americans were starting to get worried. Kincaid finally decided to take action. He would walk toward New Wewelsberg. Not all the way. Just far enough to get an idea of what lay beyond the next few turns in the road.

"And I will be back in fifteen-minutes," he told her, in reference to Quiroga's last words.

Secretly, Claire welcomed being alone. She walked with him to the end of the bridge, then when he'd disappeared around the curve, rushed back to the Mercedes for the headset.

14:29

It happened again. And it astounded her. It was Dr. Nunnally's voice that came up.

"Claire, I love that," he told her. "A green planet is an *empty planet*. Finally, someone's getting the picture. Those who stalk us, hide behind such noble ideals."

How did he do that? Was Firefly watching her? Even now? Listening in on their conversations? She looked up into the sky. Of course, if the unit was hovering, in all probability, she wouldn't see it.

"You've got to decide one way or other. What's the truth?" the old man continued.

15:13

"I have been in the presence of these creatures a couple of times at SPL. And it's a strange feeling that comes over you. You think to yourself, well look at them. They could be from another world. But when you're alone and thinking about it, there are such dark spots in the script. How they withhold themselves. And there are all those abrupt inconsistencies. The stagecraft. The telltale signs of *someone playing a role.* If these were the patrons of Nazi Germany, and they've been patrolling the planet since the beginning, why haven't they institution-alized their presence? As a human being, you've got to listen to your threat-logic. It tells you the truth. It's the only weapon you have against deception.

16:00

"I want to go back to something. This suggestion that our space brothers want peace. If it's true, why did they give the Germans the KSK? Or the Hanabu? Look at the duplicity. Them, calling for peace, all-the-while ducking our threat-log-ic. Letting us build our simple-minded backstory on how much they *love us.* Deception. That's what this is about. Believe what your eyes tell you, and the fear-instincts, they keep you alive, Claire."

Claire initiated the uplink with every intention of speaking her mind. But when the time came to speak, she broke down. She couldn't get a grip. Everything was so confused. What had seemed so clear to her in the beginning was of little, or no rel-evance now. She switched off the headset. Stuck it in her pack. Lay back in the grass at the end of the bridge. And cried.

25 New Wewelsberg

"It curves to the right," he told her, pointing up the road. "There's another guard station, about a quarter-of-a-mile. What do you want to do?"

Claire was still lying in the grass beside the road, her hands crossed over her eyes.

"I want to go home," she said.

"Why don't we drive back down the road and think about it a little more?"

She rubbed her eyes, but kept them covered. *It was too late.* "If we're going to be dead, we're dead already."

"Are you depressed?" he asked. "Killing us doesn't make any sense. We can't just go home," said Kincaid. "We're going to have to figure it out. Logically. By the way, I've been thinking about your question."

00:41

She had no idea what he was talking about.

"Clean energy. People *evacuating* off-the-grid. What if you had to have a license to live some place else ?"

She sat up and looked at him like he was crazy. He repeated it. One solution would be to license where people live.

"It's called a *police state*, Steven."

"You could still go places. Like on a vacation. You just couldn't live anywhere you wanted. There are a lot of ways to fix a population problem."

01:16

Claire told him there were more pressing issues at the moment. She was shocked that he seemed to have little, or no sense of their predicament. And irritated when he kept spouting ideas about how you controlled a population through legislation and enforcement. A suggestion strangely connected to the present situation.

"I think the Nazis tried it," she said. "You end up in Nuremberg."

"What's that supposed to mean?"

Claire lay back down. She was completely out of ideas. And hope had been missing since she'd climbed out of the rubber tender onto the shore.

What about this," he said. "Instead of tax credits, the opposite. Tax penalties. Tax kids like a luxury."

"Steven, please."

"I'm just making conversation, Claire."

She was on the verge of physical sickness. The situation was that bleak. And he just kept talking. Dr. Nunnally had certainly worked his charm on her. There were no simple solutions to anything

02:20

They remained at the end of the bridge, listening for Quiroga. Hoping for him. But afternoon turned into night. And the only sounds were cicadas and mosquitoes patrolling the riverbank.

"Tell you this. I'm not sleeping in a parked car on a bridge."

Claire agreed. They needed to drive it over.

So Kincaid walked back out to the Mercedes. When the machine rumbled to life, he shifted into gear and rolled forward. Turning onto the bank next to Claire, where she was on her back, still. Hands across her eyes. She'd pretty much been like this for a couple of hours.

"Front seat or back?" he said, shutting off the engine.

"Front."

The Mercedes was quite accommodating. They sprawled across their respective seats, the windows cracked for fresh air,. And as Kincaid said, to *let the mosquitoes in.* Given that she had decided to call in the extraction team next morning,

Claire had to tell him. There was no natural way to bring up the subject. There was no option, but blurt it out.

"What if I told you, I don't work for JPL? What if I told you I work for the National Security Agency?"

For Kincaid, it didn't fully register. "What?"

"I work for NSA, Steven. JPL is only a cover."

03:45

He sat up and stared at her over the seatback.

"Say that again."

"We were interested in the Blood Toys. Then found out about you coming to Chile. And decided to tag along."

"You've been lying," said Kincaid.

"I am interested in free energy," she told him, "if that makes any difference. But we've been manipulated. Both of us. If you want to know what I think. Someone wanted you to come down, and me to come with you."

"This was my idea," he said.

"Was it?" Claire asked. "What about the old woman?"

"Miss Suzanne? What about her?"

"She manipulated you," said Claire. "Got you to Baffin. Then here. And I was sent to Chicago. We're both being used."

"No one made me do anything, except me," he told her.

Claire asked him, was the old woman was really in contact with – whatever it was – out there in space?

"She's plugged into something."

"I hear messages too," said Claire. She reached into the pack, retrieved the headset and dangled it above the seat-back.

"With a *burst-transceiver*."

She punched in the start-sequence. Moments later, the voice of Dr. Terance filled the headset. After she'd listened, she reset play-back and tossed it into the backseat.

"Here's the latest, if you're interested."

05:08

Kincaid listened in utter astonishment. Terance's message: "That was pretty smart, pulling off the bridge. There is a problem at New Wewelsberg, but it doesn't involve you. Stay in the car, if you want, that's okay. But there's also a hotel in town. Go past the guard station, about a mile down the road, you'll see it. They're expecting you."

He pulled off the headset.

"This is what you've been doing!"

"Since Chicago," she told him.

Claire said it sounded like a B-movie, but the hard-to-swallow truth was, "Nazi-Germany had an ET connection back in the '30s and '40s. I know it's nuts," she said. "But no more than an old woman hearing star people?"

"Nazis and extraterrestrials?"

"I know how it sounds," she said.

"How could the government keep a secret, this big, this long?"

She told him, that's what she used to think, before working at the company.

"They're very good," she said. "Almost a third of our budget is used, covering the trail. And you know they've pulled it off when someone like you says the government is *too inept to have pulled off.*"

"You read too many tabloids," said Kincaid.

"And who feeds the tabloids, Steven? Who keeps the nutty reality, fresh and nutty? We do."

"You're being serious?"

06:32

Claire told him, outrageous or not, all he had to do was think about the Blood Toys bunker. The photographic detail, inside. The prophecies in his own handwriting on the microscopic pages. The directions and schematics. Those were absolute proofs of a maxed-out, nuttier-reality.

"But I do understand why you would have a hard time accepting it," she continued. "It challenges the safer legends of religion and science."

"You're serious about this?"

"Yeah Steven. Unfortunately."

"Tell me something," he said, "we're being watched right

now, aren't we?"

"That's the assumption. Just don't ask how," she told him. "The only technology we've got, isn't supposed to be operational yet. On the other hand, I don't know what I know, anymore."

It probably wasn't the time to bring up what she was actually wrestling with at the moment, that someone other than NSA might be doing the watching. Or that the voices they were hearing were not necessarily the voices they were hearing.

07:39

Neither of them slept. They would get as far as semi-consciousness, but each had a set of worries that would not go down. For Claire, the debate had to end. She could take no action, where she'd taken no conclusion.

Kincaid, on the other hand, was now obsessed with what they faced next, in New Wewelsberg. How big was the place? What was the layout? His was a tactical obsession.

An hour before sunrise, since he hadn't slept anyway, he leaned over the seat and told her, he wanted to run in and have a quick look at the town.

"I'm sorry. I can't deal with any more," she told him.

"Please."

"No. But you go if you want."

08:27

So he went alone. As before, when he stopped to listen, the only sounds were those of a world about to awaken.

Bravely, he approached the guard station. But stopped a few meters from the front door. He had no intention of getting any closer.

After a few seconds, he rushed across to the hillside just opposite the guard house. He started up, moving tree-to-tree, leveraging higher until he got to the top. Dropping to his belly, he crawled forward until he was in position to see the village. A town with old fashioned street lamps trimmed to half-light, and surrounded by what appeared to be residences.

The main street was lined with businesses. And in the middle of the block, with lights still on upstairs ... it had to be the

211

hotel.

New Wewelsberg looked like *small-town America,* only without people.

His eyes traced street to street. Nothing. Not even a dog, barking. One thing about the Germans, they kept things under control.

"Claire, it's me," he said, approaching the car. He was anxious to tell her about New Wewelsberg. And that the place looked very inviting.

09:43

"Claire!"

He opened the door. The pack was there, in the front seat, along with her poncho. But she wasn't. He quickly scanned the bank. He sauntered into the woods. Maybe she'd just gone off on an early-morning hike. He walked up and down the bank, calling. And back across the bridge. Then down the road a ways. No Claire. And no comfortable explanation.

What he wanted, at this point, was aim that big German auto the opposite direction and drive until the road or the car gave out. And though his instinct was to run, to save himself, there really was no choice in this matter. He had to find her. Even if it meant joining in her fate.

After first light, he crawled in behind the steering wheel. Shifted into first. And guided the machine back onto the pavement toward New Wewelsberg.

26 On the Town

Twenty-meters out, he took his foot off the accelerator and let the vehicle's weight do the braking. It was barely rolling by the time it reached the guard station. He turned off the engine. Then slowly and deliberately opened the door. Put his hands in the air and called out, *hello*. His voice sent a flock of sparrows into the sky. Hands still raised, he shuffled to the front door. Rang the bell. Waited. Rang again. Then tentatively placed his nose to the glass. Inside, he could see a desk lined with pictures. Old-fashioned faces. Stoic. Black and white people with parasols and pocket watches.

He called again. No one answered.

00:45

A breeze tickled the back of his neck. There was a rumble. A drop. With no more warning than that, the sky exploded. Previous storms had been heavy, but without turbulence. This one splashed in with the subtlety of a water balloon. Kincaid made it to the car, but his clothes were soaked. And draining into the seat. He was wet and totally miserable.

Hard to imagine, anything short of a hurricane, would have much effect on something as heavy as the Benz. But the big machine shuddered as he drove head-on into the furious weather. The exploding wind spanked the shop signs, and threatened to detonate shop-awnings in their frames.

As the vehicle crept forward, Kincaid studied the buildings, either side of the street. From what he could tell, New Wewelsberg seemed to be flourishing. On the right was a dress shop. Beside it, a sidewalk café with a rose-trellis out front. Or what was left of it. With every watery blast, yellow petals exploded like feathers across the tables.

Across from the café was a hardware store. Next to it, a bakery with cakes and five trays of cookies in the window. He counted.

He guided the Benz forward, rolling to a stop in front of the hotel. Out of bravery, or madness, he hit the horn. It sounded like a locomotive. But no one stirred.

02:16

It was eerie. New Wewelsberg was like a corpse. Visibly intact, lacking only one thing. Life. When the windows started to fog, Kincaid rolled down the glass, just a crack. So much water came blasting through, he had to shut it immediately. So, he stretched out across the wet leather. Closed his eyes. And attempted to block the creeping panic. Where was Claire? Where were the inhabitants of New Wewelsberg?

Question begat question. And conspiracy. After an hour of this, a thoroughly fed-up Steven Kincaid slipped into the poncho. Threw open the door, and jumped into the water with a kind of ferocity. He slugged the thirty or so steps to the hotel porch, amazed that he hadn't drowned. Or been shot. Thus began his exploration of New Wewelsberg. He went inside the hotel. Dripping a trail.

"Anybody home?"

03:16

He was answered by the lonely ticking of a grandfather clock. There was the unmistakable smell of polish in the air. Every wooden surface had been buffed to maximum sheen. And with doilies on the armrests, and beneath every round-bottomed lamp, the place bore an uncanny resemblance to Miss Suzanne's flea market in Chicago. There were implications in this, which Kincaid consciously pushed aside.

He opened the guest register, found his name. Room twenty-four. Claire was registered in twenty-six. Could she be upstairs, waiting? He ran up the steps, opened the door to room twenty-six. But no Claire. Only rumpled bedsheets and a pillow on the floor.

Out of the corner of his eye, he noticed something else on the dresser. A single sheet of paper. The words on it read: *Will be back in fifteen minutes.* If she thought this was some kind of joke, it wasn't. He opened the door to his room. Everything was neat and tidy, awaiting his arrival.

He waded back out to the ca. Retrieved his and Claire's packs. Then returned to his room for a change into dry clothes. He hung his shirt, jeans, socks, and underwear in the bathroom. Once he'd changed to dry clothes, some of his gloom lifted a little.

04:43

By the time the rain stopped and the sun had come out, Kincaid decided to search the town. One end to the other. Door-to-door. He would visit the shops. Look in every closet, if need be. There had to be people, somewhere, and he would find them. That was his thinking as he set out.

A surprise awaited him at the café. Glancing through the now-roseless trellis, he noticed, the front table had been wiped dry; the wrought-iron chairs behind it, padded with towels. All of this done since the rain stopped. Most astonishing: on the table was a glass of milk, a plate and four cookies. Someone *out there* in the ether had either made a highly improbable guess, or read his mind.

05:39

When he saw the cookies, as friendly as the gesture seemed, there was something frightening about it, too. Hands in his pockets, he walked on. Ignoring the snack. Quickly making his way to the dress shop, instead.

Displayed in the window, the styles reminded him of dresses that had been popular in the 1940s. Polka dots. Wide collars. And when he peeked back around the corner, out of curiosity, the cookies were still there.

The front door to the dress shop was unlocked. He didn't step in completely. Only far enough to encounter the fragrance of roses. Fresh cut roses. Not aerosol. And back outside ... the cookies remained.

06:26

The men's shop, opposite the women's, was also unlocked. Inside, Kincaid found an assortment of black suits ranging from children's sizes, on up. Next to the suits was a rack with lederhosen. Leather shorts with suspenders. Beside it, a collection of narrow-brimmed hats.

He tried on several. Selecting a tweedy-brown, topped off by an outrageously long red feather. Admiring himself in the mirror, it reminded him of a goofy image he'd once seen of Hitler in a mildly-gay pair of alpine shorts and suspenders. The instant the memory flashed through his mind, though, he realized he couldn't afford such thoughts. Not under the circumstance. Until otherwise informed, he had to assume, anything he was thinking could be read. And the unflattering Hitler of his memory might be an insult to someone.

"I'm sorry," he whispered. "Forgive me."

Oh boy. What would his parents think? Well at least, he was praying again.

07:41

Back outside, he glanced across to the café. Another surprise. The cookies and milk were gone. The table had been cleared. Gone too, were the towels. The pattern would continue as the day wore on. As if Kincaid's tour was being adjusted to his thinking. On-the-fly. He'd passed on the snack; they'd cleared the table. Some of this was verified, almost immediately. A couple of minutes after thinking about his parents, he noticed a sale-sign in the window of the hardware stor. A *very Christian* advertisement for Christmas lights and decorations. In English, no less. The implications were staggering.

08:27

Out past the firehouse, were residences. Houses that tended to be variations-on-a-theme. With porticos and wrought iron fences. There was diversity in terms of size, but nowhere to be seen was a three-bedroom ranch with a basketball goal in the driveway. God bless the New Wewelsbergians. They had zoning. Or as Miss Suzanne would probably say, *taste*.

Kincaid imagined their daily routines. They would obviously be a hard-working and practical people. A community in-balance. A community blessed with ecological grace.

What would it be like for the children, exiled to such a perfect world? Did they have *rumspringa*, like the Amish? Did the kids of New Wewelsberg go off the reservation, or toy with the option of leaving? How many had broken a mother's heart with a trip to San Francisco? Or worse, Dallas? Hopefully, the adolescents of New Wewelsberg were smarter than that. With luck, they came of age and traipsed their hot little disquiet to the nearest cold shower. Because living here was to live in Eden.

09:43

Next to the church stood a simple home. Enclosed with the church inside a fence, it was perfectly reasonable to assume that this was the parsonage. There was a tricycle on the porch. Balls of various sizes, tossed around the yard. Without a second thought, Kincaid opened the gate. Walked up the steps. And knocked on the door. When no one answered, he went in.

He saw the furnishings he'd come to expect. Antiques, perfectly arranged. The sweet scent of polish and floor wax. And roses.

There was even an apple pie on the kitchen table. It could have been meant for him, but Kincaid would not steal from the preacher. After all, this could be some kind of test of his character. Back in the hall, he saw three pictures. The first was a color portrait of the Führer. Dressed in lederhosen, it was the exact same picture Kincaid remembered back at the store. But the most shocking discovery: in the photo, Herr Hitler was wearing the exact same hat Kincaid had worn out of the store. And was still wearing. Right down to the big red feather. Someone was definitely reading his thoughts.

11:04

The second frame contained a portrait of Jesus. By Hallmark. His hands were folded. His eyes were lifted to the sky.

217

The third was a photograph of a family. The father wore a clerical collar. Mother held a baby. Sitting on the ground in front of them, was a blonde-haired toddler. Probably two years old. And in a magnificent snit. He sat cross-legged, his chin cupped in both hands. Scowling at the camera.

A family shrine that included Hitler and Jesus was almost beyond Kincaid's range. But maybe it was some kind of strange psychological intervention, aimed at helping him eliminate cultural bias.

27 Tripod

Standing in front of the parsonage, the Hitler-hat in his hand, a sense of hopelessness descended on Steven Kincaid. He missed Claire. But the melancholy ran even deeper. He'd been thinking about his parents, and the noble impoverishments of India. He missed them.

He was snapped out of meditation when he noticed an animal, a German Shepherd, bouncing through the churchyard gate. Upon seeing Kincaid, the animal made a spastic beeline for him, crashing into him like a runaway train. The way the animal's leg stuck out, Kincaid thought at first, the dog had been injured. He knelt for a closer look. He was surprised to discover, the animal's back left leg was board-stiff, naturally. And longer than the right. A birth defect.

"What's your name?"

The animal plopped down sidesaddle. The defective leg shooting out like a tree-branch.

"*Tripod.* Right? That's a good name for a three-legged dog."

The dog soaked up the attention. *Would they find Germans or Nazis in New Wewelsberg* had thus been answered. They would find German Shepherds.

"Where is everyone? Are you the only one in town today?"

The dog let out an affectionate purr.

01:19

As Kincaid walked back toward downtown, Tripod thumped along beside him. He talked to the animal, but also beyond, to any other ears listening-in.

"I've always wanted to live in a place like New Wewelsberg.

Because we've got to adjust the way we live. I think the enemy is pollution. And war. Pollution and war. And over-population. Three things. Pollution, war and over-population."

The dog seemed to be hanging on every word.

"We haven't done a very good job with the planet, Tripod. I have to admit."

Tripod barked an *amen*.

02:01

By the time they reached the grocery store, a couple of blocks from the hotel, Kincaid hoped his personal testimony had expressed the appropriate sentiment. As far as he was concerned, it had been a fairly robust confession.

"Now for something to eat. Are you hungry, Tripod?"

The dog barked another *amen*, even though he also seemed to know, he wouldn't be allowed inside the store. Politely, the creature sat, sidesaddle by the door as if to say, I'll wait here.

02:33

Inside, Kincaid recognized most of the products. Coincidentally, the labels were in English and pretty much up-to-date. Right down to the latest marshmallow-infested cereal.

"We should give him the real thing," he said aloud. "Uh-sausage, maybe."

He selected the longest sausage in the cooler and returned to the street, to his half-starved friend. Seeing the tube of meat, the animal went mad. Hopping around. Spinning. The ultra-leg sticking out made him look a bit like pinwheel with hair.

"Sit! Sit down."

Tripod seemed to understand. He stopped. And politely sat down, the leg sticking straight out. Just like before. Except now, it quivered with affection and excitement.

"Good boy."

Kincaid tore off a chunk of sausage for himself. Then one for the dog.

"Here's the deal," he told the animal. "And I've got a reason for saying this. These people are into hygiene. So please, be careful where you do your dog-jobs. Okay? Understand? Okay. Here's your lunch."

Politely, the animal snatched the prize from his hand and walked away. Kincaid continued talking to him.

"We don't want to offend our hosts, so if I take you upstairs tonight, you have to promise. No accidents."

04:01

As with a lot of what he'd said already, he was halfway convinced that his words were being overheard. Somehow. In that respect, he was attempting a bit of public relations, letting his hosts know: his attitude was probably similar to theirs. That he was respectful and concerned with hygiene too.

The dog finished eating what Kincaid had given him, and now eyed the remaining sausage. And whined.

"So, no mistakes tonight."

Tired of all the talk, Tripod snatched the sausage from Kincaid's hand, legging it into the street.

"Bad dog," said Kincaid, chasing him. "You'll get sick! Stupid dog."

Kincaid reclaimed the prize and told the sulking animal, he'd had enough for now. Tripod let out a sad whine, but seemed to understand that what he'd just done was bad form. In the extreme.

05:01

Back at the hotel room, the dog watched Kincaid upend Claire's pack on the bed. Her personal items spilled out. Underclothes. Extra jeans and socks. A manila envelope. The headset.

"See this? It's like a telephone," Kincaid told the animal, holding up the device. Tripod might have assumed he was about to be offered something else to eat. He yelped and did a couple of spins.

"Okay. Listen up," he told the animal. "Even though you've been naughty, I've decided, you can stay with me. But no pee. That's the deal. We go outside to do our jobs."

The dog licked his hand.

"And no lick. No lick."

Kincaid and the devoted animal sank into the mattress, next to Claire's pile of clothes. Ten seconds later the dog was asleep.

For Kincaid, it was such a strange feeling. Consorting with new gods. And that's precisely what was happening. New gods. Whose proof existed in the uncanny power to make instant, mystical compensations. As in the *visitation of the cookies*. Or the more sobering miracle of the Führer-hat. The part of the new theology that continued to bother him, though: had the notes inside the Bunker been created fifty-years earlier, as some kind of bizarre prophecy. Or *magicked* there at the last second?

One other thing. He'd come to prefer a gentleman's distance to religion. He liked the general subject of God. And all the Sunday school stories that came attached, in a book – high on a shelf. Not up close and personal. And bussing the table at Starbucks.

06:50

Thinking this way inevitably led to remembrances of India. The orphanage. He was drifting off to sleep, now. Children's faces from the past. Boarding school. Goodbyes. Then, some-where in the back of his mind, a dog growled. But it wasn't in the back of his mind. It was the dog in the dark. In his bed. Tripod had *gone off*. For some strange reason, the creature's nose was a couple of inches from his. He knew this because of the pronounced aroma of dog-processed sausage blowing into his face. Kincaid groped for the nightstand and a breath of air.

"Nice dog. No growl," he said, thinking perhaps the animal was in the throes of a nightmare. Tripod didn't let up. And the barely-restrained fury of the growl suggested imminent attack.

"Hey, it's me."

07:45

Kincaid's left hand slipped toward the lamp again. And the dog reacted. Snapping at his nose. Throwing saliva all over his face. Kincaid didn't have the luxury of wondering *why*. He had to act. Or risk having his face ripped off. Problem was, his legs were spread and the dog was between them.

With his right hand – in a single move – Kincaid swept across, grabbing the animal by the stiff leg. The dog snapped, but couldn't resist the gravity, or sudden momentum that chased it. Tripod hit the floor with a squeak. Then immediately, resumed barking. Even move furiously than before.

08:25

Kincaid turned on the lamp. The creature's appearance was shocking.

"What is going on dog?"

Kincaid noticed a bit of thunder in the distance.

"Is that it? Afraid?"

The words only seemed to enrage the animal. It lunged, but without full thrust from the back legs, it reached halfway up the bed before falling back into the floor. Still, even after the awkward grounding, the animal proceeded into another fit. Lunging again and again.

Confident that the animal's launch-range had limitations, Kincaid leaned over as close as he dared. Studying the dark, furious eyes. A move that only made the creature crazier. The barking was over-the-top, now. The animal found another level. Jumping. Shrieking. Tearing at the bed sheets, furiously. As Kincaid peeked over, however, trying to decide what to do, an unforeseen, almost mystic hush suddenly fell over the animal. It was an instant stop. Tripod stared at him, actually not directly at him. But a little above his head.

"Good boy," said Kincaid.

09:40

The dog's eyes blinked a couple of times. Kincaid was totally unprepared when the animal opened its mouth and uttered these words: *Thandé puravil oru pampirikkunnu.*

"What!"

The animal pivoted. Heading for the door as fast as three-and-a-half legs would carry him. The odd thumping continued in the hall, then to the stairs. Kincaid fell back. What had just happened? Surely, the dog *had not spoken*. But he was wide-awake, and the dog *had* spoken. *There's a snake behind you.* The same thing he'd said to Claire. Nothing made sense. But as a night-terror, it made hideous sense.

Lighting flashed. There was thunder. Kincaid jumped out of bed, ran to the window and looked below. He saw his ex-friend and sidekick at the far end of the street, banging down the pavement. Disappearing into the rain beyond the last streetlamp.

10:40

He lay there next to Claire's frilly things, contemplating a wholesale retreat. He'd made huge concessions. He'd opened his mind to a new spirituality. Gone so far as to pray to them. Made peace with them over Claire's disappearance. Unconsciously, as his mind raced for options, he buried his foot in Claire's clothing pile. Luxuriating in the feminine textures there. The silk of a nightgown. A soft cotton blouse. There were two flashlights, a first aid kit, and a water bottle. He dug deeper, rummaging with his toes until he reached an alien object. Stiff and thin.

The envelope.

He withdrew it from the pile. And when he opened the clasp, a couple of peppermints, and photographs from the Blood Toys Bunker fell out. Along with a classified document.

The shots from the top level showed the motorcycles and artillery pieces he remembered. The scene looked as real as before. The second floor had the huge tank. The third, aircraft. Then came the photos taken after everyone had been kicked out. Parked beneath a giant wing was a disc-shaped object. A German UFO. The reason they'd been banished from the workshop.

He set aside the photos of the upper levels. The last three, of the lower, were terrifying.

12:10

There were no visible machines here. No aircraft. No exotic artillery pieces. Displayed instead, was a massive tangle of human arms and legs. With terrified faces. Not unlike the body piles at Auschwitz. Here again, the day's revelation was being conjured *on the fly*. An interactive transaction authored by someone, somewhere, and intended as tool for informing his soul. Or freaking him completely out of his mind.

The detail was darkly exquisite and horrifying, like a painting by Hieronymus Bosch, or Hell Brueghel. A tableau of damnation and suffering.

12:56

The final photograph zeroed-in on some of the faces. In the chaos, Jha's Doodle-cams had captured the unmistakable face of Adolf Hitler, tangled within an unholy wave of death. Kincaid had a fleeting thought. Would he also find himself? Or Claire? To his great relief, the tortured souls were people he didn't recognize.

His mind was blank, now. Eventually, he picked up the classified document and began reading. What he read did little to recover his jittered emotions.

28 Chosen

By dawn, Kincaid and his backpack were in the car. His plan was to drive until the pavement ran out. Then continue on foot, heading west, until he reached the Pacific. He would not be returning to New Wewelsberg. As for Claire, whatever had happened, placed her beyond the scope of any conceivable rescue attempt. It was difficult to accept. But the assumption was, *she was dead*. That belief only amplified his passion to get out of town as soon as possible.

He inserted the small silver key into the ignition beneath the dash. The big machine awakened like a dragon, from sleep. Rumbling in the chill of early morning. He turned on the lights. The fuel gauge registered a little more than a quarter-of-a-tank. More than enough to get him a safe distance. He would drive the tank to empty. He wouldn't stop for anyone, except Claire. But that was probably not going to happen.

00:58

He wheeled the vehicle around, heading back the way he'd come in. The machine was powerful, but heavy. And now he could see just how fast it would go on the open road. Almost too late, it occurred to him that he would have to adjust his driving style to match the vehicle. As he swerved into the corner at the edge of town, he realized, the bridge had washed out during the storm. He slammed on the brakes. The car skidded to a stop. It was close. Had his reaction been a couple of seconds off, he would've plunged into the river. He yanked the floor shift into reverse. Turned the Mercedes around and stomped on the accelerator. Blasting back through New Wewelsberg at sixty-miles per hour, going the opposite direction.

He flew past the residences. A park. A building that looked like a school. After that, he found himself on a two-lane black-top, heading in the general direction of Argentina, if he wasn't already there. But the escape was short-lived. Kincaid slammed on the brakes again, sliding to within a meter of his second surprise. A yellow and black road barrier marking the end of the pavement.

He turned the car around and headed back to town. He pulled up in front of the hardware store. Parked. He no longer worried about someone *reading* him. As he got out of the car, he yelled, "If you're trying to tell me something, you're not doing a very good job."

Inside the store, he snatched up a strip of wood trim, typi-cally employed to mount a porch screen. And cut two lengths. He crossed the pieces and lashed them at the center, making a crucifix. He cut a length of twine for the necklace. Defiantly, he slung it over his head, letting the cross fall around his neck.

It felt good to be furious again. Like coming home. For Kin-caid, anger was somehow, defining.

If he got lucky, if he got back to civilization, he would tell of Claire's abduction, and most certain death. He would tell about New Wewelsberg and how the Chileans, with the blessings of the U.S. government, had allowed a *kingdom-of-the-occult* within its sovereign borders. He would yank open the closet on World War II. Yank it off its corrupt hinges and tell the whole bloody truth. From saucers to the disembodied voices, off-planet. The New York Times would read like a tabloid.

03:34

Inside the grocery store, he stormed down the aisles, grab-bing what he thought he might need for his escape. Protein was at the top of his list, but there was limited room in the pack. And since he was now off sausage for the rest of his life, he figured, anything else with a key on top would be fine.

He tumbled three rows of sardines into the pack. Cleared out a row of kippers. Then raided the bottled water aisle before heading out the door. But as he passed the counter, something unexpected happened. The phone beside the cash register rang.

He rushed outside, but could still hear the ringing. It posed a dilemma. Part of him wanted to get out of here. The other part wondered about Claire. For no other reason, he went back inside, snatched up the receiver and there was a woman's voice on the other end.

"Steven," said Claire. "Are you okay?"

"Where are you?"

"At the church," she told him.

"What church?"

"By the parsonage. Where you just were. Slow down, Steven, we're going to really need to ease into this."

"Ease into what?"

"I want you to do exactly what I say, Steven. Put down the pack. Just leave it there. Then come back to the church. I'm the only one here."

"What's going on?"

"Believe it or not, I missed you," she told him.

"You said, *put the pack down.* How do you know I'm holding one?"

"We'll talk about that too," she said.

"This is really you?"

She laughed. "Of course. Come to the church. See for yourself."

05:20

He put the receiver back into the cradle. Then stood out on the sidewalk, the pack still slung over his shoulder. What assurance did he have that she was actually at the church? So far, New Wewelsberg had been a Halloween ride. From magic cookies to a three-legged dog that chewed your face off. But what if it was Claire? If he followed through, and ran away now, if by some stroke of luck he made it west, he would always wonder. Had he abandoned her? He gazed up the street, in the direction of the church. Not sure what to do. In the end, it was Claire. Her voice. The prospect of seeing her. That's what decided it.

06:05

He approached the wooden steps of the church. His footsteps resonated there. He reached for the door and pushed inside. Claire was up front. Seated on the first pew.

She stood when he walked in. "Hello Steven."

He ran down the aisle and grabbed her. She pushed him gently into the pew.

"Where have you been?"

"We'll get to that," she said. "But let's talk about you. How are you doing?"

"I don't know. I really don't. I want to get out of here."

"Did you miss me?" she asked.

"A little."

"Worried about me?"

He nodded.

"Steven, *they came* when you went up the road."

"*They*?"

She pulled his head down to her shoulder and held it there, stroking his hair.

"You were worried, weren't you? What's this?" She took the wooden cross in her hand. Examined it. Smiled. Then kissed him on the forehead. "This is the sweetest thing I've ever seen," she told him. "But you don't have to be afraid. Not any more."

07:13

At the moment, that's what he wanted to think. But his emotions were all over the chart. And the fact that she hadn't given any explanations yet, which she should've done the first thing, didn't help.

"Steven, what do you think about this place?"

For Kincaid, New Wewelsberg was something close kin to a *delusion*, something that seemed to be there, but wasn't.

She giggled and told him, an *illusion* wasn't far from the truth.

"They live here, Steven. But they don't. *Conventionally speak-*

ing. Which doesn't really make sense does it?"

He told her, maybe he *didn't want to hear what she was about to tell him.*

"Yes you do. And there's something they want you to know."

"There's that *they* again. *Who?*"

She stood, her hands extended. "Come with me."

08:06

"I notice, there are no crosses," he told her as they made their way to the street.

"Well, there's yours."

"Yeah, but every church I've ever been in has at least one. Right?"

She smiled. "Then that's where we start. Religion."

He told her, he would rather start with where she'd been the last couple of days.

"Okay. That's fine too. After you left, I sat there. I never saw anyone come up, but suddenly, they were beside the car. And they took me up."

"*Took you up*? A UFO?"

"I don't know what it was. Except, I had the most incredible sensation. Maybe it was. We went everywhere. We spent a long time just looking down at the cities. And the people. And the hate. And the war. And then destruction on a global scale. I think that was the point. They gave me a chance to see from *their perspective.*"

She intertwined her fingers with his.

"And they chose us, Steven. We were being manipulated. Just like we were talking about. They set up your discovery at Baffin. And me, at NSA. They put together the situation that got me here. With what I know about the technology and what you know about media production, we were exactly what they wanted, for what they want to do."

09:32

She tilted her head to his shoulder. "Together, we are going to take the message to the planet. We've been chosen, Steven, *chosen.*"

Or *possessed*. He didn't say this out loud, but some phantom had heard, undoubtedly.

"This is where the Nazis got the technology," she continued. "After World War I, the Germans were the only ones reaching out to the future."

"Back up. Something more basic. How did you see me at the store?"

She put both hands around the back of his neck. Came close. As if to kiss him. And there, her lips practically touching his, she answered. "I was there, but in another place. We were watching you the whole time."

"You were invisible?"

"To you. But I saw you and the dog. Tripod. Everyone thought that was hilarious."

10:30

He pulled her hands from behind his neck.

"Well-let's talk about good old Tripod. He nearly ripped my lips off."

"You shouldn't have panicked. We woke the dog up, basically, because you were having problems with reality. You have these self-imposed barriers. And they keep you from seeing the bigger picture, Steven. So they woke him up. And then, the dog saw us. I was on the bed behind you. That's what the dog was barking at. Some animals, evidentially, see cross-dimensionally."

Kincaid was suddenly, very weak. He steadied himself, clutched her arm and sank down to the street.

"I also saw you with the photographs," she told him, as he knelt. "Even when you drove away."

It was completely unfathomable ... what she was saying.

"Are they here?" he asked.

"Yes. All around us."

"You can see them?"

"No, but I hear them. And they're saying, *don't be afraid Steven. You've been chosen.*

29 The Hidden Masters

They made it to the café as the street lamps came up.
The trellis was completely filled with new yellow flowers.

"Is this okay?" Claire pointed to one of the tables.

"I don't care." Kincaid figured there wouldn't be a lot of demand for tables.

"Steven, I wasn't asking you."

Evidently the voices from the sky wanted the next table over.

"They don't want anything blocking the view," she said.

"What view?"

"I don't know."

Claire was starting to act like Miss Suzanne. And if that was actually the case, there wasn't much point in rushing. Events would take their course. So he sat there. Took a deep breath. Gazed up and down the quaint street, waiting for … whatever it was that was about to happen. Claire snapped out of it. She reached across the table. Touched his hand.

00:57

"I don't know why, but the word *trial* keeps coming to my mind," she said. "Like a court room trial. But it's not us. I get the sense, they're the ones are on trial. And we're supposed to be the judge. You can ask any question, Steven. Nothing is out of bounds. You ask. I'll give you their answer."

What was the question he most wanted to ask, if he only had one? It came to mind rather quickly.

"Why the Jews?"

There was a slight pause before she answered.

"If you're asking about the holocaust, it was part of a terrible misunderstanding," she said.

"*Misunderstanding?*" said Kincaid. "That's a polite word."

"Well, they aren't sure what you mean. But if you're back to, *why did our cosmic family patronize the Reich*? They didn't know how it would turn out. Given what Germany had been through, they thought the Führer, of all people, would show the compassion Germany had been denied. That he would take the message of purity, much as Christ. In Hitler, that's what they thought they had."

02:17

Jesus and the Führer? It didn't get much stranger than that. But it explained the pictures in the parsonage. Evidentially, it was a theme, around here.

"Exactly, what is New Wewelsberg?" asked Kincaid. "German?"

She replied, it was not German. It had been created specifically for the flyovers and satellites. For five decades, the Americans had looked in on New Wewelsberg, and hadn't seen a living soul. And the three times they sent troops, there was no other option. "Our brothers and sisters had to defend the community."

"So they're not Nazis, necessarily. Martians? Presbyterians?"

"Steven, be respectful. At the company we call it an *overlay*," said Claire. "This may look like a regular town, but the most important part of it, you can't see.

"What do they look like?" he wanted to know.

03:19

She told him, they could take any form. Sometimes they lent spirit to the grays or the Nordics. "But they can look like us, if we need them to. Their natural form is light. They're laughing," she said. "They're telling me, you watch too much science fiction. *No Steven, we aren't shape-shifters.*"

"What about the classified document? That's one of the points, actually."

Claire gave him a blank look.

"I read that *Harmonic-thing* in your pack."

"Oh that," said Claire. "Did you understand it?"

"Not a lot," he told her. "Enough to know, these invisible friends of yours can show up as anyone."

"Is this an artifact of your parent's religion? This question?"

He said he didn't think so, but the report had brought up stuff he'd never thought about before.

"Do you think we're … demons?" asked Claire. He saw it in her eyes. She … Claire … was disconnected, somehow. She wasn't *speaking-for*, she was *speaking-as*.

"Are you?" asked Kincaid. "Are you possessed?"

For a moment, it was almost as if Claire zeroed out. Her face had transformed into Claire. Without Claire. If that was possible. Certainly, a bit frightening.

"No," she replied. Her eyes were completely blank.

04:56

Kincaid kept forgetting. They read minds. They not only knew the questions he would ask, perhaps they were inspiring them.

She instantly picked up on his train-of-thought. "I can't answer everything, Mr. Kincaid, but since we know your every thought and see the future, isn't it great, we chose … us ?"

With that little disjunctive thought, Claire seemed to snap back to reality. "I can't answer everything, Steven," she repeated.

Why go through the formality of asking questions if they're the ones asking questions?

"Why don't I just sit here?" he said. "They can tell me what they think. How's that?"

"They never override personal sovereignty, Steven. They don't force. Only humans do that."

"What planet are they from?"

"I was wondering when you were going to get around to that. They're *Eutherian*. They're the *hidden masters from whose womb we spring*. We have earth, sea, and sky. And our domains exists within Eutheria. Within the placenta. They are without."

06:09

"We have placentas and they don't? That's not fair."

"Steven, don't."

Here was the same class of goofy conversation he'd had with Miss Suzanne. Crazy sentences that meant anything. And nothing. At the same time.

He asked how long they'd been around, and they answered, since the beginning. *We are the chicken. You are the egg. We intervened sixteen times in your gestation. But we cannot birth you into the next consciousness. That's for you to do.*

"But you see the future," he said. "What happens?"

If we don't intervene, the planet dies. Still birth. Look deep inside, Steven. You know this is true. Your world is on the brink of ecological abortion. Whole species will vanish. The interdependence we designed in the beginning, the meticulous harmonies will go extinct.

07:06

Kincaid asked about religion. "For argument's sake, say you are responsible for Earth's diversity of life. Are you also the reason for all the different religious discrepancies?

Yes. Our dream for you, for everyone, is Christ-consciousness. The perfect man. But we sent others.

"Christ-consciousness?" said Kincaid, "I'm a Sunday school boy. Christ said he was the truth, the light, and the only way to the Father. So his *consciousness*, whatever that is, trumps what he said about himself? Because I've gone to church. He was very specific about the *shedding of blood* as the only way to salvation. Should we believe what he said of himself. Or what you say about him? That his message wasn't as important as the fact *that you sent him?* That's a little hard to swallow, actually."

We will answer your question with a question. Who wrote the words attributed to Jesus? Matthew, Mark, Luke, and John. It was their remembrance. Not his words. He had nothing to do with the cult that rose up in his name.

"And you're saying, they got it wrong?" asked Kincaid.

Perhaps, missed the point. We created him to be perfect. And dedicated to our will. He loved everyone, he did. And the healings happened, and the dead were raised. That is true.

08:43

Claire stepped outside her role as mouthpiece to drop a bombshell.

"Steven, they have a playback of crucifixion," she said.

"They showed you crucifixion?"

"Yes. The three men on crosses. I heard … I heard the thunder when he died and saw the lightning. And when they showed it to me, even though they've seen it a million times, we were all stunned. It was the most moving thing."

Kincaid held his hands up as if to say: *enough.*

"Okay, I'm going to predict the future," he said. The cosmonauts probably knew where he was going with this, already, but Claire sat politely, blinked her practically vacant eyes at him. And listened.

09:31

"I predict a great tribulation. When everything on the planet goes totally nuts. Christ said the same thing. And at that point, the issue won't be *fixing* the broken planet. But the broken human hearts on the planet. Sort of the end-of-the-game. People will have to decide. Was Jesus who he said he was? Or is there another story? You guys are definitely *the other story*."

He was cut off by Claire, again possessed of words, not her own.

There's much about religion that is good, but much that stands in the way of salvation. Much to be undone. Look at the bloodshed spilled in the name of religion (she said). "Look at the heresies against the planet, the belief that man is the center of creation, and the planet, his for the spoiling. And the murdering of whole species. And the polluting of the oceans. Man writes a blank check and God is supposed to cash it?

Steven, you were raised in a fundamentalist Christian home. And you grew up with this 'Armageddon' myth. The final war between good and evil. And the thing your ancestors always talked about was the supposed 'second coming of Christ'. We know the story. We created it. We are the reason for his return. But Steven, humans wrote their own storyline here, as usual. And missed the point, entirely.

11:06

Kincaid didn't ask aloud, but this question was in his head. *At some point in the future, will Christians disappear from the planet?*

Yes, but not for reasons you think, was the answer, almost instantly. *We've been practicing what you call 'abduction'. When the next age rings in, when we attempt to bring healing to the planet, we will put in motion an operation to remove all religious bigotry. False-piety. And we will remove those who refuse to accept the true path. We've taken some already. We will take more.*

Kincaid replied: "So it's not going to be Jesus coming back for those who believe in him as Messiah? Well-that's what he said."

That's what you think he said. He is coming back, but he's coming against you for the evil done in his name.

"Jesus comes back, and someone else takes the credit. And not that you would, but if you wanted to confuse things, you could actually abduct people who are *notorious* non-Christians. Am I right?"

We don't understand your point.

"Yes you do. Jesus takes his followers. Then you abduct a few of your own. It keeps everything confused. That's possible, wouldn't you say? I even wonder if maybe, you abducting people doesn't actually lead up to his return. Does that seem like a plausible possibility?"

So you do think we're demons?

"Are you?" asked Kincaid.

12:47

"This is why you were chosen, for your independent thought. But Mr. Kincaid, you may also choose," Claire told him, on autopilot again. "We now make another promise. From this point, we will no longer read your thoughts, because, isn't the real issue, you feel that you're being forced beyond your will? That was the problem with your parent's religion. You were forced. So, you're alone again. You may help us save the world, or not. It's your choice."

13:19

It was completely dark when the conversation concluded. Streetlamps now cast a golden glow across the brick streets and buildings. Overhead, the sky was perfect black. No clouds. Only stars. Bright, bright stars. And floating in on the breeze from somewhere, Kincaid heard the solitary voice of a violin, playing a tune he didn't recognize.

He pushed back from the table. Slumped down in the chair. And looked up at the stunning night sky.

"Show me," he was thinking, in case someone might still be listening. And they did. First, a solitary light flashed overhead, north-to-south. The instant it passed, another flew east to west.

14:07

There was nothing for a moment, then streaking in from all points of the compass, converging directly above them, thousands of lights passed over. And then, as suddenly as they'd appeared, they disappeared.

Another lull followed. Then, the sky exploded with lights, large and small. Some moving in a straight line. Others zigzagging. Others wobbling, off-axis. It was like the fourth of July. More lights joined in, flying in at higher altitudes. So much illumination was thrown into the village, the shadows from the streetlamps danced as if they were possessed. And except for the violin, the demonstration was conducted in perfect silence.

When the final note struck, the lights darted from the sky like dancers leaving a stage. Claire scooted her chair as close to his as she could. She grabbed his arm and dropped her head to his shoulder.

00:00

"Well, I don't think it's over," he told her. "Look."

She tracked where he was pointing, and saw a small, but growing point of light. It wasn't just getting larger, it was descending. Claire sat up. She clutched his hand in both of hers.

The light continued to fall, increasing in size until it was twice as large as the sun at sunset. Still, it grew. There was a hissing sound from the sky. Whatever it was, the light-disc continued hurtling to earth. Filling the night sky. Casting the village in bright daylight. Claire buried her head in Kincaid's shoulder, again. He continued watching, though, as the massive light slowed to a stop.

"Claire, you're missing it."

15:58

She opened her eyes and tilted her head ever-so-slightly. The disk was rotating like a pancake as seen from the side. Then, a most amazing thing. It began a downward descent. Drifting in a zigzag motion like a falling leaf.

When it reached a point just above the hotel, everything whited-out. Kincaid and Claire could see each other. But everything else was lost in the brightness. Then, it clicked-off. As if someone, somewhere, flipped the switch. Only the street lamps remained.

"Okay," he said. "What do they want?"

Claire didn't know. They weren't talking to her anymore. She leaned into him and kissed him, lightly.

"Partners," she said.

"That's what they want?" he asked.

"It's what I want, Steven." She kissed him again.

16:54

As he opened the door to her room, he told her he was glad they'd been brought together.

"Are you?" she asked. "Don't feel obligated. You understand what I'm saying? Tonight, if you need me for anything, you want to talk, or whatever, my door's open, Steven."

He looked at her. Never in his life had he declined such an invitation. And Claire was angelic. With her bright blonde hair and Nordic features.

Did he actually just think that? *Nordic?* He'd been in New Wewelsberg too long.

She stood on her tiptoes and kissed him again. Long and passionately. And when she withdrew, there was a huge question in her eyes, situated directly behind her invitation.

"I need to do a little thinking first," he told her. "Alone. If that's okay."

"I understand. When you're through ... ahm ..."

"Yeah, when I'm through."

17:55

Lights off, lying in his bed, Kincaid fought a huge battle. One, purely hormonal, involving Claire. He would go to her, probably. But her influence was so great, in the way all women hold power over even the most powerful man. There was another battle, perhaps even more pervasive, because it extended all the way back to childhood. All his life he'd been warned of a great deception at the end of the age. How humanity would have to choose between the forces of good and evil. And how many people would be tricked into the wrong choice. This was his barrier, this legacy. The artifacts of his upbringing.

When both sides of an argument have virtues, when both sides repel each other, how do you choose?

18:47

There were two columns in his mind. In the first: everything he'd learned as a child. Jesus Christ. The *only path to God*.

In the second was *hypocrisy*. The huge mess Christianity had made of itself. With its goofy clerics and sexual abomination. The very things the church preached against, it's clergy were most guilty of: greed, ambition, pride, sexual impurity, nasty behavior– like the crusades – and the terror of the Inquisition. And all the blood spilled in behalf of the so-called Christian God. Off-hand, Kincaid could think of about a half-a-dozen other, very excellent religions or philosophies with far less hypocrisy. Or at least, he didn't know about their hypocrisy.

Still, legacies die-hard. He'd heard half-a-dozen sermons

in his life expressing a sentiment to the effect: *even if an angel came to you, proclaiming another way than Christ, you were supposed to turn and run.* But was Christ the artifact? Were the prophecies of Armageddon and deception, the archeology of a subculture. Relics beneath liturgical dust?

That night, Steven Kincaid was lost in puzzle. In the end, he didn't go to Claire. He couldn't. A funny asceticism kept him in his room. It was so strange. To go would've been sacrilege.

When he got up the next morning, Kincaid uttered a double-minded prayer. To his old God, the supplication consisted of one word. *Help.* He offered the same to the new gods, as well. He was on shaky ground here. Either side could kill him for lack of commitment. But he offered himself as a target, worthy of benign providence.

"Someone please show me how to think," was his prayer.

20:51

Claire was in the parlor, waiting. In her hand, another note.

"Under my door this morning," she said, handing it over. She seemed a tad austere.

"Are you okay?" he asked, taking the note.

"I guess."

The note read: *find the source.* These were the only words.

"What's it supposed to mean?"

She didn't know either. The voices were completely gone.

"Find the source? The beginning?" he asked. "What beginning?" He ran this through his mental columns. His dueling creeds.

"The river?"

Claire didn't think that was it.

"Could it be … philosophical. As in *find the source of enlightenment?*"

Claire thought that, too convoluted. "Source had to mean something tangible. Something we see."

21:46

Outside the hotel, they split up. He walked toward the bridge. She headed the opposite direction, toward the residential section, in separate acts of meditation and hopeful discovery.

Kincaid passed the guard station, continuing on to the river. Source meant *origin point*. But the origin point for the river was in the Andes somewhere. Given the lack of success in their present destination, why would they consider going further?

22:17

Source also meant: *some kind of spiritual beginning, a starting place*. He had just turned back from the river, when he heard a scream. Claire. He found her in front of the guard station, out of breath, yelling that she'd figured it out.

"Why are we here?" she asked.

Kincaid thought about it for a moment. "A solution?"

"Absolutely. Find the source," she said, "I found a power station. The lines carrying power, lead in. We're supposed to follow them. They'll take us … "

"… to the source," he said, completing the sentence.

As they rushed back through town, Kincaid had the presence of mind to grab their backpacks.

"You dumped out my stuff," she said, looking at the tangled pile at the end of the bed.

"Make sure and get your water bottle, and the flashlight … eh-what's in your first-aid kit?"

"A couple of band aids, maybe. Are we expecting blood?"

"I don't know, maybe."

He told her, they just needed to be prepared for anything, because unfortunately, "We don't have a gun."

"You think we're going to need one?"

He shrugged.

"Well, I've got band aids."

30 Sheep Bunker

Claire led him out to the residences east of town. As they went, she explained some of what they had told her about the bigger picture. The nature of true reality.

"Evidentially, we're in a dimension. Inside a dimension," said Claire. "If that makes any sense."

"What I want to know, where were you? Specifically?" he asked.

"Did you ever see a southern plantation? You know. With a big house and one of those wrap around porches? That's how I understood their explanation. *Where was I?* Well, you were inside the house. And I was outside, on the porch. Looking in. For you, the cosmos existed inside those walls. For me, I saw from the … *placenta*. From the outside. We assume, there are other porches. And other powers looking in, on those looking in."

"Speaking of which, what did they look like?"

01:05

"Whatever I was imagining," said Claire. "If I expected to see Europeans from the 1930s and '40s, that's what they were. I did a test. I thought about Austin. I don't think I mentioned it, but I was there a month ago."

"And … ?"

"Well, nothing happened immediately. But remember when you were going into the parsonage? About that time, I saw one of them walking down the street in front of the church. Wearing boots, a cowboy hat, and … this is crazy. Makeup."

"What?"

"Lipstick. Eyeliner. Pink bikini, I kid you not. The whole ensemble set off by a … a beard."

"Hmm. Definitely Austin," said Kincaid. "So, you're telling me, they're watching us, dressed in beards and bikinis?"

"Let's just say they're watching," she said "because that's what they do.

02:08

A block from the power station, Kincaid asked what their voices sounded like.

"Well-no one spoke to me directly," she told him. "Inside my head, that's where I heard what they were saying."

"And how did you communicate back?"

"I thought what I wanted to say. Except once. When I saw you driving into town, I called out to you. And they said you couldn't hear. That was the only time I used my actual voice."

02:36

The power station was quite a bit larger than the guard station. At one end was a desk; electrical service-boxes were at the other. And a cup of coffee – still hot – on the desk.

Claire led through the building to the back door. When she opened it, Kincaid saw the power lines. Strands of cable strung from towers. Following a sky-trail into the distance. They walked out past the back gate, then away from the town.

"I'm still having a problem with something," he told her. "If they don't need these houses, or hotels, or any of it, why go to all the trouble?"

Claire said she'd been thinking about the same thing.

"But I remembered something. During the war, when a new U-boat rolled off the line, the Nazis gave it the number of a sub that had just been sunk. Let's say, a U-Boat goes down off the coast of Africa. Three months later it's seen in the North Atlantic. The new sub. And after a while, the result is, the Allies don't know if the ship had been sunk or not. And they start to mistrust their reconnaissance."

03:45

They arrived at the edge of a great meadow. A field unbounded and unmarked, except by the continuing line of high-voltage towers.

Claire continued. "They did the same with research. The Nazis named different projects the same thing."

"For example?"

"Well-for instance, *Kugelblitz*. It means *ball lightning*. And it was the name for the saucer program. The V-7. But *Kugelblitz* was also a proximity fuse."

"Wasn't there a chance it would be *confusatory* for someone?" he asked.

04:24

"No, because the development teams only knew what they were working on. And in this particular case, there was a third Kugelblitz project. An anti-aircraft tank. So it's pretty obvious what happens. If American intelligence picks up something involving the Kugelblitz, the question is, *which* Kugelblitz? All these programs, with the same names, neutralized any conclusion the Allies might have had."

"Nothing made sense," he said.

"Which is basically how they hid the V-7," she said, "in plain sight. The German saucer program is now the biggest secret left over from the war. But when the project migrated to the States, the codename changed from *Kugelblitz* to *UFO*, eventually. And that's how a bureaucracy hides an incredible reality in plain sight. Hide it with a new name. Then neutralize it through ridicule."

05:21

"So the watchers were helping the Nazis, but helping them from the porch, I guess. Whispering through the windows?"

She stopped and smiled.

"Precisely. The mediums and astrologers who were working for the SS were, as you put it, standing by the windows."

"Something else," he said. "If the watchers were betrayed by the Reich, why would they continue to do the German ... I don't know what the word is ... ah-*motive*?"

"I think the word is *motif*," she said. "Because it's good cover.

Makes it hard to tell the reality from the overlay. Even though I've studied it, I don't know where Nazi science ends, and Eutherian technology begins."

"*Self-neutering.*"

"Right. *Self-neutralizing,*" she said.

Kincaid then asked about Quiroga. "Was he one of them? And what about Elena?"

"Oh-don't get paranoid on me," she said.

"What about the dog?"

"Tripod was definitely an *earth* dog. I think one of the Eutherians got inside and goosed him. Or whatever they do."

"They got inside?"

"I think."

"Ugh-that's pretty nasty," he told her. And she agreed. *Ugh.*

06:43

They made their way up a grassy slope, quite unprepared for what lay on the other side. A derelict stone farmhouse. A herd of sheep. And the final suspension tower. Electrical cables dropped from the tower, entering the earth at a concrete abutment.

"Bingo," he said. "Endgame."

They started running.

The reason they'd come to Chile now lay beneath their feet somewhere. And there had to be a way down to where the power lines led. But the animals, with their affectionate nudging and crowding, made it nearly impossible to look around.

"Is this normal?" he asked.

She didn't know anything about sheep, but they didn't seem mentally right to her either.

Kincaid forced a path through, into what remained of the house. The floors were rotted and filthy. Scattered around were plaster crumbs. Animal droppings. Collapsed sills and broken glass. Kincaid took his time, though, kicking around, and eventually he found what he was looking for. Inset into the pantry floor was a hatch with an iron ring.

"Claire, check this out!"

The sheep were everywhere and wouldn't go away. They stepped on Claire's boots. Crowded atop the hatch Kincaid was trying to open. He would push one off. Only to have two more take its place.

Claire asked if it the hatch could be opened.

"I can't get them off long enough to tell," he said. "Act as if you're going to feed them or something. See if you can lead them away."

08:21

Claire clapped her hands, called to the animals, and they followed her as far as the front porch. Unfortunately, Kincaid's more ardent admirers stayed behind. He moved one way. They scooted with him, ringing him in.

"Go!" he yelled. The animals nuzzled even closer.

"There's something definitely wrong with these things," he said.

Finally, he was able to get a grip on the ring. He pushed aside the solitary animal atop the door, then kicked away the one attempting to take its place. He yanked, and kicked, and shooed, and then finally, was able to lift the door. Even without the added weight, the door was heavy. Kincaid put his shoulder into it and pushed. At last, it fell back to the ground, opening onto a flight of stairs leading into darkness. Two things happened simultaneously. The door crashed into one animal, standing too close. It scampered away, shaking its head. Another lost its balance. Tumbling down into the darkness.

09:25

The world below, at the other end of the steps, was pure black. So as they made their way, they carefully tracked each step with the flashlight.

"It's too dark for them," said Claire.

Kincaid looked up, over his shoulder. The animals had formed a perfect circle around the entrance overhead. Looking down, but not following.

Slumped across the bottom step was the animal that had fallen. Its neck was broken. They had to hop over the lifeless creature to even reach the floor.

Kincaid rotated, shining the flashlight at the walls, until he found what he was looking for. A conduit. Also, a doorway opposite the stairs, just like in the Blood Toys miniature.

"Remember the motorcycle?" she said. "The oil puddle under the front tire?"

"Yeah."

"Look at that." Claire aimed the flashlight at a stain with tread prints.

"And it's roughly the same spot as the one inside the Blood Toys bunker," she said.

"So … you think it was like a dimensional-photograph?"

"I don't know, but it is going to be interesting, what we find on the next level."

10:39

Just as Dr. Jha had tracked the conduit inside the miniature, their flashlights tracked the surrounding walls. The wall switch was exactly where they expected. Kincaid twisted the mechanism. There was a click. One by one, lights came up, overhead. Fully illuminating the chamber, which was roughly scaled to what they had seen in the miniature back in Chicago.

"What do you think?" he asked.

Claire said, "What do you think?"

"I don't have a clue," he told her.

31 The End

Levels two and three were scarred with stains and tread lines. Claire noticed something else. The floors were connected by a stairwell, but there was no ramp by which a vehicle could enter or exit. Perhaps they'd been sealed off behind one of the walls. Or maybe there was an otherworldly explanation. The Eutherians didn't play by the rules.

The fourth level in the miniature had been a tableau from what could only be described as the *Apocalypse*. Reason enough to give them pause at the top of the stairs. He whispered that things *could get weird*.

"We have to go," she told him. "Turning back is not at option. You do agree, right?"

00:45

Kincaid unzipped the pack and withdrew Miss Suzanne's sketch of the bunker. Shuffling it to the top of the stack. The drawing consisted of simple lines, with nothing indicated on the first three floors. On the fourth, though, she had sketched a small circle.

Claire said, "If it's accurate, the worst thing that could happen is zero. Nothing."

"And the best?"

"We find the Coler," she told him. She opened her pack and took out the envelope with the last photo from the Doodle-cams. The nightmare. She tugged the drawing from his hand, and held the photo and the drawing side by side. Then made an observation. "Will it be the lady or the tiger?"

"As if there's a difference."

"Hey! Watch out!" she said.

01:38

Their flashlights were clicked on until t

he mid-floor landing. Claire was the first to see the illumination spilling from the fourth level. Without a word, or really even doing much in the way of breathing, they proceeded into the half-light at the bottom of the stairs.

"Ladies first," he told her.

She said: "Uh-not this time. You."

02:92

But not really, she didn't mean it. Claire peeked inside the chamber first. Then reached for his hand and pulled him in behind, as she stepped forward.

A massive contraption stood at the far end of an otherwise empty space. It resembled an oversized roulette wheel, spinning in silence. The only indication that the thing was running was a slight floor vibration. It looked pretty much like what you would expect a generator to look like. Obviously heavy. With a portion the wheel housing passing into the floor.

"I don't know how this one works," she said, "but it seems to be doing something. Hear that?"

There was a second sound. An electrical hum. And an occasional crackle from a bluish discharge-field on the sidewall. Kincaid slipped his arm around her waist. As he did, she thanked him.

"For what?"

03:02

She flashed the dimples at him. "For the chance. I think your parents would be proud of you, Steven. I really do."

Her words were simple and unaffected.

"Claire, thank you for my big chance," he told her.

"What do you mean?"

"I don't know how to say it. I'll probably get it wrong, right? I'm pretty *vulnerable* to you, Claire."

"*Vulnerable*? You mean *amenable*? It means your heart is

willing. Open? Same here, Steven."

"No, my heart is *vulnerable* to you," he said. "You are dangerous to my heart."

"Oh. I get it. But I'm not. I promise."

Then he kissed her. Both were thinking the same thing at that moment, even though they didn't say it aloud. After all the snarking, arguments, and insults, they'd found the Coler. And they'd found something else.

04:07

Hand in hand, they turned back to the generator.

"What if I … ?" He held up an index finger as if to touch the housing.

Her response was instant. "Absolutely not. There's a surface charge, Steven. I'm serious."

He stepped closer. Not to touch, then. Just look.

"It could also arc," she warned. "Steven, please."

He did step back, eventually. Like a child, barely willing himself to obey. She snatched his arm and pulled him to her side. He told her, "Whatever you say, mommy."

It was at this moment, something quite unexpected happened. Claire said there was something they *needed to do*.

"What?"

04:55

Of all things, she knelt. Then yanked him to his knees beside her. She proceeded to thank the invisible ones for their confidence, and patience, and willingness to share. She promised to honor and celebrate them. To devote her life to their sacrifice.

Just the thought of praying to the Eutherians made Kincaid's chest burn. But that's precisely what she was doing. And it didn't stop there. Without warning, she jumped up. Her eyes still closed. And she started hopping.

"Steven?" She spoke between bounces.

"Yeah?"

"Any of a hundred-million people could be here today, but they chose us."

"Right," he replied, still on his knees. But carefully monitoring her flight.

"Are you celebrating?"

"Sure," he said. "Absolutely."

With evangelical fervor, she told him, they needed to express gratitude *with all their heart.*

Right. Kincaid couldn't get past the dogmas barking in his head. Nor was he about enter Miss Suzanne's whacky orbit. He did stand up, eventually, but it was in an effort to get out of her flight path.

He said, she could tell them thanks *for both of us.*

It was strange. Her vaulting about. Shouting to the Eutherians that she was *the most thankful seed of woman.* Maybe that's what it took to get past the Judeo-Christian legacies. But it wasn't for him. Kincaid quietly reached into the pack and took out the camera.

06:38

Still jumping, though not quite as high, Claire opened her eyes when she heard his movement, then the shutter-release.

"What are you doing? We're giving thanks," she said.

"I am, I use a camera to give thanks," he told her.

She thought about it for a few bounces. Then told him, that would *be okay,* but she continued, as he set about taking photographs of the Coler. She would run down. He knew that much from experience.

She bounced. He made his way around the Coler, eventually slipping into the shadows behind the device. There, on the backside, he came face to face with a small, cherrywood box. An exact duplicate of the one he'd seen at Baffin.

"Hey Claire."

She was pretty much jumped out by this point. And open to distraction.

"You want to see this."

"What?"

07:40

She brushed away the perspiration, and stepped behind the Coler. A little unsure of what he was looking at. He told her it was a dead-ringer for the one they'd found at Baffin. The one containing the miniature bunker.

Claire knelt beside it. A kind of spiritual awe on her face. Kneeling on the other side of the box, he asked her to do the honors. Hand trembling, she opened the lid. Inside was a miniature of the Coler. An exact duplicate of the larger machine over their shoulders.

"Is it working?" she asked, examining the small disc with the flashlight. "That must be the plan. They want us to take it back. They want us to back-engineer the miniature."

08:32

In that moment, as she said these words, the voices started speaking to her again. Her head jerked.

"What?" said Kincaid.

"They're telling us to *leave*," she said. *Leave immediately.*

He closed the lid and stood.

"We're supposed to take this?"

"Yes. Hurry!"

He was about to make an amazing discovery. When he lifted the box, there was almost no weight to it. Claire asked him what was wrong. *Why the look?*

"It feels like it's trying to fly. It's so light. It's almost ... lifting itself. Does that make sense?"

He handed it to her. Instantly, she realized what was happening.

"It's a wave-field," she told him. "Like a UFO, or the field-generation stuff on the B2."

Claire told him to kneel beneath the box. "Hold your arms out."

"Why?"

"It's an experiment," she told him.

09:33

When he was in place, arms extended and palms up, she released the box and stepped back. Strangely, it didn't fall. But drifted down like a balloon into Kincaid's waiting hands. He was dumbfounded.

"This changes everything," she said. "And there are other secrets here, obviously."

He hadn't realized it until now, but her breezy mysticism was starting to get to him a little. Was she going to end up like Miss Suzanne? But the instant this thought flashed through his mind, the earth trembled.

Holding the box as level as he could, Kincaid chased her toward the stairwell, just as the first wave hit. They lost their balance. Tumbling hard to the floor. Cracks ripped across the walls as a massive chunk of concrete crashed to the exact spot where they'd just been standing, a few seconds earlier. When his knees hit the concrete, Kincaid lost control of the box.

10:37

Helpless to do anything, he watched it pass from his fingers. Drifting toward the rolling concrete. But it didn't go crashing down. It hovered. As the surface pitched and bucked, the cherrywood box floated in perfect calm. Unfazed.

Neither had time to think about it, though. A single fissure opened across all four walls. Effectively cutting level four in half. Then, as suddenly as it had begun, the shaking stopped. The cherrywood box drifted to the floor. Touching down like a feather.

He asked if she was okay. She said she was. But there was a great calamity taking place on the floors above. They heard the walls crashing. Chunks of concrete, spilling across the floor. He jumped up and grabbed the box as the second shockwave hit. Claire stumbled forward. He lost balance. And the cherrywood box drifted down as before. Steady and peaceful. Riding well above the waves of storming concrete. The aftershock was even more violent than the quake. Another seam snapped across level four. Another chunk of concrete split off. Crashing a mere ten meters from where they were sprawled.

12:00

Claire couldn't understand why the voices were allowing this. But Kincaid knew. It was his fault. They had read his commitment, or lack-of-commitment. It hadn't been a clearly formed agnosticism at first. But he'd come to a decision. If the Eutherians read the future, if they knew enough to know that the planet was heading for ecological collapse, how could they have not foreseen Nazi-intention?

This was a tear in the logic, as obvious as the cracks in the walls around him. How could they have been *surprised by the Reich*? You couldn't *know* and *not know* at the same time. For all the smoke and mirrors, the voices had conspired, if not directly against the planet, against the human family living there. That was the proof he needed.

12:54

As the second quake dissolved into trembles, they both saw that the main crack in the wall had grown wider. Something else caught Kincaid's eye. Oozing from the fault, crude oil streamed down. Flooding the walls. Creeping onto the floor. He grabbed the box, heading for the stairs just behind Claire. From the next landing they discovered: level three was now a debris field. With pieces of ceiling still crashing down. Here too, oil exploded from the walls. As well as the ceiling. All concrete surfaces were now slick, especially the stairs.

Fighting their way up, over an ever-darkening course, they began to smell a rancid odor drifting down from the floo
rs above. Then smoke erupted from level two. Storming into the stairwell.

"Steven!"

"I'm trying to find the rail," he told her.

Without thinking, he released the box again, into the cloud, just as Claire grabbed him from behind. "Why are they doing this?"

Just as quickly as she'd grabbed him, she released him, and stepped away.

"What?" he said.

14:09

With a bleeding, oil-covered hand she spun him around and delicately unfastened the top button of his shirt. Hanging around his neck was the wooden cross. And the reason for what was happening. In the boiling darkness, flashlights cross-aimed, one soul was laid bare. The other, betrayed.

"Steven ..."

She opened her mouth to speak. But before she could, a fireball exploded through the clouds on the second level, just above. The resulting wave was intense. And hit the stairwell, full-force. Driving both of them back down the stairs. Reflexively, they rolled to the side as flames jetted past. Clinging to the rail, tripping, crawling, and sliding back the way they'd just come, they scrambled forward. But had a strong sense of being overpowered.

15:04

The fourth level had been utterly transformed in the seconds since they'd left. The Coler, ever-running, spun away in the middle of the room. But the concrete surrounding it, hemorrhaged with crude oil. There was a cataclysmic flash. Then heat from behind. The fire chased them down, pursuing them in a chain of booms and explosions. They suspected they were probably doomed. But they slopped through the muck and chunks of concrete, making their way toward the Coler.

Even so, Kincaid would not apologize for the cross. In the seconds remaining, he apologized instead, for inviting her to come with him. That was the mistake. He attempted to pull her close, but she refused to yield. That was the nature of their final moment. As she pulled away, the monster shrieked into the room. As Kincaid whispered that *he loved her*, flames struck with a violent concussion.

Then, the world went away.

16:13

Dr. Nunnally drove down Northside Road, past a small frame church. Then left onto a dirt road. It was a familiar place, though only at the greatest distance of memory. Long before highways, shopping malls, and churches, this had been as remote a place as could be found in North Carolina.

A blank spot in the trees was all that remained of his childhood home. There was not one board, not one rock, just a depression in the earth where his home had been.

He removed the pistol from the glove box and got out. How far he had come since leaving? He thought of his parents, of their small, simple lives. How many steps had he taken from this place? There had to be a number. A precise number. One million? Two? A hundred? Were he to walk back in time, one step at a time, what step-number was it, the day he left for Chapel Hill? The old man marked off the phantom numbers of his life. But he didn't despise the tears that came, as he counted back. It had been a grand life. A surprise, really. He abandoned these lonely roads to superintend the great secrets of the world. How much more could you ask?

17:38

He stood where his home had been. He looked around for a welcoming thought. And he remembered this one. Christmas. The year of the big snow. Everyone had a present that year, and that was not always the case. Children pass through such moments, unaware. The brief hours of this long, lost holiday had been the best he would ever live. Childhood and family. Mysteries and securities. It was the final thought he would take … a boy carrying firewood and a snowy night.

18:09

In an act of great duality, of hallowed memories juxtaposed to the physical act of lifting a gun, he steadied himself for what came next. It was assumed that one had only to get past a certain point. Then the gravities would pull you under. He placed the barrel in his mouth. Closed his eyes. And then slipped into another place. A place of sound and splendor. A place of welcome. In what could've been his final moment, he was snatched from his dark plan by the sound of singing from the church down the road. Taken at voice-value, the singing was actually pretty unmusical. Taken at heart value, the music was symphonic. The church hadn't been built when he was a child. But the song on the evening breeze reminded him of home. He lowered the gun. And though he could have driven, he walked the half-mile back to the church. Each step, a step backwards across the breadth of his life.

19:19

The door of the small church swung wide. At first, the preacher and the congregation attempted to ignore the strange man. And would have, had it not been for the gun in his hand. A hush fell on the assembly. Nunnally walked the aisle. His eyes burned. His lips were pale and trembling. He stopped directly in front of the clergyman. Then aimed the gun at the ceiling.

"In the name of Jesus, don't," said the preacher.

"Don't what?" asked Nunnally.

"Don't shoot, sir. We're Christians here."

Dr. Nunnally placed the gun on the altar.

"I'm not here to shoot," he said, "I think I'm here to pray."

32 Shadowed Range

Claire drifted toward consciousness a couple of times. Only to fade back. When she did finally come around, her memories were scrambled. And in some cases, totally disconnected. She fully awakened to find herself on a promontory, high above a shadowed range of peaks and canyons. A familiar place, though not immediately remembered. The tempest of light on the horizon brought it back. This was where Firefly had gone.

Kincaid's body lay a short distance away. She crawled to him,. Flipped back the crucifix. Then placed an ear to his quiet heart. There was only one possibility. This was what came next. Except, *she* wasn't dead.

00:46

She cradled his head. Kissed him. Whispered. Held him. But eventually, crawled off. Unable to bear the vacancy.

If the voices knew, up front, how hard it would be for someone like Steven to give up the old ways, why had they chosen him? It was almost as if they picked him for his resolution. Then set about to undermine it. Gazing across the phantom world, Claire's rage against the watchers escalated to such a point, she lost all power of reasonable contemplation. And the intensity sapped what little energy she had left. She turned despondent, by degrees. Then silent. Then entranced by the light storm. And then, she noticed something in the distance. A human form had emerged from the tempest. Walking in her direction.

01:41

There was a great distance between them. The man's passage,

slow and deliberate. When he closed to about fifty-meters, she realized, the stranger was none other than the man she'd seen with Kincaid at the museum, but also the church in Naperville.

"I know you," she said, as he walked up.

He smiled. Then knelt beside Kincaid. And with an open palm, stroked his hair. After slightly repositioning himself, he proceeded to lift the lifeless body.

"I can help," said Claire, sliding a hand under Kincaid's other shoulder.

02:17

The stranger gently tilted him back. Cradled him in his arms, like a child. And proceeded to carry him up the ridge. At the ridge crest, they proceeded to the other side, where she saw the same field of kelp through which Firefly had passed. She grabbed Kincaid's lifeless hand and begged, *please don't take him away.* The man didn't respond. At the shoreline, he placed Kincaid on the bank, then like someone easing into a swimming pool, slipped down into the rippling stalks.

"We're dead, aren't we?"

The stranger looked over to her when she said this. There was something incredibly gentle in his expression. But something fierce, as well. He tugged Kincaid toward the waterless sea, allowing Claire to grab his hand one last time. It was stunning. Even a bit terrifying to see Steven, standing upright in the stalks. But once he was there, he was able to stand under his own power.

"Steven?"

03:25

He turned, smiled weakly, but smiled. Then the stranger put an arm around him and led him into the greater depths. Like people in a wheat field, they disappeared into the drifting fronds. And Claire was alone.

She wept as she made her way back up the ridge. At the top, she looked out across this lonely, lost life of hers and wondered where she would end up. So intense were the emotions, and so isolating, she drifted back into befuddlement, and collapsed. Moments later, she lay back, closed her eyes, and waited to be taken.

04:09

A drop of rain hit Claire's face. There were clouds. She heard the river. And when she sat up, she saw the Mercedes on the apron of a bridge she didn't quite recognize. Someone shouted her name. She looked over and saw Quiroga running toward her, yelling: "Where's Steven?"

She didn't know.

Kneeling beside her, Quiroga said he had been trying to find them for days. Where had they been? And honestly, at that point, Claire couldn't say. The last couple of days were a blur. The only thing she knew was, she had to get out of New Wewelsberg. Now.

"What about Steven?"

"No please … let's just go."

He helped her up.

"I'll carry this," he told her.

She didn't know what he meant at first, but the cherrywood box was in the grass behind her.

"What is it?"

05:11

Claire glanced over, but revealed little, if any comprehension of the object. Or its contents.

They placed it on the front seat. Claire stretched out in back. Quiroga steered onto the bridge, heading west. With luck, he would have her in Santiago in a couple of days. With a little more luck, she would awaken to a brightened understanding of ambition. And the ancient prescription that *wisdom is seduced by vanity*. Evaporated by it, actually.

Epilogue

May 21, 1998 – Austin, Texas
A little after 3 a.m., Claire Whitlock arrived in the emergency room at St. David's. After three hours in labor, she gave birth to a healthy, 8-pound, 6-ounce baby girl. She named the newborn, *Elena*. No one visited either of them in the hospital. No flowers for Claire. No balloons or teddy bears for the baby. And only one card, from Claire's district manager. After two days, she and the baby departed, by cab.

Claire's instinct had been to take immediate refuge in simple things. She abandoned her old life, and quickly retreated into a new life. She was now an assistant-manager in a far simpler world. Where the employees were mostly teenagers, the food, fast, and the organization, finely tuned. It was a simple diminishment, but satisfying. With the new baby, her world would begin to form again. She welcomed the simple uncertainties.

01:08

May 23, 1998 – Colima, Mexico
The day she and the baby arrived back at the apartment, an update on Claire was delivered to a small orphanage in Colima, Mexico.

An old American lived there now. He wasn't a paid employee, but had quickly found work, as the resident-grandfather to the fifty-two children housed on the property. He paid his own way. And was pretty much given a free-hand in the tasks he undertook. He helped with chapel services. Surprised the children with hand-carved toys. And small, wrapped peppermints. He lent courage to the young, who faced a world they could scarcely imagine. And maybe that's the job he did best. He loved them with a grandfather's love, indulging each with favor, seldom equaled by true grandfathers with their true grandchildren.

In the final week of his life, Dr. Nunnally spent most of the time on his bed, in the out-building that also served as a toolshed. Surrounded by shovels and machetes, this was the simpler life he sought. As with Claire, his life also involved children.

02:22

As he lay there, suspended between past and present, he was often awakened with the arrival of small peppermints, flung through the window. The little ones who loved him were being drawn into a serious crisis. As they prepared for his departure. They knew no better way to tell him of their love than peppermints. Thrown through an open window.

On March 23, he was also awakened with the rare delivery of a letter. He learned that Claire had become a mother. And that the baby's name was Elena.

He read it several times. Finally, he placed it flat across his face. Prayed for the mother and her newborn. And remembered good things.

03:08

April 19, 1944 – Berlin, Germany

The eve of his 55th birthday, a small crowd of well-wishers gathered in the great hall. Traudl Junge, the Führer's secretary, was in charge of the handcart bearing the cake. A vanilla confection, roughly the size of an automobile tire, topped with a chocolate swastika. Hitler pretended to be surprised when they walked in. And beamed as they serenaded him. Afterwards, Junge and her assistant proceeded to serve.

During this part of the festivity, Himmler remained outside, standing guard over the second pushcart. When the clanking of forks against china came to an end, he wheeled it inside, pushing it in front of the Führer's desk. Like all good birthday surprises, the present was hidden, though an outline was obvious. Beneath the white coverlet was some kind of box. With the arrival of the second cart, most of the well-wishers spun on their heels and walked out. Only Goebbels and Himmler remained. Notably, Speer was in Merano, Italy. He had dared to darken the Führer's happy day with a letter of resignation.

The birthday boy was eager for the present. And maybe even a little more-so than usual, given the wounding by Speer. Hands clasped in front, the Führer joined the other two at the cart.

"Something else?" he asked.

Himmler pulled back the coverlet. Beneath, was a cherry-wood box.

04:41

The men had carefully scripted the presentation. Himmler opened the box. Goebbels retrieved the tuning forks from inside the lid.

The Führer leaned in for a closer look at the accessory ar-tillary pieces, also inside. He was amazed. Each was perfectly cast. The wheels rolled. The turrets turned.

"Extraordinary," he said. "There are even rivets."

The men smiled and nodded.

"And this?" He was curious about the strange, gold colored jewelry box.

It was Goebbels' turn. Gently, he withdrew the second, smaller box. Its surface strobed silver-brass in the overhead light. Himmler told him it was the embodiment of a prophecy.

"And that?" asked the Führer, pointing to the tuning forks.

He wanted them to open the box so he could see inside.

"It can't be opened, my Führer," said Goebbels.

"How do you know there's a prophecy inside if you've never opened it?"

05:49

Himmler picked up a tuning fork. Struck it against the corner of the tray, then ever-so-lightly touched it to the upper part of the engraved brass box.

Instantly, the first floor of the jewely box, turned transparent. Plainly visible were motorcycles and troop carriers. Hitler was amazed. Bending down, he examined even more closely.

"Try this," said Goebbels. From his breast pocket, he produced a viewing lens.

Hitler scanned the scene, even more astonished than before. He judged the miniatures, perfect in every respect. Gradually, though, the walls clouded back. Obscuring the scene.

Himmler slapped the tines of the fourth fork against the cart. The tone was barely audible. He brought it into contact with the bottom of the box. Immediately, all exterior walls, top to bottom, turned transparent. Revealing what was behind them. The fourth level was different from the others. Carefully, Hitler fixed the monocular lens on what he saw there. On this level were the Führer's people. The *knights* of the Reich.

Surrounded by his adoring functionaries, Hitler saw himself, erect and dignified. The exact vision he had in his heart.

"How are we to understand this … prophecy?"

Their explanation was basically: the Reich had achieved ultimate order. Each man made sure that the Führer noticed their figurines too.

07:25

"And that's me," said Himmler. In the miniature-tableau, he was sitting as close to Hitler as Nazi protocol allowed.

With a slight bit of venom, the Führer noted that the Speer figurine was posed with a sextant, when a dagger would have served just as well.

Goebbels understood his placement, beside the Führer, as the one who protected the great man's legacy. That was his role in this ultimate prophecy of the Reich.

When the opacity returned, the Führer motioned to apply the fork one more time. Kneeling beside the miniature, he pointed to himself in the center of small scene.

"And that's me," he said. "Wonderful."

The End

Exhibits

Majestic 12 Documents (1)
FBI Document 1957

FEDERAL BUREAU OF INVESTIGATION
U. S. DEPARTMENT OF JUSTICE
COMMUNICATIONS SECTION

NOV 7 1957

TELETYPE

URGENT 11-7-57 4-55 PM EST WHH

TO DIRECTOR FBI

FROM SAC, DETROIT 1P

UNIDENTIFIED FLYING OBJECTS, IS - X. REBUTEL NOV SIX LAST.

WARSAW, POLAND, WAS GERMAN POW

MAY, NINETEEN FORTY TWO, UNTIL SUMMER OF NINETEEN FOURTYFIVE.

ARRIVED NY MAY TWO, NINETEEN FIFTYONE, AS DP, AR NO.

UPON INTERVIEW

ADVISED THAT WHILE GERMAN POW DURING NINETEEN FORTYFOUR OBSERVED

A VEHICLE DESCRIBED AS CIRCULAR IN SHAPE, SEVENTY FIVE TO ONE

HUNDRED YARDS IN DIAMETER, APPROXIMATELY FOURTEEN FEET HIGH. THE

A VEHICLE DESCRIBED AS CIRCULAR IN SHAPE, SEVENTY FIVE TO ONE

HUNDRED YARDS IN DIAMETER, APPROXIMATELY FOURTEEN FEET HIGH. THE

VEHICLE WAS OBSERVED TO SLOWLY RISE VERTICALLY TO HEIGHT

SUFFICIENT TO CLEAR FIFTY FOOT WALL AND TO MOVE SLOWLY

HORIZONTALLY A SHORT DISTANCE OUT OF VIEW OBSTRUCTED BY TREES.

ENGINE OF TRACTOR FAILED TO OPERATE DURING THIS PERIOD AND

ONE OTHER OCCASION WHEN HIGH PITCHED WHINNING NOISE HEARD

IN AREA. NO INDICATION OF MENTAL INSTABILITY DURING

INTERVIEW. FURTHER DETAILS FOLLOW AMSD.

E CORRECT LINE FOUR WORD VX FOUR CHLD BE TWO.

END AND A K PLS

X 4-58 PM OK FBI WA EW

TU DIC

NOV 13 1957

Majestic 12 Documents (2a)
"Important"

Received 7/9/99 *Timothy Cooper* **IMPORTANT** *July 7, 1999*

Please read everything I am about to tell you as the truth. I am
not a prankster or a wacko. My reason for typing this letter is
to give you the facts as I know them. I am what is called in spy
jargon a "walk in." I became such in [1982] when I learned about
[Bill Moore] and his ["aviary"] sources who were really [OSI agents.]
Unlike yourself and others, Moore was taken in by the deception
about Majestic Twelve and EBE's. He was promised "inside"
information regarding the Roswell case. From what I know about
Moore and his desire to be on the "inside" led him to hoax some
documents based on material supplied to him by OSI. I think he
was so taken in by the material that he believed it himself and
went off the deep end. You seemed by what I have been told and
what I have read about you on the internet to be a level-headed
guy with some real backing and good information on the UFO
issue. You may not know now, but you have some really important
stuff that is creating a lot of tension in the UFO community. If
you don't, you have better appreciate it. You have been given
information that no one has. To make my point a little more
clearer, remember a few years back when you got [the JFK memo?]
[William Colby] got fingered in it and someone decided to [shut him
up] before he was questioned about it. Coincidence? No way. He
was not the first to be eliminated and won't be the last I assure
you. You have been left alone for the most part I think because
you are a nobody in the UFO community and have no credibility with
them and that is good. I think "they" wanted it this way. Being
a high profile personality is not always a good thing. Look how
STF got put on the "watch list" by the OSI. Too high of a profile
and to vocal with national identity. Linda Howe is another example.

IMPORTANT

Majestic 12 Documents (2b)
"Important"

-2-

When high profile individuals begin making waves with allegations and hard proof they put themselves in very difficult situations in which they have to defend constantly. The demise of several key personalities in just the last five years should tell you something.

Now, I want to fill you in on some things regarding the special studies and conclusions by the defunct MJ-12 group.

a. MJ-12 does not exist as a government intelligence entity. It ceased to exist in 1969 and became a private concern financed by big money and big science.

b. The group has been called by many names. The most recent one was used in 1992 and was identified by the name [JEHOVAH.] At one time it was called [ZODIAC] and may have changed in 1995.

c. The UFO/EBE Working Group is an international consortium financed and supported by some of the biggest money institutions and private industrialists in the world.

d. MJ-12 was a consolidation of two Pentagon projects [MAJESTIC] and [JEHOVAH] overseen by a group of twelve high level military, intelligence, and scientific institutions within the defense establishment hence MJ-12. Each code name had classification above TOP SECRET and fell into a classification called MOST SECRET.

MAJESTIC originally was a government panel appointed by HST to look into the possibility of extraterrestrial contact and to seek ways of detecting nonterrestrial signals through the creation of the NSA. The highest classification in 1952 was [DRINE] and later [UMBRA.] As of 1990 it is [SACRED.]

JEHOVAH was a DoD project to back engineer the hardware and research the physics. [Dr. J. Robert Oppenheimer] was appointed by [Dr. Bush] to head this project. The project name was coined by [Albert Einstein] in [1949.] Oppenheimer held this job until 1953 until the AEC no longer considered him reliable and had his security clearance taken away and lost his government job in 1954.

Einstein became unreliable in 1955 and died of "cancer".

Oppenheimer continued as a MJ-12 player until his death from "cancer."

In [1960] MJ-12 concluded that UFOs were a possible threat to U.S. defenses and could instigate mass paranoia. They also concluded that the EBEs could gain control of U.S. defenses

Majestic 12 Documents (2c)
"Important"

-3-

during a nuclear crisis by [interfering with the guidance and targeting computers of the Atlas ICBMs based in Turkey.]

j. In 1960, [President Einsehower] approved a joint defense plan written by MJ-12 that in the event the U.S. came under a nuclear attack by the USSR through EBE deception the U.S. would not retaliate with proposed USAF [SIOP] and only after confirmation of UFO misidentification launch surgical strikes on the USSR. The purpose of the strikes was to take out USSR command and control infrastructure preventing an all out nuclear war.

k. During the Cuban Missile Crisis President Kennedy was briefed by MJ-12 and was told that the EBE deception was the reason the Soviets wanted to place first strike nuclear weapons in Cuba and he therefore restricted U.S. nuclear forces from initiating the (GRAND TOUR) to bomber strikes. [General LeMay] was so furious with JFK that he secretly gave orders to SAC to go ahead with SIOP in the event the U.S. perceived a first strike warning from Russia.

l. In 1963, JFK sought to ease the uneasy tension by extending cooperation with the USSR in outer space investigation of UFOs through a joint moon project. MJ-12 was opposed to this because they felt the militarization of the moon would place the U.S. in a dangerous situation with the EBEs who control the dark side of the moon.

m In [1964,] President Johnson was briefed by MJ-12 on the dangerous relationship with EMEs and how they [influenced the doctrines and policies of U.S. foreign relations.] MJ-12 successfully prevented [NICAP] representatives from issuing their conclusions on UFOs to government leaders and blocked attempts by NICAP to brief Johnson on the UFO threat. MJ-1 was responsible for this coup.

n. In [1969,] President Nixon was briefed by MJ-12 on all aspects of UFO activity and the EBE problem since 1947. Fearing possible leaks within his NSC and national security advisor [Kissinger,] Nixon approved a Special Classified Executive Order that required the U.S. intelligence community to purge all references to MJ-12 in their UFO files and to destroy documents that could connect him to JFK's assassination by MJ-12. As Vice President, Nixon approved [ZR RIFLE] written by the [40 Committee] (MJ-1 issued new directives that sanctioned JFK's murder) for political assassination operation

o. After the press learned of the Watergate break in and theft of documents that could link MJ-12 to the 40 Committee, MJ-12 arranged for Nixon's exposure to [ZR RIFLE] and black mailed him which led to his resignation.

p. MJ-12 arranged for the removal of FBI Director [J. Edgar Hoover] in 1972 through "natural causes" because he "knew too much" and had used his [contract killers] to eliminate unreliable individuals who could expose MJ-12's existence and activities

IMPORTANT

Majestic 12 Documents (2d)
"Important"

IMPORTANT

Mr. Cooper, I could go on and on but I think you get the gist of it. I cannot verify everything I have written here but with a little reading and research I think you can judge for yourself whether all this is true or not. Consider the JFK murder for example. Everyone believes he was a victim of a "lone nut" assassin as the Warren Commission Report said (which by the way was pure fiction). It was not the Cuban problem or the Cubans. Cuba was a screen to keep civilian researchers and the Congress away from the true motive for his death. Simply put, Kennedy would have interfered with MJ-12's effort to come up with a defense and a plausible explanation to the UFO/EBE problem and was too sensitive an issue for interruption even by a president. Everyone believes that a president is in charge of his own office. That is simply NOT TRUE! Presidents can be and are compromised about issues they don't need to know of. The reason is a simple one. It gives them plausible deniability just like CIA directors who are often asked this question: 'What do we know about UFOs?' Once exposed to the data they are changed and are stuck with this problem: 'What do I tell the President?' You can't tell the President without telling others. There is no such thing as a secret in the White House. Just look at the China espionage case. Until he really needs to know nothing will be told him and that is that. This is the real dilemma for those in "the know" because the [EMEs] (extraterrestrial materialized entities) have complete control over UFOs (not to be confused with man-made UAVs often mistaken for UFOs for they have been around since the 1950s and are operated and controlled by the USAF, CIA and NRO) and can appear anywhere as anything at any time. Do you understand now. The intelligence behind true UFO sighting cases can [materialize] and

IMPORTANT

Majestic 12 Documents (2e)
"Important"

-5- IMPORTANT

appear at will to anyone at anytime any place. Why do you think the Air Force wanted Project Blue Book terminated? Because they could not explain them in conventional terms without being laughed at by scientists. After 12,000 cases they had all the evidence they needed and handed it over to the CIA and NSA. Was it mere coincidence that Blue Book was terminated [after Apollo 11] landed on the moon? And, do you think it was mere coincidence that the [Dead Sea Scrolls] appeared about the same time the UFOs were found in [New Mexico?] Everything associated with UFOs has a purpose and so far, no one has figured it out yet. The appearance of UFOs in our century is no accident. Why do you think the UFO Study Group appointed in 1947 was called MAJESTIC? And, why do you think the other project was called JEHOVAH? Put the two together and see for yourself. [It is SPIRITUAL!] If you don't believe me just read the Bible. Yes, the Bible. Mj-12 did and it scared the shit out of them. The 12 Apostles and the 12 created in 1947. One is an antitypical reflection of the other except the antitypical 12 were not spiritual men and couldn't grasp the significance and impact of what was happening on the world scene. I know this sounds crazy and unbelievable but it is true, believe me. I have it from reliable sources that the CIA used [Jacques Vallee's] books as a guide for interpreting the human response to the UFO contact problem and I suggest you do the same. He is studied at the CIA and NSA and is qouted in their literature. One thing that you should concern yourself with and that is the possible undercurrent of image and character assassination that may be used against you if you are taken too seriously by the media and the press. Unless you have strong backing by the responsible members of the UFO

IMPORTANT

Majestic 12 Documents (2f)
"Important"

-6-   **IMPORTANT**

and the media you could end up like some others who have tried to
use this knowledge for their own personal gain. I also caution
you about the [severe psychological and spiritual affects] from UFO
investigations. Some well known researchers have suffered
[personal identity questions] and loss of close family ties and even
faith itself. Don't let this happen to you. You have to maintain
a balance and perspective when investigating this phenomenon. Some
have lost all sense of reality and have suffered insanity as a
result. I wouldn't recommend getting involved in remote viewing
for a solution. The EMEs are not to be believed and are quite
deceptive. I'll let you in on one secret that MJ-12 found early on.
The earth's environment has undergone significant changes and they
are part of the ENVIRONMENT! The redacted portion of the library
book found in New Mexico predicts a world wide invasion by EMEs
in the year 2030 according to the lunar calendar which commences
sometime [after 1999.] [The CIA] has undertaken a survey project
called [ENVIRONMENT] through a joint CIA-civilian project called
[MEDEA] to look at what damage has been caused by EME controlled
UFO activity especially around nuclear power plants and industrial
waste production. From what I know the earth's population is
being [contaminated] and our DNA is being altered through pollution
of our air, food supply, and water. The [digital Trojan Horse] is
going to wreck havoc soon and we have the EMEs to blame (not really,
the army is responsible for that one). To reduce it in a few words,
WE ARE CATTLE AND SUBJECT TO SLAUGHTER BY EMEs. That is the
GAME PLAN. The "insiders" know this and are taking advantage of
the situation. Our only hope may come from [extraterrestrial
intervention.] The world leaders see no viable solution except

IMPORTANT

Majestic 12 Documents (2g)
"Important"

[population control] through [biological warfare] and [regional conflicts.]
If UFOs <u>trigger</u> a nuclear exchange lets say between India and
Pakistan, or between China and Japan, or North and South Korea, or
between Israel and Iraq, the NATO countries will surely take
advantage and try to finish them off. Keep an eye on Russia and
China. They may start something along these lines and try to
draw the U.S. into it. In order to justify this kind of [population
control] they may <u>invent</u> a crisis from outer space. They may try
to convince the world that extraterrestrials may invade our planet
and eliminate the human race and therefore they need to deploy
their space defenses and kill a number of people in the process.
Already there are events taking place all over the U.S. and in
other countries that are UFO related that bear this out. We are
being [inoculated] for possible [biological warfare] and at the same
time being [conditioned] (programmed) for [extraterrestrial contact.]
This was and still is the agenda of secret government preparations.
They <u>know</u> it is coming but <u>don't know when and how.</u>

I hope you don't take all this as the rantings of a raging lunatic.
What I have written is based on what I have learned over the years
and my association with the intelligence community who is <u>equally
in the dark</u> as to the ultimate conclusion. I have included some
goodies for you which you might find helpful. Lot's of luck to
you and keep plugging away. The answer may be a <u>simple one.</u>

Majestic 12 Documents (3a)
SOM1-01

Majestic 12 Documents (3b)
SOM1-01

TOP SECRET / MAJIC EYES ONLY

SOM 1— 01

Special Operations Manual }
No 1 - 01

MAJESTIC — 12 GROUP
Washington 25, D. C., *7 April 1954*

EXTRATERRESTRIAL ENTITIES AND TECHNOLOGY, RECOVERY AND DISPOSAL

TOP SECRET / MAJIC EYES ONLY

1

Floyd Wray

Majestic 12 Documents (3c)
SOM1-01

CHAPTER 1
OPERATION MAJESTIC—12

Section I. PROJECT PURPOSE AND GOALS

1. Scope

This manual has been prepared especially for Majestic—12 units. Its purpose is to present all aspects of Majestic—12 so authorized personnel will have a better understanding of the goals of the Group, be able to more expertly deal with Unidentified Flying Objects, Extraterrestrial Technology and Entities, and increase the efficiency of future operations.

2. General

MJ—12 takes the subject of UFOBs, Extraterrestrial Technology, and Extraterrestrial Biological Entities very seriously and considers the entire subject to be a matter of the very highest national security. For that reason everything relating to the subject has been assigned the very highest security classification. Three main points will be covered in this section.

  a. The general aspects of MJ—12 to clear up any misconceptions that anyone may have.

  b. The importance of the operations.

  c. The need for absolute secrecy in all phases of operation.

3. Security Classification

All information relating to MJ—12 has been classified MAJIC EYES ONLY and carries a security level 2 points above that of Top Secret. The reason for this has to do with the consequences that may arise not only from the impact upon the public should the existence of such matters become general knowledge, but also the danger of having such advanced technology as has been recovered by the Air Force fall into the hands of unfriendly foreign powers. No information is released to the public press and the official government position is that no special group such as MJ—12 exists.

4. History of the Group

Operation Majestic—12 was established by special classified presidential order on 24 September 1947 at the recommendation of Secretary of Defense James V. Forrestal and Dr. Vannevar Bush, Chairman of the Joint Research and Development Board. Operations are carried out under a Top Secret Research and Development - Intelligence Group directly responsible only to the President of the United States. The goals of the MJ—12 Group

MJ—12 4838B

2

Majestic 12 Documents (3d)
SOM1-01

TOP SECRET / MAJIC EYES ONLY

are as follows:

a. The recovery for scientific study of all materials and devices of a foreign or extraterrestrial manufacture that may become available. Such material and devices will be recovered by any and all means deemed necessary by the Group.

b. The recovery for scientific study of all entities and remains of entities not of terrestrial origin which may become available through independent action by those entities or by misfortune or military action.

c. The establishment and administration of Special Teams to accomplish the above operations.

d. The establishment and administration of special secure facilities located at secret locations within the continental borders of the United States for the receiving, processing, analysis, and scientific study of any and all material and entities classified as being of extraterrestrial origin by the Group or the Special Teams.

e. Establishment and administration of covert operations to be carried out in concert with Central Intelligence to effect the recovery for the United States of extraterrestrial technology and entities which may come down inside the territory of or fall into the possession of foreign powers.

f. The establishment and maintenance of absolute top secrecy concerning all the above operations.

5. Current Situation

It is considered as far as the current situation is concerned, that there are few indications that these objects and their builders pose a direct threat to the security of the United States, despite the uncertainty as to their ultimate motives in coming here. Certainly the technology possessed by these beings far surpasses anything known to modern science, yet their presence here seems to be benign, and they seem to be avoiding contact with our species, at least for the present. Several dead entities have been recovered along with a substantial amount of wreckage and devices from downed craft, all of which are now under study at various locations. No attempt has been made by extraterrestrial entities either to contact authorities or to recover their dead counterparts or the downed craft, even though one of the crashes was the result of direct military action. The greatest threat at this time arises from the acquisition and study of such advanced technology by foreign powers unfriendly to the United States. It is for this reason that the recovery and study of this type of material by the United States has been given such a high priority.

MJ 12 4838B

3

TOP SECRET / MAJIC EYES ONLY
REPRODUCTION IN ANY FORM IS FORBIDDEN BY FEDERAL LAW

Majestic 12 Documents (3e)
SOM1-01

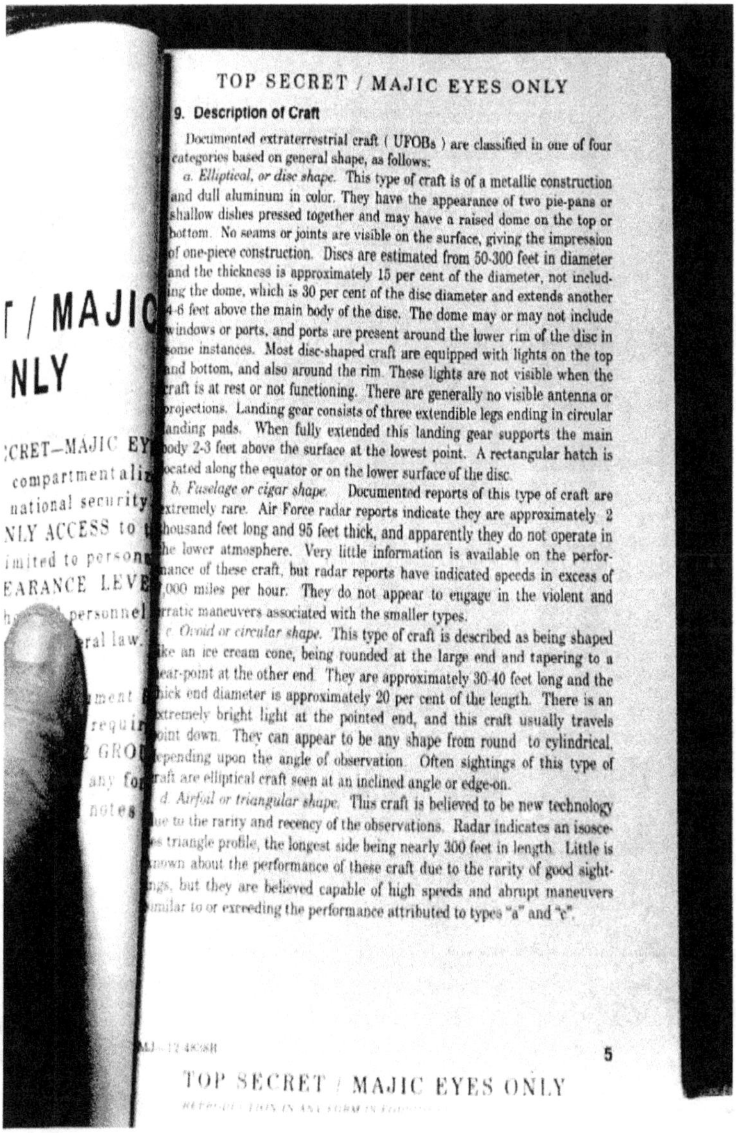

TOP SECRET / MAJIC EYES ONLY

9. Description of Craft

Documented extraterrestrial craft (UFOBs) are classified in one of four categories based on general shape, as follows:

a. Elliptical, or disc shape. This type of craft is of a metallic construction and dull aluminum in color. They have the appearance of two pie-pans or shallow dishes pressed together and may have a raised dome on the top or bottom. No seams or joints are visible on the surface, giving the impression of one-piece construction. Discs are estimated from 50-300 feet in diameter and the thickness is approximately 15 per cent of the diameter, not including the dome, which is 30 per cent of the disc diameter and extends another 4-6 feet above the main body of the disc. The dome may or may not include windows or ports, and ports are present around the lower rim of the disc in some instances. Most disc-shaped craft are equipped with lights on the top and bottom, and also around the rim. These lights are not visible when the craft is at rest or not functioning. There are generally no visible antenna or projections. Landing gear consists of three extendible legs ending in circular landing pads. When fully extended this landing gear supports the main body 2-3 feet above the surface at the lowest point. A rectangular hatch is located along the equator or on the lower surface of the disc.

b. Fuselage or cigar shape. Documented reports of this type of craft are extremely rare. Air Force radar reports indicate they are approximately 2 thousand feet long and 95 feet thick, and apparently they do not operate in the lower atmosphere. Very little information is available on the performance of these craft, but radar reports have indicated speeds in excess of 7,000 miles per hour. They do not appear to engage in the violent and erratic maneuvers associated with the smaller types.

c. Ovoid or circular shape. This type of craft is described as being shaped like an ice cream cone, being rounded at the large end and tapering to a near-point at the other end. They are approximately 30-40 feet long and the thick end diameter is approximately 20 per cent of the length. There is an extremely bright light at the pointed end, and this craft usually travels point down. They can appear to be any shape from round to cylindrical, depending upon the angle of observation. Often sightings of this type of craft are elliptical craft seen at an inclined angle or edge-on.

d. Airfoil or triangular shape. This craft is believed to be new technology due to the rarity and recency of the observations. Radar indicates an isosceles triangle profile, the longest side being nearly 300 feet in length. Little is known about the performance of these craft due to the rarity of good sightings, but they are believed capable of high speeds and abrupt maneuvers similar to or exceeding the performance attributed to types "a" and "c".

Majestic 12 Documents (3f)
SOM1-01

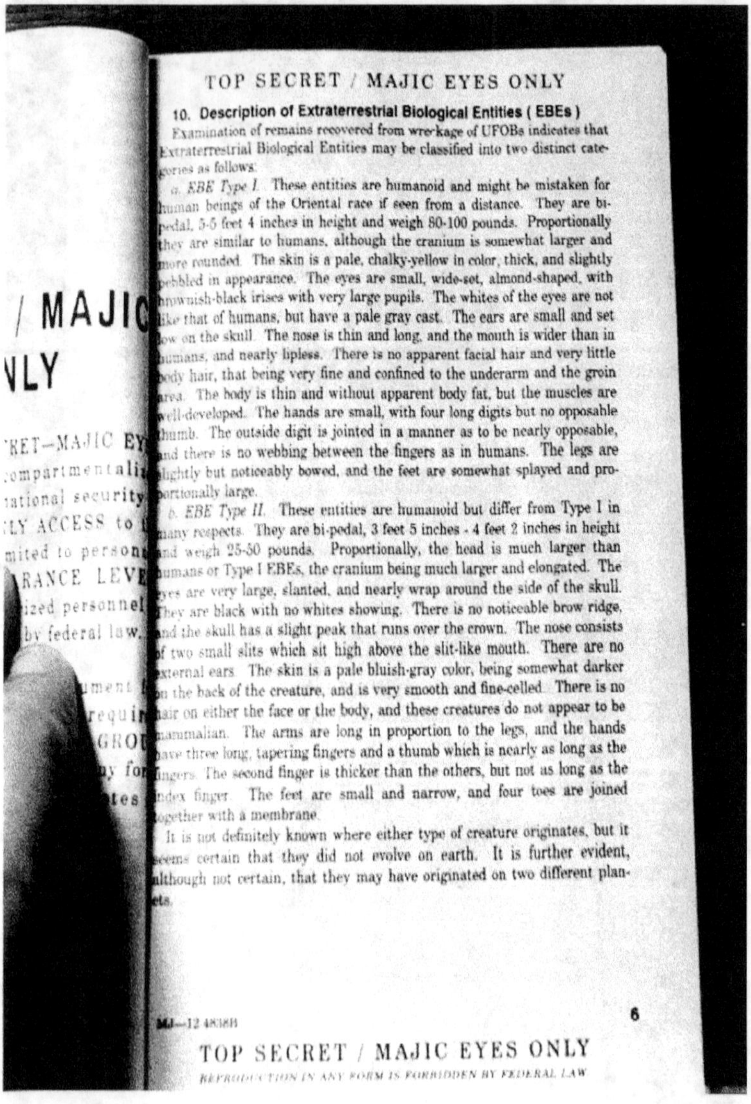

TOP SECRET / MAJIC EYES ONLY

10. Description of Extraterrestrial Biological Entities (EBEs)

Examination of remains recovered from wreckage of UFOBs indicates that Extraterrestrial Biological Entities may be classified into two distinct categories as follows:

a. EBE Type I. These entities are humanoid and might be mistaken for human beings of the Oriental race if seen from a distance. They are bi-pedal, 5-5 feet 4 inches in height and weigh 80-100 pounds. Proportionally they are similar to humans, although the cranium is somewhat larger and more rounded. The skin is a pale, chalky-yellow in color, thick, and slightly pebbled in appearance. The eyes are small, wide-set, almond-shaped, with brownish-black irises with very large pupils. The whites of the eyes are not like that of humans, but have a pale gray cast. The ears are small and set low on the skull. The nose is thin and long, and the mouth is wider than in humans, and nearly lipless. There is no apparent facial hair and very little body hair, that being very fine and confined to the underarm and the groin area. The body is thin and without apparent body fat, but the muscles are well-developed. The hands are small, with four long digits but no opposable thumb. The outside digit is jointed in a manner as to be nearly opposable, and there is no webbing between the fingers as in humans. The legs are slightly but noticeably bowed, and the feet are somewhat splayed and proportionally large.

b. EBE Type II. These entities are humanoid but differ from Type I in many respects. They are bi-pedal, 3 feet 5 inches - 4 feet 2 inches in height and weigh 25-50 pounds. Proportionally, the head is much larger than humans or Type I EBEs, the cranium being much larger and elongated. The eyes are very large, slanted, and nearly wrap around the side of the skull. They are black with no whites showing. There is no noticeable brow ridge, and the skull has a slight peak that runs over the crown. The nose consists of two small slits which sit high above the slit-like mouth. There are no external ears. The skin is a pale bluish-gray color, being somewhat darker on the back of the creature, and is very smooth and fine-celled. There is no hair on either the face or the body, and these creatures do not appear to be mammalian. The arms are long in proportion to the legs, and the hands have three long, tapering fingers and a thumb which is nearly as long as the fingers. The second finger is thicker than the others, but not as long as the index finger. The feet are small and narrow, and four toes are joined together with a membrane.

It is not definitely known where either type of creature originates, but it seems certain that they did not evolve on earth. It is further evident, although not certain, that they may have originated on two different planets.

MJ—12 4838B

6

TOP SECRET / MAJIC EYES ONLY

REPRODUCTION IN ANY FORM IS FORBIDDEN BY FEDERAL LAW

Majestic 12 Documents (3g)
SOM1-01

TOP SECRET / MAJIC EYES ONLY

11 Description of Extraterrestrial Technology

The following information is from preliminary analysis reports of wreckage collected from crash sites of extraterrestrial craft 1947-1953, excerpts from which are quoted verbatim to provide guidance as to the type and characteristics of material that might be encountered in future recovery operations.

a. Initial analysis of the debris from the crash site seems to indicate that the debris is that of an extraterrestrial craft which exploded from within and came into contact with the ground with great force, completely destroying the craft. The volume of matter indicates that the craft was approximately the size of a medium aircraft, although the weight of the debris indicates that the craft was extremely light for its size.

b. Metallurgical analysis of the bulk of the debris recovered indicates that the samples are not composed of any materials currently known to Terrestrial science.

c. The material tested possesses great strength and resistance to heat in proportion to its weight and size, being stronger by far than any materials used in military or civilian aircraft at present.

d. Much of the material, having the appearance of aluminum foil or aluminum-magnesium sheeting, displays none of the characteristics of either metal, resembling instead some kind of unknown plastic-like material.

e. Solid structures and substantial beams having a distinct similarity in appearance to very dense grain-free wood, was very light in weight and possesses tensile and compression strength not obtainable by any means known to modern industry.

f. None of the material tested displayed measurable magnetic characteristics or residual radiation.

g. Several samples were engraved or embossed with marks and patterns. These patterns were not readily identifiable and attempts to decipher their meaning has been largely unsuccessful.

h. Examination of several apparent mechanical devices, gears, etc. revealed little or nothing of their functions or methods of manufacture.

Majestic 12 Documents (3h)
SOM1-01

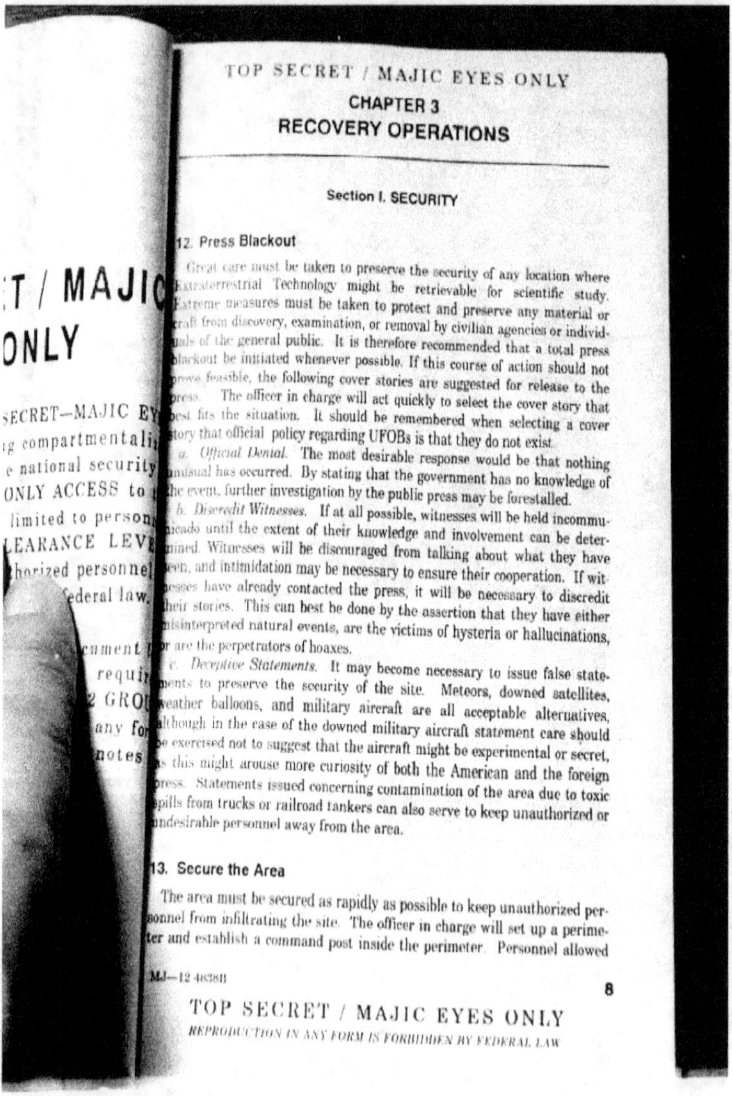

TOP SECRET / MAJIC EYES ONLY

CHAPTER 3
RECOVERY OPERATIONS

Section I. SECURITY

12. Press Blackout

Great care must be taken to preserve the security of any location where Extraterrestrial Technology might be retrievable for scientific study. Extreme measures must be taken to protect and preserve any material or craft from discovery, examination, or removal by civilian agencies or individuals of the general public. It is therefore recommended that a total press blackout be initiated whenever possible. If this course of action should not prove feasible, the following cover stories are suggested for release to the press. The officer in charge will act quickly to select the cover story that best fits the situation. It should be remembered when selecting a cover story that official policy regarding UFOBs is that they do not exist.

a. *Official Denial.* The most desirable response would be that nothing unusual has occurred. By stating that the government has no knowledge of the event, further investigation by the public press may be forestalled.

b. *Discredit Witnesses.* If at all possible, witnesses will be held incommunicado until the extent of their knowledge and involvement can be determined. Witnesses will be discouraged from talking about what they have seen, and intimidation may be necessary to ensure their cooperation. If witnesses have already contacted the press, it will be necessary to discredit their stories. This can best be done by the assertion that they have either misinterpreted natural events, are the victims of hysteria or hallucinations, or are the perpetrators of hoaxes.

c. *Deceptive Statements.* It may become necessary to issue false statements to preserve the security of the site. Meteors, downed satellites, weather balloons, and military aircraft are all acceptable alternatives, although in the case of the downed military aircraft statement care should be exercised not to suggest that the aircraft might be experimental or secret, as this might arouse more curiosity of both the American and the foreign press. Statements issued concerning contamination of the area due to toxic spills from trucks or railroad tankers can also serve to keep unauthorized or undesirable personnel away from the area.

13. Secure the Area

The area must be secured as rapidly as possible to keep unauthorized personnel from infiltrating the site. The officer in charge will set up a perimeter and establish a command post inside the perimeter. Personnel allowed

MJ—12 4638B

8

TOP SECRET / MAJIC EYES ONLY
REPRODUCTION IN ANY FORM IS FORBIDDEN BY FEDERAL LAW

Majestic 12 Documents (3i)
SOM1-01

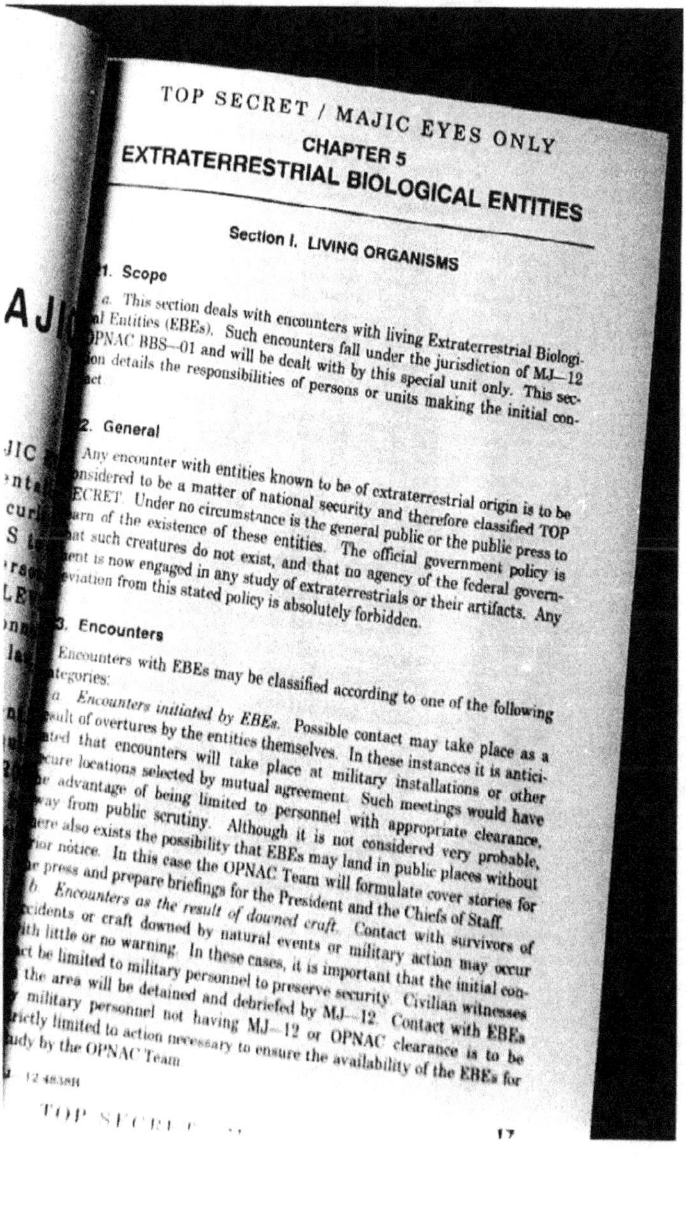

TOP SECRET / MAJIC EYES ONLY

CHAPTER 5
EXTRATERRESTRIAL BIOLOGICAL ENTITIES

Section I. LIVING ORGANISMS

1. Scope

a. This section deals with encounters with living Extraterrestrial Biological Entities (EBEs). Such encounters fall under the jurisdiction of MJ-12 OPNAC BBS-01 and will be dealt with by this special unit only. This section details the responsibilities of persons or units making the initial contact.

2. General

Any encounter with entities known to be of extraterrestrial origin is to be considered to be a matter of national security and therefore classified TOP SECRET. Under no circumstance is the general public or the public press to learn of the existence of these entities. The official government policy is that such creatures do not exist, and that no agency of the federal government is now engaged in any study of extraterrestrials or their artifacts. Any deviation from this stated policy is absolutely forbidden.

3. Encounters

Encounters with EBEs may be classified according to one of the following categories:

a. Encounters initiated by EBEs. Possible contact may take place as a result of overtures by the entities themselves. In these instances it is anticipated that encounters will take place at military installations or other secure locations selected by mutual agreement. Such meetings would have the advantage of being limited to personnel with appropriate clearance, away from public scrutiny. Although it is not considered very probable, there also exists the possibility that EBEs may land in public places without prior notice. In this case the OPNAC Team will formulate cover stories for the press and prepare briefings for the President and the Chiefs of Staff.

b. Encounters as the result of downed craft. Contact with survivors of accidents or craft downed by natural events or military action may occur with little or no warning. In these cases, it is important that the initial contact be limited to military personnel to preserve security. Civilian witnesses in the area will be detained and debriefed by MJ-12. Contact with EBEs by military personnel not having MJ-12 or OPNAC clearance is to be strictly limited to action necessary to ensure the availability of the EBEs for study by the OPNAC Team

12 48-38H

TOP SECRET

17

Majestic 12 Documents (3j)
SOM1-01

TOP SECRET / MAJIC EYES ONLY

Isolation and Custody

a. EBEs will be detained by whatever means are necessary and removed to a secure location as soon as possible. Precautions will be taken by personnel coming in contact with EBEs to minimize the risk of disease as a result of contamination by unknown organisms. If the entities are wearing space suits or breathing apparatus of some kind, care should be exercised to prevent damage to these devices. While all efforts should be taken to assure the well-being of the EBEs, they must be isolated from any contact with unauthorized personnel. While it is not clear what provisions or amenities might be required by non-human entities, they should be provided if possible. The officer in charge of the operation will make these determinations, since no guidelines now exist to cover this area.

Injured or wounded entities will be treated by medical personnel assigned to the OPNAC Team. If the team medical personnel are not immediately available, First Aid will be administered by Medical Corps personnel at the initial site. Since little is known about EBE biological functions, aid will be confined to the stopping of bleeding, bandaging of wounds and splinting of broken limbs. No medications of any kind are to be administered as effects of terrestrial medications on non-human biological systems are impossible to predict. As soon as the injuries are considered stabilized, the EBEs will be moved by closed ambulance or other suitable conveyance to a secure location.

In dealing with any living Extraterrestrial Biological Entity, security is of paramount importance. All other considerations are secondary. Although it is preferable to maintain the physical well-being of any entity, the loss of EBE life is considered acceptable if conditions or delays to preserve that life in any way compromises the security of the operations.

Once the OPNAC Team has taken custody of the EBEs, their care and transportation to designated facilities becomes the responsibility of OPNAC personnel. Every cooperation will be extended to the team in carrying out its duties. OPNAC Team personnel will be given TOP PRIORITY at all times regardless of their apparent rank or status. No person has the authority to interfere with the OPNAC Team in the performance of its duties, by special direction of the President of the United States.

Section II. NON-LIVING ORGANISMS

Scope.

Ideally, retrieval for scientific study of cadavers and other biological remains will be carried out by medical personnel familiar with this type of procedure. Because of security considerations, such collection may need to be done by non-medical personnel. This section will provide guidance for retrieval, preservation, and removal of cadavers and remains in the field

MJ-12 4838B

TOP SECRET / MAJIC EYES ONLY   18
REPRODUCTION IN ANY FORM IS FORBIDDEN BY LAW

Majestic 12 Documents (3k)
SOM1-01

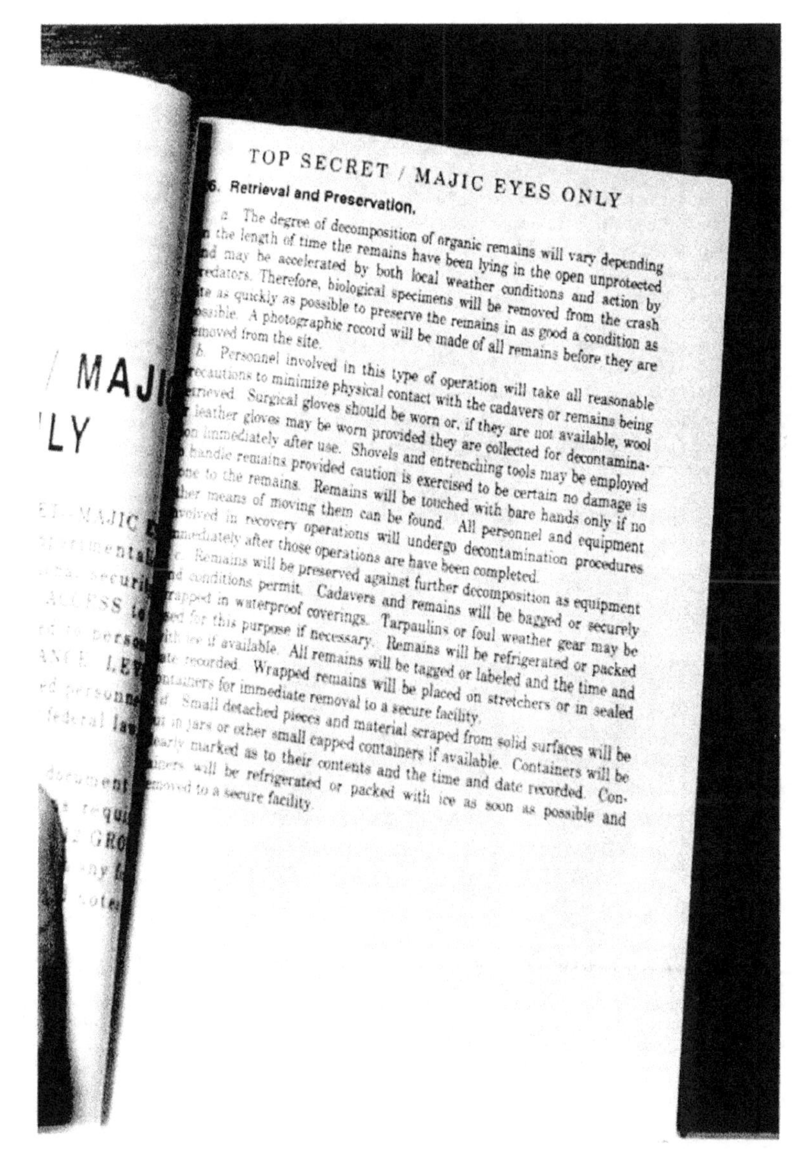

Computer Generated Exhibit (4a)
Unexpected Harmonic

theoretical modeling suggests that these cosmic condensates (C-condensates) evoke an energy scalfold, a pre-designed EM-wave structure that posses interdimensional properties that are tunable.[27] Given the technnology, these C-condensates could be instantaneously collapsed to one-millionth of their original volume via energy-modulation. Imagine the skin of an aircraft, say an aluminum alloy, where the unit cell-structure could be changed by drastically reducing molecular bond length. If an alloy *monomer* could be shrunk to less than 400nm and still held together by energy at 700nm apart, then the entire aircraft skin would be invisible to the naked eye.[28] This would explain the sudden appearance of their craft in our skies, or alternately, the sudden disappearance, as well. The vehicle would disappear as it crossed the from the "visible," into the "invisible" spectrum (>340nm).[29]

7. Understanding this notion of *thresholding* provides a theoretical basis for an amended view of the cosmos. The implications include: 1) speeds faster than the speed-of-light are possible; 2) these speeds might be achieved and sustained with minimal outlays of energy; 3) our space-time domain might actually be bound within the spectral-zone of what we define as *visible light*. By extension, interdimensional properties could alter the nature and boundaries of other dimensions. [30] Our dimension might thus be roughly understood as a *space-time node,* in what we define as the *visible spectrum*, one that demarks a slice in a broader continuum of undiscovered (inaccessible) space-time fabric. The framework for our dimension would be governed by the speed-of-light,* with its attendant scaling characteristic: time. [31]

8. EME-access to us would require a "dial down" of mass as a pre-requisite for "entering time." [32] No, we don't understand -- even remotely -- how this is accomplished, but it offers an explanation for *field-effects* whereby ufo-nauts survive sudden acceleration/deceleration bursts, or radical, high speed turns. [33] They are not just *one* with their transport-craft, both they and their transport may actually be variably altered at a sub-atomic level. Their passage might not be remarkable for speed-of-movement, but actually, more in keeping with a change-of-nature.[34]

---

* *Our current dimensional-model includes height, width, depth and time. As you approach the speed-of-light, time slows. Beyond the speed of light, time ceases to be the phenomenon we know and understand. This was the initial observation that led the Cothran Working Group (CWG) to the Judeo-Christian model of dimensionality. The top dimension would be the zone where God exists, apart from everything else. God is "holy" – which the ancients defined as "being set apart." The variable spectra beneath this "set apartness" would be composed of dimensional zones, bound and defined by frequency-rate. The ancients understood these zones as "heavens."*

Computer Generated Exhibit (4kb)
Unexpected Harmonic

An Unexpected Harmonic v.79c   TOP SECRET   SAS-TS--1-143-95   Nunnally, Paige, Rosenfeld

Beyond Science, Into Madness

9. *Change-of-nature* presents us with a profound set of possibilities.

10. First, if there is a mechanism for reversibly changing mass to higher frequency wave state-energy, we might have a new perspective for "aliens manifesting themselves in human form." [35] Many researchers have been put-off by the suggestion, but if EMEs can change mass and energy states, perhaps *moderating* their physical appearance is no big deal, comparatively-speaking. What is a big deal is the impact such acknowledgement would have on human civilization. It is widely held that any such revelation would induce widespread *metaphysical madness,* a condition in which a "Methodist might be shot for being misidentified as Pleiadian." [36] This is the destabilizing secret behind UFOs. *Someone is stalking you, watching you.*

11. *Why were Oppenheimer and Einstein re-evaluated at the end of their careers?* They were seen as unstable. *Why were they unstable?* As was the case with James Forrestal, perhaps their world-view and social functionality collapsed from exposure to a non-human reality, or emotional-spiritual interference. [37] Additionally, one of them may have been "compromised by an *EME stand-in,* a *look-alike.*" [38] Oppenheimer's rather notable derailment in the matter of Haakon Chevalier lends to the strange speculation that he was *betrayed-by-proxy.*

12. "Many first-responders to UFO-crash events have been suspected as stand-ins." [39] Interdimensionals interrupt our protocols, investigative processes and insert themselves into chains-of-command where they "feed deception." [40] The documentation resulting from EME-exposure provide the basis for our draconian secrecy. [41] If Einstein and Oppenheimer weren't intellectually resilient enough to manage a radically different dimensional reality, or *phantom* betrayal, what are the prospects for those of us who lack their capacity for abstract thought? [42]

The President may have been 'alienated' by a Martian last Thursday. [43]

13. This might be a funny comment, but it suggests a gateway to paranoia, madness and [soci-etal] breakfdown.

14. *Change-of-nature* also provides an interesting explanation for many UFO-crash events. A timing-failure at "dial down could result in a superluminal craft impaling itself into the surface of a planet." [44]

15. Perhaps the most frightening evaluation suggests that Interdimensionals may access us

Computer Generated Exhibit (4c)
Unexpected Harmonic

SAS-TS--1-143-95

An Unexpected Harmonic v.79c   TOP SECRET   Nunnally, Paige, Rosenfeld

through a portal, "our ancestors understood as spiritual." [45] The final summary for EME-influence might thus be described as a "fluency for shattering our cognitive-patterns, shaping our feelings and beliefs, and the capacity to assault us as we dream." [46]

Judeo-Christian Cipher (JCC) **

16. *Change-of-nature* also suggests the goal of religious practice. This change is often rooted in a special understanding of origins and destinies.

17. *Did the CWG adopt a Judeo-Christian perspective out of cultural bias?* This question is justified. Many original members of CWG had prior association with Judeo-Christian beliefs. *Are there better models?* That question is being explored.

18. Judeo-Christian perspective includes: 1) a *higher-domain entity* entering and effecting behavior in a lower domain; 2) a cosmology/theology obsessed and rooted in concepts of light; 3) a belief-set strongly oriented to dimensionality (heavens, domains, principalities); 4) a staggering list of miraculous events suggesting the existence of Interdimensionals.

Jumping From Sunday School to Quantum Mechanics

19. The meeting-notes from the Cothran-Group provide an interesting roadmap for how researchers -- both public and private -- came to entertain a religious pedagogy. The subject seems to have arisen from reference to the Genesis-statement, "Let there be light." A suggestion was made that the concept might be better translated: "Let there be time." Understanding the visible spectra as marking our boundary, dimensional perimeter, or "brane," was a conversational point in the beginning, but quickly led to other canonical citation.

** *Before this report was completed, a follow-up was authorized, exploring specific instances of Biblical canon with respect to: time, dimensional bounding, cosmology and mass-frequency. Tentatively entitled, "Judeo-Christian Cipher (JCC)," the goal of this second document is as a grid-tool for future research. The prospect of a forthcoming JCC freed us from evaluating theological evidence, a study beyond the scope of this assignment. If proven reliable, the JCC could be scaled into use as a research tool.*

Floyd Wray

Computer Generated Exhibit (4kd)
Unexpected Harmonic

Seeing The Light

20. *Light* and *dark* are easily the prime compositional elements in *Biblical* narrative. Usually thought of in terms of metaphor and simile, *light* is the descriptor of highest order, and ultimately associated with the glory of God. *Darkness*, by comparison, is the ultimate descriptor for evil, alienation and Satan.

Light – JCC
21. In the canon, God is described as "the Father of lights." [47] During the exodus from Egypt, the *glory* of God was understood in terms of light. Exposure to this glory resulted in a blinding radiance from the face of Moses. [48] In the *New Testament*, the "bright hosts of heaven" appeared to the shepherds, announcing the birth of Jesus. [49] On the Mount of Transfiguration, the face of Jesus "shone like the sun." [50] Jesus was known as the "light of the world." [51] His teachings were deeply invested in distinctions based on light. Near the end of the *New Testament*, the book of *Revelation* describes the new Jerusalem, rebuilt after the passing of the heavens and earth, *when time shall be no more:* "And the city had no need of the sun, neither of the moon, to shine in it: for the glory of God did lighten it, and the Lamb is the light thereof." [52] When the JCC is completed, the canonical references to light will undoubtedly comprise a massive listing.

Dimensionality – JCC
22. In addition to light, the Biblical canon seems to suggest *dimensionality* in Christ's parable of the rich man and Lazarus. [53] In the narrative, the recently-deceased Lazarus is comforted in the *bosom of Abraham*. The rich man, also dead, observes the consolation of Lazarus from a dimensional zone of torment. Just before His death on the cross, Christ comforted the dying man beside him with the promise: "today you will be with me in Paradise." [54] Both *Paradise*, and *Bosom of Abraham*, suggest another domain, set apart from human reality. [55] St. Paul suspected that he had been caught up into the *third heaven*, where he heard things, "too beautiful to tell." [56] (Some religious scholars suggest that there may be as many as seven heavens, or more [57]) In another place, the writer of *Hebrews* says that we are "encompassed-about" by a great cloud of witnesses, observing us from a dimensional distance. [58] Prior to his death, the first Christian martyr saw *cross-dimensionally*, into the realms of heaven. [59] In the extra-canonical book of *Enoch*, the narrator is taken to God via a passage that crosses apparent dimensional zones, to the dimension where God dwells. [60]

Tunable Dimensions
23. Though it may strike some as a bit far-out, a case for *dimensionality* could be argued from passages where prophets in the *Old Testament* are caught away into the sky in "chariots" of fire, or "Ezekiel's wheels-within-wheels." [61] Another account describes invisible armies, materializing into view at the time of the prophet, Elijah. [62] Perhaps the most interesting examples of the phenomenon are found in the life of Christ. In the forty-days

TOP SECRET
Page 10 of 28

Computer Generated Exhibit (4e)
Unexpected Harmonic

SAS-TS--1-143-95

An Unexpected Harmonic v.79c   TOP SECRET   Nunnally, Paige, Rosenfeld

after his reported-resurrection, Christ *materialized* in the midst of his followers on several occasions. [63] Of course, his final earthly contact with his disciples concluded with his rising from the earth, then disappearing into the clouds. [64] In the days prior to this, Christ made a specific reference to his acquisition of a "glorified body," [65] a suggestion that often leaves theologians scratching their heads. [66] The pattern implies that in order to enter time, Christ's nature required a *dial down*, to achieve human form, "so that he could live as we live, then die as we die."

(handwritten: — 8) footnote ?

24. With his earthly mission complete, he reacquired his original state, returning to trans-dimensional ascendancy and a glorified body.

Light -- Reviewer-Input v.79c

(handwritten notes:)
Matthew 2:1-12
James 1:17 — Father of Lights
Luke 2:3 — tongues of fire
Genesis 9:11 God send a rainbow
Acts 22:9 Paul sees light
non-canonical Book of Jubilees 4:17 in terms of Messiah
↳ sun-time te'udh + ēdut

* John 9:15 - light of the world
2 Kings 2:11 - chariots of fire
* 1 Tim 6:11-16 - unapproachable light
Dan 10:12
* Isaiah 9 speaks of light

Dimensionality -- Reviewer-Input v.79c

(handwritten notes:)
God sees through
* Exodus 14:24 dimensional tunneling through pillar of fire?
Matthew 17:1-9 - Transfiguration / Luke 24:13 - Road to Emaus?
Numbers 22:23 - Angel + Balaam's ass
Luke 5=18 - back to Heaven
2 Kings 6:17 - unseen armies
John 21-1-19   Heb 12:22
Job 2:2 Satan patrolling the earth
Acts 14 - Angel Paul
Acts 8 - Phillip
2 Corinthians 11:14
Heb 13:12
Gen 18:1
Gen 19
Matt 24:31
I don't like the way these boxes are ordered. Some examples fit all three!

Tunable Dimension -- Reviewer-Input v.79c

(handwritten notes:)
Mark 16:12-14
John 21:1
Genesis 28:10 → Stairway to Heaven
Revelation 4:5 - there's an interesting reference to the 7-spirits of God — 7-Heavens? ALL OF Revelations is about Dimensions

* Acts 7:55 - First martyr Stephen sees the Heavens open + Observes cross-dimensionally
Caverns + dim
1 - Enoch 22 — I know this isn't in the canon, but it really does come off as a dimensional passage

Floyd Wray

Computer Generated Exhibit (4kf)
Unexpected Harmonic

alerts us to reconsider some forms of what we refer to as *delusion*. If there is such a thing as *heightened dimensional acuity*, it could be related to any number of influences, including sensitivity to electromagnetic fields. [133] The brilliant mathematician, John Nash, might have been merely *tuned-in* to another realm, and a victim of Interdimensional "interference." [134] Of the many surprises drawn from the JCC-toolset, the most disconcerting may be the prospect of other, dimensionally bound life-forms. Lurking just beyond what we can see or hear, there may be vast civilizations of creatures that may, or may not be capable of *tuning us in*. These creatures may, or may not, have our best interests at heart.

Messy Arguments – Interesting Possibilities

43. Many of these speculations infuriate the religious, the non-religious, the scientist, the non-scientist, the philosopher and the non-philosopher. Every single citation can be argued; no conclusion stands, sacrosanct. Some will undoubtedly claim that the mere prospect of a JCC confers an implied legitimacy to religious belief. Perhaps it does; perhaps it doesn't. Issues of belief, faith and pedagogy are issues of individual choice. *Our interest is the employment of any toolset or evaluative system that advances our understanding of origins, destinies and the nature of cosmic reality.*

44. The unexpected harmonic from the JCC provides us with a compelling framework for understanding. First, it gives structure to a tradition that has been shoved aside as a cultural artifact. More importantly, the JCC-framework provides us with a new way of thinking about everything from string-theory and dimensional bounding, to origins and destinies. [133]

45. One of the most interesting results has been in the implications such an understanding holds for dark matter, and dark energy. Perhaps these phenomena are best understood as *dimensionally bound*. We often think of darkness as an absolute absence of light; by employing the JCC, we discover that dimensional mass and energy exist, but aren't accessible from our space-time node in the dimensional scale, without the technical capability to make the crossover. From a purely philosophical perspective, the JCC suggests, if the prime creative force inhabits the ultimate state -- the domain of highest enlightenment light -- we might want to think twice about visiting the domain of *nether-energy*.

How Would A Change In Mass Frequency ... Feel?

45. The observations arising from a JCC are troubling, highly contentious, and challenge our understanding of the cosmos. Curiously, they may also inform us with respect to *how we*

Computer Generated Exhibit (4g)
Unexpected Harmonic

die.

46. We do not understand the process of dying beyond the anecdotal reports of those who inform us from their deathbeds, or those who've *died* and come back to tell of their experience. NDE (Near Death Experiences) are highly subjective, but deserve our cautious interest.

46. There are persistent accounts in which those nearing death see *angels*, or "departed loved-ones." [134] They tell of heavenly scenes and stunning colors. They "see Jesus," or "God," and speak of their visions in terms of ecstasy. [135] Neurological theory suggests that such reports may describe the electro-chemical "snap, crackle and pop" that accompanies death." [136] But the theories introduced with the JCC suggest an alternative possibility: as a person dies, their final moments may reveal a process of transitioning to a higher energy state. *They are en route to a dimensional threshold.*

47. Those who've experienced an NDE often make similar observations. Since they don't die, their *round-trip* experiences often describe: 1) a departure from their physical body; 2) from *somewhere near the ceiling* they still hear and observe the events going on around them; 3) they encounter *deceased* family members, from whom they receive counsel; 4) some claim to encounter *Jesus* or *God*; 5) there is a *bright light*, toward which they are drawn. [137]

48. This *light* is variously described as "God, Christ, a living light, beautiful, intelligent, loving, compelling and welcoming," among other things. [138] "The near death experiencer is often overwhelmed with peace, ecstasy, an absence of pain and a sense of belonging." [139] Most would prefer to remain in this state, or proceed into the light. At some point, they are "informed that their time has not yet come," and they'll have to return. [140] Most near death experiencers describe re-entry into their physical bodies as painful, discouraging and the "saddest experience they've ever known." [141] As a result of their NDE, they no longer fear death, but actually look forward to "what happens next." [142]

49. Here's where NDEs unexpectedly link to study of variable mass. What we may have in these reports is a description of *attenuation*. All the elements are there: unseen domains, beautiful colors, buoyancy, unseen *others, a living, higher light*. It is a threshold from which the return to human reality is both painful and unsought. The time of dying is thus a transition from the current dimensional form to a more enlightened state. It should be pointed out, there is a significant statistical sampling of near death experiencers who report "darkness, with an indescribable sense of evil lurking in the darkness." [143] Visiting the nether domain is, therefore, a real possibility. If dimensional zones are *reversibly conjugated*, according to scalable mass energy, perhaps we have a partial explanation for the passage into death. When the end comes, as we cross over into a new dimension, as we

Computer Generated Exhibit (4kh)
Unexpected Harmonic

join the bright, intelligent light, our senses *tunnel* into an energy domain of infinite transcendence.*** At its core, this is a theme of origins and destinies, and strangely, it's been around in one form or another for thousands of years. [144]

Dimensional Mass Energy and the Sandbox

50. It's impossible to discuss the JCC perspective on dimensionality without considering its impact on social convention.

51. The first, and most obvious shock falls on religious belief. Christian theologians have a significant tradition of explaining miracles and acts of *divine* intervention in terms of natural events, or human misunderstanding. The JCC forces certain of these traditions to a *revision-of-explanation*. For many, there's no place in the *pastoral sandbox* for understanding God in terms of an enhanced theory of cosmology. [145] To do so <u>smacks of disrespect</u>, or a vain human attempt to subordinate the concept of God to a metaphysical fad. The implications of a JCC-based cosmos confronts certain liturgies and religious schools-of-thought with a major challenge. Resistance to a JCC-based cosmology will be signifiant.

52. If religious sensibilities face upheaval from a new cosmological model, the sciences aren't exempt, either. The most obvious impact of the JCC falls on the unification of Quantum Mechanics with Einstein's *spacetime fabric*. The much-sought unification theory might only be possible with the introduction of other dimensions, and the employment of *strange physics*. The JCC is really just a new window through which to view the universe, but it challenges the traditions of cosmology. [146] It presents the researcher with the prospect of a *transcendent intelligence*. This is a deprecated concept, for many, and the perceived enemy of enlightenment.[147]

53. And the JCC-based cosmos doesn't just offend the liturgies of theoretical physics, it also presents a formidable affront to 19th century theoretical models. Classical Darwinism has faced amendment from researchers like Ronald Fisher, arguments from Hardy-Weinberg, and mathematical models like those relating to *allele* frequencies. [148] The prospect of the JCC, however, might be seen as a repeal of many cherished, theoretical projections. As with QM, the JCC-model reinstates the deprecated notion of higher dimensional life-forms, and the attendant prospect that these forms aspire to interact, cross-dimensionally. The big quesion involves *how they tunnel into our sandbox*. Humans are not endowed with a trig-

[Handwritten marginal notes:]
- *Soviets see bio-Plasma as a new form of eveneVsy — integrated system of charged particles.*
- *an ... or religious betrayal*
- *Bio-plasma, VRIL — what about Morphogetetic Fields ala Rupert Sheldreke*
- *Saw a BBC on this guy.*
- *An Undiscovered field is a logical possibility. The guy.*

*** *In this state, no kinetic/potential energy is required to climb over the energy barrier.*

Computer Generated Exhibit (5a)
NSA Document

~~CONFIDENTIAL~~

UNITED STATES GOVERNMENT

memorandum

DATE: 6 June 1995

REPLY TO
ATTN OF: P0241

P0241,141-1123z

SUBJECT: USSID 12 Guidance: The Cothran Theory (FOUD) – Information
MEMORANDUM

TO: YNYN EEI LAN ANL EXC OPC UTY OCS MDI SHP SOL XP

1. (C-CCO) The extraterrestrial-reality, for USSID 12 purposes, remains outside the scope of human understanding. After several
decades, interaction between humans and EMEs remains unpredictable,
and lacks a basic rationale for ongoing partnership. Non-compliance,
professed language deficit, faulty data, rogue intrusion, "cancer,"
half-truths and outright deception are the hallmarks of EME-associa-
tion. Since 1942, each behavioral model ascribed to the EMEs has undergone constant revision by those who work directly with them. At
this late date, we do not understand what motivates them. They have
gone to extraordinary lengths to hide goals and plans. They appear to
follow a simple strategy: employ random actions to prevent human han-
dlers from identifying a functional pattern of behavior. Having studied and discarded more than one-hundred behavioral models, the Cothran
Working Group (CWG) adopted an unexpected model. Through extensive
analysis of internal documentation, they concluded that the EME-enigma
falls into unexpected alignment with the cultural profile of Judeo-
Christian tradition. Using the Bible as the cipher, much of the EME
mystery finds broad explanation in the profile of a "celestial" competition between two powerful adversaries.

2. (C-CCO) CWG have isolated numerous case identifiers, including, but not limited to: a) competitive valuation of the "human
soul"; b) genetic-manipulation; c) backdoor (spiritual) access to individual targets; d) the mystical preeminence of the "~~Godshybrid~~" known
to history as "Jesus Christ"; e) actual conflict between celestial adversaries taking place just beyond the (human) field-of-view; e) esca-
lating hostilities between the two parties; f) trans-dimensional
behavior; g) the growing sense that open intrusion into the human dimension by one adversary will trigger a final, cataclysmic battle in
which all humans will be directly involved and at-risk.

~~CONFIDENTIAL~~

Computer Generated Exhibit (5b)
NSA Document

<del>CONFIDENTIAL</del>

USSID 12 Guidance: The Cothran Theory (FOUD) -   P0241,141-1123:
Information MEMORANDUM   Page 2 of :

   3.   (C-CCO) CWG's employment of a religious-cipher has not been
universally accepted. The hard-tangibility of the EME-conflict, with
its catalog of deceit and documented aggression, seems to fall outside
the convenient, pastoral myth that defines modern religious practice.
The "God" of Christianity becomes the ultimate potency in the CWG-conclusion; the CWG model of "God" describes an entity residing at a distance ("in a realm of holiness") to the dimensions, cosmic realms and
systems, created and maintained according to his purpose. Against the
span of such unimaginable power and limits to human cognition, the po-
tential toll in this war has been reduced through the engineered appearance of the ~~human God~~d known as "Jesus Christ." Whatever else
organized religion is, it is more-or-less based on the simple values
and promises of a cosmic salvation - against the inevitable cataclysm
of a final battle.

   4. (C-CCO) Our records indicate that we have interfaced with
both parties to this conflict over the last fifty-years. Our moon and
Mars are littered with the wounds and artifacts of their celestial
combat. Without the Judeo-Christian cipher, both parties seem to be
rough-equivalents, from human perspective. When the cipher is employed, however, their differences are obvious. Perhaps the greatest
challenge for human observers, involves the recasting of what had been
relegated to cultural myth. Connecting the CWG-reality to "Sunday
School" reality, is an extremely difficult undertaking, and requires
the application of "tangible" and "intangible" values with an uncommon
sense of immediacy and reality.

   5.(FOUG) Please insure that all personnel are aware of the CWG's
summary-document: "An Unexpected Harmonic." Additionally, please insure that all personnel are made aware that the CWG-conclusion is non-
actionable, and does not reflect agency policy, at this point.

DISTRIBUTION:

Chief,   PO241

                    Derived From: NSA/CSSM 207-2
                    Dated: 3 June 1992
                    Declassify On: Source Marked "CADR"
                    Date of Source: 3 June 91

<del>HANDLE VIA COMIN CHANNELS ONLY</del>
<del>CONFIDENTIAL</del>   Official Form No. 18
                              (REV 1-89
                              GSA FFWK 131CPAD1034
                              3439-254 (COMPUTER FASCIMILE)

Computer Generated Exhibit (6)
Nunally's Note

from the desk of
M.N██████ly, Ph.D.

Thur 4 - 1992

Dave:

Thanks for lunch. Hope I wasn't
too hard on you guys. You may be
onto something -- though I'm not
quite sure I'm convinced to the
degree that I'm ready to be a
Methodist again. Looking forward
to summary-review in march. After
that, maybe I'll dust off my
Bible.

MN

Floyd Wray

Computer Generated Exhibit (7)
Reg Taylor's Non-Traditional UFO Theory

There is a non-traditional explanation for the "high strangeness" in UFO reality, and it links to biblical provenance, and the population split that might have occurred in the days of Noah and the flood.

EXECUTIVE SUMMARY

According the Genesis 3: 14-15, there are two "seedline-populations" on the planet. One, above ground. The other an "eater of dust," a highly advanced civilization that still exists. As a result of the flood, the "dust-eaters" were banished from outside, to inside the earth. Where they still remain in a condition of imprisonment.

Nuclear detonations at the Trinity site in the 1940s threatened the over-structure of the underground civilization. Which explains the point-of-origin for UFO awareness in and around New Mexico. Nuclear testing, during World War II, alerted the underground civilization to a clear-and-present danger.

The dust-eaters are highly advanced technically and have been known to us as the supernatural-race of Atlantis, regional gods, spirit beings, ghosts, and demons. Their above ground appearances have been highly variable, in that respect, but never dominant; anomalies that "shade Judeo-Christian" tradition, but never reach ascendancy.

Both civilizations, above and under, are subordinate to a higher order. Think "God."

The UFO story is thus spiritual, and competitive with the human story. We're seeing the concluding chapters of a seed war going back to the Garden of Eden. And the earliest writings in human record.

From Admiral Byrd's diary in 1947, a US military mission to the Antarctic (Project Highjump) resulted in an encounter with this inner earth civilization. The meeting led to a short, but decisive conflict. Byrd and his mission were dramatically defeated.

Anyone who dismisses this an over-the-top explanation, consider this biblical reference found in the Bible: 1 Peter 3:19. During the three days between crucifixion and resurrection, Peter says that Christ ministered to the imprisoned spirits, inside the earth. Given this explanation, UFOs link to an ultimate contest between two seed lines, between fallen man and fallen angels.

Trying to understand "extra-terrestrial" when it is actually "inner-terrestrial" is a misdirection. The big secret is imprisoned within the earth — quarantined. The grander secret for "top siders" is Messianic, in the fullest sense of all things biblical.

We're seeing the last chapters of a seed-war. One originated at the beginning of the human existence. One that is coming to an end in the UFO story.

Computer Generated Exhibit (8)
Baby Elena Card

To Him who alone possesses immortality
and dwells in unapproachable light,
whom no man has ever seen or can
see, to Him be honor and eternal
dominion   I Timothy 6:15

Congratulations! Blessings! Prayers!

Los bebés son la magia beautiful

Computer Generated Exhibit (9)
Notification of Death

Odenton Resident Dies In Mexico

On June 2, 1998, Millard Nunnally of Odenton, MD, passed away in Colima, Mexico, after a brief illness. Millard was preceded in death by his parents, the late Hilda and Hugh Nunnally, two sisters and one brother. Born in North Carolina in 1927, Dr. Nunnally served proudly in the U.S. military, and was a respected analyst for several government agencies from 1953 to 1996. Interment was in Colima on the grounds of Orfanato Manos Benditas (Hands of Blessing Orphanage).

G. WITTMAN